IT'S A
Love/Skate
RELATIONSHIP

Skate

RELATIONSHIP

CARLI J. CORSON

HARPER

An Imprint of HarperCollinsPublishers

Library of Congress Cataloging-in-Publication Data

Names: Corson, Carli J., author.

Title: It's a love/skate relationship / Carli J. Corson.

Other titles: It is a love/skate relationship

Description: First edition. | New York : Harper, an imprint of HarperCollins
    Publishers, [2025] | Audience term: Teenagers | Audience: Ages 13 up | Audience:
    Grades 10–12 |

Summary: "In this queer romance, a hockey player must trade her hockey stick for
    figure skates—and just might fall for her ice princess skating partner"—Provided
    by publisher.

Identifiers: LCCN 2024005401 | ISBN 9780063370869 (hardback)

Subjects: LCSH: Lesbian teenagers—Juvenile fiction. | Figure skating—Juvenile
    literature. | CYAC: Lesbians—Fiction. | Teenagers—Fiction. | Ice skating—Fiction.
    | LCGFT: Lesbian fiction. | Romance fiction.

Classification: LCC PZ7.1.C672962 It 2025 | DDC [Fic]—dc23/eng/20240705

LC record available at https://lccn.loc.gov/2024005401

Typography by Julia Feingold

24 25 26 27 28 LBC 5 4 3 2 1

First Edition

To Mom and Dad, who are always on my team,
and to Veronica, my game changer

One

Okay, so I'm beyond shitty at math, but even I can't screw up this equation currently ripping me in half: the Blizzard's hockey rink seats about 2,400 spectators, which means there are roughly 1,200 people cheering for me to score . . . and 1,200 people screaming for me to choke.

The announcer's voice booms through the speakers as spectators register my presence on the ice—this time in a crucial spot. *"With under two minutes left and a tie score, coaches signal for a line change. Rising-star junior Charlie Porter hops the boards to join her brother, team captain Mac Porter, along with the rest of the first-line shift for the Cranford Caribou."*

It's a miracle I hear him over the roar of the crowd, and that roar is no surprise—our snowy 'burb of Winthrop, Vermont, is best known for the extreme competitiveness between our public and private schools, guaranteeing jam-packed bleachers for any matches in our hockey-crazed town. Seriously, our rivalry? I'm talking decades of grade-A, grass-fed, organic-as-hell *beef*.

And this isn't just any game.

Each Labor Day weekend, the Winthrop Cup is up for grabs— one trophy tiered like a shiny silver wedding cake but oh-so-much sweeter. The winners house the cup in their school all year-round, and we're rocking a five-year domination streak, the cup serving as the centerpiece in our Cranford trophy case.

My maroon-and-silver-clad Caribou squad leans over the boards from our bench, sticks and gloved fists pounding in support.

I've been kicking ass on second-line shift all night—so much so that Coach Doug pulls back our out-of-gas starting right-winger and sends me out with the first line in such a crucial spot.

Mac knocks my helmet with his. "You ready to bring this cup back home where it belongs?"

My smirk twists behind my wired helmet cage. "Hell yeah. The hardware's not going anywhere."

"Just remember—no showing off," Mac warns, like always.

I snort, playfully shoving him. "Like it's my fault my stick-work's better than yours."

"She's not wrong, Big Mac," our left-winger, Matty Cann, pipes in with a wink through his rec specs, always eager to rile his captain.

Our speediest defenseman, "Flyin' Brian" Gates, grunts in the affirmative. He doesn't talk much.

Mac whacks Matty's chest protector with a gloved backhand. "Line up for the face-off," he commands, and I turn to do the same before Mac snags my elbow. "Hold up." He leans in and lowers his voice, nodding toward the stands. "On second thought . . . maybe show off a little bit? Scouts in section 104, six rows up. Wasn't gonna say anything in case it would psych you out, but—if you see your shot, take it. Show 'em the Porter way."

My stomach flips. "Cool. Cool, cool, cool. No problem. I totally got this."

Mac already scored his full-ride scholarship, so it's my turn to make an impression if I've got any chance at scoring an acceptance into a D-I school and playing competitive hockey post–high school.

"Here we go, Little Porter!" Goalie Nicole Vesper bellows from our net before the crowd noise swallows whatever further encouragement she shouts.

I turn and point my stick Nicole's way as a nod of acknowledgment. She's a senior in all the brainiac classes, so we're not super tight, but on our ice, girl game respects girl game. And for the record I'm not, like, *actually* little. I'm five eight and pretty damn buff. Unfortunately, the rest of my team isn't exactly Shakespearean or Snoop Doggian when it comes to doling out clever nicknames.

While the refs conference pre–puck drop, I steal one more glance toward the stands—this time at Dad's regular seat. He's on his feet with the rest of the spectators, leaning forward and clapping hard in support like always.

My chest deflates as my gaze lands on the empty seat beside him—one we were told to save because Mom, and I quote, *"Wouldn't miss it for the world! xoxoxo."*

Then I hate myself all over again for believing she'd actually show up this time.

"Focus up!" Coach Doug paces along the bench behind my teammates, competitive anxiety written all over his grizzled face.

Shoving all nonhockey-related thoughts into my brain basement, I crouch into ready position and pop my mouthguard back over my teeth. My dark, messy braid falls over my jersey's number 4. I'm breathing heavily from a hard game fought, a pink flush painting my white cheeks, when a grating voice cries out from enemy territory.

"We're five on four with a little girl at winger! Crush that ladybug and let's get this dub!" The Winthrop High Snow Leopard goalie, Konor Stratford, wears a captain's *C* patch affixed to the upper left chest of his green-and-gold jersey. With his long black hair, obnoxiously chiseled cheekbones, and that smarmy-as-hell glint in his eye, he's basically a defective Disney prince.

His mind games won't work on me. I'm not some sort of amateur, after all. The scouts in the stands are paying just as much attention to me as they are to all the other juniors and not-yet-committed seniors.

The ref finally approaches center ice and holds the puck out over the face-off circle.

To the right of Mac at center, I square off against a towering Winthrop winger, Gavin Davis, crossing my stick with his.

"It's over, sweetie," Davis taunts. "Cup's gonna look shiny as hell in our trophy case."

"Yeah? You mean the one with all the cobwebs and dust bunnies?"

The referee drops the puck and the clock resumes ticking down.

I lunge my full weight into Davis's body to knock him off-balance, ducking low with sharp skating and striding backward into defensive positioning. Breathing hard through my nostrils, I time Davis's windup and dive to deflect his slap shot from the point; the puck ricochets off my padded hip and sails into the plexiglass.

Caribou and our supporters erupt into cheers as we gain puck possession.

I tap my stick twice against the ice—the universal *I'm Open* signal—and Gates looks past me, instead shuffling the puck to a double-teamed Mac. Growling a few unholy swears, I shift to guard one of the defenders instead.

Mac—with impressive accuracy despite being bullied against the boards—jabs the puck between his legs.

His pass hits square on my stick's tape.

A bolt of newfound energy powers my skates, hammies and quads burning as I push the puck over our blue line toward center ice.

The play-by-play announcer's call booms louder. *"Here's Charlie Porter with the puck—and wow, she can really fly! Porter makes a slick move and spins past the last Winthrop defender, and she's on a breakaway with a chance to win it all for Cranford!"*

Twenty-four hundred people shout as my legs pump harder, sweeping down ice with the crunching *whoosh* of Snow Leopards hot on my bladed heels.

Konor Stratford's smug-ass grin plasters behind his goalie mask as he crouches into ready position, eyes tracking my impressive, intricate puck dribble. Keeping up speed, I soar over the center-ice red line before flying into enemy territory—and that's when his taunts rise above the roaring crowd. "Show me what you've got, Ladybug!" He slams his thicker goalie stick against the ice, flapping his glove. "You gonna shoot glove side or stick side? You're a show-off with that fancy stickwork—you're gonna go glove, right?"

Handling the puck like a muscley magician, I deke hard—rearing back and faking a slap shot to Stratford's glove side—selling the psych-out beautifully.

Stratford lunges left, exposing his stick side—right as Gavin Davis catches up with me from behind.

Davis spears his stick between my skates and hooks my ankle, tripping me up.

It's an obvious penalty. The ref's gonna blow his whistle any second and I'll get a penalty shot—

But the whistle doesn't come.

Instead, I fling a backhanded shot toward the exposed net as I fall forward, seemingly in slow motion. Thanks to Davis's illegal hook screwing with my timing, the angle's off for my shot.

And unfortunately for me, I'm *extra* garbage at geometry.

The puck flies toward the narrowing window between Stratford and the post and—

Ping!

The stinging clink of puck smacking goalpost pipe echoes throughout the rink, eliciting a choir of groans and pitiful cries from my teammates and our supporters.

I hit the ice with a full-body thud, slamming my gloved fist onto its unforgiving, scratched-to-hell surface before scrambling back to my skates and powering my legs in a desperate attempt to catch up with the Winthrop counterattack.

Too late.

Not only did I blow a huge opportunity, but the ominous clinking fail combined with the missed penalty call shifted the energy and momentum in favor of the Snow Leopards. So much so that twelve seconds later—

"Gooooal! It's a buzzer-beating, game-winning goal for Gavin Davis, and the Winthrop High Snow Leopards will carry the Winthrop Cup back to their school for the first time in five years!"

Dropping back to my knees, I bow my face into my gloves as the celebratory chants of our rivals loop inside my helmet and I will myself not to puke on the ice.

When I summon an ounce of courage to lift my head once more, Mac and Coach Doug stand toe to toe with the refs, arms flailing at the brutal injustice. It's pretty damn clear by the referees' inaction they didn't see Davis hook my skate. My whole team files out from the bench with their heads hung.

Almost my whole team.

Mac's heavy hand drops to my shoulder and grabs my jersey, tugging me back to my skates. "C'mon, let's get out of here."

"I had him beat," I croak, shaking my head in disbelief. My focus flits to the scouts in the stands as they chatter close, pointing to the clustered Snow Leopards and ignoring me completely.

"The refs missed the hooking call, yeah. Nothing we can do about it now." Mac clearly tries keeping his voice even for my sake, though he can't fully mask the disappointment drenching his words.

Even without the blown penalty call, I could've been faster. I could've taken the shot sooner—an unhindered shot that might've sailed home. If I hadn't been so showy. *But it worked*, my gut argues back. I had him beat. A wide-open net. If it wasn't for Davis—

My stick drags between my skates like a tail between my legs on my way back to our bench. A sickening dread weighs heavy in my gut as I affix my blade guards and tread slowly away from the ice and into our team's locker room, bracing myself.

"Not your fault," Mac mumbles, sticking close to me while Coach Doug launches into his verbal assault.

Yeah, the refs blew the damn hooking call, but that's no excuse.

Plenty of other opportunities you didn't capitalize on.

They wanted it more than you did.

Selfish hockey. Of course, he along with everyone else looks at me on that last one—as if they wouldn't have attempted the same exact shot on a breakaway.

Remember this feeling. Use it as fuel for the upcoming season.

Coach Doug's postgame beratement cycles on repeat through my head as I shuffle into the girls' locker-room showers with Nicole and the quiet sophomore girl on our team, taking much-needed space from the guys. Nicole, encouraging as she is, knows better than to try and cheer me up so soon after an epic failure.

Scrubbing the sweat from my skin does nothing to rinse away the humiliation of blowing the game-winning shot—despite the missed penalty call. The penalty I can't help but wonder if the refs would've called on one of my male teammates. No point dwelling on that, though, right? Proving sexism is damn near impossible without making it sound like an excuse, and I don't make excuses.

Twenty minutes later, with my hair still damp beneath my backward hat, I dread-tread into the lobby to meet up with Dad and Mac.

The Blizzard's lobby is a central hub for the entire skating complex—the hockey players, parents, and spectators from the hockey rink; the figure skaters and public skaters from the other rink. There's a snack bar, a skate-rental window, and, upstairs, a gym and pro shop. The open area between the two rinks serves mostly as a chill social space for parents waiting for their kids' practices to finish. Tables and chairs stand around the ice arena's pride and joy—an eight-foot-tall marble statue of local legend Glenn McGarrity, who grew up in the Blizzard and played almost two decades in the NHL, and was eventually inducted into the Hockey Hall of Fame.

Now the lobby's crowded with lingering players and fans, a nauseating amount of Winthrop High green and gold bustling around in continued celebration.

I grip my hockey stick harder as I spot Captain Prickface himself—Konor Stratford—along with his assbag first mate, Gavin Davis. Davis extends his beefy arm to take a selfie while he and Stratford kiss opposite sides of the Winthrop Cup.

I make a mental note to douse the trophy in bleach when we win it back next year.

Standing on tiptoe and craning my neck to try and find my family, their grating dude-bro voices carry my way.

"Look who it is! Hey, Ladybug!" Stratford swaggers over with the cup perched on his hip. "Another year, another disappointing, overrated Porter. Pro tip—maybe get some shooting lessons from someone other than your big brother."

"I had you beat," I snarl, my eyebrows drawing tight. "You know I had you beat."

He shrugs me off. "Doesn't matter if you blow your shot, does it?"

"*Ping!*" Gavin Davis mimics the puck-on-pipe noise, setting my teeth on edge. "Some advice? Leave hockey to the men. Why don't you take up a girly sport like softball or knitting—"

"Wow, shit-for-brains. Could you be more sexist?"

"Hey, seriously?" Mac steps up beside me. "Don't pretend like she didn't go toe to toe with you each shift. She was all over you—you never even got a decent shot off till the end."

Davis huffs, his cheeks blazing. "She got lucky a couple times, that's it." His irritated gaze fixates on me and he tilts his head to the side. "Y'know, you're not bad-looking without the hockey pads.

I wouldn't mind you being all over me in a different way. . . ." A predatory grin twists up his chapped lips as he leans in and lowers his voice. "I could show you how to put that filthy mouth of yours to better use, if you—"

Crack!

The force of my right hook knocks Gavin Davis into the horde of Snow Leopards behind him.

One of them takes in the sight—Davis clutching his bloody lip, me still bowing forward with my fist clenched. "Whoa, holy shit! Did she just—"

Gavin Davis spits a mouthful of blood on the floor, eyes flashing. "You wanna play hockey like a man, Porter? You're gonna fight like one, too."

"Gav, don't!" Stratford reaches for Davis, but not in time.

Davis cracks his knuckles as he barrels forward like a pissed-off bull and tackles me to the floor.

Mac reacts a beat too late; as he lunges to pull Gavin off me, Nicole and Matty Cann snag him by the arms. Flyin' Brian Gates shoves the nearest Winthrop player instead.

The cracking voice of a preteen rink rat erupts through the space. "*FIIIIIGHT!*"

Green Winthrop letterman jackets and maroon Cranford hoodies dive into the fray, pent-up on-ice frustrations exploding in a chaotic fog of testosterone and resentment. A flurry of flinging fists and elbows catch cheeks, chests, and solar plexuses on both sides, yelling and screaming easily overtaking the elevator music streaming from the snack bar as non–hockey players get caught in the cross fire.

Meanwhile, Davis and I roll around fighting for the upper hand. I use his momentum to pin him onto his back, straddling his waist. His elbow catches my jaw as he attempts to block my strikes.

Davis emits a wheezy, egging cackle through bloodstained teeth. "Oh yeah! Hit me again, baby! I like it rough!" He bucks his hips up into mine and I strike him again, ensuring his left eye will be swollen shut for a week.

I'm dimly aware of a sudden, rushing shatter nearby, but I'm too caught up with trying to simultaneously hurt Davis and not get my teeth knocked out from his counterstrikes to investigate.

The piercing shriek of a whistle causes the chaos to instantly pause—hockey players reacting to the universal play-stoppage sound like Pavlov's dogs.

Registering my position, I scramble off the panting Gavin Davis and my attention snaps to the upstairs overhang, where Bobby, the rink manager, stands with his knotty old hands curled around the railing, a frown deepening within his white beard as he scans the disarray below: A mosh pit of bruised and bloody bodies frozen midfight. Faces screwed up with pain, guilt, shock, or a mashing of all three. The ransacked snack bar looted and raided for ammo—Twinkies and stale hot dog buns pilfered as makeshift projectiles scattered on the ground.

The Glenn McGarrity statue knocked off its pedestal, pulverized into a pile of marble chunks and slowly settling dust.

"Who the hell's responsible for all this?" Bobby scans the scene below.

A moment of awkward silence passes.

"It was her, Bobby. Charlie Porter." Konor Stratford flings his snitch-ass index finger at me from a few yards away, where he crouches beside a red-haired girl wearing a green-and-gold track jacket, white figure skates with lilac blade guards, and extreme distress written all over her heart-shaped face. She squeezes the hand of a blond guy writhing in agony while clutching his left skate.

And while I'm hyperaware of the dozens of judgmental stares following Stratford's finger and pouring into me from all around the lobby, I'm pretty damn certain none hold anywhere near the same level of undiluted fury as the death glare from the redhead in the figure skates.

Two

After a brief conversation with Bobby, I'm slouching in the back seat of Dad's old Jeep Cherokee with half a tissue shoved up my bloody left nostril and an ice pack resting over my throbbing knuckles.

"Ten thousand dollars," Dad mutters—mostly to himself, under his breath—as he drives the familiar route through town toward our quiet neighborhood. "Ten . . . thousand . . ."

"Dad." Mac sits in the passenger seat sporting a fresh bruise on his cheek. "We worked it out. Charlie's gonna pay off her debt by working at the rink."

"That's a shit ton of rink coffee I gotta sell," I mumble, picking at my thumb's cuticle as I frown out the window. I didn't even protest the arrangement from Bobby, who took pity on me once he recognized me as the player who blew the Winthrop Cup game for her team. His offer was generous, considering he could've probably pressed charges for property destruction or whatever.

"About ten thousand cups, to be more specific," Mac clarifies.

A dollar per cup. Right. *Math.*

"Then they'll buy a new Glenn McGarrity statue and everything'll feel back to normal."

I snort. "Maybe for you." He's not the one who has to face our classmates as the school's biggest disappointment tomorrow.

"What the hell were you thinking, kiddo?" Disappointed Dad Eyes flicker through the rearview mirror. "Picking a fight like that. That Davis kid is a good head taller and a hell of a lot thicker than you. Do you know how many people got hurt back there? I raised you better—at least good enough to know to keep the damn fights on the ice, where it's socially acceptable."

I lift my injured hand to sandwich the ice pack between my knuckles and my jaw. "I didn't mean for other people to get hurt." Porters are notoriously bad at talking about feelings, but my "why" was probably a perfect shitstorm of factors: Missing the cup-winning shot. Blowing a huge opportunity to stand out for the scouts. Letting myself get goaded by those douche nozzles. And Mom . . .

Apparently I'm a fan of kicking myself when I'm down, because I check my phone again and pull up our message chain. Her last text, sent last night, included an obnoxious amount of kissy-face, hockey-stick, and trophy emoji. It's only a matter of time before the apology call comes through.

My phone pings with a Bestie Group Chat notification, both Jade and Emily texting to ask if I'm okay, though neither of them could make the game.

Shitty news travels fast.

"If you heard what he said to her, you would've beaten the hell out of him too," Mac assures Dad. "I would've if Charlie hadn't literally beaten me to the punch."

I fire back a quick assuring text to my friends while Dad mumbles under his breath, though he doesn't actually protest. We all know Mac's right. Davis deserved what he got. But none of those other people did, and I spend the rest of the ride home racking my single brain cell for ways to make amends.

We pull into our driveway and despite my sour mood, a wave of grounding relief relaxes my aching body as I hop out of the car and lumber toward the house.

Casa de Porter is an old two-story colonial with rusty copper-colored brick, plum shutters, and a covered front porch. I've lived here my whole life and grew up watching our huge dogwood tree change colors, lose its leaves, and regrow them from my bedroom window. Our neighbors are pretty chill; most of them are super into decorating for holidays and some have cute dogs. Mac and I take turns keeping our yard looking fresh.

Being home is the only thing that can settle me the way the ice does—as long as I ignore the specific dogwood branch once holding our tire swing where my mom used to push me until I was five, when she decided to hit the family redo button with some guy she met during a rehab stint.

Anyway. I drop my cadaver-size hockey bag in the garage, at least having the presence of mind to unzip it so I can air out my sweat-caked protective pads.

"Gonna make herb chicken tonight," Dad says as I'm halfway up the stairs.

"Cool," I croak, heading straight into my bedroom.

I face-plant into my gray comforter, hoping I'll pass out and wake up and today will only be a nightmare. At least Dad and Mac know to leave me alone when I'm wallowing in Grumpville. Small mercies.

Tap tap.

Or not.

Ugh. "What?"

Mac steps in wearing his Minnesota Gophers Hockey T-shirt—from the Division I university he signed a letter of intent to play for after high school. "I'd tell you not to be too hard on yourself, but you won't listen to me anyway."

My eyes roll back into my skull. "I'm gonna take a nap."

"Good. Sleep it off. Just wanted to give you this." He flings a rolled-up garment at my head. "I know how much you missed it."

I unroll my freshly washed purplish red polo shirt with the Cranford logo embroidered on the upper left chest. "Thanks."

"I've got our khakis on the ironing board. I'll press 'em out after dinner."

"Thanks, Mr. Mom. I missed looking like Jake from State Farm." As far as school uniforms go, it's not the worst. At least Cranford doesn't make me wear a skirt.

"Hang it up so it doesn't get wrinkled," he says, backing out before pausing. "Oh, uh—and maybe turn your notifications off tonight? Between the game and the fight—"

Oof. "Right. Got it."

In my dreams, I go viral for sinking a sick trick shot or delivering a brilliant body check.

Instead, I'm Hockey Rocky—but, like, the one where he blows the big match at the end.

Cranford Preparatory School proudly stands away from the main roads in a naturally wooded area, giving it a private, homey feel. The campus consists of several fairy-tale-vibing stone or brick buildings—some covered with ivy, all clearly labeled with gold plaques affixed to the front doors. The K–8 lower school and 9–12 upper school sit across from each other with a fountain in between, a bronze caribou statue appearing to drink from the water. The library and fine arts center share a building to the east, while the west hosts the field house, with a cleared-out area for the baseball and softball diamonds, soccer fields, and tennis courts. Across a cobblestone walkway, the dormitory houses students—some international—who board, though about half the student body in our intentionally small classes commute locally, like me and Mac.

We share a silver Honda Accord passed down from our Pop-Pop. It still smells like him—like black coffee and chocolate scones and blue-collar political rants. Mac parks among the Audis and BMWs and other luxury vehicles belonging to our classmates. We've always been scholarship kids, but it never seemed to matter to anyone here.

Mac spots nonhockey friends in the parking lot, jerking his chin upward at them before checking back with me. "You good? Or—"

"I'm good," I assure him. The last thing I need is a pity escort through the front doors of a school I've grown up in. Blowing out a hard, steadying breath, I pull my crossbody bag across my chest and grip the strap a little tighter than usual as I trudge into the building.

The main lobby boasts polished hardwood flooring and walls featuring gilded portraits of Cranford's founders, the lighting warm and natural. To the right, administrators and their secretaries bustle about in the main office, and to the left . . .

Shit. The gaping hole in the middle of our trophy case is more glaringly obvious than I thought it would be. There's even a faint outline in the shape of the tiered trophy from where the sunlight faded the background paper behind it—an extra reminder of where it belongs. Had belonged.

"It'll be okay, Char. I bet they'll shuffle things around—maybe give our basketball championship trophy center stage for once." Emily Berry-Crane steps up beside me and wraps an arm around my back. She's a full head shorter than me and rests her own against my shoulder. "Sorry I missed it yesterday. My dads would've both been heartbroken if I bailed on the family Labor Day party. Brian texted me as soon as he could." Brian as in Flyin' Brian, my teammate and Em's boyfriend of six months. "You okay?"

I sling my arm across her shoulders in a half hug and briefly rest my cheek atop her hair, sighing. "Yeah, I wish more people missed it. Maybe once we kick off the regular season and get some dubs under our belt, people won't be as butt-hurt about the cup." I peer over my shoulder in time to spot a few of my teammates striding by, two delivering pity waves and another outright glaring.

Desperate for a topic change, I step back and take in Emily's first-day-of-school look. We all wear some variation of the standard uniform, of course—but now she's got purple streaks in her jet-black hair. "Whoa, that looks *so* good! How was the big fam reunion?"

Emily brightens at the compliment, dramatically tossing her hair over her shoulder. "Thanks! It was fun! Except my cupcakes crumbled while I was icing them so I couldn't bring a dessert. . . ."

"Aw, shit. Again? Did coconut or almond screw with you this time?"

"Chickpea flour. I'll try almond or coconut next time." Emily's diabetic and loves sweets. Her current life goal is to concoct her own grain-free, diabetic-friendly baking recipes to compile in a cookbook or a blog. I'm one of her de facto taste testers, along with—

"Is it true? Our very own Charlie Porter took down *the* Glenn McGarrity statue?" Jade Douglas, the third leg of our tripod, strides forward with all the confidence of a runway model. She opts for the pleated skirt over khakis, and literally nobody can blame her, considering her dark brown skin is flawlessly smooth, which honestly isn't fair.

"Jade!" Emily and I rush toward her and pull her in for a hug.

"Well?" she asks when she pulls back, leveling an intense Mom Look at me.

Groaning, I clap my free hand over my forehead. "Technically *I* didn't knock it over, someone else—"

"Yeah, but you started the chain reaction!"

"Don't beat yourself up too badly about it," Emily says. "Everyone knows Glenn McGarrity was a misogynistic jerk anyway." She turns back to Jade. "How was your flight yesterday? We missed you so much all summer!"

Jade's a boarding student from the *Hotlanta* suburbs, and she winces every time I call them that. Her painted lips purse. "Delayed, of course. I was hoping to get to Charlie's big game."

I shrug. "Seriously, you didn't miss much."

"You can't blame yourself, Charlie. Mercury's in retrograde, so that explains a whole lot. Not only the rough game, but my cupcakes and Jade's flight delay," Emily explains with a sage nod.

My lips roll inward as Jade outright snorts. Her scientifically gifted mind short-circuits whenever Emily reasons anything using astrology. "We had some nasty storms down in Georgia. It's still hurricane season."

"Well, I'm glad you made it in before today," I say, softening as I glance between my two best friends. "Kicking off junior year would've been weird as hell without both of you."

"Speaking of weird as hell . . ." Jade nods toward the front door. "What's your dad doing here?"

"What?" I whirl around and spot him wearing his regular work gear—an old plaid shirt with a dirt-smudged vest on top, well-worn jeans, and his mud-caked construction boots. "Uh—hi?" Blinking hard as he approaches, I quickly check inside my bag. "Are you here for Mac? I didn't forget my lunch or anything."

"Mornin', girls." Dad nods toward my friends before refocusing on me. "No, I'm here for you. Got a call from your secretary this morning asking me to come in. Not sure what—"

"Mr. Porter." Dean Quigley, Cranford's headmistress, steps out from the main office into the lobby. She wears her typical navy blazer and pencil skirt with heels, her gray-streaked hair pulled back into a bun so tight it makes her eyes pop out behind her thick-framed glasses. "Charlotte."

I grimace at my given name. "Hey, Dean Quigley."

The Quigs motions toward the door from which she appeared. "Thank you, Mr. Porter, for arriving on such short notice. If you'll both please step inside my office, there's an urgent matter I need to discuss with the both of you."

Emily and Jade look at each other before glancing back at me.

I shrug. "I'll catch up with you guys at lunch, I guess?"

They linger for a moment, a combination of curiosity and protectiveness radiating from their postures.

"Welcome back, ladies. Get to class." Dean Quigley brandishes her hand dismissively and ushers me and Dad inside, down a narrow corridor, and back into her spacious office. "Please, have a seat."

I drop into the leather chair, which squeaks as I sink lower and cross one hand over my stomach.

Dad rakes a hand through his hair and remains standing. "Is this about what happened at the rink yesterday? As you know by now, Dean Quigley, Charlie's temper gets the best of her sometimes. But she was goaded into it."

Dean Quigley walks around her mahogany desk and eases into her wingback chair, keeping her perfect posture rail straight as she folds her hands over her closed laptop. "Words should never lead to flying fists, Mr. Porter. And despite the hockey game having been complete, she was still acting as a representative of this school community. Legally, she had no right to strike the Winthrop boy. And the chaos it sparked thereafter . . . we've been dodging local news networks since dawn."

Dad squeezes my shoulder. "I'm not here to make excuses for Charlie's behavior. She'll accept whatever consequence you deem appropriate."

I grumble under my breath.

"I beg your pardon, dear?"

"I'm sorry, Dean Quigley, but he really did deserve it for the gross thing he said to me."

Dean Quigley rubs her temples. "Be that as it may, Miss Porter, you and I both know this is not your first offense. Unfortunately I have no choice but to revoke your athletic scholarship and suspend you from Cranford for six months."

Ice rushes through my veins and I bolt upright, my jaw falling unhinged. "*What?* You're *suspending* me? That's not fair!"

No school for six months means I'll miss the entire ice hockey season.

I'll miss playing for the college scouts—miss my shot at a scholarship I desperately need if I want to play at the next level.

Dad quickly backtracks on his "whatever form of punishment" or whatever he claimed seconds ago—clearly he doesn't think the consequence fits the supposed "crime" either. "Hold up now, Dean Quigley. You've known our family for a decade. My kids grew up in this school. Her friends—her life—is here at Cranford. You can't—"

"I assure you I can," Dean Quigley says, softening a hair in the next beat. "I truly am sorry it's come to this. But after receiving a scathing phone call from the president of our board of directors, I must take sharp action. With so many injured as a result of her impulsivity, along with what I've been informed is a rapidly spreading video of the incident on social media . . . it's terrible PR, and our numbers are dangerously light as is. A revocation of any scholarship funds along with a six-month suspension is written in our school's behavior policy as a consequence for an infraction of this magnitude." She pauses, pinching the bridge of her nose for a beat. "If Charlotte can keep her record clean wherever she attends the first six months of her junior year—and if she maintains at least a B grade point average—I will be happy to readmit her to Cranford for the spring trimester. That, I feel, is more than generous."

"It is," Dad assures her, patting my back. "More than generous. Thank you, Dean Quigley. Let's go, Charlie."

I scoff. "But—"

"We'll talk more at home, kiddo." Dad ushers me out of the office.

As we push through the heavy double doors, Jade and Emily leap from the chairs where they ignored Quigley's directive and loyally waited outside.

I swallow hard and shake my head, walking by them as shame, rage, and regret battle for dominance in my body. All the while, I desperately try not to picture my best friends at Cranford without me—eating lunch, hanging out between periods, and making new memories for almost an entire school year.

Three

Mac waits until we wash up and settle in for dinner before launching the Porter Family Brainstorm Sesh. "So? What are we gonna do to overturn the Quigs?"

I avoid Mac's eyes from across the table, my jaw firmly clamped as I'm forced to unlock my arms to spoon mashed potatoes onto my plate.

"Pass the peas, would ya?" Dad extends his hand as Mac passes them off.

My brother waves his fork in a small, circular brandish—like a wand that'll magically get us talking. "Well?"

Dad scratches his scruffy chin. "There's nothing we can do. Even if we somehow manage to get her unsuspended, I can't afford to send her without the scholarship money. It'll be okay. Charlie's just—gonna take a little break from Cranford."

"Two-thirds of the school year." An unfortunate math fact I understand simply because I'm used to demolishing two-thirds of a pizza in one sitting. Now I swirl my fork through my mashed potatoes, too nauseated to actually eat them. "Suspended until next spring, and I've still gotta be Bobby's rink bitch, too."

"Hey now. Community service is good for anyone," Dad says, as though it would somehow make it enjoyable or rewarding or whatever. "At least you're a minor, so it won't go on any sort of permanent record. Bobby's grateful to have an extra pair of hands for a while. He wants you to start tomorrow morning."

"Seriously? Already?"

Dad rests his hand over mine. "It's not fair, but life's not fair sometimes, and we can't do a whole lot about this. Sooner you start at the rink, sooner you'll earn back what you cost 'em. Quigley said she'll have you back after six months, and until then . . ." He hesitates before continuing. "I'll enroll you in the public high school."

The clang of my fork striking the side of my ceramic plate makes both Dad and Mac flinch. "Wait, *what*? You want me to go to school with that prick who goaded me into the fight? No way!"

Dad winces. "It's not great, I know. But I can't afford another private school without financial aid, and it's way past application deadlines. Not to mention they probably won't accept you anyway, with your . . . less-than-stellar behavioral record."

"This is bullshit." A pesky lump of feelings lodges in my throat.

Mac hums as he cuts into his chicken breast. "What about virtual school? That's a thing, right?"

"Oh. Yeah!" A spark of desperate hope flickers. "Virtual school's good with me. Not like I'd have a social life at Winthrop anyway. Might as well turn into a homeschooled hermit."

Dad considers for a few seconds before shaking his head. "Let's be real, kiddo—you can barely get yourself motivated to do your work with teachers in person. Try Winthrop, see if you can steer clear of their hockey team. It's a big school with over a thousand kids. I'll get you registered in the morning."

I shove my napkin from my lap back onto the table with more force than necessary.

Dad frowns. "You're not gonna eat?"

"Not hungry." I push back through my heels, the chair-sliding squeak setting my teeth on edge. Trudging upstairs like a pissed-off troll, I slam the door behind me and curl up on my bed.

My phone chirps twice.

I ignore my friends' texts, too busy wallowing in my shitty situation. My *shituation*, if you will.

Not long after, a soft knock raps on my door. "Can I come in?"

Mac. Again.

"Why?"

It's not a no, so he pads inside on his weirdly hairy Hobbit feet and drops onto the foot of my bed. "This sucks."

"Yeah."

"Was kinda hoping you'd start on my line for my senior year."

I twist to face him. "Is that supposed to make me feel better?"

Mac shakes his head, his hair—the same dark brown shade as mine—falling into his eyes. He rakes it back. "No, sorry. My point is—you'll get your shot when you're back next year. I know it sucks, but if you keep up your regular workouts, run drills at the pond with me when it freezes over again, you'll come back and blow 'em away better than before. That should be your focus."

I pick a loose thread on my blanket. "I'm barely gonna have any time to show my stuff to the scouts."

"Yeah, they won't see you this season—but they'll get a glimpse early next year. They won't give all their spots away by then. Besides, you're a stubborn-ass Porter. If you put your mind to something, you'll do it no matter what. And listen, I know I've said it before—but I would've taken that shot yesterday too."

My gaze levels on him. "Which shot? The backhander where I hit the damn post and lost us the Winthrop Cup, or the one where I broke that skeeze's face and got my ass kicked out of school?"

"Both," Mac replies without blinking. "I know it doesn't feel like it, but for what it's worth—I think you did the right thing. That's probably why Dad didn't ground you on top of everything else."

"I guess."

He reaches toward me with his freakish wingspan and ruffles my hair.

I swat him off. "Dude—"

"I'll train with you extra, okay? We can keep up your cardio with nighttime jogging or hit the gym at the Blizzard when you're not on shift."

My nose scrunches. "Ugh, stop being nice to me."

"Hey, don't get used to it. You'll hate me again when I'm skating circles around you on one-on-one drills this winter."

"Yeah, that's better." Sighing, I flop back onto my pillow. "Now get out. I gotta get up extra early for community service before my first day at my *awesome* new school."

Bzzzzzz. Bzzzzzz.

My phone alarm buzzes under my pillow as ass o'clock strikes again.

I should be used to it, since practices usually start before sunup, but the ungodly hour hits different when I'm not waking up for hockey. I'm half conscious as I pull on my coziest ripped jeans and a plaid shirt with my leather jacket over the top, snag a pack of strawberry Pop-Tarts, and head out the door. The sky hovers inky black overhead as I ride my bike through our sleeping town.

I've never stepped inside the Blizzard without my massive equipment bag slung over my shoulder or a meticulously taped-up hockey stick in hand. When I push into the main entrance instead of the players' side door, tendrils of dread and regret curl around my heart and squeeze.

No hockey for a whole damn season.

Finding the main office, I linger for half a minute before awkwardly knocking on the doorframe.

"Who'zit?" The gruff response belongs to Bobby, now sporting a flat cap along with a pair of suspenders under a patchwork cardigan.

"Hey. Charlie Porter. I'm here to work for you?"

Recognition lights up his face. "Ah, yep. Ten thousand buckos."

A dry, strained chuckle puffs free. "Yeah. I'm still really sorry about that, by the way."

"You may've started the fight, but you didn't push the damn thing over, did ya? I appreciate the extra set of hands." He pushes up from his squeaky desk chair and lumbers toward me. "A hockey girl, eh?" A fond glint sparkles in Bobby's eye before he waves me along. "C'mon, I'll show you around."

Touring a place I've spent half my life training in definitely feels weird, but I can't help but notice how much I don't know about the Blizzard—mostly how I've only ever spent my time on the right half of the rec center, the hockey rink, as opposed to the figure skating/public skating rink on the left. At first glance, both rinks seem similar; upon closer inspection, the other rink lacks hockey nets, red and blue lines painted on the ice, and plexiglass safety shields to protect spectators from ricocheted pucks.

Bobby walks with a slight limp and explains my duties: sweeping up the stands and indoor grounds, cleaning up after birthday parties, taking out the trash, and wiping down gym equipment. I'm also charged with snack-bar shifts and sharpening skates in the pro shop.

He teaches me how to use the cash register and we work out a daily schedule with service hours both before and after school along with some weekends.

"So basically I'm gonna be best friends with the dumpsters out back."

Bobby claps me on the shoulder. "I pay my starting staff sixteen bucks an hour, so we'll get these hours cleared for you soon enough." He enters the supply closet and extends a broom. "Let's get you started." Bobby leads me back through the double doors to the figure skating rink.

This time, it's no longer empty.

A middle-aged white woman with a pinched, serious face stands at center ice on chunky-heeled boots instead of skates. Red hair twisted into an elegant low bun, she wears heavy makeup caked over her white skin along with designer jeans and a thick sweater as she scrawls furious notes on a tablet.

The viper girl who crouched beside Konor Stratford when he narced on me skates out toward the older lady. Today she wears a fitted green Winthrop High hoodie with black yoga pants and white skates.

I catch a glimpse of her face—which is actually really pretty when she's not firing death rays from her eyes like a scary, shrimpy Superman.

Bobby reads the unspoken question on my face and leans in. "Alexa Goldstein. She's a damn talented pairs skater. That's her partner, Frankie Drake." He nods toward the boy who'd been clutching his ankle in the aftermath.

Frankie's wearing a crewneck sweater and leaning hard on crutches as he stands off-ice, looking on from the half wall. He's got light brown skin and his frosted hair curls in a Greek-god kind of way. Frankie and Alexa nod along to the older woman, who motions to her tablet before gesturing out to different points on the ice.

"That's her mom?"

"Yep. Geri Goldstein and her partner won a bronze medal in the '98 Olympics. Now she coaches her kid. These two're on the same track. They're damn good. Took first place at regionals a half hour before the lobby turned into a wrestling ring."

Oh. So that was the "big figure skating event" happening in the other rink while we lost the Winthrop Cup.

The seriousness of whatever's going on keeps my voice at a hushed whisper. "They're all business over here, huh?"

"You noticed, eh? Unlike you hockey hooligans, figure skaters rent out the rink by the hour, and it ain't cheap. The Drake boy busted his ankle in the fight. He won't be skatin' for a while."

My stomach plummets as I recall Frankie's face screwed up in agony. "I was hoping it wasn't as bad as it looked."

"They'll work through it. That Alexa—she's a real firecracker, just like her ma." He motions toward the stands. "Sweep up each row. I'll need you at the snack bar after."

I salute Bobby and climb to the top of the bleachers to start working. I don't eavesdrop, like, *on purpose*, but Geri Goldstein's commanding voice booms through the entire rink.

"Welcome to auditions." She greets the seven skinny dudes skating onto the ice one by one. They position shoulder to shoulder in front of her and Alexa.

"We're grateful you answered our call today on such short notice. As talented singles skaters, you have an incredible opportunity to get a taste of pairs skating"—she motions to her daughter—"with an Olympic-level skater on track to place high at sectionals, along with medaling at the national championships this competition season. Alexa is in need of a temporary practice partner for approximately three months while her competition partner heals from injury. As stated in our email, you will be compensated for your time while gaining extra skills and conditioning for your solo endeavors."

Blah blah blah, rich people and their rich sports. Not that hockey's cheap—but I've always worn hand-me-down pads. Making a mental note to find Frankie Drake later on to apologize in person, I pop my earbuds in and crank my music, effectively drowning Geri out to work through my cleaning tasks. My attention occasionally flickers down toward the ice, where the auditioning dudes take turns showing off their skating skills—impressively high and graceful leaps, cool spins, and extreme flexibility making me wince.

I'm nearly through sweeping when each male skater steps up to Alexa one by one. They take her by the waist and attempt to lift her off the ground.

And one by one, they fail.

I can't help it—after the last one hoists her up only a few inches and immediately drops her back to her skates, I burst out laughing. I don't notice at first thanks to my blaring music likely screwing up my eardrums, but my cackle echoes throughout the rink, and everyone—all of the puny-armed dudes, Geri Goldstein, Frankie Drake, and Alexa herself—snaps their gaze up at me.

Snagging my buds from my ears, my face warms and I grimace. "Oh. Shit. Sorry."

"You there," Geri snipes, her tone icy as she marches toward me with a hand at her hip. "Come down here."

"No thanks."

"That wasn't a refusable request."

The way she snaps her *t* sets my teeth on edge and I slowly amble down the steps until I reach ground level. "I said I'm sorry, lady. I didn't mean to—"

"Who are you working for?"

I blink and motion to my broom. "Huh?"

She scoffs. "I wasn't born yesterday. You're spying."

"Spying?"

"From another club! We know your game. They're sending lookouts younger and younger these days. So who do you work for? Let me guess—Elena Ingleborg hired you to scope out our new training partner, hm?"

Alexa at least notices the complete puzzlement on my face—not unlike when I'm taking a math test—and gently takes her mother's arm. "Mom . . . she's not a spy. Her name's Charlie Porter and she's a hockey player. From *Craaanford*." The way she mockingly sing-songs my school's name sends my eyebrows flying northbound. "She started the fight in the lobby where one of her teammates fell on Frankie and broke his ankle."

My ears burn with shame at Alexa's callout. "Yeah, I'm not a spy. I mean, that sounds pretty dope, career-wise—but there are clearly more interesting things to spy on than cringe ice skating auditions." I cut a glance to Frankie across the ice, sincerity lacing my tone. I'd planned to apologize one-on-one, but I can't bite it back now. "I'm *really* sorry about your ankle. Seriously. I didn't mean for anything like that to happen. You didn't deserve—"

"*Sorry* won't fix any of this," Alexa snaps, her voice as frigid as her withering glare. After a beat, Alexa's head tilts to the side, irritation creasing her brow. "Did you call my mother's auditions *cringe*?"

My ears warm beneath my hair. "I mean, yeah. Those guys sucked, right? Not the skating part, obviously—but they couldn't lift you up. I don't know shit about pairs skating, but isn't that kind of important? Maybe you should require, like, at least one bicep in your next audition call."

The auditioners cry out in protest.

Geri's nostrils flare, but she can't argue my point. She turns back toward them and holds up her hand to effectively cut their yelling. "You're all dismissed. Thank you for your time. Don't call us, we'll call you."

I turn to continue my sweeping, until—

"You're a hockey player. So you can skate." Geri's eyes tour my torso as she sizes me up like a Thanksgiving turkey.

"Yeah, I can skate. But not like her." I barely glance at Alexa.

"Nobody can skate like Alexa," Geri says, pride pulling across her painted lips. "You're strong, though. I bet you could lift her up."

"One-handed. So what?" I blurt, puffing out my chest a bit. A second passes and realization creeps in. "Whoa, wait. Are you trying to—"

"That's a *hard* no from me," Alexa cuts in, hands anchoring on her hips. "Seriously, Mother? Did you not process the part where she's the *reason* we're in this position in the first place? We'll audition another round of figure skaters."

Geri turns toward Alexa, softening her tone. "She's not the one who fell on Frankie. There's nobody else who can help us. All pairs skaters with upper body strength are committed to partners for the season. Remember—she doesn't need to make the jumps, she only needs to be good enough to help you practice your lifts and time out the new choreography until Frankie's healthy."

"Give hockey girl an audition!" Frankie calls from across the ice, amusement sparkling in his eyes.

I shake my head at Frankie Drake. "I'm with Little Miss Ice Princess on this one. Thanks, but no thanks."

"See? We're in agreement," Alexa says. But she can't seem to stop running her mouth as she studies her freshly manicured cuticles. "It's a shame, too—I heard she got herself kicked off her team for what she did, so she has *loads* of free time now without her hockey season. Besides, there's no way she's actually strong enough."

Her bitchy barbed retort spikes a flood of white-hot annoyance rushing through my core. I drop the broom and hop the boards, my well-worn low-top Converse landing on the ice. Stepping up to Alexa—who stands a solid three inches shorter than me, even when I'm not on skates—my hands reach out and hover over her waist, pausing before actually making contact. I don't want to touch her— part of me thinks I might turn to stone or something if I do—but Porters never back down from a challenge, direct or indirect as they may be. "May I?"

Alexa merely shrugs. "Go ahead, give it your best shot. It'll need to be a little better than the one you missed in the cup game," she drawls back with an air of taunting boredom, her own hands anchoring on my broad shoulders.

My larger hands plant at her sides. Channeling pent-up She-Hulk energy, I retaliate with a cocky smirk before hoisting her skyward with little effort, holding her there for good measure.

Alexa's elbows lock and her lips purse in the same way her mom's did earlier. "Congratulations," she deadpans. "You've proved you're all brawn, no brains, just like I assumed you were."

While Alexa's completely unimpressed, Geri lights up. "What did you say your name was?"

"It doesn't matter," I say, easing Alexa down despite the intense urge to drop her on her snooty ass. "I gotta get back to work."

"We'll pay you," Geri blurts. "I'll double whatever it is you're making here. Three months—before and after school, occasional weekends. It's a great opportunity, even for a hockey player—"

"I said no thanks." Like hell I'd help anyone from Winthrop— especially a spoiled brat who thinks she knows anything about me.

Alexa sniffs, sending me off with a dismissive regal wave. "Forget her. We'll find someone else. A real *winner*."

It takes all my willpower to not flip her off after climbing back over the boards and snagging my broom. I shoulder through the double doors linebacker-style and open the snack bar instead.

I'd rather sling cheap coffee and stale pastries to grouchy, under-caffeinated hockey parents than spend one more minute with Alexa Goldstein.

Four

Irritation festers while I finish my shift, morphing into straight-up anxiety as seconds tick by to the start of my first day at Hell High.

Mac's double-parked against the curb with my bike already hooked onto the rear rack.

I manage a half-hearted "hey" while dropping into the passenger seat and handing off one of two hot chocolates, which he accepts with a grateful grin.

"You're seriously wearing that?"

"Jealous?" I pluck the collar of my leather jacket.

Mac snickers as he drives out of the Blizzard's parking lot. "Well, you definitely look . . . comfortable."

Summoning the most obnoxious fake enthusiasm ever, I thrust my fist upward. "Hell yeah! I'm living that public school life now, baby! No uniforms! Freedom of self-expression and more reasons for bullies to screw with me! *Wooooo!*" That much snark tanks what little energy I have left and I sink lower, cracking the window.

Mac shakes his head. "They won't mess with you. If they do, they'll have to get through me first."

"Yeah, thanks—but you're across town. Besides, I can fight my own battles, remember?"

He shoots me a look.

"*Ugh*, I know. Not that I'll be fighting. I don't wanna be stuck there for my senior year, too."

"Damn right."

My guts churn harder as Mac approaches Winthrop High. The

boxy, beige brick building stands before its massive parking lot, a few bikes chained to the racks near the stairs. Traces of poorly power-washed graffiti linger above the overgrown bushes lining the lower windows. So many damn windows. Three floors of them, a few with rusty air conditioner units sticking through. I pick at a frayed thread on my well-worn messenger bag resting across my lap, hesitating.

"Oh, here. Dad went to the district admin building to register you this morning and they emailed your schedule." Mac snags a folded piece of paper from the visor over his head, handing it off. "So what's your game plan for day one? Get a feel for the place, try and blend in?"

My bitten-down black-painted fingernails drum against my thigh. Pulse quickening, I survey the students—my new temporary classmates—as he idles in the drop-off lane.

A group of thicker dudes in green-and-gold Winthrop jackets strolls in front of our car, swaggering toward two cheerleaders already in uniform. On the first day. Seriously? What are they cheering for—not forgetting how to read over the summer?

With a huff, I snag my Cranford Hockey snapback from my bag and shove it onto my head backward. "I'll never blend in with them."

Mac claps me on the shoulder. "Give 'em hell, Little Porter. Not literally, though."

I shove him back before steeling my nerves and stepping out of the car. "Thanks for the ride, Turdburger."

Keeping my head down, I climb the stairs and enter Winthrop High School for the first time ever, attempting to ignore the burning sensation of several pairs of eyes searing into me. A caribou lost in a snow leopard den.

Taking a few strides down the main hall, I stop in front of Winthrop's trophy case, nestled between two sets of forest-green lockers.

The Winthrop Cup stands front and center, gleaming with fresh silver polish.

Taunting me.

My fingers curl tighter around the strap of my messenger bag, my shoulder and neck muscles tensing with a fresh injection of shame and regret.

Sucking in a sharp breath through my nostrils, I force myself to keep walking, unfolding my schedule.

Homeroom—Mr. Healey—Rm. 320

"Is that the hockey chick from Cranford?"

"I heard she got expelled for punching out Davis."

"Yo, I saw that video! Girl's got a nasty left hook. . . ."

"Can you imagine showing your face here after missing that shot?"

Cutting the onlookers the deadliest glare I can muster, I tug my earbuds from my pocket and hook them in place, cranking my music louder while hiking up the stairs two at a time.

Finally, I find my homeroom—which, for the record, feels nothing at all like "home" with its tiny window, cold metal chairs with attached desk trays, too-bright fluorescent lighting beaming down overhead, and corny-ass motivational posters crookedly duct-taped onto white cinder-block walls. Students chat in small groups sitting or standing around.

I drop into a chair in the back corner, hoping to stay invisible for as long as possible.

A middle-aged man wearing a sweater the same shade of gray as his walrus mustache strides in a minute later. "Settle down, juniors." He opens a laptop and eases into the cushioned chair behind the desk. "I don't care if you stand or sit, listen up and let me take attendance.

Then you can do whatever till the first bell rings."

Mr. Healey begins reading names aloud, students responding in kind.

"Here."

"Here."

"Present."

"Here!"

"What's up, Mr. H.?"

"Charlotte Porter?"

"Here," I say. "And it's Charlie."

"*Ping!*" Someone bursts across the room, earning a round of mocking laughter from most of the others.

My lips press into a tight line as I trace my calloused fingertip over the vandalized initials carved into the desk.

Mr. Healey settles everyone down and finishes taking roll. Then everyone returns to their conversations, ignoring me.

Well, almost everyone.

"Bold move, wearing that loser hat around here."

My hardened gaze snaps toward the voice behind me.

One of the underevolved Winthrop hockey players whose name I don't care to learn struts by me, thankfully not sticking around for a conversation.

I wouldn't have given him the satisfaction anyway. Instead, I study my schedule—or at least pretend to, hypervigilant of everyone else around me. Wishing I could just fade into the background for six months.

The bell beeps and I wait until everyone else files out before stepping back into the now packed halls. My attention shifts between the painted directional arrows and room numbers as I round the corner and pull to a sharp stop.

Konor Stratford casually leans against a locker in his Winthrop

Hockey jacket, a captain's patch sewn onto his sleeve. His black hair shines with so much gel, like he attempted to filter himself in real life.

His arm slings casually around a petite-framed girl with wavy red hair.

Alexa Goldstein. Instead of her figure skating gear, she wears a fitted purple top, light denim jeans, and gold sandals showing off a fresh pedicure.

A bitter snicker puffs past my lips. *There's* a match made in hell.

My instinct tries tugging me in the opposite direction until I spot the number on the classroom door just past them. The class where I need to be. Instead of attempting to find some sort of detour route, I square my shoulders and hold my head high as I stride past Konor and Alexa, pretending I don't notice them despite their annoyingly commanding presence.

Stratford's voice calls behind me. "Is that . . . no way! Ladybug, wait up!"

My teeth grind and I ignore him, ducking into biology and bee-lining toward the back row.

To my great displeasure, Konor Stratford rushes inside and eases into the desk beside me. "Heeey, Porter!" His tone drips with mocking glee.

My arms fold over my chest. "Get away from me."

"Aw, why? We're both Snow Leopards now! You're gonna have to ditch that lame-ass hat, though."

I refuse to give him the satisfaction of rising to his bait. Not this time.

And I sure as hell will never be a Snow Leopard, no matter how long I'm stuck here.

The bell beeps again and I cut him a hard look. "Don't you have your own class to get to?"

"This *is* my class." He kicks back, fishing his crumpled schedule from his jacket pocket and offering it as proof. "Tried this one last year, but . . . y'know. Science is hard. So. Redo."

"Great. Lucky me." As I glance around, the rest of the desks fill in. Effectively trapped next to him, I remove my notebook and pen.

His lips curl with mischief. "Plus, this class is the shit because of Mrs. *Milf*ord. . . ." Konor lets out a low whistle as the teacher steps inside.

She's hot.

MILF hot.

Oh. That's a fitting last name.

My face heats upon thinking it as I tear my gaze away from the front of the room.

Like a rich lady's Yorkie, Stratford keeps yapping. "Redoing a class isn't a big deal. I bet you wish you could redo things, huh? A couple of your recent, regrettable life choices spring to mind. . . ."

Pinning Konor Stratford with the stoniest scowl I can muster, I lower my voice. "Shut up. Seriously. Find another seat tomorrow. I'm not sitting next to you for six whole months."

Konor visibly deflates, his hand bracing over his chest. "Does this mean you won't be my lab partner, Ladybug?"

Thankfully, Mrs. Milford's presentation connects from her laptop to the Smart Board and she begins her welcome spiel.

Every ten minutes or so, Konor emits a faint *"Ping!"*

His taunting sets my teeth on edge, but I don't react.

I won't rise to it. I can't.

By the time class ends, bottled rage thumps through my veins. I bolt from the classroom and Konor Stratford. Ducking into the nearest bathroom, I swipe open my phone to send a scathing text to my dad for putting me in this position.

I swipe away Mom's second attempted bullshit-apology call and click my text notification instead, opening my group chat with Jade and Emily.

They sent a selfie of the two of them wearing Cranford polos and matching frowns, holding up a sign reading "We miss you already!" with a doodled heart and crossed hockey sticks.

Tears sting my eyes and I blink furiously to keep them at bay.

My thumb hovers over my phone's keyboard but I leave the photo of them on read, emotion lodging in my throat.

After bio and my decompressing mini meltdown in the bathroom, I mostly dissociate through English and algebra. Then, with my earbuds cranked too loud, I make my way to the cafeteria. One look inside the jam-packed, noisy-as-shit (even over my blaring music) space, I nope right out and about-face, heading as far away from that social-disaster land mine as possible. Cowardly? Probably, but I prefer thinking of it as proactive. No doubt I would've wound up in an argument—verbal or physical—with one of the trolls from the Winthrop Hockey table. That's how I find myself standing before two double doors beneath a sign I never thought I'd voluntarily approach, much less enter.

The library.

With a quick glance over my shoulder, I enter the space and keep my head down, moseying through the stacks before finding a relatively isolated table. Perfect. I drop my messenger bag decorated with pins and patches—some frayed at the edges—onto the table and retrieve my bagged lunch.

I'm shoveling half my turkey and cheese sandwich in my face, rock music still thumping in my ears, as I unlock my phone once more to a text from Mom.

It's a picture of Kylie, my seven-year-old half sister I barely know. She's posing in a pink tutu and a T-shirt that says "Second-Grade Superstar," flashing a gap-toothed smile at the camera.

Beneath the pic, Mom writes:

(10:47 a.m.): Ky-bear says she hopes you're having a great first day of school too, Char Char! We miss you and Macky!! Xoxoxox

First of all, it's technically my second day of school. She doesn't know about the whole transfer situation yet—Mac and Dad both know better than to tell her before I do.

Secondly, we're only four hours away. If she genuinely misses us like she says she does, she'd make an actual effort to—

"*Dude!*" A tap on my shoulder sends me flailing, the damn chair nearly flipping sideways before I manage to steady myself with my palms smacking flat atop the table. I yank my earbuds out and simultaneously glower and grimace as I crane my neck to blink up at the two people now hovering over me.

Frankie Drake, with his crutches tucked under his armpits, has a judgmental look in his eyes undercut by a note of genuine amusement coloring his expression. "This is a library, Charlie Porter."

I frown. "Uh, yeah. I kinda got that by all the books and shit."

Frankie snorts. "I mean, you can't eat in here." He points to a sign I missed clearly stating *No Food or Drink.*

My eyes flicker down to what's left of the half sandwich in my other hand, crumbs sprinkled across the wooden table. "Oh. Got it. No worries, I'll clean up after myself."

The cute curvy girl standing beside Frankie wears a black dress featuring a neon-green and orange skull print, fishnet stockings, and blue hair twisted into a cool braided bun. She speaks up next. "You do that. We don't have a million janitors like you probably do at your rich-people school."

Seriously? "I'm not rich. And I'm pleased to report we clean up after ourselves at Cranford, too."

"Your cafeteria food's probably edible, at least," Frankie muses. "So you got a pretty shitty deal out of that messfest over the week-end, huh?"

"Not as shitty as you," I volley back, my gaze dipping down to the boot affixed around his injured foot. For all my harsh consequences, at least I don't have any broken bones. I apologized across the ice earlier, but it didn't feel like enough. With a wince, I look back up to him and wholehearted sincerity coats my tone. "I really am sorry, Frankie. Big-time sorry."

Frankie allows my apology to sink in for a few seconds before he softens, too. "Thanks. I know. I was pretty furious and mopey for a few hours after, but it turns out I'm not mad about taking a break from my super-intense on-ice training schedule for a couple months." His chest puffs out. "Besides, I'll be back better than ever in time for competition season, which is the fun stuff."

"Of course you will." Skull-dress girl hooks her arm through Frankie's. She hesitates before reaching out to tap one of the pins on my bag—the flag boasting red, orange, white, and pink stripes. "I've got one of those too," she shares in a surprising show of near-instant solidarity I've never really experienced, considering all the accepting straights in my life. "I'm Cyn."

"Cyn," I repeat. "Like Cindy? Cinderella?"

Her face contorts. "Just Cyn."

Frankie mostly manages to muffle his cackle. "*Cyn*thia and I should return to the front desk."

She shoots Frankie a hard look. "Whatever, *Franklin*. I'm supposed to be restocking."

Solidarity softens my face. "I'd take Cynthia or Franklin over *Charlotte* any day." I pause. "Wait, you're the librarian?"

Cyn nods. "You could say I'm one of them. They budget-cut the official librarian position a few years ago. Now they let the tutoring club supervise book checkout in shifts throughout the day. Free child labor for the school district, looks good on our résumés and college apps. Win-win, I guess?"

"Huh." I glance at Frankie. "So you're a tutor, too?"

This time, Frankie laughs loud enough for Cyn to elbow his arm. "My beautiful hyperactive brain can't think of anything I'd like doing *less* than tutoring. I'm here probably for the same reason as you—avoiding the caf."

"We eat in the back office," Cyn explains. "No greasy fingers anywhere near the books."

I wipe my hand on my shirt.

Frankie snickers. "Something tells me Charlie never had any intention of touching a book."

My lips twitch to match Frankie's. "You're not wrong."

"You're welcome to join us tomorrow, if you want." Cyn points to a door on the back wall. "In the office. For lunch."

Frankie arcs his neatly shaped eyebrow at Cyn for a beat before looking back to me. "Of course, yeah! You can totally eat with us. We know what it's like to want to avoid certain people."

For the first time since I threw that fateful punch and my world caved in on me, my shoulders slacken with a sharp injection of gratitude and relief. Frankie and Cyn will never replace Jade and Emily—but having allies at Winthrop? On my first day? My tight-lipped smile pulls wider. "That'd be cool. Thanks."

The duo returns to the front desk and I make sure every crumb ends up in the nearby trash can. With a few minutes left until World Cultures, I take out my phone once more. I leave Mom on read to return her text later and tap back to my bestie group chat.

Snapping a quick selfie wearing an exaggerated frown and pointing to my backward Cranford hat, I send it along with a text:

(11:53 a.m.): miss you nerds too.

And I do, more than I care to admit to myself. On day one of my suspension, I already miss my girls like a visceral ache. I miss Cranford's quiet campus and my favorite teachers—even if I regularly gave them hell both academically and behaviorally. I miss hockey and my teammates, my body craving skates on my feet and a stick in my hand, yearning for another intense matchup—which I won't be seeing until next season.

It's tempting to blame Gavin Davis, but my temper got me into this, I remind myself as I hook my earbuds back into place. Casting Frankie and Cyn a head nod on my way out, I step back into the halls, rounding the corner in time for another Winthrop Hockey dick to lower his shoulder and check me back into the nearest row of lockers.

Crash!

My bag and hat hit the floor while I stumble, yet miraculously stay upright.

"Oops! Sorry, Porter! I tripped!" he cries over his shoulder, his buddies cackling like a pack of stoned hyenas.

Jaw clenching as I pick up my hat and my bag from the floor, I resist the urge to storm after them and instead mutter phrases so vulgar, I swear Dean Quigley's clutching her pearls all the way across town.

Seriously, screw this place.

Five

I push myself through days two and three at Winthrop. Despite my thirty-minute reprieve spending time with Frankie and Cyn for library-office lunches, everything else sucks snow-leopard balls— the classes, the homework, the teachers, and mostly my new classmates, who continue either taunting or ignoring me, depending on how much they care about sports.

It's way worse than Coach Doug's suicide drills, which without fail make at least three of my teammates puke on the ice. Unfortunately, even with that comparison, pleas to Dad aren't enough to yank me out of there yet. Apparently three days isn't "giving it enough of a chance."

Frankie's homeroom sits across from mine and he mercifully sticks by me on our walk to first period.

I brace myself for Konor Stratford's obnoxious callout when he spots me down the crowded hall.

Instead, Alexa takes his arm and steps up on tiptoe to kiss his cheek, whispering something before turning toward us with her chin in the air. Striding forward in an uppity strut, her red high ponytail sways in steady rhythm as she approaches. "Franklin, my love," she says, pulling him in for a one-armed hug while not deigning to spare me the slightest glance. "How's the pain today? Still manageable?"

"Yep! Needed to ice it when I got home yesterday because of swelling but not too much pain." Clearly sensing lingering tension from Wednesday morning's audition crashing, Frankie clears his throat. "I'm just walking Charlie to class."

Alexa's prissy smile flickers into a sneer before relaxing once more. "How chivalrous of you. Personally, I don't believe she deserves your forgiveness so quickly, but you've always been so understanding. So charitable. Always looking out for the strays."

My eyebrows fly toward my hairline. "Strays?"

"Yes. A stray is a noun, plural 'strays.' Someone abandoned, not where they belong." She reaches out to smooth Frankie's collar. "Surely *Charlie* can read a map and follow directional arrows—or should I not assume as much, after she's taken what must be dozens of knocks to the head?"

"You *do* know that shit-for-brains you're dating is a hockey player too, right?"

"Konny's different," Alexa snaps, finally firing a piercing glare in my direction. She softens again as she refocuses on Frankie. "Anyway, I wanted to make sure you were okay . . . and remind you to stay vigilant. I'm not completely convinced she's not a spy."

I snort. "So am I a brainless jock or a Black Widow spy? Seems like you can't make up your mind."

"You're a pest either way," Alexa snipes back, giving Frankie's arm a squeeze. "Take care of yourself—and watch your back. I'll text you later."

Frankie's lips clamp together as if he's struggling not to interject, but he gives a dutiful nod in return. Once she storms off, he exhales in a strained chuckle. "Sorry about that. She's pretty protective of me."

"Protective or possessive? Does she try to control all the people you hang around?"

"Not all of them. I know you don't know her enough to see it, but Alexa's a good person; I've been her partner for years. She just—she's really intense about holding grudges and stuff. I've never been injured this bad before, and all the uncertainty is really rattling her. But I'll ask her to chill. I know you've got enough going on right now."

A good person? I cast Frankie a skeptical squint. "Nah, it's cool. Queen bees like that don't bother me."

Once Alexa returns to *Konny* Stratford, she casts one final warning glare at me over her shoulder.

I blow her a kiss in return.

Alexa huffs, whirling back around so violently she nearly whips an underclassman with her ponytail.

"It's actually kinda funny watching girls like that lose their shit when they don't get the reaction they want."

Amusement dances in Frankie's eyes and he shakes his head, fondness written all over his face. "Watch your back, Charlie. You don't wanna mess with Lex too much."

"Thanks, but I can handle her. I'll see you at lunch?" Hopefully the Ice Princess doesn't talk Frankie into revoking his library lunch invitation. I'll be even more pathetic sitting alone.

"You got it. See ya there."

No matter how cool Frankie's been, I can't forget he'll always be on Alexa's side no matter what. He's her partner.

And I'm the one who screwed over her skating season.

Saturday morning at the Blizzard, I complete my regular cleaning tasks and trudge from the dumpsters to the lobby, moving slower than usual; the *stressy depressy* brain gremlins take up residence in my head, a weird sluggishness weighing down my limbs.

No surprise, really. I haven't been off the ice for this long since I caught the flu in fifth grade, and as it turns out, working at the Blizzard without being able to skate reroutes me deeper into Sadville.

"You gotta be shitting me," I grumble under my breath, spotting the forever-long line waiting for the snack bar—me—to open. There's no way this many parents are lazy enough to not stop at 7-Eleven or Starbucks on a Saturday, right? Everyone knows rink coffee is comparatively garbage.

Forcing my scowl into a pained smile, I rush behind the counter, wash my hands, and push up the service window to get to work.

Coffee. Danish. Coffee. Banana. Hot chocolate. Bagel. Coffee. Coffee.

"Looks like this slo-mo snack-stand girl could use some help," calls a voice about four customers back in line.

My nostrils flare. The last thing I need is someone being a dick to me right now. "Are you serious? I can handle—"

"Surprise!"

Annoyance instantly washes away, relief tinging my tired laugh. "You guys are the worst."

"You love us," Jade corrects, tugging Emily along as they barge into the cramped snack stall with me. "Put us to work, Porter. How can we help?"

No longer as bothered by the line of undercaffeinated, disgruntled hockey parents, my heart swells.

"Um. I'll take the register and food if you guys can manage coffee, tea, and hot chocolate?"

Emily salutes me. "Fab! We're all over this barista business!"

"We make it look damn good, too," Jade adds as we fall into an easy, efficient rhythm.

With two extra pairs of hands, the line shrinks quickly.

We serve what must be the two hundredth cup of crappy coffee when Emily checks the clock. "I need to get to basketball practice."

Practice. What I wouldn't give for Coach Doug to kick my ass on-ice right now.

Jade checks her smartwatch. "And I should hit the library.

Not sure why I thought it was a good idea to sign up for four AP classes. . . ."

I wince. "*Four?*"

"You've met my parents," Jade reminds us. Last year, Dr. Douglas and Mama Douglas flew up to visit Jade and took us all out for a five-star steak dinner. It was *awesome*.

"We know you'll ace 'em all." Emily takes my elbow. "Come with us to the fair tonight?"

"Tonight?" Oh, right. The Winthrop Fall Festival. "Wait, no—it's on Winthrop grounds. You guys can't expect me to go back to that school on my day off!"

Jade checks my hip with hers. "Hey, it's not their event. It's just held there 'cause the grounds are big enough. It's a tradition! Plus, you think we're gonna let you mope around without us on weekends? You got a tough deal from Quigley, but we sure as hell won't let you avoid us for six months."

"You can't say no. Jade already got permission to leave campus *and* there'll be funnel cake," Emily reminds me with a knowing grin. "You *love* funnel cake."

Those brain goblins whisper for me to reject their offer, but I know I need to fight back against the sloth-like funk I've been drowning in. Besides, it's not like they'll accept no for an answer. And I do happen to love funnel cake. "Okay, yeah. I'm in."

Emily whoops while a victorious smile stretches across Jade's lips.

"We'll pick you up around seven," Jade promises. "Prepare yourself to get your ass handed to you on all the games."

I playfully roll my eyes and thank them for their help before they head out. Then I begin restocking hot chocolate packets. The lull in customers pulls my attention toward the hockey rink, despair blossoming fungus-like in my chest as I lean harder over the counter, watching an intramural hockey team run drills. A longing frown deepens as I yearn to join them, a fresh round of bitterness and regret boiling in my stomach as my brain battles my heart for dominance.

Think of the fair! Think of your friends! Don't think of hockey! Funnel cake, bitch!!

I pluck a rag from the sink behind me and begin wiping down the countertop.

"*There* you are." The familiar no-nonsense tone hooks my attention. Unfortunately, it's too late to duck and hide from the Ice Queen herself.

My customer service smile is so phony I'm not sure why I bother trying. "Hey, Mrs. Goldstein. I'm about to close up. Coffee?"

Geri's face twists as though she'd sniffed fresh dog shit. "Mrs. Goldstein is my mother, Charlie."

"Oh." I should probably sound more apologetic but I'm not.

In my periphery, Alexa lingers near the figure skating rink doors, but I refuse to so much as glance in her direction.

"I spoke with Bobby," she says. "He agreed that if I make a sizable donation toward the funding of a new Greg Mc-Whatever-His-Name-Is statue, he'll allow you to finish your community service hours by skating for me. As Alexa's practice partner."

I freeze. "Whoa, what? You did that without asking me first? Why would you—"

"You're an athlete, are you not? A hockey player, yes, but you're not allowed to skate. Not here, anyway. It must be killing you."

My spine snaps straighter. She's right, of course—but I refuse to give her the satisfaction of a verbal answer, even as my traitorous jaw twitches. "Alexa made it pretty damn clear she doesn't want my help. And no offense, but I'd rather spend time with the dumpsters out back."

Geri's perfectly painted lips purse. "I won't apologize for my daughter's assertiveness."

I scoff. "That's what you call it?"

Geri simply pauses for a moment, raising a gloved hand and pulling the glove off one finger at a time. "What if I sweeten the pot?" She extends her phone across the counter, scrolling through a list of contacts. "You seem like a go-getter, Charlie. Someone with her sights on a dream greater than peaking as a high school athlete. Say . . . a college career? The US Women's Olympic Team? If you're talented enough, which . . . I've asked around. Word in the rink is you're quite skilled, if a bit showy and impulsive. And junior year is prime for scouting, is it not?"

My nostrils flare at the reminder, cheeks burning. "Yeah. But I'm gonna miss this season, so I can't play for the scouts."

"Unless," she starts, motioning to her phone, "I make a call. I have personal connections to higher-ups in the athletic departments at several universities. Division I schools. I could set something up for you with at least three programs. Make sure they see what they need to see. You'll get a real chance to prove yourself before all their roster spots are filled."

My heart skips a beat. "That's—really? You can do that?"

"I can. *If* you help me in return." Geri pockets her phone. "You may not care for Alexa personally, but I'm offering a business relationship. An opportunity to strengthen your skills for your own sport. Skates need to stay sharp, do they not?"

"You'd go through all this trouble for me? I'm the one who put you in this position, remember?"

"I'd go through this trouble and more for my daughter, yes. You've clearly shown remorse for what you've done, and if Frankie forgives you, that's all the more reason you should agree to this. You miss it, don't you?" She pauses, her eyes tracking hockey players through the glass double doors leading to the hockey rink. "It's a shame you're afraid to spend time with my Alexa. Three months until Frankie's back—three months of intense practice in a sport requiring even more conditioning than hockey."

Resting my hand atop the bag of stale-ass hot dog buns, my brain works to process Geri's response. "Wait. You think I'm *scared*?"

Geri holds up both hands. "I'm only calling it like I see it."

"I'm not afraid of anyone," I all but growl, my focus darting toward the figure skating rink to lock onto Alexa as though that would prove I'm the opposite of afraid.

Alexa stands by the doors with her arms folded over her chest, tapping her toe as she meets my eyes with yet another withering glower.

As if she's trying to brainwash me into rejecting her mom's offer.

My expression sours . . . until a muted whistle from the hockey rink pulls my attention to the other side of the complex again. Hockey practice jerseys sweep down ice and my heart thumps harder.

Three months of learning how to figure skate and putting up with Alexa the Ice Princess rather than working earsplitting children's birthday parties and wrestling leaky garbage bags into dumpsters. Keeping myself in shape on-ice instead of selling overpriced Gatorade and folding clothes in the pro shop upstairs. Geri's promise to land me a scouting tryout for not one but *three* D-I schools.

"Well?" Geri eyes me expectantly, extending her hand across the snack bar counter without her phone this time.

It's kind of a no-brainer, isn't it? I'm an athlete through and through. If I can't play hockey, I might as well train my ass off until I get back to my team. And how can I ignore Geri's connections?

Plus, I'm not scared of anyone—especially Alexa Goldstein.

My head jerks upward in a clear nod. "Yeah. Okay, fine. I'll do it. Thanks, Mrs. Golds—I mean, Geri?" I take her hand and initiate a firm shake.

Her mouth twists into a hungry grin—like maybe I sealed a pact with the devil. "Call me Coach."

Obvious strain underlies my stunned smile. "Coach. Got it."

"We'll start Monday morning at five thirty sharp. I'll leave a pair of skates and appropriate training gear for you in the locker room. What size boot are you?"

"Ten. Um . . . appropriate training gear?" My brow knits. "If you try and make me wear a tutu or tights or whatever, I'm out."

"You don't need to worry about that. Just don't be late." She takes three steps away from the snack bar before turning back. "And Charlie?"

"Yeah, Coach?"

"Get a good night's sleep the night before." Her eyes flash with terrifying determination. "You're gonna need it."

Six

"So, let me get this straight . . . ," Jade says as Emily scans for a parking spot back at Winthrop High. I'd spent the ride to the fair recapping everything about my convo with Geri Goldstein after they'd left the snack bar. The deal. "You agreed to let some Karen and her Karen Junior daughter turn you into a girly ice skater for three months? And she *says* she can get you a shot with big-level scouts? How do we know she's telling the truth?"

"She's an Olympic bronze medalist," Emily reminds Jade. "Which means her connections must be legit, right?"

"I don't think she'd screw me over. She's asking a lot of me."

Jade hums. "Still sounds a little sketchy. You should get all this in writing, make her sign it."

I smirk. "Maybe Mama Douglas is right about suggesting you go prelaw in college. . . ."

"*Ugh*, nope! Not gonna happen." Jade points left. "There's one, Em."

"Got it." Emily guides her Prius into the parking spot. "What did your dad and Mac say about all this?"

"They're worried I'll get hurt," I say, recalling the conversation over dinner an hour ago. "But when I explained Geri's terms with the scout connections and how it'll keep me in much better shape than at-home workouts with Mac, they were cool with it."

Emily cuts the ignition and we all hop out of the car. "Good! At least they're supportive. And you're not competing or anything, just practicing—so you don't need to do any of the risky jumps and twirls and stuff, right?"

"I think so, yeah." Despite knowing I don't have to enter the building this time, a sense of dread churns in my stomach as I glance upward. Even after sundown on a weekend, the gross vibes hit the same.

Jade strides around to our side of the car and glares at the massive brick building with its snow leopard statue mounted proudly in front of their flagpole. "It's still so weird that you go here now," she says, tugging the tie from her hair twists and checking her reflection in Em's side-view mirror. "And I hate how the fair's held here too. Should be somewhere neutral. Lip gloss?"

Emily skips over to accept the tube. "Charlie's here *temporarily*," she amends while swabbing the glaze over her lips. "I mean, they couldn't fit a Ferris wheel and everything on Cranford grounds, y'know? And this is open to the whole town. It's for all of us." She offers me the lip gloss next.

I cast her an offended look and swat her hand away. They both know I don't do lip gloss. Pulling a tube of ChapStick from my frayed jeans, I apply the cherry-flavored balm over my lips instead. Then I adjust my backward Cranford cap and force my focus on the fair. "Let's do this."

Flip-flops slap beneath our feet as we approach the red, orange, and yellow balloon archway. Circus tents of varying sizes canopy across the expansive fields and a Ferris wheel rotates in the distance, along with a carousel spinning at the same tempo on the opposite side. Pop music blares through rigged speakers and food trucks stand throughout.

Emily audibly inhales, exhaling with a happy sigh. "Smells like fun."

"Smells like oversaturated buttered popcorn and dudes wearing too much Axe body spray." I wave a hand over my nose as a group of middle school boys pass by.

"This way." Jade loops her arm through mine and leads us toward a canopied booth where about a hundred old-fashioned glass bottles stand at attention in a perfect square. "I've got a pretty good feeling about whooping both your butts at ring toss."

"Step right up," drones the booth operator. Her attention remains on her phone while she smacks her gum. "Three bucks for ten rings. Hook seven and win a fish." She vaguely motions to the wall of bagged multicolored betta fish.

Emily gasps. "Oh, they're cute!"

Jade surveys the game with her typical analytical eye. "This'll be cake. I'll hook more than the both of you combined."

"No chance." Plunging my hand into my pocket, I retrieve three crumpled dollar bills and flatten them on the booth's ledge in exchange for ten orange plastic rings.

Emily and Jade swap their cash for blue and green rings respectively.

We stand side by side, tossing rings one at a time. We all hook our first ring, earning a fist pump from Emily.

"Caribou-yah!"

Jade and I wince at the corny Cranford mascot cheer she adopted during third-grade field day.

"What if we all win a fish? They can be fish besties!"

"You can't put them all in the same tank," Jade says. "They'll eat each other."

Emily's eyes pop wider. "Seriously?"

"It's true." Jade glances over at the suddenly distraught ray of sunshine, offering her a playful elbow nudge. "Is your boo coming tonight?"

At the mention of Emily's boyfriend, she seems to shake herself out of thinking about fish cannibalism. "Brian's coming with some of the hockey guys a little later."

"Mac included," I add, flinging another ring. It misses, plastic clinking the rim of a glass bottle. My face twists. "I hate that sound."

"That's my favorite sound in the world," a deeper, familiar voice drawls behind us. "The sweet, sweet sound of puck on pipe."

"*Ping!*" another guy chimes in beside him.

We whirl around, instant glares shifting on all of our faces.

"Hey, Ladybug." Konor Stratford stands before us flanked by four of his teammates, Alexa tucked beneath his arm. "Check it out," he says, extending his free arm and twisting it enough to display the new patch embroidered on his jacket: *Winthrop Cup Champions*.

My molars grind hard. "There should be an asterisk after 'Champions.'"

Alexa's giggle carries a mocking undertone. "*Someone's* a sore loser."

Okay, so I'm a little bit of a sore loser—but I can't let Alexa Goldstein, of all people, know she's right. So instead, I bark a bitter laugh and roll my eyes. "I don't dig losing because someone cheats and the ref doesn't make the right call on a hooking penalty, *Alexa*." Her name spits off my tongue in the tone of a hurled swear.

I name her on purpose, Jade and Emily both snapping their gazes onto my profile from either side. Yep, she's the one. The bitchy Barbie I agreed to help.

"Hey, I didn't cheat!" Gavin Davis steps forward, his eye still sporting a purple bruise from last weekend's punch. He scans my girls and changes trains. "Your friends are cute, Porter." He visually tours Jade and Emily and licks his lips. Gross. "Aren't you gonna introduce us?"

His question makes my skin crawl and I protectively step forward. "No chance."

Under the bright field lights, the jagged scar on Davis's jawline shines pink against his pale skin. I make a mental note to find out who put it there and ask Emily to bake them a thank-you cake.

"Gloating isn't a good look on anyone," Jade says, ignoring Gavin in favor of pinning Konor and Alexa with a hard stare.

"Aw, c'mon now." Konor raises his free hand in a show of truce. "We're not only here to remind you of our excellent victory. Where's the town camaraderie? It's the Fall Festival! You ladies should hit the rides with us. Let's be friends."

"*Hard* pass." He's probably just trying to wingman for Sir Hooks-a-lot. I nod back toward the booth bottles. "Ignore them."

"Or," Davis offers, motioning to the next booth over, "I could challenge you to a water-gun race? Give you a chance to redeem yourself?"

"No thanks!" Emily says, slipping an arm around my middle and attempting to tug me in the opposite direction.

I don't budge.

Jade groans. They know I can't resist a challenge.

A chance to best Davis at something? It's not hockey, but I'll take any win I can get at this point. My mouth curls into a competitive twist. "Let's go."

"Don't beat her too bad, bro," Konor calls as we all stride toward the next booth. "She's helping out my girl. Can't bruise her ego much more."

Alexa cackles. "Don't worry about that. My mom hired her, not me. She'll punk out in two weeks tops, and I'll find someone better."

I cut a glare over my shoulder as I step beside Davis. The booth allows room for eight players per match, but this race will be only the two of us, our supporters surrounding us from behind in a semi-circle.

The booth operator collects our dollar bills and motions to the targets in each of our lanes. "Better your aim, faster the ball rises. Ball hits the top first, you'll win a prize." He nods toward the rows of stuffed animals.

Gavin winks at Jade. "I'll win one of those teddy bears for you, gorgeous."

Jade recoils as though she sniffed his sweaty hockey pads. "I'm good."

"Ready?" The game operator steps on the two release pedals to activate the water guns tethered to the booth by a short rope for me and Davis, both of us crouched in the ready position as we take aim at our targets. "Go!"

Kshhh!

A loud rush of water shoots from our guns at the same moment.

"C'mon, Charlie!" Emily cheers.

Jade joins in. "You got this, girl!"

"C'mon, man! Stay focused!" another Winthrop hockey crony calls.

Davis flinches and falls behind.

Triumph flashes in my chest as the ball in my lane rises notably higher than Davis's.

Alexa runs her mouth behind me. "I mean, can you even *picture* her on figure skates? There's not a graceful bone in that body."

Konor laughs. "Not one. It's a little freakish for a girl to be *that* muscular, don't you think, babe?"

Their verbal venom strikes me square in the back, hard enough where it pulls my attention and triggers my fury.

Hard enough where I no longer give a shit about racing Davis.

I'm dimly aware of Jade and Emily verbally erupting in my defense to tell them off—and yet before my single brain cell musters a complete thought, I'm turning and firing the water gun directly at Konor and Alexa.

Alexa shrieks as though I'm actively murdering her, darting behind her boyfriend and using him as a human shield.

The game siren blares. "Hell yeah, I won!" Davis declares, though nobody else cares about the game anymore.

The booth attendant cuts the water.

"What the hell was *that*, Porter?" Konor croaks, peeling off his soaked jacket and wiping the water from his face. When he shifts, Alexa comes into full view looking like a drowned rat. Or more like a drowned red panda.

"Oh my *god*, she's a menace!" Alexa's sputtering in shock, her perfectly styled hair now drenched and sticking to her cheeks. Her light blue top clings and reveals the outline of her bra beneath. She clutches her arms over her chest, undiluted rage etched through her daggered glare and chattering teeth. "You'll pay for this, Charlie Porter," she snarls before taking Konor's hand and striding away, the gang of snow leopards trailing after them.

I set the water gun back on the booth ledge, admiring my handiwork as Alexa attempts to wring out her hair while staggering off.

Jade and Emily are still laughing when they hook their arms through mine and guide me toward the food trucks.

"I think you earned a funnel cake for getting through that without throwing a punch. My treat," Jade insists.

"They deserved it," Emily pipes up in support. "You totally had Davis beat again, too."

"Damn right I did."

We're in line for treats when Mac rushes toward us, Flyin' Brian and Matty in tow. "What the hell happened, Char? We saw Stratford and Davis on our way in—they said something about my sister being unhinged—and Stratford and his girlfriend looked like they hit up a waterslide fully clothed."

"They deserved it." I repeat Emily's declaration with a slight shrug. "Don't worry, booth dude was cool. I'm not gonna get in trouble or anything, it's just water."

Mac visibly relaxes. "You're so damn chaotic."

"And we share genes, so what does that say about you?"

Emily leans into Brian. "You guys should've seen the looks on their faces. Maybe one day they'll learn how to stop running their mouths."

"Unlikely." Jade buys a round of funnel cakes, cotton candy, and a huge bag of popcorn.

Our Cranford crew spends the rest of the night enjoying the cool autumn breeze, the games and rides, and each other's company.

I'm midair on the Ferris wheel popping wisps of pink spun sugar into my mouth as my mind replays Frankie's warning. *"Watch your back, Charlie. You don't wanna mess with Lex too much."*

Would Alexa retaliate in school somehow? Would her mom make me pay on the ice on Monday morning? Probably. Whatever.

The horrified look on her prissy, too-pretty face was definitely worth it.

Seven

Monday morning, I report directly to the Blizzard's figure skating rink and duck into the locker room. Geri left a bag for me labeled with a magenta Sharpie—training clothes and a pair of brand-new black figure skates. When I emerge in my uncomfortable gear, Geri stands at center ice in a navy sweater, studded jeans, and tall, flat boots, with a tablet clutched to her chest.

Alexa—decidedly much drier than the last time I saw her—stands beside her with her hands on her hips, her upper lip curled with impatience. "You're two minutes late."

I step onto ice for the first time in over a week, which should absolutely be a happy moment for me regardless of whatever I'm about to endure.

Instead, I'm tugging at the black spandex riding up my ass crack in a super wedgie, grumbling as I glide toward them. "Didn't realize these pants would take a full two minutes to actually pull on, so."

A wolf whistle carries from the stands. "Lookin' good, Charlie! Work that spandex, girl!"

I thrust a thumbs-up at Frankie, relief soothing over my tense neck and shoulder muscles. At least it's not me and the Goldstein girls alone.

Alexa huffs. "Be grateful we didn't insist on you wearing nude tights and a rhinestone-encrusted leotard."

"Probably a good idea—you know, *not* pissing off the person who's responsible for lifting your ass into the air for the next three months."

"Yes, well. *I'm* not neuron deficient."

Refusing to give her the satisfaction of reacting to yet another verbal barb, I glance down to my black figure skates—smoother and narrower than my well-fitted hockey skates. I tap the blade's jagged toe pick against the ice. Unlike my perfectly snug hockey boots, the figure skates squeeze my feet all wrong, pinching and rubbing in all different spots.

"You'll break the skates in after a few weeks," Geri assures me.

"What about these pants? Kinda feels like I'm wearing an adult diaper." At first glance, my bottoms look like regular shiny yoga pants—but according to the tag I pulled off, they're lined with three millimeters of neoprene, a synthetic rubber designed to "reduce impact velocity."

Translation: my ass will surely be hitting the ice hard and often, and the pants are supposed to make sure I'm able to walk the next day.

"You could let her wear her hockey pants," Frankie offers with a teasing grin.

Geri waves him off. "They're for the best. You'll thank me later." She takes one firm step toward me. "We're going to give you a crash course in the basics of pairs figure skating today, Charlie." She pauses. "Starting with stroking."

I snicker, slamming a hand over my mouth in a failed attempt to muffle the noise.

Alexa tips her head back. "Seriously? Grow up."

Geri levels a stern look at me. "Stroking," she enunciates sharper, quirking a perfectly shaped eyebrow my way as though daring me to laugh again, "is what we call skating in sync with your partner. There are different types of stroking, and we'll start with the basic forward version." She taps her tablet and turns it to face me.

On screen, a pair skates in perfect tandem while holding hands, gliding around the perimeter of the ice—almost as if they're exact shadows of each other. Alexa's eyes pierce through me as though making sure I'm engaged in the lesson.

"Notice their form here," Geri says. "As you're standing in for Frankie, watch the male skater in particular. Note how he positions his body slightly behind his partner at each corner and twists his torso so she can cross over smoothly."

Alexa continues. "The trick is in the grip. The hand-holding position determines if our shadow tracking is correct. If not, it'll feel awkward and the execution will appear too stiff or too loose."

A smirk twitches at the corners of my lips. "Avoid stroking too stiff or too loosely. Got it."

Frankie cackles, though immediately ducks behind the boards when Geri levels him with a nonverbal warning.

Alexa pins a withering glare on her mother. "I told you she wouldn't take this seriously enough."

"Get to work," Geri snaps. "Link hands."

Alexa takes a deep, steadying breath, bracing herself as though she's about to reach into a barrel full of hungry piranhas—and extends her slight, manicured fingers toward me.

I slowly reach out to take her hand. Mine's notably larger, with bitten-down nails, my fingertips calloused from years spent gripping hockey sticks.

Alexa frowns and mutters under her breath as she tugs, leading me toward the perimeter of the oval rink. "Ever heard of hand lotion?"

"Ever heard of a muzzle?" I fire back through clenched teeth.

"Start with slow strokes, Alexa Michelle," Geri calls. "On my count. Push off on your right leg first. And . . . one, two, one, two . . ."

"I got this," I assure Alexa—because how difficult can skating in sync with someone actually be?

We start off pretty damn smooth. I easily follow Geri's rhythmic counting, my weird skates hitting the ice in steady rhythm with

Alexa's. As we approach the rounded corner, I lag back a bit like the dude in the video.

Except my toe pick catches the ice unexpectedly, sending me falling out of count.

"*Shit*," I hiss, stumbling on the crossover. Tripping over my own damn skates in a wildly humiliating fashion, I hit the ice hard. For the record, the neoprene crap sewn into my pants doesn't help at all; the impact on my left butt cheek radiates into my hip.

"You let go of my hand," Alexa says, hands braced on her hips. "Never let go of my hand."

"What did you want me to do—pull you down with me?" I climb back to my skates and brush off the frost from my left side.

Alexa shrugs. "That would've been perfectly fine. I'm not made of glass."

"No? And yet you couldn't handle getting sprayed with a little water. . . ."

"That wasn't *a little water* and you know it!"

"Run it again," Geri commands, ignoring our banter. "As many times as it takes."

It takes eight more bungled attempts with four more wipeouts for me to get the hang of leading Alexa through a semiclean crossover stroke, which isn't nearly good enough for Geri, who remains at center ice barking corrections to fix my form throughout.

"Keep your head up, Charlie!"

"Don't sickle your free foot!"

"Skate through your hips, not your shoulders—there's nobody to check into the boards over here!"

After forty-five minutes, here's my first takeaway:

Alexa Goldstein is a control-freak dragon in princess form, just as intense if not more unforgiving than her mother.

"You'd crush it as a hockey coach, y'know," I pant at Coach

Geri, dragging my achy legs in long gliding strides past her once she calls time on practice.

"They could never afford me," she sniffs. "Same time tomorrow. We'll pick up right where we left off."

"You did good for your first practice, Charlie!" Frankie calls from the stands.

"Below average at best," Alexa amends.

I pop on my blade guards for the short trek from the ice to the locker room while Alexa lingers to no doubt complain about me to her mom. Once safely away from the dragon ladies, I flop onto the locker room bench, blinking in confusion.

A faint floral scent wafts in the locker room air—I must've not noticed it before when I rushed to change into my new practice gear. Having grown up used to musty postgame stench in both boys' and girls' hockey locker rooms, I can't help but croak out a delirious laugh.

I might only be a few dozen yards from the rink where I grew up, but it's like I traveled to another dimension, with snippy girly girls and yoga pants from hell.

I yank off my skates and socks, noting the bright blisters littering my feet where my figure skating boots rub in an entirely different way than hockey boots.

I can't even blame my feet. I'm equally as irritated and confused.

Snagging my gym bag, I carefully slide into my shower flip-flops and shuffle into the adjacent bathroom, choosing a stall and turning on the water before stripping down. Stepping beneath the rushing lukewarm spray, I bow my head and allow the water to wash over me. A grumble escapes as I lather my coconut-scented shampoo through my hair, my open feet wounds stinging and muscles I never knew existed beginning to ache. My head spins with Geri and Alexa's brutally blunt feedback and all the new terms and techniques I learned on day one. A cold rush of dread floods my veins upon remembering I committed to enduring this again tomorrow—and several days per week until Frankie Drake's return.

Am I regretting this commitment already? Oh yeah, you bet. It kinda tracks though, considering my not-so-smart decision-making lately. If nothing else, at least I'm consistent.

Like if I wrote an autobiography, its title would be:

Yikes, Girl: The Not-So-Hot Shots and Many Misses of Charlie Porter

I rinse my shampoo and apply leave-in conditioner, then squirt some body wash onto a rag before being wrenched from my thoughts.

"Those look painful."

Gasping, I damn near choke on hard township water as Alexa's voice carries into my shower. I relax a beat later, registering her presence in the stall beside me.

Specifically, her ankles and dainty, small feet sporting a few freckles on top, both visible beneath the single stall wall separating us.

Our naked selves.

Holy shit. Focus up, Porter.

"Uh. What?"

"Your feet." Her words snap impatiently and bounce off damp tile, carrying with an echo. "The more you skate on those boots, the more comfortable they'll feel."

The casual tone in Alexa's voice low-key blows my mind.

Because we're high-key naked.

I've never had a naked conversation with anyone.

One time Emily tried to FaceTime me and Jade from one of her "bomb-ass bath-bomb baths" (her words), and I told her she's a creep and she should call me back later.

Play it cool, Porter.

"Yeah, I know. I've broken in new skates before. I'll be fine." I rush to scrub the sweat from my body. Logically I understand Alexa can't see through walls and it's not like a sudden tornado will sweep through and break the partition between us.

But *still*.

There's also a tiny, terrible part of me now wishing *I* could see through walls, but the instant I think it, guilt twists up my gut and deep shame rushes through my veins. Not, like, religious guilt or homophobic guilt or anything like that—I just don't wanna objectify girls the way guys do. But sometimes it's hard not to have those thoughts when a girl is, like . . . *really* pretty.

Alexa may be a bitch, but she's a *hot* bitch. And I have eyes, okay?

"You can quit if it was too much for you today," Alexa casually continues, her tone making it clear that's very much her wish. "Figure skating requires much more discipline than hockey. I thought it might be too challenging."

I huff. "Don't you worry about me. I can handle—"

Thbbttt!

An unmistakable fart sound emits from Alexa's stall.

Alexa sputters, horror tinging her tone. "Oh my god, I swear that's my conditioner bottle!"

A booming snort-laugh tears through my vocal cords and reverberates off wet tiled walls.

She groans. "Shut *up*! Oh my god, you're *so* immature. . . ."

"Oh, come on, farts are funny whether they're real or not."

It's Alexa's turn to scoff. "You're the most annoying human I've had the misfortune to meet."

I'm sure she hears the smirk in my tone. "Now I'm kinda picturing your farts like rocket fuel, launching you into the air for your fancy jump-twists—"

"*Grow. Up.*" The Ice Princess cuts me off. Music blares from her stall in the next beat, effectively cutting off any chance I had to retort.

I rinse the soap from my body and shut off the water a minute later, toweling off faster than ever and pulling on clean boxer briefs, my jeans, and a faded old band T-shirt with my plaid shirt open on top. Then I wring out my hair onto the floor. It'll air-dry wavy and a little frizzy, but I don't care; I'll braid it when I'm bored in class later.

Then I amble back to the locker room.

Letting my sore feet fully dry, I lower back onto the bench. I'm reaching under my T-shirt to apply my deo when Alexa emerges from the bathroom wearing a short yellow bathrobe with its tie secured around her waist and her hair twisted up in a light blue towel.

My hand contracts like it's suddenly possessed, the plastic deodorant cap popping from my fingers. I curse as I bend over, scrambling to find it beneath the bench.

"You're going to clean those out, right?" she asks, snagging a white tackle box with a red cross symbol on its lid and easing down beside me.

My gaze follows hers to my battered feet. "I cleaned 'em in the shower. . . ."

"You need antiseptic spray or they could get infected."

"I'm fine, know-it-all." I reach for a Band-Aid, ignoring the antiseptic.

Alexa swats my hand away as she primly perches on the bench and crosses her legs, angling her body toward me. "Stop. Let me do it."

While she fishes through the kit, the front of Alexa's robe opens probably more than Alexa realizes. As soon as I catch the barest glimpse of her bra strap and a hint of cleave, my eyes snap to the ceiling. *Jesus, Porter. Chill.* Refocusing on my foot situation, I shift and kick my right ankle up over my left knee, clearing my throat. "Wow, you won't even let me put my own Band-Aids on? You really are a control freak, huh?"

"Your feet are more valuable to me than the rest of you. Also, you're long overdue for a pedicure—or at least a toenail trim," she notes, a flicker of disgust crossing her face.

"Maybe I like them this way," I counter, though she's not wrong.

"Ew." Alexa uncaps the antiseptic spray, spritzing the disinfectant into my open sores.

I suck in a sharp breath and emit a slew of unholy swears on my shuddering exhale.

Amusement stretches across her lips. "The big bad hockey player can't handle a little sting, huh?"

"You're a goddamn sadist," I growl. "But it's fine." My pinched tone betrays me and I offer a cool shrug. "Surprised me, that's all. I'm good."

"Mm-hmm." Alexa continues disinfecting my wounds on one foot before fishing out some Band-Aids. "Neosporin quickens the healing process." She squirts clear gel from the tube onto the center of the bandages. Methodically, she sticks them over each of my open sores, then snaps her fingers. "Switch."

I shift on the bench and allow her to repeat the process for my other foot.

"Your feet are weirdly big," she muses aloud.

Another mischievous grin flickers at the corners of my mouth. "Well, you know what they say about girls with big feet."

"Big egos?" Alexa volleys back, making quick work of patching up the rest of the blisters. "There. All done. Change your Band-Aids after school and let them air out overnight."

My nose scrunches as I peer at my bandaged feet. "Cool. Now I've got Frankenstein feet."

Alexa raises her pointer finger. "You mean Frankenstein's monster's feet."

"Huh?"

She heaves a heavy sigh. "Victor Frankenstein was the name of the scientist, not the monster. Frankenstein created the monster."

I blink like a tired llama with a hint of impishness. "So you're telling me you're a nerd?"

Alexa presses her palm to her forehead, though I swear I spot a flicker of amusement in her expression before she schools her lips into sourpuss mode again. "I'm a nerd because I like to read? Does that make you a jock because you play hockey?"

"Umm, yes?"

"Labels are unnecessary. You can be athletic and not be a jock. You can love reading and not be a nerd. You can wear black nail polish and not be a goth or whatever." She taps my dark-painted thumbnail. "People love to categorize people in boxes with neat little labels. But humans are way more complex than that."

I consider for a moment. Honestly, it's damn near impossible to focus on much of anything with Alexa Goldstein sitting beside me wearing a bathrobe. "You're the one stereotyping me as a brainless jock," I mutter. Reaching for my socks, I carefully slide them over my newly bandaged feet. "So what's his name, then?"

Alexa unwinds her towel from her hair, damp dark red waves falling down her back. "Who?"

"Frankenstein's monster."

"Why don't you read the book and find out?" She stands and pulls her rolled-up jeans from her bag, stepping into each leg to tug them up over her hips. "Or—you don't strike me as much of a reader. Google it." With a patronizing wink, Alexa snags her makeup bag and struts back into the bathroom.

Never in my life have I ever wanted to read something so damn badly—just to prove her wrong.

Eight

Against my own expectations, I survive three weeks at Winthrop High mostly thanks to lunches with Frankie and Cyn, my efforts to avoid the Winthrop hockey team as much as possible, stress-relieving night jogs with Mac, and continuing to spend weekends with Jade and Emily.

Against Alexa Goldstein's expectations, I survive three whole weeks of figure skating—despite her constant snark and goading during practices.

It's the last Friday morning in September and after another grueling practice, I'm a sweaty mess. On the plus side, I'm less sore in general, the muscles I'm utilizing to stroke around the ice and learn spinning techniques bulking up to support my efforts. My feet are so used to being coated in Band-Aids they'll probably feel strange when I don't need them anymore.

Alexa won't admit it, but I'm definitely getting the hang of skating with toe picks.

I turn to follow her off-ice when Geri calls us back.

"Hold on, girls. One more thing before you're dismissed."

We both whirl around on our skates, cheeks flushed and fighting to regulate our breathing.

"More reps, Coach?" I pant. "Time's up, isn't it? And I'm killing it with my sit spins. . . ."

"*Killing it* is a generous self-assessment," Geri says, conceding a beat later. "You're improving, yes. I want to offer a token of gratitude for your dedication so far." She reaches into the pocket of her blazer and extends two tickets boasting the logo of my favorite pro team—Boston Fleet of the Professional Women's Hockey League.

I gasp. "Holy crap, for real?" Uncharacteristic giddiness sends me hopping on my skates. "I haven't been to a pro game in forever!"

Geri struggles to tamp down her smile. "Yes, *for real*. Franklin suggested it. The game's tomorrow night."

My eyes flicker toward the beaming Frankie. Clearly he noticed the Boston Fleet logo pinned onto my bag, and I may or may not have launched into a rant during lunch last week about how Boston's goalie totally got snubbed for the MVP award last season.

"Frankie's observant and thoughtful like that," Alexa adds.

"Thanks, Coach. That's super cool of you." I reach out to accept the tickets—but Geri holds tight to their other end before I can pluck them free.

"One condition." There are always conditions with Geri, and my head tilts to the side. "You take Alexa with you."

"Wait, what?" Alexa and I chorus—the first time we're actually in sync without eight failed attempts beforehand.

Alexa shakes her head. "No thanks. I have plans tomorrow night."

With Stratford, no doubt. My upper lip curls at the thought.

"Rearrange them," Geri replies. "I'm sick and tired of you two constantly bickering during practice. You'll go and enjoy a night out together—outside of the Blizzard and away from anyone's school grounds."

I grimace. "Kind of a waste though, right? If she doesn't care about hockey?"

Geri releases the tickets to me. "It's money well spent if the two of you can find some common ground. That's my assignment. Find something you have in common—aside from your overall athletic ability and your extreme stubbornness. I refuse to deal with two more months of you sniping at each other at every opportunity."

Alexa whines under her breath and turns sharp on her skates, heading off-ice.

I mutter another thanks to Geri, following suit.

The two of us don't speak as we wash up and get ready for school, and I'm wondering if she's dreading spending one-on-one time with me as much as I am with her. I spend the whole school day and most of Friday night curious about what negotiation tactics she's playing with her mom to back out.

She doesn't win that battle, as evidenced by my receiving no cancellation notice by either of them; instead, I receive a simple text from Alexa. No greeting, just her address.

So on Saturday night, I follow my phone's GPS app toward her home, stoked about the game despite my undoubtedly miserable company for the evening.

"Hot damn," I whisper to myself as I take a moment to admire the Goldsteins' jumbo white stone-and-stucco house sporting some cool twisty topiary landscaping, a crystal chandelier sparkling through the center upper-floor window, and an elephant-gray front door with a fancy-ass gold knocker. I wonder if Alexa's house is bigger than Jade's family estate down in Georgia.

While I consider texting to let her know I'm here, she bursts through the front door of her house and struts down the walkway. Wearing a forest-green Winthrop hoodie with a denim jacket on top and her hair pulled half back, she drops into the passenger seat of my car and immediately pulls on her seat belt. "Hopefully you're not as reckless of a driver as you are with everything else."

I snort. "Well, hello to you too, princess." She smells nice—like warm vanilla with a hint of something flowery. Inwardly scolding myself for noticing, I shift the gear into drive and pull off from the curb. "Lost the battle with your mom, huh?"

"Unfortunately for both of us, yes." She's quiet after that until a new song streams from my car's speakers. Her reddish eyebrow arches my way. "You like Taylor?"

"Huh?" Oh, the music. "It's a random Spotify playlist, but some of her songs are pretty good, I guess? I'm not, like, a Swiftie or anything." I blink, casting her an amused grin at a stop sign. "Wait. Are you telling me you're a Swiftie?"

Alexa makes a strained sound—almost as if I insulted her mother. "*Some of her songs are pretty good, you guess?* Wow. You have *no* taste. She's the most brilliant songwriter of our generation and that's a fact, not an opinion. Anyway, we both like Taylor Swift. That's something in common. Mission accomplished."

"Okay, that's a stretch, but I'll play along. Now you don't have to talk to me the rest of the night." It shouldn't bother me. I should actually be relieved, right? So why the hell does my stomach clench? Whatever. I don't need to talk when I get to watch my favorite team.

We're halfway there when Alexa reaches out to turn up the air conditioner.

"You're kind of overdressed—layers wise, I mean, if you want to leave your jacket in the car. The rink won't be that cold." She should know that, having grown up in an ice rink, too.

Alexa sniffs. "I'm simply prepared in case *someone* decides to dump a cup of water over my head at any point."

My chuckle erupts and I shrug. "Don't start nothing, won't be nothing."

She groans.

We arrive at Boston's home ice arena—the Tsongas Center in Lowell—and I lead Alexa inside with our tickets in hand, a rush of excitement shooting down my spine as we take our seats ten rows up near center ice. The team's banner hangs overhead as they skate around the right-side goal for warm-ups. "They're favored to be the Walter Cup champions this season, y'know."

Alexa's expression remains unimpressed. "What's with you hockey players and your obsession with cup-shaped trophies?" She peers onto the ice, her gaze shifting to the team toward the left. "The purple team any good?"

"Minnesota? Yep. Their captain is pretty much the best player in the entire league."

Alexa eyes me. "So is this part of your plan? Try to get good enough to make one of these teams?"

"Oh, I'll get here someday," I assure her, cockiness sharp in my tone. "That's the dream, anyway. College hockey, then the bigs." Flinging a finger gun toward the women's pro teams, I unzip my jacket to reveal my hunter-green Fleet T-shirt beneath.

The refs gather and whistle for the starting face-off while I tip my head back and cheer with the rest of the crowd. *"Let's gooooo!"*

Alexa flinches and whips out her phone, muttering something under her breath about Ibuprofen. She's the only one not watching as the puck drops for the two teams to begin their match, and I couldn't give less of a damn. It's her loss, I tell myself as I lean forward in my seat, cheering for my team.

Throughout the first period, I'm laser focused on the game—high-fiving strangers within reaching distance when our team scores, booing refs for bad calls, filming a few video clips and sending them to Mac during play stoppages.

It's during the first intermission that the jumbotron screen lights up on the scoreboard, highlighting the best plays during the first period and engaging fans with interactive trivia games.

Alexa remains locked in on her phone—until I react near frantically beside her.

I straighten my posture, whip my jacket off, push up my sleeve, and flex my bicep.

Attention finally pulled from texting her boyfriend, Alexa's eyes damn near bug out of her head. "What the *hell* are you doing?"

My free hand points to the jumbotron, where the crew chooses flexing fans at random to display in their MEGA MUSCLES frame. "I'm trying to get on the Flex Cam!"

Alexa slinks lower in her seat. "Oh my god, you're *so* embarrassing."

"Why? Because I've got a *freakish* body?" I pin her with a rare serious look, calling Stratford's shitty insult back to mind.

Alexa softens, a quick wince flickering across her face. "Charlie, I'm—Konor shouldn't have—"

"C'mon, man! I'm right here!" I cut her off with a cry, bouncing back to flex mode and praying to the hockey gods for my five seconds of fame. Unfortunately, the camera operator doesn't choose to highlight my guns for the crowd. With a defeated sigh, I pull my jacket back on and drop back into my seat as the second period begins. "Weak. You want some popcorn or something?"

My attempt to keep the subject away from Stratford and their taunting from the fair makes Alexa deflate—with regret or relief, I'm not sure.

She nods. "Sure, I'm a fan of popcorn."

"Hey, there's another thing we've got in common. I'll be right back." Popping up from the seat, I head toward the concession stands and return just in time for Boston to score another goal.

This time, Alexa's watching intently, curiosity bordering on confusion swirling in her eyes. "I don't get it," she mumbles, reaching over to pluck a few warm and buttery popped kernels into her mouth. "Thanks."

"The puck went into the other team's net. That's a goal," I explain, clawing a handful of popcorn and shoving it into my mouth like I'm a toddler.

Alexa's head tips back with impatience. "I meant I don't get *them*. A team full of women. How they just . . . get along like that, work together. Like they're all friends or something."

"They're teammates and probably friends off-ice, too. Good teams usually are." I take a moment to consider Alexa's question. That's when I realize I've never seen her hanging out with anyone besides Stratford and the hockey guys, or Frankie in the Blizzard. "Not a lot of girl-on-girl support in your sport, huh?"

Alexa releases a few notes of a biting chuckle. "You have no idea how bad it is. Back when we lived in New Hampshire, Mallory Ingleborg—she's a pairs skater with her brother—she was my best friend. At least I thought she was. Turned out she got close to me because she was trying to beat me. She psyched me out before a big competition, got in my head and told me I didn't even have to try too hard to win, which somehow messed with my mindset and—" She cuts herself off. "Whatever, I'm better than her. Being friends with girls is not worth the drama. With school and training and my mom's curfews, I don't even have *time* for friends."

I blink owlishly. "Everyone needs friends." I can't imagine my life without Jade and Emily. My teammates, too, even if some of them are still a little pissed at me. And though it's new, I'd dread my days at Winthrop a million times more if I didn't have Frankie and Cyn.

"Agree to disagree." Snagging some more popcorn, Alexa tosses a piece up into the air and catches it in her mouth. It's probably her attempt at a topic change, but I can't resist a challenge—even a non-verbal one.

So I toss a kernel even higher and catch it with ease.

On her next attempt, Alexa flings a piece of popcorn even higher . . . and it bounces off her chin, falling to the floor.

I smirk. "You almost had that one." Then I toss mine as high as she just did, snagging it from the air with my tongue.

"Show-off," she mumbles, though there's no sting in her tone this time. She even keeps her phone in her pocket and settles in to watch the game.

After the refs blow their whistles to signal the end of the second period, more trivia questions pop up on the jumbotron. Then another frame game appears—this time it's the Kiss Cam. The camera operator pans to several couples, waiting for them to kiss each other to coax applause from the crowd.

I laugh along . . . up until Alexa and I pop into frame.

Since the camera focused on straight-looking couples the past four turns, the entire crowd cries even louder in encouragement.

A panicked laugh bursts from my throat. *"Seriously?"*

I watch Alexa on the big screen lighting up with shock.

The crowd chants. *"Kiss her! Kiss her! Kiss her!"*

Seconds feel like minutes and I shake my head, doing my best to maintain my chill on camera. Eventually the camera operators will take a damn hint and move on, right? Except they don't.

"Jesus, people. *Fine.*" Alexa rolls her eyes before shifting in her seat, leaning over to press two fingers beneath my chin and plant a lingering kiss to my cheek.

I'm dimly aware of the screeching wolf whistles surrounding us as my face turns as red as a goddamn tomato, my fist clenching so hard around a handful of popcorn, the kernelly treat crackles to dust.

For the entire third period I keep my eyes locked on the ice— though, honestly? I can't seem to focus on much other than the remnants of Alexa's lip stain tingling against my skin.

Nine

"Hold up . . . she *kissed* you? Like, with her lips?" Emily's face shines with delight behind her raised mug of chai tea.

It's Sunday afternoon and the three of us chill in a round booth at the Winthrop Beanery, our favorite homework hangout spot. Textbooks, school-issued laptops, notebooks, and pens litter the table around our caffeinated and/or sugary drinks, my hot chocolate towering with extra whipped cream.

"What else do you kiss someone with, Emily?" As Emily's expression shifts to resemble the smiling purple imp emoji, Jade realizes the error of her question and holds up her hand. "On second thought, don't answer that. I'm good with not knowing the specifics of whatever you get up to with Flyin' Brian." Jade sips her latte and refocuses her attention toward me. "So do we still hate Alexa? What's going on?"

"I mean, yeah? Just because she thawed out a little bit doesn't erase how she's been treating me, right? She was weirdly quiet on the ride home, staring out the window. She still probably hates me."

"It doesn't erase the past month, no," Em agrees. "But maybe she's slow to warm up? She wouldn't have kissed you if she genuinely hated you." She pauses. "Oooh, if you find out her birth date and time, I can do her whole star chart! That might help you figure out some of her motivations and what sets her off and stuff."

Jade shakes her head, though fondness clearly underlies her exasperation. "Not the star charts again."

Emily levels a heatless glare at Jade. "Of course you don't

believe. You're a Capricorn sun." She hums and takes a thoughtful sip of her tea. "And Alexa must have a Virgo placement somewhere in her chart; that would explain her perfectionism and some of her prickly behavior. . . ."

I sigh. "Can we change the subject, please?" I'm so damn tired of thinking of Alexa Goldstein. I think about her even when we're not skating together—replaying our conversations in my head, trying to mentally chess-move how she might zing me during next practice and how I can cleverly retort. She's obviously under my skin and it's beyond exhausting. "Tell me what's been going on with you guys. Anything interesting happening at Cranford? Did the Quigs find another student to focus all her disciplinary efforts on? She must be so bored without me there." Then I shift to Emily and Jade in turn. "How're the grain-free baking attempts going? Did you draw me anything cool lately? I could use some artwork for my dinged-to-hell locker."

While Emily shares details from yesterday's bake-athon with support from Flyin' Brian, Jade retrieves her sketchbook and pencils from her bag and begins sketching while we chat; she keeps her work in progress tilted toward her so I can't see it until it's finished. As if I'd peek or something. *Psh.*

I savor these weekend hangouts more than ever now that I don't get to see my girls during the week. We're mostly through our hot beverages when Jade's phone lights up on the table.

Our eyes dart to the screen, Jade's dad popping up as an incoming call.

Jade drops her pencil and closes her sketchbook, straightening her posture before answering the FaceTime. "Hi, Daddy!"

"There's my baby girl!"

Emily and I obnoxiously squish against Jade until we're in frame.

"Hey, Dr. Douglas!" I call with a wave.

"Charlie and Emily! How are you young ladies doing? Keeping my little girl on track?"

Emily rests her head on Jade's shoulder. "She's the one who keeps us on track!"

Dr. Douglas chuckles. "Her mother and I would expect nothing less."

Jade leans both left and right to shoulder us out of frame, exasperated fondness stuck on her face. "How are all y'all doing at home?" Her southern accent always cranks higher when she's talking with family. It's adorable.

"Good, good. Had the cousins over last night for dinner. We miss you."

"I miss y'all, too. I miss Mama's cooking most of all, though."

While Jade catches up with her dad, I slowly reach toward her sketchbook, pinching the corner.

Jade doesn't miss a beat, chattering on while snatching my wrist midgrab.

I pout and settle back with my hot chocolate, opening my biology textbook to study instead. Last week's pop quiz on mitosis earned me a D for "didn't digest shit in class," so I know I need to try a little harder. My return to Cranford in the spring depends on it.

Em and I work quietly, and we both tune back in when Jade's mother's voice carries through the phone.

"Remind her about the summer program applications, Edward!"

Jade stiffens. "I heard her. Tell Mama I didn't forget."

Dr. Douglas's pride carries in his deep voice. "I know you didn't. We've got all the faith in the world you'll get accepted—and not just because your old man's a proud alum."

Jade works harder to keep her spirits up for the remainder of their call. If her dad notices, he doesn't mention it. When she hangs up, she takes a deep, steadying breath and sinks back against the booth.

Emily's face scrunches. "You didn't tell them about RISD yet, huh?"

Jade shakes her head. "Still waiting for a good time to bring it up."

"There's probably never gonna be a perfect time," I say. "Pretty sure they'll notice they're cutting a check for the RISD fine arts summer session instead of Haverford's science camp."

"I'm applying for both," Jade says, pulling her sketchbook back in front of her—finally allowing us to see the cool dragon sketch she's working on, smoke billowing out of its ears. "Maybe I won't even get into RISD, and then I won't need to face Hattie's wrath when I tell her I want to be an artist and not a scientist or a lawyer."

Nudging Jade's nondrawing arm with my elbow, I cast her a firm nod. "You know we've got your back, right? If art's your passion, you should totally go for RISD. I mean, obviously you've got serious skills." I tap the corner of the sketchbook page. "That's gonna look *so dope* in my locker."

She continues shading the dragon's scales. "You try telling my parents that. They'll explain how mortifying it would be introducing the Douglas children—the heart surgeon, the entertainment lawyer, the soon-to-be civil engineer . . . and the starving artist. Not that my parents would ever let me *starve*, but you know . . ."

"You've got time," Emily reminds her. "And we're here to help. However you need us."

Jade nods. "I'll hold you both to that."

I'm halfway through my walk home when my phone buzzes in my pocket. Glancing at the screen, I blow out a hard exhale before accepting the call.

"—a venti iced mocha latte with extra whip, one pump mocha—" Mom smacks her gum on the other line.

I frown. "Mom?"

"That'll be six seventy-nine, please pull around."

"Oh, hi, hon! I'm at the Starbucks drive-through"—as if I couldn't figure that one out on my own—"just thought I'd give you a call while I'm out running errands. How ya been, Char?" She pronounces the *Ch* like *Sh*—one syllable away from the full name I despise. It sets my teeth on edge every time.

"Fine," I say, not bothering to tell her about the whole suspension fiasco. "Just walking home from meeting Jade and Em at the Beanery. How're you? How's Kylie?" Maybe it's dickish of me, but I never ask about Rick, her new husband. Well, not *new* . . . but newer, I guess.

She answers in the plural anyway. "Me and Ricky are good! Ky-Ky's *loving* second grade. She's got a great teacher and some really nice friends in her class."

"Yeah? That's great." Mom doesn't hear my lack of enthusiasm. She never does. And I fully realize it's super immature for me to be jealous of a seven-year-old, but sometimes I can't help it. She's the redo daughter. The kid who fits into Mom's life in her new town, with her eight-year sobriety chip and clean slate.

"What about hockey? Your brother mentioned something about you not playing this season? What's that about?"

Dammit, Mac. "Oh, uh—yeah, just taking a little break from the team. Gotta focus on schoolwork. Y'know, college applications at the end of this year and all."

"What a responsible choice! I'm sure you'll get yourself into a great school, just like Macky. Do you think you'll follow him out to Minnesota?"

If she really knew me at all, she'd recognize my lie for what it is.

I guess that's the good thing about her living in upstate New York. "I don't know, maybe? Kinda depends on if I get a scholarship." My stomach sinks, recalling how I took my own fate out of my hands and now my future's hanging on toe-picked figure skates and girly Goldsteins.

It's a risk, bringing up something about myself. I know Mom will inevitably twist the focus to Kylie, but I clear my throat and give it another try anyway. "I actually started figure skating, since I'm not playing hockey. To keep myself in shape and stuff. Thought it'd be good to learn something new." It's half the truth, anyway.

"Figure skating? Wow! That's—" she pauses, then her voice simultaneously muffles and carries. *"I asked for extra whip. Be a doll and add a little more? Thank ya much!"*

I kick a rock on the path home, mumbling under my breath.

"That's *wonderful*. Kylie wants to ski, but I think it might be a little too dangerous for her. Don't you think that's a little too dangerous for a seven-year-old? Kid's a whip, let me tell ya—picks up things so damn fast. Dance, gymnastics, now skiing. God, now I'm having flashbacks of fighting with your father about you and your brother starting hockey too young. . . ."

I pull the phone away from my ear and drag my hand down my face, running through a round of breathing exercises before lifting the phone once more.

She's back to yammering on about Kylie skipping ahead two levels in gymnastics.

Somehow, I manage to dissociate until she rambles to a pause. "That's great, Ma. Listen, I gotta go do some more homework and stuff."

"Oh, of course you do! Okay, hon. *So* good to hear your voice. Let me know when we can make some time to meet up again. Maybe around the holidays?"

"Sure, sounds good. See ya." I end the call, guilt and relief intermingling in my chest as per usual. She'll make plans, then she'll break them 80 percent of the time. At least I know by now never to hold my breath.

One of those cartoony gray storm clouds hangs over my head when I turn onto our street and find Mac in the driveway wearing his hockey gloves.

"There you are." He takes one look at me and winces. "Let me guess—you picked up the phone when Mom called?"

I snort. "Does that mean the golden child actually let her go to voicemail for once?"

"Nah, I missed her call while I was in the shower, figured she'd try you next. Didn't call her back yet."

"You're a dick for telling her I'm off the team."

Mac squints. "Sorry. She kept asking about you. I could only put it off so much. We both know I'm a shitty liar." He crouches to pluck my hockey stick from the lawn and tosses it to me.

I catch it one-handed, dropping my book-filled bag on the leaf-littered grass with a heavy thump.

Maybe it's because I'm on feelings overload thanks to Alexa being weird and Mom pissing me off again, but reuniting with my hockey stick lodges emotion tight in my throat—like I suddenly swallowed a hockey puck.

Mac shuffles the street puck toward me in a sharp pass and I instinctively receive it in a soft cradle stop.

Dribbling the puck back and forth, I shift to the side, rear back, and fire a slap shot at the target—the plastic goalie net we regularly drag in front of the garage, which earned several dozen dents in the cracked white paint thanks to our practicing over the years.

My shot sails true, the puck hitting the netting and rolling back down the driveway on its side. I snag it before it rolls into the street, scooping it up onto the flat edge of my stick's blade and tossing it into the air a few times like a pancake in a frying pan.

"All right, fancy pants." Mac folds his gloved hands atop the butt of his stick and leans his chin into them. "Wrist shot, upper stick side."

Despite the location change and my temporary reprieve from the team, Mac's still captain. And while I wouldn't think twice about defying my brother's orders on literally anything, I can't shake off a senior teammate even if we share DNA. It's hockey team law. With that in mind, I quit puck juggling and shoot a wrister; the puck once again finds its mark in the upper right corner of the net and pops back to me.

"Good. A month away and you haven't lost your edge. Now a backhander, lower glove side."

I deke to my right before flinging the puck with my stick's outside blade, the more challenging shot no match for my determination.

"Beautiful." Mac steps between me and the goal, crouching into ready position. "Let's add a defender to the mix."

For the next hour, everything stressful about the past few hours, few days, few weeks melts away—Winthrop High and their cockroach-infested hockey team, Alexa and Coach Geri, my sore-as-hell bandaged feet, and my own mom. It's only me and Mac drilling plays in the driveway. At the end of our impromptu practice, I win our one-on-one scrimmage and celebrate a little too hard, my fists pumping in the air.

"Hell yeah! Little Porter emerges victorious! Old Man Porter loses his dazzle in the face of his superior sibling!"

"Shut up, I let you win!" Mac drops his stick and shoulder checks me to the grass, and just like that, he's back in brother mode.

I'm laughing harder than I've laughed since before I got myself into this whole Winthrop mess, snagging Mac's ankle to trip him up before he can escape.

"Yo, Sonic and Knuckles!" Dad calls from the front porch, hands in his pockets as he shakes his head with exaggerated exasperation. "You can get your own goddamn grass stains out of your clothes. What do you want for dinner?"

"Pizza!" we chorus, still catching our breath as we climb back to our feet and gather our gear.

Mac rakes his hand through his hair and pins me with a competitive glare. "Rematch tomorrow?"

Duh. "You're on."

Ten

October hits and teachers swap their "Welcome back!" bulletin boards for corny, spooky themes. All of Winthrop—even the Blizzard—displays festive decorations both outside and inside shops and houses.

There's something special about autumn in Vermont, like everything's off-kilter until the season hits; the leaves start changing and the scarecrows, faux cobwebs, and orange lights bring out more childlike happiness in people. Carved, painted, or plain old pumpkins litter every step and railing. There's a cool and comforting chill in the air.

And because I am both cool and chill, Halloween happens to be my favorite holiday.

So October passes quicker than last month. In those thirty days, my figure skating improves. I master all the stroking techniques, manage not to fall out of my spins about 80 percent of the time, and start getting the hang of lifting Alexa into the air while skating at slow speeds.

We continue snarking and sniping at each other, but it's different now. Annoying little puppy nibbles rather than sharp-toothed grown-dog chomps. Not like *flirting*, which Jade and Emily wrongfully insinuated during our last Beanery homework hangout, but a sort of playful teasing among temporary partners. Competitive ribbing! There we go.

'Tis the season to swap my Cranford Hockey snapback with my Cranford Hockey beanie. I'm maturely handling occasional forced interactions with Konor in bio and unfortunate run-ins with Gavin Davis in the halls; I finally figure out the best routes between classes to avoid those to whom I'd grant the superlative of "most likely to roofie girls in college."

After the last Friday bell, I crouch by my locker shoving the books and binders I'll need for this weekend's homework into my near-bursting bag. For real, the trick to the Winthrop hockey team's leg muscles? Fifty-pound backpacks.

"Charmander!" Frankie's smile shines pearly as ever as he crutches toward me and leans against the locker beside mine. Lately he's been alternating my nicknames based on different evolutions of the same Pokémon. I forget which evolution that particular one is, but I know it's the dope orange dragon, so I don't mind it.

"Hey, Drake." I push to my feet.

"We made it through another week," he says, hooking his thumbs through the straps of his JanSport. "And I know I missed practice this morning, but a little birdie told me you're improving on your sit spins."

"A little birdie, huh? Don't you mean a bloodthirsty vulture?"

Frankie laughs. He's grown used to me bitching about Alexa, and he and Cyn don't seem to mind giving me space to vent—even if Frankie keeps trying to convince me she's not totally evil. "Got any big plans for tomorrow?"

"Tomorrow?"

Frankie motions to the skeleton propped up on a hay barrel outside the chemistry lab—surely donated by the science department.

"Oh, right. Actual Halloween." I shrug with the shoulder not weighed down by a million pounds of books. "I'm gonna head over to Emily's to give out candy. And by 'give out candy' I mean eat half of it."

"You don't go trick-or-treating? Legally we're still kids, so why not go around and score a whole pillowcase full for ourselves? Me and Cyn are gonna hit up the rich neighborhoods for some full-size bars. I've got a costume and—"

"What's it gonna be, a fairy?" Gavin Davis cuts in as he stops a few lockers down, opening his own to check his ugly mug in the mirror. "Not much of a costume for someone like you, though."

Frankie's entire demeanor shifts, his shoulders hunching as he shrinks and stares at the floor.

Meanwhile my spine snaps straighter, on high alert, my inner viper ready to strike. "Wait—does this tool bag say this kind of homophobic garbage to you regularly?"

"I ignore it, Charlie. I'm a pacifist." He musters a slight shrug.

"Yeah? Cool. I'm not." Without much concern for my own well-being, I stride up to Gavin Davis, grip him from behind, and slam his broad back against the nearest locker, holding him there with my forearm across his beefy neck.

"Porter, what the *hell*—"

"Mess with Frankie again," I snarl, my eyes blazing. "I dare you."

"You're already on thin ice here," he wheezes. "Gonna make another stupid mistake?"

"You mean deliver a well-deserved consequence for shit you shouldn't be getting away with?" My forearm presses harder into his throat as I lower my voice to a dangerous whisper. "Mess with Frankie again and I'll finish what I started at the Blizzard. Say whatever pervy shit you want to me—but nobody messes with my friends."

Davis scowls and raises both hands. "Fine, Porter. Get *off* me."

I step back and cross my arms over my chest while Davis turns and barrels down the hall, calling over his shoulder, "Crazy bitch."

That's where I spot Alexa—who casts Davis an equally threatening death glare.

Then she shoots me a look I've never seen from her before.

It takes me a minute to register it for what it is.

Gratitude.

She nods firmly in thanks before heading off.

"Didn't need you to do that," Frankie says, though his body sags with relief. "I've got threatening arms too, remember? I don't want you getting in trouble again because of me."

"But you're a pacifist, you said so yourself. Besides . . ." My eyes flicker down to his boot. "Least I can do."

"I told you to stop apologizing for that," Frankie says.

We walk side by side toward another weekend of freedom, taking a deep breath once we pass through the double doors. I wish I could bottle the perfect crispness in the air and take hits from it during the gross, humid summer months. "Have fun with Cyn tomorrow night. Score me some Reese's Cups if you can?"

"Will do. And wish me luck, would ya? I've got my big follow-up appointment with my ortho doc tomorrow."

"Yeah? Good luck, dude! Happy Halloween."

Frankie steps in and pulls me into a hug lasting an extra beat longer than it needs to. "Happy Halloween."

The next night, Mac drops me off at Emily's house on his way to some seniors-only party.

The Berry-Cranes live in a cozy eggshell-blue townhome. Emily is an only child and her dads both teach in the township next to ours. Their house is always the most decked out for every holiday, so Jade and I love scoring invites for any occasion—especially since one of Em's dads is a *Top Chef*–level cook. Because of the geographical and also neighborly closeness of the families in this particular community, it's a hot spot for trick-or-treaters on Halloween night.

Jade and I chill on the porch steps with the candy bowl between us, taking turns pinning hard stares on greedy children who snag more than two pieces. Emily—wearing a cat ear headband with painted whiskers streaking across her cheeks—returns with a tray. She hands each of us a cup of hot cider and her latest baking attempt wrapped in a napkin.

"Okay, guys, try these! The cider's courtesy of my dad, and the pumpkin chocolate chip cookies are courtesy of *moi*."

"Ooooh, I'm ready." I share a private, bracing look with Jade as we accept our treats.

"Pumpkin chocolate chip, huh?"

Noting Emily's hopeful stare, I make sure to control my facial reactions.

"They're not perfect," she warns, dropping to sit on my other side, then pulling the candy bowl onto her lap.

"Not . . . bad," I croak, sipping the cider to provide enough moisture to help me swallow the sandpapery masticated crumbles. "A little dry . . ."

"*A little?*" Jade coughs.

Emily deflates. "Damn. Almond flour's the *worst*. I'll try something else next time."

"No, hey!" I lean over to playfully nudge her shoulder with mine. "The flavor's solid! It's the consistency. The pumpkin and dark chocolate together are . . ." I bring my fingertips to my lips, making the chef's kiss gesture. "You're so close to cracking the grain-free-flour situation. Once you do . . . you'll have a hundred recipes and you'll need a whole damn encyclopedia to publish them. Jade'll draw you some super cool cover art."

"Damn right I will." Jade finishes her cookie in solidarity.

Emily sighs with contentment. "Thanks, you guys." She nods toward the sidewalk, where various groups of trick-or-treaters amble in both directions. "So what's the new total?"

Jade lifts her phone from her lap. Her mouth moves quietly as she counts her tallies. "Four Batmen, two Supermen, two Harley Quinns, five Iron Men, seven Black Panthers, three Captain Americas, two Thors, one Loki, one Hawkeye—the Kate Bishop version, highly approve—and nine Spider-Men."

Emily emits a low whistle. "What'd I tell you? Marvel kicks DC butt every year. Pay up."

"Hey, the night's not over yet. Plenty more kids in costumes hanging around." I pause. "There seriously need to be more girl superheroes. If I see one more Disney Princess, I'm gonna chuck candy at their parents."

Jade snorts. "And make the little girls cry? What's the word for Halloween Grinch?"

"Asshole," I supply. Jade and Em chuckle into their cider cups.

"Where's your Wonder Woman costume, then?" Jade asks.

"At the dry cleaner's, obviously. It's been a busy week fighting crime in this dangerous suburbia."

"Trick or treat!"

Jade grins at three kids running up Emily's walkway, their chaperone hanging out by the fence. "Wow, okay. So we have a zombie, a rock star, and a . . ." She squints at the little boy with random socks attached to his footie pajamas, his hair styled straight up and out to the sides.

"I'm static cling," he mumbles with a world-weary sigh. Clearly he's been receiving many confused looks and questions from Em's neighbors.

I can't suppress my snicker. "Aw man, I hate static cling! Scariest costume of the night. Here, take more chocolate." I reach over and claw a handful from the bowl, dropping it into the kid's candy sack.

He lights up. "Thanks!"

As that trio retreats, a little girl skips up the path wearing a snowman costume. *"Trick or treat!"*

"Oh, I love Olaf!" Emily bursts.

"You *are* Olaf." I nudge Emily, addressing the little girl. "You wanted to be the snowman over the blond queen who can freeze things with her fingertips? I mean . . . that's a respectable choice, I guess." I raise my hand for a fist bump; the girl giggles and bumps back.

"Ladybug?"

Glancing behind her, my lips twist into a pained scowl.

Konor Stratford stands at the end of the walkway—his slicked hair tucked beneath a snow cap tipped with a pom-pom. He wears a fur-trimmed tunic along with light blue pants.

My laughter echoes into the foggy night sky. "Sweet Ugg boots, Stratford."

"Kristoff's a good sport," Alexa says as she approaches to stand beside him. She's dressed in a blue-and-black Princess Anna dress with a pink cape flowing behind her in the light breeze, her natural red hair woven into a loose braid over her shoulder. "We're taking Konor's sister around. Where's your Halloween spirit, Charlie?"

My back straightens. "Uh . . ."

"She's Wonder Woman incognito," Jade supplies, extending the candy bowl to Olaf.

Emily nods. "Her outfit and Lasso of Truth are at the cleaners. It's been a rough week."

"Dealing with you guys," I mutter for my friends' ears only.

Alexa's eyes brighten with fond amusement. "Is that so?"

"Konny?" Stratford's sister turns toward him. "I gotta go to the bathroom."

Emily pops up. "Oh, she can use ours!"

He shakes his head. "Thanks, but we're not far. We've been out awhile anyway. Pretty sure we scored enough candy to hold us over through Christmas. What do you think, Olaf?" When his sister agrees, he takes her hand and glances at his girlfriend. "Ready to head back, Lex?"

Alexa hesitates. She peers back at me and my friends.

For a suspended moment I'm transported back to the Boston Fleet's ice rink, recalling what Alexa offhandedly mentioned about not needing friends. The flash of sadness in her eyes. Maybe that's why I'm blurting out words before they filter through my brain.

"You can hang with us, if you want?"

I feel Em's and Jade's shocked stares piercing me from either side—not out of annoyance, but curiosity . . . and maybe a pinch of teasing-flavored delight?

"Yeah, totally!" Emily waves her over. "We've been wanting to officially meet Charlie's new partner!"

I refrain from elbowing her. "Temporary figure skating partner." An important distinction.

Jade slides away from me on the step and pats the spot between us. "You're more than welcome to join us."

Alexa appears to internally war with herself for another few seconds before crouching to give Konor's sister a hug and standing on tiptoe to brush a kiss to her boyfriend's cheek. It's a quicker peck than she laid on me during the Fleet game. Not that—you know. Simply an observation.

Konor's eyes flash with disappointed irritation before he nods, unwrapping the Winthrop-green scarf from his neck and draping it over Alexa's shoulders. "Okay. See ya Monday."

"I'll call you tomorrow." Alexa turns and glides forward, smiling in a more genuine way than I've seen from her. "You must be Jade and Emily. So nice to finally meet you." She extends her hand to shake Jade's hand. Then she lowers herself to the space offered and reaches across my lap to shake Emily's hand.

I blink at her in bewilderment. I didn't really think she'd accept my invitation.

Alexa puffs out a laugh tinging with . . . nerves? Then she nudges me. "Don't make this weird. You hang out with Frankie all the time at school. It's only fair I get to know your friends, too."

"I'm not making anything weird," I insist, smoothing my expression into a much cooler one as I lean back and rest my elbow on a higher step.

"We've heard so much about you," Jade says, a spark of mischief in her eye.

I fire a warning glare in her direction, my ears warming under my beanie.

"So you're turning our Charlie into a figure skater," Emily says.

"Only as much as she'll let me. She's turning herself into quite a training helper." She cuts me a look that's a little guarded, yet holds not a trace of disdain. It's *weird*.

"Can't believe our bruiser hockey babe is becoming a graceful ice princess. . . ."

Playfulness overtakes Alexa's expression. "Well, nobody said anything about Charlie being graceful—"

I scoff. "Wow. Rude."

"—but she's a fast learner, that's for sure."

Eager to turn the topic of conversation away from my figure skating attempts, I tour my pointer finger in an oval around her. "Speaking of princesses. What's this costume situation you've got going on? *Frozen*? Really?"

Alexa holds up her hands. "In my defense, Konor's sister picked the theme. Besides, there aren't many options out there for redheads.

I've already been Ariel, Merida, Max from *Stranger Things*, Jessie from *Toy Story* . . ."

"You should do Poison Ivy," Jade interjects. "And Charlie could be Batwoman. You two could really *go at it together*—"

"Fighting crime!" Emily specifies. "Dynamic duo for sure."

I'm seriously going to murder them.

Alexa hums. "There's an idea. Maybe next year."

Not really, though. We both know as soon as Frankie heals up, we'll avoid each other for good.

I know I should be relieved. Thrilled, even! Yet the reminder sparks a rush of weirdness down my spine that I don't have any desire to unpack right now.

"You could've been the moose," I say. "Tucked your hair into a little moose hat. I'm just saying."

"Not a moose." Emily snickers. "The character's a reindeer, Charlie. His name is Sven."

"Whatever." I snag a bite-size Kit Kat from the bowl, tear it open, and pop it into my mouth.

Alexa laughs. It's the first genuine, carefree laugh I've heard from her, and it strikes strange in my chest. "This is so nice, hanging out with you guys." She turns to me, her expression softening and her lower lip catching between her teeth for a beat. "Thanks for letting me stay here. I really do appreciate it."

While I get how Alexa's extending some sort of olive branch, I know better than to fully trust it. "Must be a nice change of pace from spending so much time with those shit-for-brains bullies."

Alexa deflates some. "They're not all bad. I'm working on Davis, I promise. After what he did to Frankie yesterday—which I wanted to thank you for—"

"You don't need to thank me. He's my friend now too, remember?"

She nods. An awkward hush falls over the stoop.

Emily pushes to her feet, wiggling her empty cup. "I need a refill before more trick-or-treaters swing by. Alexa, you want some cider? It's homemade."

"Oh, sure! That'd be great. Thanks."

Another hour passes—mostly with Jade and Emily talking Alexa's ear off. (Let's be real. It's 75 percent Emily talking Alexa's ear off.)

The later crowd brings middle schoolers and some shady high schoolers in masks and hoodies shamelessly trick-or-treating for free candy.

Throughout the rest of our night, Alexa eagerly joins into our deep conversations on how there needs to be more gender-neutral Halloween costumes and whether or not we believe in ghosts. (We're split: Emily and I believe. Jade and Alexa do not.) We finish our ciders and pocket a few mini chocolate bars for ourselves.

"Well," Alexa starts, standing and smoothing down the skirt of her costume dress. "I'm almost at curfew. Thanks again for letting me spend time with you guys. I'm really glad I got to meet you both." She flashes a grateful grin at Jade and Emily.

"Do you need a ride?" Emily asks, hitching a thumb toward her car parked in the driveway.

"Thanks, but I'm not far. I'll walk."

"I'll walk you." I stand and shove my hands into my front pockets. The last thing I need is something happening to her on the solo walk home and Geri finding some way to blame me for it.

Alexa's eyebrows arch. "You don't mind?"

I shrug. "No, I mean—lots of zombies and ghosts and super-villains out tonight, so . . . safety in numbers and all, right?" My dad joke pairs with a soft wink and semi-sticks its landing.

Alexa looks as though she's about to protest but bites it back and instead waves goodbye to Emily and Jade.

"See you nerds later." I throw a peace sign over my shoulder and lead Alexa onto the sidewalk.

"I'm this way," she reminds me, heading to the left.

Most of the trick-or-treaters are calling it a night, families extinguishing porch lights and closing front doors behind their storm doors. The fogginess mostly dissipates and a nearly full moon hangs overhead, providing a substantial natural glow combined with the few streetlights we pass. The temperature notably drops this time of night. The chillier air stings my cheeks in a pleasant way.

Alexa removes Konor's scarf from under her arm and wraps it around her neck.

The sight of it—his presence lingering on our quiet walk—prickles beneath my skin.

"So you're really into him, huh?" I grimace the instant the question flies past my lips.

"Konor? Yes. I know you have the whole hockey rivalry thing and his friends are . . . less than civilized, so I understand why you think he's a huge jerk. But he's really a good guy."

My jaw sets. "If you say so."

"Not all hockey players would dress up like that for their little sister. He even posed for pictures. It was adorable."

I want to tell her all the shitty things he says to me in class—how he goes out of his way to remind me of my blown shot, continues to mutter comments about my appearance—but I figure it'll only come across as pathetic and she'll probably rationalize them as part of our hockey beef anyway, so I don't. Instead, I mentally kick myself for bringing him up in the first place.

Alexa checks her watch and sighs. "I can't believe I still have a curfew. I'm almost *seventeen*. My mom's the worst."

My eyebrows shoot northbound and a dismissive snort escapes. "No, she's not."

"She is, though! Do you know how hard I had to fight to even have some semblance of a normal life by going to school? She wanted me to do some sort of virtual learning program so I'd have more time for practice." Alexa pulls a face. "She texts me every hour when I'm not with her or at school. She never backs off."

Sarcasm saturates my reply. "Oh no, how *terrible* that your mom cares about you. She's the *worst*. Allow me to play the world's smallest violin." Pulling my hands from my pockets, I mimic doing just that.

Alexa's hackles rise. "I was only saying—"

"What? Your mom wants the best for you. She's training you to be the best of the best. You're her entire world—anyone who knows her can see that. Hell, she even puts up with you having that prick of a boyfriend—"

She freezes on the sidewalk, her hands planting on her hips. "Oh my god, of *course* you're bringing up Konor again. Maybe *you* should date him since you're obsessed with him."

Her words strike me in the gut and I choke out a bright, strained laugh. *"What?"*

"You bash him every chance you get! I know you're only doing it because you're jealous of him. It's not his fault he's better than you at hockey."

"Jealous? There's no chance in hell I'd ever be jealous of him." I take a step back and fold my arms over my chest.

"You totally are and it's so obvious." Alexa steps back and crosses her own arms seemingly without thought. Even off-ice, we fall into sync with mirroring. "He is, isn't he? Better than you."

"No," I growl back, fingers curling into fists beneath my folded arms. "No, he's not. I had him beat on my breakaway and—" I shake my head. "Forget it. Believe what you want. You've never even seen me play, so stop acting like you know me."

"Stop acting like *you* know *me*," Alexa fires back, her glare harsher and more practiced than mine. "I had fun tonight, you know—for the first time in a really long time, thanks to you and your friends. I thought we were starting to—" She cuts herself off, blinking back tears to stop them from falling.

My heart fractures at the sight—but then I remember what a spoiled brat she is. "Stop acting like you suddenly give a shit about me. I've been helping you out and you've been a complete bitch to me since we met."

Her eyes narrow harder. "You're only helping me because my mom said she'll hook you up with the hockey scouts, so don't pretend like *you* care about *me*." Alexa wipes away a traitorous tear with her knuckle.

We stare at each other in silence for a few prolonged beats until Alexa ducks her head, storming away from me with her pink Princess Anna cape and Konor Stratford's scarf billowing behind her. "Don't follow me, Charlie." Her voice breaks on my name.

The sob she chokes carries on a chilled breeze between my ears and plays on a loop as I hang my head and walk myself home.

Eleven

Sundays are supposed to be my sloth days.

Instead, I find myself in front of Alexa Goldstein's mini mansion, my hands shoved into the pockets of my leather jacket. Rocking back on my heels, I note the deep-purple and red shades of the trees in her neatly landscaped lawn, wondering how often they hire landscapers to care for their yard. It's impossible to picture Geri or Alexa pushing a lawn mower.

Their landscapers swing by at least every three weeks, I conclude—clearly stalling.

I slept like crap last night thanks to Alexa's barbed words, her heart-wrenching cry. What she accused me of. The way I overreacted and started the fight. I'm forced to conclude she's not *totally* wrong.

Okay, well—she's wrong about Stratford being better than me at hockey, but everything else.

I was wrong. I'm sure as hell not jealous of Stratford, but I am kind of jealous of Alexa's relationship with her mother, and I can't blame her for bitching about Geri when she has no idea about my abandonment issues. Even if I'd told her, the level of my problems doesn't diminish her problems. I also know if I want to keep our deal so I can stay in top hockey shape and earn my scouting tryout Geri promised, I can't let our fight fester.

Finishing my mental pep talk, I trudge up the stone path, step onto the front porch, and summon the courage to ring their doorbell. Then I step back, my hand finding my pocket once again.

Geri opens the door wearing less makeup than usual, eyebrows climbing. "Charlie," she says, emphasizing the first syllable of my name even more in greeting. "How can I help you?"

I muster a tight-lipped grin at the ex-Olympian. "Hey, Coach. Sorry to bother you, but I'm wondering if . . . Is Alexa home? I really need to talk to her for a minute."

Geri hesitates.

Alexa probably told her about our fight.

"I got it." Alexa taps Geri's shoulder and casts her a nod, closing the door behind her after Geri retreats. She's wearing yoga pants with a cream-colored cable-knit sweater and a pair of narwhal slippers—purple with silver horns.

She crosses her arms over her chest as she did last night, waiting. *Right. Get on with it, Charlie.* "Sorry, hey. I know it's still early."

"I'm awake. What can I do for you?" Her tone carries sharp and businesslike. Like before.

Despite Alexa's colder demeanor, I straighten my posture and pull my hands from my pockets, forcing them to hang lifeless at my sides. Defenseless—which is high-key terrifying but suddenly feels important. "So I came here to be a Zamboni."

"What?"

"Y'know." I shrug. "Smooth things over?"

Alexa tries but ultimately fails to bite back her grin. "Wow. That was really awful."

"Made you smile though, didn't it?" I shift my weight from one foot to the other. "I came here to apologize for being a dick last night. I shouldn't have brushed off you getting annoyed with your mom and I'm sorry. My own mom sucks and I was just projecting or whatever it's called." Reaching upward, I rub at the back of my neck and exhale on an anxious chuckle. "I guess that's what my old therapist would've said."

Alexa's gaze trains on my face during my apology—as if searching for keywords or a certain magical phrase. After, her posture relaxes and she offers a slow nod. "Thank you." She pushes a stray red curl behind her ear and heaves a sigh. "I owe you an apology too. I overreacted, and I shouldn't have accused you of being jealous of Konor. That was pretty low for me, and I didn't mean it. So I'm sorry, too."

I focus on Alexa's brown eyes and spot a few flecks of green in the natural morning light. I wasn't expecting an apology in return, but her words wash over my heart like a balm, soothing the lingering sting from the night before. "Thanks." A beat passes. "So we're still on for practice tomorrow?"

Alexa nods, palpable relief radiating between us. She hesitates before stepping back and opening her front door. "Wanna come in? Mom's making hot chocolate."

My shoulders sag as more tension floods away, but a new injection of nerves infuses through my core. Goldsteins in their natural habitat? Curiosity wins out. "Oh, hell yeah. What kind of weirdo turns down hot chocolate?"

Stepping inside, I can't help but marvel at the extreme contrast between our homes. While my house sits smaller, more cluttered, and cozier, the Goldsteins' contemporary-style home boasts a formal entryway with shiny dark hardwood flooring and a grand staircase with intricate iron spindles, that crystal chandelier even more breathtaking from the inside. "Whoa."

"Can you take your shoes off? Mom's pretty anal about tracking dirt through the house."

"I heard that, Alexa Michelle," Geri calls from an adjacent room.

"No problem." I brace one hand on the back of the door and yank off my Converse, relieved my socks—while mismatched—lack holes today. "Got a spare pair of narwhals for me?"

"I forgave you. Don't push it." Alexa hangs my jacket on a coatrack. "Kitchen's this way."

We pass through a white-columned archway leading into a spacious kitchen with dark granite countertops and tall, white wooden cupboards. "Hot damn. Your house is sick."

"We consider it healthy, but thank you." Geri carries the pot from the stove toward the kitchen island and pours frothy milk into three ceramic mugs. "Whipped cream or marshmallows, Charlie?" Then she opens the stainless steel double-door fridge, returning with a canister in one hand and a 'mallow bag in the other.

"Hmm . . ." I follow Alexa's lead and hop onto one of the stools, stirring the cocoa powder into the mug and watching the milk darken. "Both, please?"

Geri slides both toppings across the counter.

Alexa plucks a mini marshmallow from the bag and tosses it into the air, catching it in her mouth.

I mimic her actions with ease, answering the unspoken challenge like I did before with the popcorn.

"You two should be doing that in sync by now," Geri notes as she stirs her own morning treat.

Alexa and I groan in unison.

"Mom, it's Sunday."

Geri hums. "I suppose." She cups a few marshmallows and pops them into her mug. "I'm off to drink this with a nice soak in the tub. Enjoy your morning, girls."

"Thanks, Coach." I raise my mug in an appreciative toast while Alexa reaches over and squirts a heavy dollop of whipped cream into it. "Sweet."

"Literally. C'mon, I want to show you something." With our mugs cradled carefully between our palms, Alexa leads me into the living room and nods up at the wall. "I figure a fellow athlete would appreciate seeing this in person." Geri's Olympic bronze medal hangs on display in a glass case alongside a picture of her young twentysomething self posing with her partner.

"Holy shit," I breathe, my tone reverent. "That's incredible."

"Yep." Alexa radiates with pride.

"You'll get one of your own someday. You and Frankie." I deliver a careful hip check to Alexa, minding the hot chocolate.

"You think so?" It's a rhetorical question. She knows so. A competitive glint flickers across her expression. "Let me show you what we're up against. Sit with me."

I join her on the plush charcoal-colored sofa, sipping my hot chocolate while Alexa sets hers atop a coffee table coaster. She pulls her laptop over her legs and opens a browser, clicks into her search engine, and begins typing.

Squinting, my head tilts toward the screen. "What the hell is an Ingleborg?" I blink. "Wait, you've said that name before. Is that the girl who psyched you out before that competition?"

"Yep, my ex–best friend turned nemesis. The Ingleborgs— Mallory and Mason—are a sibling pairs team. They're our biggest competition every year. They train out of New Hampshire and they've got their own private ice rink in their backyard. Here." Alexa clicks one of the videos and angles her laptop toward me.

Together we watch Mason and Mallory Ingleborg's free skate from last year's national championships. They skate as exact complements to one another—shadowing and mirroring flawlessly, each movement in perfect sync. They land side-by-side double and triple jumps like they could do the same in their sleep. And when Mason tosses Mallory into the air, he lifts her without a hint of strain or struggle.

"Frankie and I almost edged them out last year at nationals. We lost by a tenth of a point. I've never seen Mom so furious with the judges."

"Oof, that's brutal. You'll beat 'em this year."

"I like your optimism, Porter."

"Those Dingleborgs are going down," I say with a firm nod. "After all, your last name isn't *Silver*stein, is it?"

Alexa groans at the dad joke and shakes her head, trying to hide the reluctant fondness in her expression behind her mug. "You know, I really appreciate your enthusiasm," she says, her eyes suddenly sparkling with mischief. "Especially when you've got whipped cream right here. . . ." She reaches out and brushes the pad of her thumb just beneath my lower lip.

I suddenly forget how to breathe for a few seconds as my cheeks burn.

"There." Alexa brightens, pulling back. "All gone. Now you may proceed with your battle cries on my and Frankie's behalf."

A pressured laugh escapes and I glance away, remembering oxygen is a thing I need.

While my short-circuited brain reboots and I scramble for a reply, her doorbell mercifully chimes.

Alexa taps her finger to her chin. "Wow, the morning of unexpected visitors. Too early for Girl Scout Cookie season, right? I'll be right back." She pushes up from the couch and disappears around the corner. A moment later, her gasp echoes. "Frankie!"

At Alexa's cry, I ease up from the couch and pad toward her, waving to Frankie from the hallway.

Geri's voice carries from the staircase as she descends in a floor-length terry-cloth bathrobe. "How are you feeling, Franklin? Recovery still on track, I hope?"

Frankie frowns. "That's why I'm here. I met with the orthopedist, and the bone didn't set right. I need another surgery." He pauses as both Goldsteins visibly crumple. "I'm so sorry. I won't be back in time for sectionals. I thought I would be. I hoped . . ."

"Of course you hoped. This isn't your fault," Alexa reassures him. Her words pinch with sorrow. "We'll get 'em next year, okay? Don't you worry about it."

Geri chimes in. "You take care of that ankle. One day at a time."

They chat for another minute before Frankie leaves.

Alexa closes the door behind him and stumbles toward the staircase, dropping onto the bottom step and burying her face in her hands. "That's it. Season's over."

"Not necessarily," Geri says, rushing to sit beside Alexa and wrap her arm around her shoulders. "We'll keep you trained up with Charlie's help, put out farther-reaching advertisements for competition partners for sectionals, and hope Frankie's back in top form by nationals."

Alexa sniffles. When she raises her head, her eyes shine with tears. "Everyone's paired already. It's *November*. Sectionals are in four months."

"Why can't I do it?" I burst, piercing through their panic bubble as the two redheads appear to remember I'm still here.

They blink at me.

Geri rubs soothing circles on Alexa's back. "We're so grateful for your support, Charlie. And while you're learning far faster than I thought you would, a temporary training partner doesn't need to make the jumps. A competition partner . . ." She shakes her head. "There's not enough time."

I step forward. "So make time." One look at Alexa's devastated expression and my eyes narrow with intensity, a fire igniting in my chest. "Make me good enough, Geri." At first, I'm not totally sure why my words spew out with such desperate determination, figuring it's the acknowledgment of an actual Olympic medal hanging on the wall in the other room urging me to jump all in without much forethought—but then I remember I'm a competitor at heart. If someone tells me I'm not good enough to do something, I crave success more than anything. Then there's Alexa sitting there looking absolutely crushed and for some reason I don't really understand, I instantly want nothing more than to fix this for her. For *them*. Her and Geri. "I'm all in if you want me. Sure, even with training I still might not be good enough, but I want to try."

Alexa stares at me with a mixture of shock and awe written on her blotchy face. She wipes at her tearstained cheeks, glancing up at her mom. "She can do it. She's too stubborn not to."

Geri considers me, head tilted to the side. "It would take more than morning practice. We'll need to train after school three days per week on top of that and extend on weekends. And—there's more to it. You don't skate with enough emotion, Charlie. Judges grade performance as much as technique. You'd be committing to more than you're ready for."

I shake my head. "I can't play hockey until next school year. Hockey was my life. And now I want to know how far I can take this. I want to know what I can do in this sport, too." My focus shifts between both Geri and Alexa before settling on the coach. "Please. Let me try. I'm asking you to kick my ass into competition shape."

"All we need to do is place fourth or higher at sectionals to secure a spot at nationals. Frankie will be back for nationals," Alexa reminds her.

Geri rubs her chin. "All right, Charlie Porter. We'll start on competition-track training tomorrow morning."

Alexa rises and steps forward to take my hands in hers. "Thank you." Her watery expression locks on my shell-shocked one, gratitude lighting up her whole face.

I release a weak chuckle, slightly stunned at myself for committing to something so intense with so little forethought. "Don't thank me yet."

Geri stands behind her and snags her tablet from the entryway table. "If you thought I was hard on you before now, you better buckle in. You'll hate me every single day leading up to competition day in February, but if we do this right, it'll be worth it." She taps on her screen, displaying a video of pairs skaters launching themselves into the air, twisting two or three full rotations, and landing with a smooth, single crunch. "Now's as good a time as ever to start you on understanding jumps."

Alexa and Geri lead me to the kitchen table.

I settle down with my not-so-hot chocolate.

"There are six main types of jumps," Alexa explains. "Toe loops, salchows, loops, flips, lutzes, and axels. . . ."

My eyes glaze over as Alexa describes the subtle differences between the jumps. When she's done, the information she rattled off jumbles in my brain bowl like alphabet soup. "Can you maybe write that down for me?"

Flushing, Alexa puffs out a soft breath of laughter. "Sorry. Don't worry. We'll take it one step at a time."

Geri agrees. "We'll start on basic jumping mechanics and work through the different jumps as you progress. Hold on to your little beanie, Charlie Porter." A scary intensity returns to her expression. "Tomorrow we'll get you airborne."

Twelve

Geri declares Mondays, Wednesdays, and Fridays two-a-days, meaning two hours of on-ice training—one before school and one directly after.

After leaving Alexa's house, I hit up the Beanery for our regular homework hangout and I tell Jade and Emily my new plan. They're cautious but supportive, as I knew they would be. Turns out they really like Alexa after spending some time with her, and they credit the figure skating opportunity as the thing keeping my spirits up during my time away from Cranford.

I don't necessarily know when the shift happened from tolerating to enjoying figure skating, but leave it to my girls to call my ass out when I get a little too animated describing all the sweet new moves I've learned.

The nerves kick in the next day after my first two-a-day, when I plan on telling Dad and Mac about my way more intense commitment.

Thanks to Dad pulling a double shift on Sunday, the three of us aren't home together until Monday night.

The kitchen smells amazing, my mouth watering from the aroma of the creamy chicken fettuccine alfredo simmering on the stovetop.

Dad and Mac grab a bowl of pasta and sit down with ease.

After the two on-ice training sessions and a full day of school, every cell of my body is exhausted. Even my hair hurts, which, thanks to bio, I learned is technically dead the moment it erupts from your scalp. I trail behind and whimper through the pain as I scoop myself a bowl of chicken pasta and lower myself not unlike an old person with a bad hip, shoving an ice pack between the kitchen chair and my bruised tailbone.

"What the hell's the matter with your back?" Dad asks, pausing midreach for the salt.

Mac looks on with concern. "You're training harder," he says. "After school now, that's why you wanted me to drop you back off at the Blizzard today—more gym time? Don't make this a habit. Over-exercising isn't good. You know this."

"I'm not overexercising." I pause, making sure I've got their attention. "So Frankie has to get another surgery and I committed to skating with Alexa in competition. Sectionals, in February."

"Competition?" Dad frowns. "Which means you're learning all those flippity flips and the spinny hops and all those dangerous moves?"

Despite the throb radiating from my lower back, I laugh. "I'm not a rabbit."

Dad and Mac don't laugh along. Instead, they share a glance with matching creases between their eyebrows.

"You're not a pairs figure skater, either," Mac points out. "Not really. The practice was fine for your conditioning, but—"

"Maybe I could be, though?" I kick myself for doubting myself enough to lilt my reply into a question. I'm going to do this. I made up my mind on the spot after watching Alexa crumple on her stair-case. "I'm learning the jumps, yes. I'm getting my ass kicked and it's really hard, but I asked for this. It's been so long since I've felt this . . . this *hunger* to be great."

"That's because you're used to playing hockey this time of year and you're already great at that," Dad reasons, rubbing his eyes beneath his glasses. "Charlie . . ." I know he's concerned or annoyed because he doesn't call me "kiddo." "We're a hockey family. I don't want this pairs skating business to distract you from your goals. The scouts. You've wanted this since you were a kid. One rough landing on those figure skates and you'll pop your own damn ankle, break your arm—hell, maybe you'll give yourself a knee injury you'll never come back from."

Since Dad and Mac aren't eating, I twirl fettuccine noodles around my fork, hoping it might encourage them to do the same. We Porters are notoriously bad at reasoning when we're hungry. "Guys—I'm figure skating, I'm not doing drugs. Seriously, don't you think you're overreacting?"

"Is it because you feel bad for her?" Mac finally speaks up. "Alexa. Do you feel like you had to say yes because her partner went down after you punched Davis? Do you feel guilty?"

"What? No." I puff out a hard breath. "I mean, I did, but I apologized for that at the beginning. Mac, come on. This keeps me on the ice longer! If you couldn't play hockey for a year, you'd be itching to get out there any way you could. I understand it's a risk. I really do. But it's a risk I'm willing to take. I'm being as safe as possible, taking all the proper precautions. Coach Geri doesn't want me injured same as you. She has me practicing technique off-ice on gym mats before running it on the ice. I won't even attempt triples until I master doubles."

Dad's eyes widen. "Triples?"

"That's not as reassuring as you think it is," Mac says.

"Listen, it's just an extra couple of months until Frankie gets back. I only need to get good enough to help them qualify for nationals in the spring." I turn back toward Mac wearing a pleading look. "C'mon, Turdburger. Picture it: I'm flying down ice with you behind me, then I leap and split the defenders with a double axel, completely confusing them while dropping the puck back to you. No defense. Stunned goalie. He shoots, he scores!"

Mac levels me with a look. "That's not real life, Charlie. That's in the *Mighty Ducks* movie."

"The *best movie of all time* though!" I lean forward, gesticulating with my fork. "It can totally be done. And if I don't incorporate straight-up figure skating moves into my hockey play, I'll still be better balanced and stronger."

"I'm not saying no. Let me sleep on it," Dad says, heaving an audible exhale as he spears a piece of creamy chicken from his bowl. He grumbles under his breath loud enough so we can hear. "You two make my hair grayer every damn day. . . ."

Mac guffaws. "Hey, it's not me! I'm the well-behaved one, remember? Your grays are ninety percent Charlie."

"Can't argue with that." Relaxing into a snicker, I preen up at Dad. "Good thing gray looks good on you, Pops. You're turning into a real silver fox thanks to me. You're welcome."

We finish dinner in a heated debate about the Bruins. I offer to wash up and pack the leftovers before we all head upstairs for the night.

The next morning well before sunup, I'm only half awake as I trudge downstairs with my school clothes in my bag. I shuffle into the kitchen to grab another pack of strawberry Pop-Tarts, freezing when I spot my lunch prepacked on the counter beside a box of those break-and-shake ice packs. The note propped beside it is written in Dad's hasty scrawl.

GIVE 'EM HELL, KIDDO.
—DAD

The following four days serve as a harsh reminder about how damn hard and unforgiving solid ice actually is. While I'm able to land single jumps with relative ease thanks to my hockey experience, doubles require far more discipline, balance, and strength—and my dozens of attempts leave me bruised and aching all over. As it turns out (pun fully intended), jumping on-ice puts pressure on different parts of my skates, which signals the return of Charlie Frankenfoot. Or—Frankenstein's monster's foot? I keep forgetting to google that.

Once again coating my feet in Band-Aids, I wear extra-thick socks beneath my loosened kicks as I shuffle through Winthrop's hallways on Friday morning with a handful of jumping lessons in the books.

I'm mentally quizzing myself on the inner/outer blade takeoffs and landings for each type of jump when my phone buzzes in my pocket.

> **Alexa** (9:06 a.m.): I'm sending you links to some of my favorite yoga sessions.
> Make sure you do one per night. They'll help your soreness.
> I'll know if you skip. 😌

I groan into my phone. Yoga? Seriously?

Alexa's somehow simultaneously gotten nicer and more intense after I committed to competing with her. She critiques my form as much as her mother, yet she makes an attempt to compliment any improvements she notices. Her texts are probably supposed to be helpful and well-meaning, and yet I've never read a smiley-face emoji as threatening before now. This morning, she brought me one of her protein-packed green drinks as an alternative to my morning hot chocolate. It tasted like someone's lawn—specifically, the patch of grass where the dog shits.

I'm about to fire off a reply when—

"What's up, Charizard!"

"Jesus!" My hand flies to my heart and I puff out a hard breath, glaring at Frankie. "Don't scare me like that."

"No problem." Frankie leans against the locker next to mine, his lopsided smile ever-present on his face since I agreed to step in for sectionals. "How d'you want me to scare you next time, then?" His expression sobers when he notices I'm a little rattled. "You okay?"

"Yeah, I'm fine. Alexa wants me to do *yoga*."

"Yoga's good for you!"

My upper lip curls. "So they say. What about you?" I nod down to his hard cast, newly plastered onto his leg after a second surgery earlier in the week. "Lunch has been weird without you. Cyn has a new fandom girlfriend she won't stop talking about."

"I know, she texted me about it. I'm all good now! On the road to recovery for real this time. Got some quality pain meds." He leans down and knocks the hard fiberglass.

"You gotta let me sign it."

Frankie narrows his stare, fishing into his pocket for a Sharpie. "Only if you promise to not draw a dick on it."

My face falls as I snag the marker and drop to my knees. "You're no fun, Drake." After a moment's hesitation, I uncap the marker with my teeth and messily print across his casted instep.

YOU SHOULD SEE THE OTHER GUY!
—CVP

Beside my initials, I draw a hockey stick with a dash for a puck beside its blade. I'm no artist like Jade, but it's clear enough.

While capping the marker I spot Alexa's signature up higher, her handwriting predictably neat. She doodled an impressive figure skate beside her signature, too.

I'M FRANKIE DRAKE! I'M A BIG (K)LUTZ!
♥LEX

I snort. That's so damn cute.

. . . Not that *she's* cute. The pun is cute. And the drawing.

Pushing back to my feet, I silently swear at the haunting cackles of Jade and Emily suddenly bright in my head.

"Did you get my text with the yoga video links?" Alexa asks as we sit side by side on the locker room bench, lacing up our skates.

"Yoga video links?" I feign ignorance, knowing she'll see right through me. "No, sorry. I was just following the rules. We're not allowed to have phones out in school, remember?"

She elbows me. "Liar. Since when do you follow anyone's rules?"

I fire a slick pair of finger guns her way. "Let's do this. I'm determined to land one before the weekend."

Almost an hour later, I grimace as my ass hits the ice for what must be my forty-sixth fall of practice.

"You need to hit that toe pick harder, Charlie. Watch Alexa again."

Frankie extends a water bottle over the boards, and I chug before handing it back.

"During her leap," Geri continues, "her legs cross at the ankle, arms tuck tight into her chest to increase spin velocity—two rotations in the air—and she lands clean, popping both arms out to slow and steady herself. It's physics."

"I suck at physics." I pant while bracing my hands on my knees, suddenly wishing I had Jade's gifted science brain.

Alexa once again demonstrates the double toe loop I've been working on all week. Then she skates over, clapping me on the back. "You're doing great."

"Really? You make it look so easy and I haven't landed one yet," I remind her, brushing the ice flakes from my pointlessly padded pants while I drag my exhausted body back to my starting point.

"You will if you keep trying. Once you get a feel for it, the other jumps will happen a little more naturally."

Geri steps toward me. "In pairs competition, jumps are performed in two ways. In side-by-side shadow jumps, the judges base the value and grade of the awarded points on the partner who is less successful in execution, even if the other partner's jump is flawless."

An anxious laugh bursts free. "Oh, awesome! So the jump score's on me, no pressure."

Geri either doesn't notice the strain in my voice or doesn't care. "In throw jumps, you'll methodically toss Alexa into the air in a jump assist. She'll complete her jump as though she made it herself, but with the added height there are extra stylistic points to be earned. Alexa can either land the jump on the ice, or you'll catch her midair. We'll get there eventually." She waves her hand dismissively. "For now, double toe loops until our ice time is up."

Glancing at the clock, I nod before throwing myself into more double toe loop attempts. On my first try, I over-rotate. On my second, I don't uncross my skates fast enough to land upright. Both result in hard falls plus a skinned, bloody elbow.

Alexa remains laser focused as always but uncharacteristically patient, gently pointing out my missteps each time. She never once shows an ounce of frustration or disappointment—both of which bubble up through my eyeballs.

"You're so close! You're gonna stick one before we leave today, I know it!"

"You don't know *everything*!" I snap, immediately tugging at my low ponytail and willing myself to chill. "Sorry. I appreciate the help, I just—I need coaching, not cheerleading. I need you to keep telling me what I'm doing wrong and how to fix it, okay?"

Alexa simply allows me to work through my outburst, nodding. "You got it. Pull your arms in tighter next time." She dramatically tosses her ponytail over her shoulder. "Besides, the cheerleaders couldn't handle me."

I snort laugh. "You don't do team sports anyway."

It happens on my next attempt. My game face carries me through, all of their coaching notes swirling in my brain as I skate forward to gain momentum, shift into backward positioning, crouch, launch up from my toe pick, tuck my arms into my chest, cross my skates at the ankle, rotate all the way around twice in the air before—

Crunch!

Whoosh!

I land hard on my back leg, my arms flinging out to assist my balance while I coast to a wobbly finish. It takes a second for me to process not crashing on my ass again, then I gasp. "Oh shit, I did it!"

Alexa claps, hopping like an eager bunny on her skates.

Frankie whoops and cheers from his supportive spot in the stands.

"Sloppy," Geri clips. "But it's a start. Now land two more before our time's up."

I grimace.

"Alexa, I want three squeaky-clean triples from you. You're not getting off easy because we're molding a new skater. Jumps and then we'll call it a day."

We take turns.

Alexa performs a beautiful triple lutz.

Then I skate hard, picking up speed before shifting to skating backward. Glancing over my shoulder, I once again hit my toe pick and land another barely stuck double. "Boom! Triples, here I come."

Alexa laughs and high-fives me.

Coach Geri emits an exasperated sigh, though she can't fully bite back the pride flickering at the corners of her mouth.

Thirteen

In the two weeks after Dad, Mac, Jade, and Emily support my decision to pursue this figure skating thing full-throttle, we all get swept up into our typical November cyclone of busyness. Mac and I do our best balancing schoolwork with kicking up practice hours for our winter sports—both my hard-core training with Alexa and stealing some driveway sibling stickwork time together. Dad takes on extra hours at work to earn more money for the holidays. Mom doesn't call, but I don't expect her to during this time of year. She's too caught up in chasing Kylie's latest big-time athletic potential and ignoring mine, after all.

It's the middle of the month when Geri plans a "field trip" for me and Alexa. I'm forced to bail on this week's Beanery date with Jade and Em as Geri drives us from Winthrop to a Metro-North train station in Connecticut on Sunday morning.

"Are you gonna tell me where we're going now?" The Goldsteins had been annoyingly zip-lipped since they asked me to get permission from Dad to spend a whole Sunday away.

"Here are your tickets," Geri says, extending the envelope to Alexa. "Go on, you can tell her."

We step out of the car on the same side and Alexa all but squeals. "We're hopping on the train going to New York City! Mom booked us a matinee to see *Wicked*!"

"*Wicked*?" My head tilts to the side. "The movie?"

Alexa huffs impatiently. "Why would we go all the way to New York City to see a movie, Charlie? I'm talking about *Wicked*, the

Tony Award–winning musical on Broadway." She pauses. "Have you ever seen a Broadway show? Or any musical anywhere?"

Oh. Theater. Right. "Emily's into acting, so I've seen some of her shows at Cranford. Never a Broadway one."

Alexa lights up. "Never? Trust me, you're in for a treat! *Wicked*'s amazing. Funny and poignant, and the songs are the best."

"Got it. I'm adding a point to your nerd card," I fire back.

Geri strides around her car and tucks a travel pack of Kleenex into Alexa's pocket. "Don't forget your tissues," she says with a teasing grin. "Something tells me Charlie's a crier."

"What? *Psh*, I am not!" As we approach the train platform, I take note of Alexa's outfit. She's wearing a burgundy dress with black leggings and flat riding boots, her long red hair styled down with a headband and a dark yellow scarf around her neck. "Am I, uh, dressed appropriately for a Broadway show?" I peer down at my blue plaid shirt cuffed halfway up my forearms, dark jeans, and combat boots loosely laced, my hair neatly brushed, for once, beneath my regular beanie.

"It's a Sunday matinee, you're fine," Geri assures me, leaning over to press a kiss to Alexa's head. "You've got your itinerary. Call or text me if you need anything. I'll be here tonight after my shopping day in New Haven to pick you up." She eyes the two of us, landing on me. "And stay out of trouble."

Faux innocence lights up my face as I raise two fingers to my brow in a jaunty salute. "Sure thing, Coach. Thanks." I can't pretend I'm excited to see a Broadway show, but I'm legit hyped to spend a day in New York City. Even if it's another obvious attempt to help me and Alexa "bond" or whatever. Not like I dread spending time with her the way I used to.

"Bye, Mom!"

The train approaches minutes later and Alexa leads me into

the nearest car. "C'mon, I need seats facing forward or I'll get nauseous." She finds a pair of open seats and drops into the one nearest the window. "It's a two-hour ride, so get comfortable."

"Cool, I'll take a nap." I settle my bag onto my lap. "I'm surprised your mom's not chaperoning us."

"She wanted to," Alexa says. "But she planned a whole day for herself in New Haven—meeting up with old friends and stuff—and she thought it'd be a good idea for the two of us to spend more time together off-ice instead." She removes a paperback book from her bag along with her on-brand earbuds. While she thumbs through her music app, I peer at the book cover.

"Whatcha reading, dork?" There's a dude and a woman sharing a saddle on horseback, the man's bare arms wrapped around the woman's middle as they lock dreamy eyes. I snicker. "Whoa. *That's* not school-assigned reading material." Dawning mischief spreads across my face.

Alexa scoffs, slamming the book face down on her lap to hide the cover. "Charlie—"

"Is it *X-rated*?" My eyebrows waggle.

Upon my probing, Alexa's cheeks redden toward the shade of her hair. "No! It's *really well* written—"

"Erotica?"

Her eyes flash dangerously when an older couple peers over at us from across the aisle. "*Shhh!* It's *tasteful historical romance*!" she hisses. Adorably flustered, she rakes a hand through her hair. "You're *so* annoying. Just go to sleep, would you?"

"My pleasure. Enjoy your *tasteful historical romance*."

Part of me—the quiet, responsible part I don't usually listen to—knows I should spend at least part of the ride catching up on studying or replying to texts and emails I've fallen behind on due to my packed schedule. Instead, I give in to the call of sleep knowing

I'll want as much energy as possible to spend the day exploring New York City.

I wake to shoulder taps.

"Charlie. Wake up, we're almost there."

Flinching and wincing at the crick in my neck, I stifle a yawn with the back of my hand before stretching my arms upward. Blinking out the window, I squint. We're in pitch-darkness, bright train lights flickering down overhead. "What the hell?"

"We're underground. Penn Station is the next stop."

"Oooh, right. Haven't been here since I was a kid." I tap the closed book in her lap. "Did you finish? Was it *steamy*?"

Her eyes roll. "Yes, I finished. Here." She opens the lip of my bag and shoves the book inside. "If you're so curious, why don't you read it?"

"Ugh." I yank the book from my bag like a blistering hot potato, setting it back atop her lap. "Romance is cringey enough, but *straight* romance? Gross."

Alexa's eyebrows arch, amusement pursed on her lips. She looks as if she wants to say something else but decides against it, dropping her gaze into her bag and swapping her book for a small notepad. "Here's our rough itinerary for today."

10:00—Museum tour—American Museum of Natural History

12:30—Lunch at La Masseria

2:00—*Wicked*—Gershwin Theatre

5:30—Dinner at Marseille

7:30—Board train for CT

I know I should be grateful, but I can't help but frown. "A museum? Snoozefest." Then I skim the rest of the itinerary. "Those lunch and dinner places sound pretty ritzy. . . ."

Alexa opens her mouth like she's about to argue—but decides against it. "You said you haven't been here since you were a kid?"

"Nope. And all I remember is lunch at Applebee's and the ESPN store. Oh! And the M&M's store. Dad was obsessed. That was *awesome*."

"It is pretty fantastic." She hums. "You know . . . Mom won't necessarily care if we go somewhere else. Aside from the show, I mean." A flash of rebellion sparks in her eye.

I gape, my hand flying over my heart. "*Alexa Michelle*," I breathe, mimicking Geri's go-to full-naming strategy when Alexa gets overwhelmed or puts a toe pick out of line. "Are you suggesting we *deviate from the agenda*?"

Alexa stands and nudges me into the aisle when the train stops. "I'm simply saying I'm not necessarily in the mood to visit a museum either. Not that there's anything wrong with them." She grabs my arm as we shoulder through the tourists herding toward the escalator leading up to Penn Station's ground floor. "I propose we go shopping instead."

"Shopping?" My nose wrinkles. "Not really a fan of shopping either."

A scheming sparkle flickers in her eye. "You will be. Trust me."

Stepping outside Penn Station, I'm immediately taken aback by just how *huge* everything is—the looming buildings, the cattle-packed sidewalks, the bumper-to-bumper traffic. Chatter surrounds us in multiple languages; blaring car horns range from sharp to faint, near constant in the background.

"This way!" Alexa keeps her hand locked in the crook of my elbow as we walk. It's nice. Safety-wise, I mean. Getting separated here would really suck, even if we both have phones. A short while later, she pulls to a stop and points across the street.

I follow her finger and gasp. "The Nintendo store! How'd you know I was into video games?"

"You've got a Bowser pin on your bag. And one time you wore mismatched Mario and Luigi socks to the rink." Her perfect teeth glint against the reflecting sun. "What can I say? I'm observant. And now *I* have a reason to call *you* a nerd."

A strange rush of fondness floods my system, but then I reason Alexa's probably super observant in general. Not only with me. "Dude, call me whatever you want!" I don't even care about going full-on gamer geek, rushing into the store and not bothering to tamp down my excitement as I check out the displays, clothing, and toy merch. I'm fascinated by the encased retro Nintendo gaming systems dating back to decades before I was born. Mac and I share an old PlayStation with our controllers so worn they're literally duct-taped together, so the gamer girl in me—always present despite my lack of playing time lately—rushes toward the Nintendo Switch play area. Alexa and I take the Switch Joy-Cons and battle it out in a few Mario Kart races with children and their parents looking on.

She predictably plays as Yoshi and I always choose Bowser because he's the shit. Tuning out the rest of the crowded store, we each win one race and decide the winner of the third is the true MK champion.

"You choose the map, m'lady."

"Rainbow Road, in your honor." Alexa tosses me a cheesy wink.

"Oh, excellent, my home turf. You're going down, Goldstein."

We crouch into ready position as the traffic light on the screen ticks from red to green.

By the third lap she's beating me, which is absolutely unacceptable. I've been playing Mario Kart with Mac since I was old enough to hold a controller. Unwilling to give Alexa the pass to dunk on me all day, I steer a little too hard—and my body "accidentally" knocks against hers.

"Ugh, *Charlie*!" She staggers to the side, Yoshi flying off the track while Bowser soars across the finish line. "You cheater!"

"Victory is mine!" I pump my fists into the air before turning and high-fiving the people gathered around. *"Bow-ser! Bow-ser! Bow-ser!"* They chant along with me.

Alexa plants her hands on her hips, shaking her head while huffing in admonishment. Despite my shifty move, she can't seem to keep the exasperated fondness from her face. "Cheating will get you nowhere in life, kids!" Handing off her Switch Joy-Cons to one of the children, she snags my wrist. "C'mon, Bowser. You're disqualified, so I win by default. Also, I'm hungry."

We're laughing together as we exit the store, arguing over the merits of my win while heading toward Times Square.

After a delicious lunch at a cool Mexican joint where Alexa and I engage in an intense debate over soft-shell versus hard-shell tacos, we stop into a couple stores—the Disney Store and M&M's World, where I buy Dad an overpriced bag of rare-colored peanut M&Ms.

I treat Alexa to a massive bakery cupcake, and we devour our dessert in line as we wait for the Gershwin Theatre doors to open.

Alexa gets our tickets scanned and we accept our Playbill programs, finding our seats in the center *mezzanine*—which is apparently a fancy way of saying "upstairs." She leans toward me as I'm taking in the opulent, old-school vibe of the theater.

"Are you ready to have your mind blown and heart explode from experiencing your very first Broadway show?" Leave it to Alexa to make it sound super intense.

"Ready or not, here I am." I lift my Playbill. "What's this one about, anyway? It's a riff on *The Wizard of Oz*, right?"

Alexa flips to the cast page and points out actor headshots. "It's about the witches of Oz back when they were in school—the Wicked Witch, whose name is actually Elphaba, and Glinda the Good."

"Oooh, a prequel?"

"Mm-hmm. I won't spoil you on the rest. You'll have to sit back and enjoy the show."

I smirk, leaning closer. "Does this production have any *tasteful historical romance*?"

Alexa swats my arm with her Playbill and turns her attention forward as the curtain rises.

The show's pretty good. Gotta admit I spend half the time stealing side-glances at Alexa's profile, more amused by her extreme reactions than the story—the way she mouths along to the lyrics, how she laughs along with the jokes, how her breath catches when Elphaba kisses Fiyero during their big corny love song, the way her eyes gloss over when Elphaba and Glinda sing their best-friend song before parting ways at the end. She moves to grip the chair's arm where my hand has been resting since the second act started. I fully expect her to flinch away from the contact . . . but she doesn't. She simply leaves her hand resting atop mine, and that's when my insides randomly squirm.

We've never really made skin-to-skin contact outside training, but we've held hands every practice.

This? I mean . . . we're not holding hands. She's basically using my own forearm as her armrest, which isn't a big deal at all. So why the hell am I hyperfocusing on it?

I'm still overthinking things when the curtain falls to end the show.

The spell seems to break when Alexa glances over at me, tears streaming down her cheeks. She bursts into a watery laugh and rummages in her bag for a tissue. "God, what's *wrong* with you, Porter?

How can you not cry after experiencing something like that?"

Shit. I can't exactly tell her I low-key stopped paying full attention at some point during act two. Instead, I offer a casual shrug. "Because I'm not a theater nerd like you?" I don't want her to think I'm ungrateful or whatever, so I clap as hard as everyone else when the cast emerges to take their bows. "It was pretty dope, though! I liked the music. Glinda was hot."

Alexa leaps to her feet for the ovation, firing an unimpressed look at me while I follow suit in a much more chill fashion. "Maybe we can meet her at the stage door. You can slip her your number."

I snort. "*Ha.* I'm pretty confident in my ability to woo the ladies, but shooting my shot with a Broadway star who's (a) almost definitely straight and (b) very likely not interested in breaking the law by dating a minor sounds like the perfect recipe for rejection."

"Well, that's her loss," Alexa notes as she ushers me from our seats toward the exit.

"One thing did bother me about the end, though."

Alexa's eyebrows shoot northward. "What's that?"

"Elphie had much better chemistry with Glinda than Fiyero. I get that I'm probably gay-biased or whatever and it's only my opinion, but—"

"No, you're not wrong. Lots of people think that, too. There's a bunch of Gelphie fan art and fan fiction and stuff online."

"*Gelphie*?" I blink hard before unfiltered delight shines over my face. "Fan art? Fan fiction? You *nerd*!" I check my hip against hers, cackling. "Queen of the nerds."

Alexa shoves me back, her cheeks pinkening. "I didn't say I *read* any—"

"Uh-huh, suuure."

"Shut up, Charlie."

That's when I realize Alexa hasn't mentioned Konor Stratford all day. She barely checked her phone aside from sending a quick check-in text to her mom. It's weird considering her phone was basically glued to her hand during our trip to watch the pro hockey game. Not that I'd dare bring him up and risk ruining this surprisingly nice day trip.

We step onto the street and, thanks to daylight savings, the sun's already setting between two skyscrapers in the distance. "So what now? Wanna hit up that fancy-sounding restaurant on your mom's list?"

"*Bleh*, no thanks. I'm still full from lunch and that supersize cupcake." Her lower lip catches between her teeth—something she does whenever she's conflicted or deep in thought. "I was hoping maybe we could head back toward Rockefeller Center?"

I shrug. "Sure, I'm down for whatever." We walk several blocks in comfortable silence, Alexa humming the tune from one of the *Wicked* songs. I'm assuming Alexa wants to see the famous Christmas tree, but maybe that's not up until after Thanksgiving?

Alexa doesn't mention the tree. Instead, she leads me toward an outdoor ice rink in front of the Rockefeller building, a golden statue of a chiseled dude erected directly behind it. She brightens. "I've always wanted to skate here."

A sharp laugh bursts past my lips. "Are you kidding me? It's our day off from skating and you want us to skate?"

"*You* don't have to," she counters, eyeing the rink itself. It's around dinnertime, so the ice isn't too crowded. She approaches the skate-rental window and I follow along.

"Yeah, I won't. Giving these puppies a well-deserved break." I point to my boots. "Can't imagine those rental skates are gonna feel half as comfy as your expensive ones back home."

Alexa shrugs off my concern and rents a pair of skates. She drops onto a bench to swap her footwear, a strange sort of determination in her eyes. "I've never skated without my mom watching," she says, a wistful lilt in her tone. "I've always wanted to free skate without running a routine, without working toward some sort of immediate or future goal. Mom always says it's an unnecessary risk, but *look* at it." She pauses tying her skate to gesture at the iconic ice rink before us. The position of the setting sun sets off purple and orange hues in the dusky sky. "It's *beautiful* here. I can't remember the last time I've skated only for fun."

"Look at you, breaking the rules."

"*Bending* the rules. I'll only be out there for ten minutes or so, but I'll kick myself if I don't seize the opportunity. *Someone* must be a terrible influence on me."

"Hey, I get that I'm the rebel between us, but *you're* the one who decided to go rogue today." I promise to keep her boots and her bag safe, holding tight to our belongings as I step up to the rink's half wall.

She hooks her earbuds in place and selects a song from her phone before securing it in her pocket.

"Which Swiftie track did you pick?" I call out as she steps onto the ice, sticking out her tongue at me instead of replying.

Alexa's entire demeanor shifts once her blades hit the ice; she visibly relaxes, a serene expression overtaking her typically highly expressive face, and I wholly understand what she's feeling in this moment. The peacefulness overcoming a skater when we're where we feel the most free. The most daring. The most at ease. Hockey player, figure skater. Rink, pond—doesn't matter. A skater's at home when we're gliding on glass.

She solo-strokes a warm-up lap before picking up speed and performing an unchoreographed improv skate, attracting the attention of casual skaters and off-ice onlookers. I lean my forearms over the side, admiring her soaring double and triple jumps, her dizzying perfect spins. The uninhibited joy radiating from her movements, away from coaching and critique and the pressure of podiums and partners. The unfiltered emotion in her face, her limbs, surely leftover from those she experienced during the show. She hits that perfect flow and succumbs to it. It might be the first time Alexa Goldstein ever gives up control. She allows the music, her skates, to take over.

I can't tear my eyes away. She's mesmerizing.

She twirls to a stop at center ice with her chest heaving, cheeks rosy and bright from the early evening chill. Alexa's always been pretty, but this is the most beautiful she's ever looked, and I forget I'm supposed to be breathing. Returning to herself with a few slow blinks, she finds me in the audience and pins me with her widest, most genuine grin.

The force of it damn near knocks me sideways as my heart trips harder. What the—

Oh.

Oh *shit*.

Fourteen

Registering my pointless, doomed crush on my skating partner (who's *probably* 100 percent straight and *definitely* already in a relationship) triggers my body breaking out into a cold sweat on our walk back to Penn Station. I blame my uncharacteristic quietness on exhaustion, though for once I can't sleep on the train, my mind spinning. Alexa's the one who falls asleep using my shoulder as a makeshift pillow. It's not the most comfortable positioning for me, but I don't have the heart to wake her. I don't want her to move away.

Okay, no, I'm not doing this. I need to chalk it up to Alexa's skating ability—that's what made me feel so much. She's trained most of her life to make audiences feel that way. What I need is one good night's sleep, then I'll be over it.

I'm grateful when things return to normal once we're back at it the next morning, and after a few more days, *this bitch* starts landing her doubles pretty consistently. They're nowhere near clean enough for Geri's ultrarefined palate. Once my leg muscles grow accustomed to the pain and strain of double jumps, Geri decides to inflict torture on my arms.

Swapping skates and neoprene wedgie pants for normal workout attire, Alexa and I meet in an empty Blizzard gym on Thursday morning.

"Run it again, ladies." Geri paces up and down the side of the training mat like a Chanel-clad shark scanning for chummed water.

It's been thirty minutes and our skin glistens with sweat. Thankfully I'm wearing a black muscle shirt to significantly reduce the appearance of my pit-stain situation while silently thanking the deodorant gods as I sweat more than I do during our on-ice practice.

Not that my partner's in much better shape, but Alexa some-how manages to smell just as good as she did when we started. How unfair is that?

Focus, Porter. Lifts and throws, not your partner's cute frizzy curls escaping from her hair tie.

Alexa wipes her palms on her outer thighs. "I'm not getting too heavy for you, am I?" A cheeky, challenging grin twists up her lips.

"I could say a dickish dude thing like maybe you should lay off the cheeseburgers, but I won't."

She elbows my side.

"Girls." Geri's hands plant on her hips. "Again."

"Sorry." I step back toward the center of the mat as Alexa retreats toward the edge.

Then I begin the count. "One, two, three!"

Alexa runs toward me and leaps into my arms. I catch her waist and once I hoist her into the air, she springs into the lift, easing the transition. Her left hip perches on my right shoulder, and with the support of my hand on her thigh and my firm grip around her mid-dle, I launch her skyward with a pizza-dough-type twist.

Alexa spins two full rotations, traveling midair to where she started before awkwardly landing on both feet.

"Keep your head up, Charlie!" Geri snaps.

"That was good, though! We just need to make sure you throw me at a slightly higher angle so I can complete my last rotation." Alexa blows a stray lock of damp hair from her forehead.

"Got it. I'm a little out of gas for more throws," I admit, breathing hard and shaking out my arms.

Geri nods. "That's fine. The last thing we want is for you to keep throwing Alexa without enough force and risk injury to both of you. We'll practice lifts for another ten minutes or so. If you think you can?"

"Yeah," I croak. "For sure."

We run the four different lifts and holds we have yet to practice in the rink, needing to make sure the mechanics are flawless before throwing skates and solid ice into the equation.

In our final attempt, Alexa jumps at me and we transition into a hold—this time, a dip. Her body slides down my front and I catch her thigh with my strong grip while Alexa, with impressive control and core strength, keeps her body rigid and points her toe like a ballerina. Her hand anchors around the back of my sweaty neck as I gently dip her downward.

We're panting hard, noses nearly touching—and our gazes lock.

Suddenly I forget how to inhale, and I wonder if my cheeks are as red as Alexa's.

From exhaustion and heavy breathing, obviously. *Not* from my weird feelings I absolutely need to get over ASAP.

Geri clears her throat.

I jolt back to awareness and help Alexa upright. "How was that one?" My voice breaks on the last word and I clear my throat. "No drops that time."

"Incredibly sloppy." Geri scrawls more notes on her tablet. "It needs to look like one seamless movement. I can see you counting the steps in your head like it's work. Every move must appear fluid and effortless. And keep in mind—during competition, those pained expressions need to look like genuine smiles."

"Mom." Alexa sends Geri a pleading look.

Geri relents, tucking her stylus away. "It's better. Much better than last week."

Grinning, I snag my water bottle and squirt a stream of cold water into my mouth as though I'm wearing a caged helmet.

Hockey habits die hard.

"But we truly do need to start working on your gracefulness—or lack thereof. We'll arrange dance classes for you in the next couple of weeks."

"Dance classes?" I cackle, nudging Alexa's elbow with my own. "Your mom's hilarious." I instantly sober at the stoic look on Geri's expression. "Whoa. Shit. She's serious?"

"Dead serious." Geri glances up at the clock. "Cooldown time. Good effort today, both of you." It's as good of a compliment as I'll get from Geri, and I nod in acknowledgment as she struts out of the gym.

Good effort, she says. Not good work. Because my work still isn't nearly good enough for competition. Maybe it's Porter stubbornness or maybe it's my natural athletic drive or some combination of both, but with each improvement I make, I never let myself truly bask in the win. Instead, I only focus on other things I need to fix. My body tells me I'm transforming—muscles I've never needed for hockey strengthening and defining as evidence of my hard work. Yet I know I'm still nowhere near where I need to be, which roils my insides. At least I have time. Two and a half more months to get good enough.

Alexa drops to the mat in a wide straddle. "Don't forget to stretch," she reminds me for what seems like the hundredth time since our training started. "Yoga poses!"

"I'll do another one of those yoga videos later. Gonna hit the showers. Enjoy your yoga, yogi."

I trudge into the locker room with typical post-training heavy limbs, trying not to think about whatever the hell wishful magic trick my brain played on me at the end of that last lift.

Because for a split second, it kind of looked like Alexa might be a little bit into me, too.

⛸⛸⛸

Every school day I thank the scheduling gods Frankie and Cyn have the same lunch period as me. Considering my borderline grades, it's a little bit ironic I enter the library every day. Even if it's only the back office and I have yet to check out a book for myself.

Cyn's giddy as she scrolls through her girlfriend's Instagram, showing us her favorite pics with each pause.

Frankie pops a potato chip into his mouth and leans forward, ignoring the more nutritious aspects of his meal. "So let me get this straight. . . ."

"Gay," I correct with a wink.

"Okay, yes. Let me get this gay. There're no homophobes at Cranford? Like—*none*?"

"Sounds fake," Cyn chimes in.

I shrug. "Not really? Super small school, lots of my classmates board from all over the place so there's a lot of diversity, y'know—in general."

"How idyllic," Frankie says with a dreamy sigh. "And before you ask—"

I open my mouth and immediately close it.

"—*no*, Gavin Davis has not bothered me in any way since you fully slammed him into the lockers with your bruiser bodyguard–bouncer babe act."

Relief washes over me and I take a too-big bite of my turkey and cheese sandwich.

"Wish I could've seen it," Cyn says. "Oooh, look at this one! My favorite." She holds up her phone to display a picture of a cute Indian girl on a hike.

"She's adorable." Genuine happiness for Cyn shines in my eyes. "Damn long distance."

Cyn gives a wistful sigh. "For real, girl." She sets her phone down. "What about you? You've been here long enough now to have someone catch your eye."

"Me?" My chuckle means to be dismissive but instead blurts out with a slight strain. "Nah, everyone outside this room is still my enemy. Besides, I don't have time for any of that with my new brutal schedule."

"Speaking of that brutal schedule . . ." Frankie finally picks up his plastic fork and begins swirling it around in his grilled-chicken salad while pouring ranch dressing on top with the other hand. There's a suspicious twist to his mouth for a fleeting instant before he rolls his lips inward. "You and Alexa seem to be warming up to each other."

My attention drops to my sandwich. "I guess? Turns out we're a lot more productive when we're not actively hating on each other."

"Does that mean you still passively hate each other?" He pauses. "Or do I spy with my pretty little eye a friendship blooming through a crevice in the ice?"

"I don't know if I'd call it *friendship*." I can't. Not when, deep down, I know there's something different about my relationship with Alexa from what I've had with any friend. I simply don't get crushes on my friends, as much as I keep trying to talk myself out of this one.

"What would you call it then?"

"Hmm . . ." I scarf another obnoxiously large bite of sandwich to buy myself some time, chewing and swallowing hard, then chugging some water before responding. "A professional truce."

Frankie snickers. "Okay, stubborn. You're totally friends now, which is super adorable, by the way. But deny it all you want."

"I will, Franklin," I declare, snagging the apple from his lunch bag and biting into it.

The next day after Saturday morning on-ice training, I'm hunched over Emily's kitchen counter beside her, a tablet streaming her "Baking Beats" Spotify playlist. The kitchen's a mess—dirty bowls, measuring cups and spoons, and some batter drippage every which way. Grain-free flour snow-dusts the counter and our aprons. Emily's rocking a powdery streak across her cheek.

Jade sits across from us in the flour-free safety zone, leaning back in one of the kitchen island stools, her sketchbook resting on her propped leg while she draws. I hope it's another dragon, but I know it's pointless to ask before she's ready to show us.

Emily clutches the wooden spoon as a makeshift microphone, singing along to one of Beyoncé's classic tracks. Jade and I sing backup, Jade's head bopping along to the beat.

While I help gather the batter-spattered kitchen gadgetry and transfer it to the sink, the song fades out and I toss Jade a curious look over my shoulder. "Not to sound like Hattie, but how are those summer-program apps coming along?"

"Finished the science-program application—the essay was cake. The RISD app is finished but I've gotta work on my portfolio pieces. I'm supposed to feature one piece getting to the heart of who I am as an artist and a person—whatever that means. I've got time, though—the whole package isn't due till February first."

"You'll crush it," Emily pipes from where she's crouched by the oven. Straightening, she wipes her hands on her apron. "Not only the portfolio, but your conversation with your parents when you go home over winter break, right?"

"Em's right, girl. Gotta rip that Band-Aid off." I'd know, as I've become something of a Band-Aid connoisseur over the past couple of months. According to my sound logic, Jade is her parents' youngest and only daughter, so they love her too much to abandon her. "Dr. Ed and Hattie are intense, but once you show 'em your work and explain how badly you want this, they'll be cool with it. Even if it takes them a little while to get used to the idea." I cast Emily a quick wink. "And I bet that's regardless of whether or not Uranus is in Gatorade."

"Retrograde." Emily flicks a chocolate chip at me. "And it's not, for the record."

Jade snags the ricocheted chocolate chip and pops it into her mouth. "Yeah, winter break. That's probably a good time to mention RISD. I'll think about it."

I'm nearly finished washing the dishes when my phone pings with a text.

Emily peers at the notification. "Ooooh. It's your *girlfriend*."

Ever since I told them about our NYC day (*date*, they insisted almost immediately), Jade and Em saw right through my attempts at brushing off or downplaying my own feelings. So while I didn't confirm my inconvenient crush, I didn't convincingly deny it either.

Jade snickers behind her sketchbook. "Booty call? We all know Stratford's too damn self-centered to be gifted in that area. . . ."

Emily laughs along. "Stratford probably kisses like he's a lizard snatching flies. Alexa's *totally* curious about the Charlie Porter Smooching Experience. . . ."

The tips of my ears burn. "Shut up, you guys. Finish washing your own damn dishes." Drying my hands on a decorative hand towel, I toss it at Emily's smug face before turning to my phone to swipe open the message.

Alexa (1:19 p.m.): Hey! I know it's last minute but do you have plans for tonight? Konor's throwing a party at his dad's lake house and he told me to invite whoever I want. I know you don't really get along, but maybe this is a good chance to get to know each

other outside of school and hockey? Bring Emily and
Jade too!

A grim shadow contorts my features as I consider the offer.

"What is it?" Jade pauses her sketching.

Emily frowns. "You okay?"

"Yeah, I'm good. Alexa invited us to Stratford's house party tonight."

Jade recoils. "Pass."

"Yeah, but . . ." I pocket my phone and move to the drying rack, plucking another towel and starting to dry the dishes one at a time to work out some sudden restless energy. "I don't know, I have a weird feeling. I don't trust those guys with Alexa and what's bound to be a shit ton of booze."

I mentally shush the little devil on my shoulder sounding suspiciously like Frankie. This doesn't mean we're *friends*.

Em nods. "So . . . are you gonna go?"

"Ugh. Maybe I'll swing by at some point, just to make sure she's okay?"

Emily and Jade share another look, conniving smirks morphing across their faces.

"What?"

"Oh, nothing . . ." Emily singsongs.

Jade cackles. "You've got it bad, girl."

"You *so* do!"

I loosely backhand Emily on her apron-covered boob—which only serves to make her laugh harder. "Dude, shut up. That's not even—"

"You broke your own rule though," Jade continues as though I didn't just tell her to shut up. "Never fall for a straight girl."

Emily jumps in. "Maybe she's not straight, though! We don't know for sure."

140

"Lay *off*, you guys." I turn away from them and double down on dish drying. "Not that it matters anyway. She's got a tool-bag lizard-kissing boyfriend."

"For now," Jade adds, tapping the butt of her sketching pencil against the counter. "I don't like the idea of you entering a Snow Leopard den alone, though. So we'll go with you tonight."

"*Caribou-yah*, of course we will! We've got your back." Emily holds up a batter-caked whisk. "Going to a Winthrop party sounds like *whisky business*."

Jade and I groan.

I text Alexa back.

(1:24 p.m.): cool, we might stop by. lmk the address.

Sliding my phone into my back pocket, I thank my loyal friends, unable to ignore the sinking feeling of tonight's party almost definitely being some brand of shitshow.

Sort of like poor Emily's newest cookies, which emerge from the oven looking more like hockey pucks.

"Solid effort," I say. "Back to the drawing board. Or, uh, baking board?"

"It's Queen Bey's fault," Jade says. "You got too into your booty pops and vocal riffs, forgot to set a timer."

"We'll try this one again next time." I pull pouty Emily in for a side hug. "C'mon, let's go watch a *British Bake Off* episode. It'll be a much-needed mood booster for all of us before we take on a Winthrop party tonight."

As predicted, Emily's baking-fail-induced melancholy rebounds during the show as she soaks in every cheesy second of it.

Jade scrolls through socials on her phone, ignoring the episode.

I drape across the couch and snooze through it.

Fifteen

Eight hours later, my low whistle blows visible in the frigid air. "Hot damn. Stratford lives here?"

We stand together outside the modern structure boasting floor-to-ceiling windows, sharp corners, and a balcony wrapping around the entire second level. Like a ritzy adult tree house overlooking a lake, already frozen solid thanks to a recent record-breaking cold snap. The dull thrum of pumping bass pulses from inside, muffled music echoing down the car-packed street where we parked Emily's Prius.

"Crashing a Winthrop party. Definitely our brightest idea," Jade declares. Her parents granted my dad and Emily's dads permission to sign her out of the Cranford dorms overnight on weekends, and we spent the past hour back at Emily's house getting ready.

"We're not crashing. Technically, we were invited," I remind her as we stride forward, Jade's and Emily's heels clicking on smooth pavement.

"By Alexa, not by Stratford," Emily says. "It'll be fine. Maybe it'll even be fun!"

We head up the walking path to the front door and push inside. The party is well underway. Music blares louder while people mingle in small clusters holding different-colored Solo cups.

At least I recognize some people from Winthrop who aren't on the hockey team.

"All right." I nod toward the kitchen. "Let's—"

"Drinks!" Emily takes our hands and tugs us toward the booze.

A keg barrel sits on the tiled floor beside the counter where various bottles of hard liquor stand intermingled with fruit juice cartons.

"Uh, beer?"

Both Emily and Jade shake their heads.

"Fruity it is. You guys go for it, I'll drive us home."

I look on with fond amusement as they consider how to craft their concoctions—debating mixers, arguing over vodka-to-fruit-juice ratios.

"Craaaanford Prep School babes!" Gavin Davis strolls over, his face reddened and the top few buttons of his shirt open, like it's some sort of invitation as opposed to a flashing sign to immediately bail. He raises his cup in one hand and two fingers on the other. "I come in peace."

Jade and Emily cast him a hard glare over their shoulders.

My jaw sets. "You stay away from us, we'll stay away from you. Got it?"

"Whatever, Porter. There's much hotter tail to charm the dresses off of than your friends anyway." He snags an unopened bottle of vodka and shuffles back out of the kitchen.

Once Emily and Jade finish mixing their drinks, we take a slow lap around the first floor of the house, marveling at how *nice* everything is.

"So Stratford's a confirmed spoiled rich boy, no surprise there." I peer into an open doorway where stairs lead into a basement, music thumping harder below.

"Let's check it out," Emily says as she takes Jade's hand and tugs her down the steps.

I hesitate before realizing Alexa could be in the basement. All I want to do is make sure she's okay, then we can duck out. In the meantime, it can't hurt to let my friends have some fun.

Someone swapped the basement bulbs for black lights, which cast a neon-purple glow on the crush of bodies dancing to a pretty dope mash-up. Then I spot the DJ setup in the corner, where Stoner Todd from my English class works a turntable and a glowing beat pad with impressive skill.

Emily and Jade flank me, swaying together while sipping from their cups.

"Hang on, nerds. You know I'm not big on dancing. . . ." Stoner Todd's cool fade into a new track makes me halt my objections and I give in and dance with them while my eyes slowly adjust to the darkness. Then I strain my neck in hopes of catching a familiar flash of red hair.

Eventually, Jade spots a group of guys who "look like hot swimmers" and tugs Emily along. "C'mon, Em. Let's make some new friends."

"I have a boyfriend!" Emily reminds Jade as she stumbles after her.

"You can still wingwoman for me, right?" Jade waves me off. "Go find your girl!"

"She's not my—" They're gone before I finish my protest. Grateful for the dancing break, I wedge between two couples attempting to swallow each other's tongues and climb the stairs. Blissfully cooler air hits as I pop into the kitchen to snag a water bottle before wandering into the living room.

There she is. Curled up with Stratford on the couch.

My left eye twitches.

Several Winthrop Hockey goons lounge around with cups in hand, girls perched on their laps.

Alexa lights up like a freakin' firework when she sees me.

"Charlie!" Pushing to her heels, she sways on the spot before stumbling over, falling forward into my arms with a giggle. "Oops, sorry . . . good thing you're good at catching me now, huh?"

"Whoa, yeah, I got you." Locking one arm around her middle to keep her steady, I study her face. "You okay?"

Up close, her eyes shine glassy and her serene expression plus the booze on her breath answers my question.

"Welllll . . . I'm kinda drin-um-drunk. Definitely breaking, not bending, the rules. Don't tell my mom, okay?"

I only half manage to bite back my grin. "I won't tell your mom."

"What's up, Ladybug?" Konor kicks his ankle over his opposite knee, arching a caterpillar brow. "You trying to steal my girl at my own party?"

"Well, I *am* better company, so."

Alexa slumps harder against me—sort of like she can't find her own center of gravity—so I uncap my water bottle and pass it to her. "Drink some of this."

She takes a few heavy gulps. "It's been a fun night. Isn't this place great?"

Grudgingly, I nod. "Yeah, it's impressive."

"It's my dad's place," Konor says, pushing to his feet as he swaggers toward us. "Want another drink, babe? I'm gonna get her a refill." He glances back to his friends. "You guys want anything?" Then back to me. "How about you, Porter?"

I frown. "Pretty sure she's had enough, don't you think?"

The dudes snigger in a skeezy choir. A *deplorus chorus*, if you will. Gavin's salacious energy radiates creepily from the armchair. "Your girl looks like she's *ready for bed*, Stratford."

"I *am* kinda sleepy," Alexa slurs in agreement, resting her head on my shoulder.

Konor's cheeks redden and he palms Davis's skull, shoving it aside with a laugh. "Chill, bro."

My stomach lurches at the insinuation.

"You wanna head upstairs, Lex?" He reaches for her hand.

I smack it away. "Dude."

Konor blinks. "Is there a problem, Ladybug?"

"Yeah." I tighten my hold around her waist. "She's wasted."

"So? Most of us are, if you haven't noticed," he says, motioning around the room before snagging Alexa's hand successfully this time. "Babe? Let's go."

"She's not going with you," I growl through clenched teeth, refusing to release her.

Konor barks a few notes of mocking laughter. "Excuse me? She's *my* girlfriend, Porter."

For now, Jade's voice echoes in my head. "And she's my . . . friend, clearly too drunk to consent to literally anything right now."

Alexa's eyelids flutter closed.

I gently tap her cheek. "Lex? Hey, wake up."

"Hmm?" Her eyes open. "Oooh, hey you!" She chuckles, looking back and forth between me and her boyfriend. "You hockey players are soooo silly. Why can't you all just get along?"

I level a "told you so" glare at Konor. "Sorry not sorry, Stratford. I'd be a shitty friend if I left her with you like this. She's coming with me."

Konor's gaze darkens and he yanks Alexa's hand hard.

She gasps and stumbles into his arms. "Konny—"

"I don't know what the hell you think you're playing at, Porter. But this is my house. My girlfriend. You can leave if you want. Door's that way." He pauses. "As a matter of fact, get the hell out."

I stand my ground, arms crossing over my chest. "Not without her."

Leaning in, Konor lowers his tone and hisses through gritted teeth. "Listen up, you little dyke—"

"Konor!" Alexa gasps, mouth agape as she blinks blearily up at her boyfriend.

I suck in a sharp inhale through my nostrils, my cheeks flaring as fury bubbles in my stomach and lodges in my chest. My fists clench beneath my crossed arms so tightly my nails bite crescent-moon shapes into my palms.

"M'gonna go with Charlie," Alexa declares, shoving out of Konor's hold and returning—albeit clumsily—to take my arm. "That's a horrible name you called her. We're gonna have a serious talk about that tomorrow."

"It's fine," I insist, knowing it's very much not fine, but I've got more important things to focus on at the moment. "Let's get out of here, okay?"

"You wanna *go*, Porter?" Konor cracks his knuckles, firing icy daggers my way.

I level a hard look at him. "Seriously? You wanna fight me? You're drunk, I'm not. I'd have you on the ground in a heartbeat."

"You wish," Konor spits. "I'm too much of a gentleman to hit a girl—even if you're only half one. I'm talking hockey." He glances back to his buddies, all leaning in and encouraging him with nods while sniping more insults my way. "Thanksgiving morning. Hopkins Pond. Dawn. Bring your eight best, I'll bring mine. I'll wall your ass out again, show you who's ice boss for good."

"Charlie, don't." Alexa curls her hand tighter around my bicep. "He's just baiting you—"

"You're on." The opportunity for Winthrop Cup revenge proves too sweet to pass up. "C'mon, Lex." While I'm supporting her around her middle, we walk off and find Jade and Emily in the kitchen.

Emily's refilling her drink, bopping along to the music streaming from the open basement door while Jade sits across some swimmer's lap at the kitchen table, apparently trying to eat his face.

If I wasn't so frazzled and trembling with simmering rage, I'd laugh.

"Charlie? What happened?" Emily's happy, serene expression twists with concern.

Registering Emily's tone, Jade disengages from the swimmer and startles at the sight of me supporting an unstable Alexa Goldstein.

I barely unclench my jaw. "We gotta go, okay? Right now."

Without hesitation, Jade pushes up from the dude's lap and Emily, leaving her cup on the counter, fishes her car keys from her wristlet and presses them into my palm. "We're gone."

"That *asshole*," Emily whispers after I recount what went down in the living room, her rare swear full of conviction from the passenger seat.

"He's never said anything that mean. M'really sorry." Alexa sits behind me, reaching over to rest her hand on my shoulder while I drive away from the party. "And I didn't mean to drink so much. Whatever they mixed for me . . . sweet but kinda deadly." She gasps. "Kinda like you!"

Despite the white-hot irritation still swirling through me, my lips twitch into a weak smile. "I'm not sweet. These two are, though." I nod to my right.

Alexa scoffs. "Yeah, okay. Deny it all you want, but I know the truth, my knight in shining beanie." She bats her eyelashes up at me through the rearview mirror in an overly dramatic fashion.

I really hope my friends miss the warmth pinkening my cheeks—swatting Alexa's hand away as she attempts to pinch one. "*Stop.* You're so weird."

Alexa sits back and giggles. "So you guys are gonna crush 'em, right? On Thanksgiving?"

Jade nods. "Our team will shut them up hard."

Emily cuts me a look. "Mac might kill you, y'know."

"Yeah, but he'll play. He can't resist a challenge."

"Porters." Emily mumbles fondly. "Drop me and Jade off at my house, Char. You can bring my car back tomorrow."

"Sounds good." My eyes flicker back toward Alexa in the mirror. "Want me to drop you at home too?"

"Oh, nope! No. Negative. Nooo way. Mom would kill me if she saw me like this. Can I stay at your house? I maaay have told her a little fib that I was gonna crash there anyway. . . ."

My jaw falls dramatically slack. "Alexa Michelle." I once again repeat her mom's tactic. "You *lied* to your mother?"

She squints guiltily. "Yes. Yes I did. So can I?"

My shrug is chill. Chiller than chill. "Sure." My grip tightens on the steering wheel and I pretend not to feel Emily's smug stare locked on my profile from the front passenger seat.

We listen to the radio for the rest of the ride with Alexa singing adorably off-key, much to the amusement of my friends.

I drop them off and park Emily's Prius in front of my house.

"Oooh, I've never been here!" Alexa pipes as she bounces on the seat.

"It's half the size of your house." I help her out of the car. "Let's see if we can get inside and upstairs without waking my dad."

Alexa snickers and then gasps. "So we're like spies?"

"I mean, you're not . . . *not* allowed to stay over? I just don't wanna wake him and explain. It's fine. Try staying quiet, okay?"

Alexa nods and we get inside. She nearly wipes out on the stairs, but I catch her around the waist—a new habit, apparently—as we climb.

"You're supposed to be the graceful one between us, remember?" I whisper.

"Still am!" she whispers back, brightening as we step inside my bedroom, eyes widening with booze-infused wonder. "This is *so* cute! A hockey star in her natural habitat." She stumble-skips to my bed and drops onto one side, dazedly beaming as she visually tours my bedroom—Boston hockey posters tacked on the walls, dozens of hockey trophies and medals lining my shelves, the pile of not-quite-clean-but-not-yet-dirty clothes heaped beside my hamper.

I snag my softest faded camp T-shirt and a pair of mesh shorts from a drawer and set them on the bed.

Alexa kicks off her heels and turns her back toward me, sweeping her hair toward the front. "Can you unzip me, please?"

"Huh?" I blink hard, my throat tightening as I process the request. "Oh, yeah. Sure." Relying on the dim lamplight on my bedside table, I anchor one knee on my mattress and clasp the dress zipper between my semi-tremoring thumb and forefinger. The tip of my thumb brushes against the soft skin over her spinal column as I work the zipper downward.

I swear she shivers.

Or maybe my brain's simply screwing with me once again.

"All set," I croak, turning back toward my dresser and grabbing another T-shirt and my Wonder Woman–patterned sleep boxers. "I'll, uh, give you some space to change." In the bathroom, I change into my pj's and toss my hair into a messy bun, wash my face, and brush my teeth.

After a quick mental pep talk, I pull the door open to find Alexa standing in the hallway.

She leans against the wall with a sleepy smile stuck on her face. It's actually unfair how cute she is wearing my clothes. "My turn?"

"All yours, yep. Found a packaged toothbrush from my last

dentist visit and left it on the counter for you." While Alexa washes up, I snag an extra comforter, quilt, and pillow from the hall closet and spread them out on the floor beside my bed. Then I drop down, settling into it.

Alexa returns and quietly closes the door behind her before eyeing me on the floor. "What are you doing?"

"Practicing my double axel. What does it look like I'm doing?"

"Smart-ass. I mean, why are you on the floor?"

"You're the guest," I say with a shrug, reaching up to pat the lip of my mattress.

Alexa's expression flickers with confliction, but she decides not to argue and settles atop my bed instead. "What a gracious host. Thank you."

"So what was your plan? Staying with Stratford tonight?"

"Mm-hmm. Up till he was a jerk to you. Gonna have a long talk with him about it tomorrow, I promise." She yawns, settling beneath my blanket and turning on her side to peer down at me. "Told my mom I was gonna have a sleepover with you. And look, now it's not a lie!"

"What if she called me and you weren't here?"

"You would've covered for me."

My eyes roll. She's right and we both know it.

Alexa exhales dreamily. "Also I like your pillow. Smells like your shampoo. Coconutty . . ."

"You're so weird," I mutter, my stomach flipping at the compliment. "How ya feeling, champ?"

"Tired. Better, though. My head's still swimming a little." Her face scrunches. "Sorry I'm kind of a mess and ruined your night."

"Hey, you didn't ruin anything. And you're not a mess." I don't tell her my concern for her well-being was my reason for attending the party in the first place.

Not that she'd care, right? We're partners. We're supposed to look out for each other. Nothing more than that.

"Gonna close my eyes now. G'night, Charlie." Alexa rolls toward the window and pulls my blanket higher up her body. Her breathing evens out moments later.

"Night, Lex."

It takes way too damn long for me to fall asleep.

I stir when orangey sunbeams pour through my open curtains and streak across the floor at my unfamiliar eye level. Shifting slightly, my body goes rigid once I register a slender arm slung around my middle, heavy and unmoving.

Alexa breathes soft and even into my hair, her warm body pressing cozily against my back. She snuggles closer, mumbling something incomprehensible in her sleep.

Oh. Okay. This is fine.

Swallowing hard, I carefully take Alexa's delicate wrist and lift her arm enough to slip out when—

"G'morning," Alexa rasps behind me, her voice thick with sleep. She seems to process her positioning in the next beat, retracting her arm and rolling onto her back.

"Did you, uh, fall off the bed? Didn't think I'd need one of those toddler bumper-rail thingies."

Her chuckle carries with a tinge of awkwardness. "Guess so." She stretches her arms over her head.

I push onto my elbow, glancing down at her. My gaze snaps to the expanse of exposed skin between her—my—T-shirt and the waistline of the borrowed shorts. Before I can even admonish myself for looking, my breath catches at the sight of a severe scarring pattern above her hip.

The quarter-shaped patch of skin shines raw-pink and long since healed, though slightly jagged, as if picked at time and time again.

She sucks in a sharp breath as she follows my gaze, yanking the shirt down. "Don't—"

"Sorry." My cheeks flare as I rub the back of my neck.

Alexa pushes to sit up beside me, folding her legs pretzel-style as she runs her fingers through her untamed bed head. "Look, it's not—I went through a rough patch of anxiety and picked my skin a lot when I was ten, okay? I'm not—"

"You don't have to explain." Cutting in, I draw my knees to my chest. "For what it's worth, I went through a rough patch around that time too. Except instead of picking my skin, I used to pull my hair out."

Alexa softens. "You did?"

"Mm-hmm." My heart trips harder because I never told anyone about this. Well—anyone outside my family. Not even Emily and Jade. "One by one. When it got really bad I had a bald spot and I had to wear a clip-in hair piece for the second half of fourth grade. I guess it was because my mom replaced me around then. She had a daughter with the guy she ran off with a few years before."

"Oh, Charlie . . ."

I shrug. "It's history. Nobody noticed and I don't do the hair-picking thing anymore. Meds and therapy helped a lot."

"Good. Me too." Alexa twirls a lock of hair around her finger. "Thanks for sharing that with me."

Nodding, my lips roll inward as I search her face for signs of discomfort. "You okay? Last night was . . ."

"Yeah. Kinda headachy, but okay."

A small snicker passes my lips. "Yeah, well. You *kinda* over-did it. . . ."

She groans and hangs her head. "Shut up, I know I did."

"I'll let you off the hook with teasing for now out of pity, 'cause you look like you really need some Advil and water."

"Oh god, yes please," Alexa whimpers. "I really owe you one from last night, seriously."

"Don't mention it." I study her face in the morning light. I know I need to tread lightly since my Stratford bashing always puts Alexa on defense, but his actions last night were too shitty to ignore. "Hey, do you . . . remember what happened? 'Cause you were pretty wasted, and he tried to take you upstairs. Like it was pretty clear he was gonna—"

"Konny wouldn't have done anything like that," Alexa insists with a sharp, dismissive wave of her hand. "He talks a big game in front of his friends, but he'd never try and take advantage of me. I know it." The way she avoids my eyes and fidgets with the ends of her hair kind of tells me she's not fully sure if she believes her own reasoning.

"Lex—"

Her soft hand settles over my bare knee, which immediately shuts me up. When I meet her gaze again, those big brown eyes shine with gratitude. "Thank you for looking out for me. It means a lot."

Not gonna lie—my stomach drops when she doesn't immediately declare she plans to break up with Stratford, but my selfish self turns away from her so she can't see disappointment written all over my face. "I'll be right back with water and meds." I scramble off my makeshift floor bed, notably colder the instant I step away from my unexpected sleeping partner.

Sixteen

Alexa insists on making breakfast as a show of appreciation.

She's still wearing my T-shirt and shorts as she moves about our kitchen with all the confidence she carries on ice.

"Sure you don't need my help?" Aside from fetching the cookware and ingredients she requested, I've been banished to hanging behind her with my cup of tea. I sip from the Rad Dad mug I bought at one of those elementary school holiday shopping events. It remains Dad's favorite mug.

"Positive! I've got this." If her hangover medicine hasn't kicked in yet she doesn't show it, bopping between checking on the bacon sizzling in the oven, cracking eggs into a bowl, and dicing peppers and onions on a nearby cutting board.

Or—at least trying to dice them. Peering around, I wince at her technique, or lack thereof. "Whoa, hey. Hold up. You'll slice your thumb off." With a light laugh, I set my Rad Dad mug aside and step up behind her. "Let me show you a better way."

Her body stiffens as if to protest, but she wills herself to relax. "I'm doing fine—"

"Just watch," I insist, my long arms wrapping around to curl her fingers inward so her knuckles brace against the side of the blade. Then I slowly place my hands around hers to demonstrate proper vegetable cutting. "It's more of a rocking motion than straight up chopping."

I should've asked her to step aside. My front's pressed against her back and she leans into me, my chin hooking over her shoulder. "See?"

"I . . . yes. That's definitely—that's better." I'm about to pull away when she cranes her neck to look up at me. "Show me on the onion?"

"You dice, I'll guide." She begins dicing the onion, though I leave my hands atop hers—you know, to make sure she's got the rhythm down for herself.

"Where'd you take cooking lessons, Chef Porter?"

A decompressing chuckle puffs against her ear. "My mom taught me, back when she lived here. My dad's more of a grill guy—"

"Ahem."

I whirl around to find my brother lingering in the kitchen archway, a confused but nonetheless delighted look in his eye.

I hop back from Alexa like a spooked cat.

"Good morning," Mac says, heading to the coffee maker as he rakes his messy hair from his eyes. "Smells awesome."

Alexa beams between her flushed cheeks. "Hi, Mac! No worries, we're making enough for you and your dad, too." She scrapes the peppers and onions into the frying pan.

"We?" I fetch my mug of tea. "Alexa's cooking. I'm simply the sous-chef." Aside from some waves before or after training sessions, Mac and Alexa haven't really interacted. I'm not sure why this stirs my nerves. Maybe because Mac has way too much ammo to embarrass me.

"Dad's working night shift—he'll be home for lunch." Mac sets the table for three and waits until we settle in with our plates full of breakfast foods before eyeing me. "Soooo, I woke up to a weird text this morning. Something about a Cranford versus Winthrop pond match on Thanksgiving morning?"

I pause with my egg-loaded fork halfway to my mouth, wincing. "Oh, um. Yeah. So last night at Stratford's party—Alexa invited me, obviously—he challenged us to an eight v. eight. Thought it'd be a pretty good opportunity to shut those assholes up."

Mac scratches his cheek. "Sure, we'll play." He glances toward Alexa before looking back to me. "Not you, though. You'll sit out."

Alexa releases a deep exhale. *"Thank you."*

I sputter. "Wait, what? He challenged *me*!" I blink back at Alexa and soften, remembering my commitment. "Lex . . ."

"If you're asking my opinion, I don't think it's worth risking an injury," she says, nibbling on the corner of a piece of bacon.

"Completely agree," Mac says. "An unsanctioned revenge match? They'll play even dirtier without refs and you know it."

"I'll wear full pads," I offer. "I'll be careful!" As soon as the words leave my mouth, I know I'm fighting a losing battle. Hell, I've made so much progress in my figure skating even *I* know it's a bad idea, now that I've had time to process it. Before Mac or Alexa can retort, I hold up my free hand. "Okay, okay, fine. I'll let you guys handle it."

"Good call," Mac says. "We'll win the pond match. Then you'll get your own revenge the right way—by dominating the next Winthrop Cup game upon your epic return next season." He nods at Alexa. "This food's really good, by the way."

"Thank you!" Alexa digs into her eggs with palpable relief rippling from her body. "It's probably the perfectly diced peppers and onions." She taps my socked foot with her own beneath the table.

I grin back behind my Rad Dad mug.

I can't freaking *wait* to get to the Beanery to unload all this on Jade and Em so they can tell my scrambled-eggs brain what the hell it all means.

Monday morning, Alexa and I stand on-ice before Geri, waiting for her to run through today's training agenda. It's been less than twenty-four hours since I dropped her off at home and Alexa's . . . off, somehow. I thought we'd be cool after yesterday, but she doesn't hang back to wait for me to lace up my skates in the locker room and she doesn't meet my eyes now, her own somewhat puffy.

"Girls, sectionals will be here before we know it. Now that Charlie's grasped the different skating techniques"—she levels another hard look my way—"in theory, if not in practice—it's time to piece together our competition programs."

Alexa takes over, her voice raspier than usual. "We need a short program and a long program—most people call it a free skate—for competition. The short program routine lasts three minutes; the free skate is four and a half minutes."

"We'll have Alexa skate the same routines for sectionals with you as she will for nationals with Frankie—only we'll crank up the difficulty of some of the components with Frankie, since nationals are for a medal. In competition, each will be judged and scored, but the free skate, obviously, carries more weight. We need a creative theme for each—music and accompanying outfits. For our short program . . ."

Geri holds up a remote and clicks a button.

Idina Menzel as Elphaba Thropp's famous pre-intermission chorus booms throughout the ice rink.

Defying Gravity.

The shock of it damn near sweeps my skates from under me and I almost wipe out. *Oh.* So that was the actual purpose of our NYC "field trip."

Alexa takes my elbow and helps steady me.

"As you know from the show, *Wicked* . . ." Geri paces in a slow circle around us. "Is about passion. Passion for doing what's right, passion for those you care about. My hope is, now that you've mostly gotten over your childish bickering, what the judges will note as a lack in technical difficulty, we might make up for with emotion. You two . . ." She pauses, glancing between us. "Will need to sell to the audience—and more importantly, the judging panel—that you care about each other so deeply you're willing to go through hell and back together. That the love you have for each other is so powerful it can make the world a better place. Do you think you can manage that?"

Alexa dutifully nods. "Definitely."

Bats flap wildly in my stomach as I suddenly recall what her body felt like pressed up against mine in a nontraining scenario. That's right, bats—much more badass than butterflies. "Okay, yeah. Got it."

"Excellent." Geri skips to another track. "Let's begin with a few stroking laps."

Alexa's hold tightens on my hand as we skate our warm-up laps.

"Hey, what's up with you today?" I whisper once we're out of earshot from Geri.

"M'fine," she replies. "After everything this weekend . . . I told Konor I need some space."

I damn near trip over my own two skates, and I feel like a huge dick wanting to punch my fist into the air with happiness when Alexa's clearly upset. "Oh," I mumble instead. "You okay?"

Alexa shrugs. "Not really. It's not easy coming to terms with the fact that someone's maybe not the person you thought they were. Even if he keeps trying to convince me otherwise."

"Yeah," I agree as we approach Geri once more. "That sucks." I kick myself for not having anything more supportive to say in the moment, hoping Alexa senses my genuine empathy over my selfish glee. Stratford's the worst, but I don't want Alexa hurting.

Geri checks off "warm-ups" on her tablet. "Now we begin choreography. Once we establish this routine, we'll craft our free skate program. Then you'll be dreaming each step in your sleep." Fixing her hard stare on each of us in turn, her lips press into a thin line. "You've seen what Mason and Mallory Ingleborg are capable of. If we're serious about placing high enough at sectionals to qualify Alexa and Frankie for nationals, you two need to be laser focused. Is that clear?"

"Yes," Alexa responds.

"Crystal," I add with a dorky finger gun.

"Good." Geri flips around her tablet and extends it toward us. "Here's our winning recipe. I broke down the code for you next to each component, Charlie."

Alexa + Charlie's Short Program

Defying Gravity

```
ChSq1 = Choreo Sequence #1
2A = Double Axel
LzTw = Twisting Lift
SpSq = Spiral Sequence
2S + 2T = Double Salchow, Double Toe Loop
ChSq2 = Choreo Sequence #2
2Lz + T = Double Lutz, Single Toe Loop
BiDs = Death Spiral
Li = One-Handed Lift
ChSq3 = Choreo Sequence #3
```

"Damn," I breathe while skimming the list of coded jumps, lifts, throws, and spins. "That's . . . a lot."

Geri shakes her head. "The Ingleborgs will execute at least two triple jump combinations. I'm realistic, Charlie. You're capable of performing all of these elements individually—we simply need to put them together and clean them up. Remember—there's no podium at sectionals, no medals. We're not expecting first place or even second or third. We're shooting for fourth to send Alexa and Frankie to nationals."

Alexa nods. "Let's learn the steps, then we'll run it a thousand times."

"Plus a thousand more," Geri adds.

I snort, my tone dripping with sarcasm. "Why not throw an extra thousand on top of that?"

Geri's manicured index finger flings my way. "Now you're getting it."

"Surprise!"

I ease into the passenger seat of our shared car when Mac drops a Dunkin' bag onto my lap. Peeking inside, I brighten at the sight of a chocolate-frosted doughnut with sprinkles. "Oh, hell yeah! Thanks for—" I cut myself off and eye him as he pulls away from the Blizzard's curb, noting the slight strain in his profile. "Ugh, what are you buttering me up for?"

Mac winces. "Don't be pissed. I told Mom we'd spend Christmas with her this year."

"What?" I tense, whacking Mac in the arm with my bagged doughnut. "Dude, no. Absolutely not."

"We have to, Char. It's in the custody agreement—we're supposed to swap holidays between Mom and Dad every other year."

"And every other year I strategically get the shits so extreme I can't leave the house." I shake my head. "C'mon, you know it's not fair leaving Dad alone when Mom's got her new family. She's constantly bailing on our matches; we can bail on this guilt-free!"

"Dad's the one pushing us to go. He'll be okay. We can do our own Christmas with him before or after." Mac glances my way. "I miss her. I know you do, too."

Huffing, I lock my arms over my chest. "It's complicated," I grumble, shoving the chocolate-iced treat into my messenger bag for later. I may delay eating it in protest, but even I can't resist a doughnut for more than a couple hours. I'm only human, and a doughnut's a doughnut.

I'm grumpy about my impending Christmas plans when I step out of the car, pulling up short a few feet from the sidewalk.

Konor Stratford and six of his bulky teammates stand in formation, all glaring my way.

"There she is," Gavin Davis calls.

My posture stiffens. I consider bolting around them to run into the building, but it's probably better to face them head-on. With witnesses around.

Stratford stomps forward, his expression dark and full of fury. "Porter, you shit stirrer. We need to talk."

"She sure as hell doesn't have to to talk to you if she doesn't want to." Mac steps up behind me, clearly having witnessed the Snow Leopard den trap set for me upon arrival.

Konor snaps his attention to Mac. "Ah, Big Porter! Nice khakis, bro. I'm so looking forward to walling you out again on Thursday morning." He glances my way. "Both of you."

Mac shakes his head. "Charlie's out. She has a competition to prep for." He nods toward Alexa, who strides out of Geri's Lexus and stands equidistant between us, clutching her books to her chest as she looks on.

Konor follows Mac's nod, his jaw trembling at the sight of his ex-girlfriend. He swallows the lump in his throat and channels his rage back at me. "I don't give a shit about that. It's *your* fault my girl turned on me, it's your ass we're gonna sweep the pond with on Thursday."

"Did you not hear my brother? He said I'm out."

Gavin Davis leans in. "If you don't play, we'll make sure you get what you deserve in a different way." He cracks his knuckles, licking his chapped lips. "When you're least expecting it."

My grip around my crossbody bag strap tightens so hard my knuckles turn white. "Is that a threat?"

Konor sneers. "That's a *promise*, Ladybug."

Mac takes a hard step forward, reaching for Konor's throat.

I step between them, bracing my hand on Mac's chest and pushing him back hard. The last thing I need is Mac getting some sort of assault charge for rising to this shithead's bait.

The thought of falling into a Stratford-and-Davis revenge plot is more than enough to change my mind. "Fine. I'll play. You'll both regret pushing this when we smooth the ice with your butt-hurt tears after we win."

Stratford and Davis back down, rabid glee overtaking their foaming mouths.

I shove Mac back toward the car. "Go. Get out of here. I bought us some time and we'll deal with them on Thursday. They won't mess with me before then—they'll want me at full strength so I can't use any apparent weakness as an excuse."

Mac digests my logic and relents. "I'll rally the troops. We'll make 'em pay for this."

That competitive streak roars in my chest. "Damn right we will."

Alexa rolls her eyes and stomps off.

Seventeen

A two-day snowstorm hits Winthrop before Thanksgiving.

Perfect timing for the Winthrop versus Cranford rematch at Hopkins Pond.

Community volunteers shovel mountains of snow from the frozen surface so kids can skate over the long weekend. The resulting heaps cap both ends of the oval pond where, on Thursday morning, regulation-size hockey nets stand in front of each end, the gathered snow providing a natural barrier so we won't lose too many pucks on wide shots. In a couple hours this pond will be packed with skaters, but just after sunrise, it's too early for families to be out and about.

"Coach would kill us if he knew what we were up to," Mac says as we trudge from the parking lot toward the lake with skates and sticks slung over our shoulders.

"Mine too." I grimace as I think of Geri.

"So would Dad."

"Technically we didn't lie to him. We're training on the pond today. It just happens to be in the form of revenge." I haven't worn hockey skates in months, but that doesn't mess with my confidence at all. Playing hockey isn't only like riding a bike for me—it's like breathing.

"Damn right. You promise you'll wear all your pads?"

"Yeah, I will." It's the only way I can rationalize this not-so-smart decision.

Full-body gear isn't used for pond hockey. Goalies wear full padding for obvious reasons, but everyone else doesn't bother aside from helmets and hockey gloves. Without refs and strict rules like icings or offsides, gameplay tends to be more chill.

But this isn't *just* a pickup game, and it'll be as intense as any match ever gets. I'm under no delusion Winthrop will ease up on the checking. But I've always used my speed to dodge the worst of their hits, so today's gonna be fine. Better than fine.

Alexa's upset with me for changing my mind, but she grudgingly accepts my playing today after we argued about it Monday after school. Once I pointed out Stratford and his goons would probably jump me or find some other way to injure me directly if I stayed on the sidelines, she relented—while also admitting she feels guilty over putting me in this position in the first place.

Dropping onto a tree stump to pull on my protective gear and swap my boots for my skates, I squint at the empty pond. The sun barely cracks the horizon, setting off orange and yellow hues reflecting atop the ice. It's kinda beautiful.

"It's cold as balls out here." Jade blows hot air into her gloved hands as she lingers behind the bench where our players gather.

"Gorgeous morning for you guys to crush some Snow Leopards," Emily chirps beside her. She wears Flyin' Brian's alternate jersey on top of her Cranford hoodie.

Brian arrives next, carrying his hockey stick in one hand and a tray of large beverages from Dunkin'. He extends the tray to an ever-grateful-for-caffeine Jade before wrapping his arm around Emily and dropping a kiss to the crown of her head.

Our nemeses begin clustering around the bench about thirty yards away, a conveniently placed snow-capped tree serving as a natural divider.

My toes wiggle in my backup hockey skates. It's never worth using indoor skates on a pond since twigs or pebbles or other debris tend to screw up blades. Still, I've grown used to figure skates, so no doubt I'll need to pick up another box of Band-Aids later.

Whatever. It'll totally be worth it.

In addition to Brian, Mac recruited some of his senior first linemen to add some bulk to our team, along with the best from our second shift and our starting goalie, Nicole Vesper.

"What are they—" Jade cranes her neck around the tree. "Are they wearing face paint?"

Konor Stratford's forehead and undereyes shine with dark green and black paint.

"It's war paint, Cariboo-boos!" Gavin Davis leans around the tree with streaked cheeks and puckers his lips in a smarmy kiss. "Hi, Little Porter!"

Emily glares. "That's cultural appropriation, you jerks!"

"All right, Caribou." Mac stands before us on the grass wearing his blade protectors. "No refs, no rules. They're gonna play extra dirty, so be careful out there."

I pull my Cranford hockey jersey over my black compression Under Armour and chest protector.

Jade hastily braids my hair down my back.

"Look who's here!" Emily waves behind her. "Hey, Alexa!"

Alexa approaches wearing her long gray parka and tall snow boots, red hair flying free in the breeze. "Hey, guys. Good luck out there."

"Hey, girl." Jade cuts her a questioning look. "Are you rooting for us or are you rooting for them?"

It's a fair question. Even though she and Konor are on a break, Alexa still attends Winthrop High. She holds up her mitten-covered hands. "I'm only here to make sure my competition partner doesn't break any bones."

I cast her an apologetic nose scrunch. "I'll be fine. Here . . ."

Fishing into my bag, I retrieve my Cranford Hockey beanie and hand it to her. "It'll keep your ears warm."

Alexa shakes her head and shoots me an admonishing grin. "You're gonna get me in trouble."

"Maybe. But I think you like bending the rules sometimes."

"Hmm . . . maybe so." She steps forward to grasp my upper arm, leaning in close and lowering her voice. "Kick his ass, okay? He deserves it." Her expression sobers further in the next beat. "And if you hurt yourself, I'm gonna hurt you worse."

I huff a laugh. "You got it."

Alexa pulls my beanie over her hair as she strides over toward the tree, leaning into its trunk.

Emily gives a muted squeal, holding tighter around her boyfriend's middle. "Char, she was *definitely* just flirting with you!"

"Nah, that wasn't—" My ears heat despite the cold. "It's not like that."

"Looked like flirting to me." Mac grins.

Flyin' Brian nods.

I backhand Mac in the stomach before firing a quick glare to Brian. "Can we please focus up?" I shove my helmet on, glancing at the others around our pregame prep area. "Game time. You ready for this?"

The eight of us—six players and two alternates—grab our sticks and head to the pond. We remove our blade guards before stepping onto the ice, claiming the nearest net as our own. Dribbling pucks and firing quick passes to each other, we warm up by shooting slap shots and wristers at Nicole, who's sharp as hell this morning.

Thank you, hockey gods.

The rest of our teams and some classmates gather to watch in support. Word spreads pretty quickly when there's a Cranford versus Winthrop hockey match, sanctioned or not. It's something of a miracle Dad or Geri hasn't caught wind of it.

As the co-organizer of this morning's match, I skate toward unmarked center ice with my teammates flanking me on either side.

Konor Stratford does the same, pinning me with a menacing stare through his goalie mask and ridiculous face paint. "First team to five goals wins."

"We know the game." My glare flickers toward Gavin Davis as he sizes me up with the full intention of knocking me down repeatedly. "Sure you're not gonna cry to your mommy and daddy after you get lit up by a girl again, Davis?"

The burly Winthrop winger sets his jaw. "You're dead, Porter."

"Bring it on, assbag. This is for screwing my year."

Mac claps my shoulder, tugging me back. "Let's set up for the face-off."

The alternates skate toward the designated out-of-bounds area while the rest of us take our positions.

I square up as our right-winger, crouching into a ready stance.

Another familiar voice calls from the snow-caked grass.

"*Goooo, Charlie!* You got this, girl!"

Glancing over, I spot Frankie and Cyn standing by the tree alongside Alexa.

"Yaaay sports!" Cyn cries with all the sarcasm I'd expect. But she waves to me with a genuine smile.

I nod back, stoked they made it.

Perched in a lawn chair near our makeshift center ice, the same Winthrop sophomore who called the Winthrop Cup match speaks into a wireless microphone, his speaker booming onto the ice.

"*Goooood morning and welcome to this unofficial and un-reffed rematch between this year's Winthrop Cup champions—the Winthrop Snow Leopards—and the embattled Cranford Caribou! Today's matchup features unique rules in that there really aren't any.*

Let's hope clean hockey will be played on both sides. First team to score five goals earns the dub!"

Mac crouches at center ice against Gavin Davis, the puck sitting between them. Hitting the ice and tapping their sticks three times begins the match.

"And we're underway!" announcer kid calls. *"Oooh, Davis immediately levels Mac Porter with a questionable shove to his chest right off the bat. Er—stick."*

"I'm coming for you, Little Porter!" Davis shouts as he barrels into our territory.

I skate backward and stand my ground between Davis and Nicole, who's surely tracking Davis's puck dribble behind her goalie mask. Knowing the bastard's all mouth and muscle and zero grace—there's no way he'll try to deke around me.

"Now Gavin Davis heads right for Charlie Porter. He lowers his shoulder—and Charlie Porter drops even lower, wiping out Davis's legs from underneath him! Davis somersaults to the ice as the puck skids directly into Nicole Vesper's waiting glove. What a hit!"

"*Caribou-yah*, Charlie! Show him who's boss!" Emily cries from the sidelines.

Davis snarls as he climbs back to his skates.

"Vesper drops the puck and passes it to her defenseman, Matty Cann, who shovels it to Mac Porter. Mac leads the attack for Cranford, faking a shot—and passing to Brian Gates. Gates carries the puck around the net, shuffle-passes it back to Mac Porter. He guns the puck just above Konor Stratford's shoulder pad—GOOOOAL! First score of the game goes to Cranford!"

Mac throws his arms up, hugging me and Brian before skating back to center ice.

Em cheers extra loud for Flyin' Brian's assist.

The match carries on. Much like our regular-season battles,

Winthrop manages to overpower us physically while we maintain the upper hand in technical stickwork and speed. Without refs, we play even smarter to keep ourselves safe.

Over the next grueling forty-five minutes, we trade goals until we're tied 4–4, all of us sweaty and exhausted. After squeezing water through my helmet cage during a brief stoppage, I skate back onto the ice with determination shining fierce in my eyes.

My legs burn in the best way as we resume play and my stick knocks the ice twice.

"Here's Mac Porter again with the puck. He enters Winthrop territory—and drops a pass back to his sister! Charlie Porter skates hard, fancy footwork twirling around an enemy defender. She flies toward Konor Stratford, rears back for the shot, and—"

"Aaagh!" My stick clatters on the ice, echoing into the frigid air.

"—Gavin Davis delivers a brutal vertical stick slash on Charlie Porter!"

A slew of vulgar swears spills past my lips as I drop to my knees clutching my wrist.

"You piece of shit!" Mac cries, skating to my side and bracing his hand on my shoulder. "You'd be suspended for the season with a slash like that!"

Shameless glee plasters on Davis's face. "Good thing there're no refs to suspend me then, huh?" He skates toward Konor Stratford, holding out his glove for a fist bump.

Stratford laughs and bumps back.

I growl as I yank my glove off my hand while Mac unfastens my helmet and pulls it off.

"How bad is it?" Mac asks. "Can you rotate it?"

Still shaking with rage, I rotate my wrist up and down, then twist it bilaterally.

A sharp burning sensation tingles up my forearm.

"I'm fine," I lie, scowling through gritted teeth. Glancing toward the embankment, I lock eyes with a visibly shaken Alexa and deliver what I hope is a reassuring nod. She, Frankie, and Cyn now stand with Emily and Jade, concern shining on all five of their expressions.

"I've got an idea," Konor calls from down ice. "Let's give Ladybug a penalty shot! That way she can't cry and say we cheated." He taps his hefty goalie stick on the ice. "How 'bout it, Porter? This is what you want anyway, right? One shot at redemption for your embarrassing blown Winthrop Cup shot?"

Adrenaline and anger flood my system, overriding most of the pain and all of my good sense. I don't hesitate. "You're on!"

"Hey." Mac grips my elbow. "No. We gotta get that wrist x-rayed."

"I said I'm *fine*. Gimme my stick, Turdburger." I try snatching it from his hands, attempting to ignore the sharp twinge in my wrist.

He pulls my stick out of reach. "Can't let you do that. We're gonna swing by to see a doctor, then get you home so you can take a hot shower and put some ice on it."

"*No*. Mac, c'mon! Let me take the damn shot."

Mac squares his body in front of mine, blocking Stratford from view. "Charlie. Don't be stupid. If you're injured and keep going, you'll hurt it much worse. We're tied. You've got more important things going on right now than winning this match." Mac nods his chin toward a still-panicked-looking Alexa.

I follow his eyes, and at the prolonged sight of her, the raging emotions begin draining from my system so I can think more clearly. Right, *priorities*. Mac's not wrong. I don't fight him this time when he slips an arm around my middle to lead me off the pond.

"Where are you Porters going?" Gavin Davis shouts. "We've got a match to finish!"

"Game over," Mac shoots back. "It's a draw."

Stratford scoffs. "A draw? If you forfeit, we win! You know that, right?"

Mac and I ignore them. He urges me onto a bench and gently takes my left arm, frowning as he inspects my wrist. "You're already bruising."

Alexa storms over toward Davis and Stratford, flinging an accusatory pointer finger at the both of them. I can't hear what she's saying, but their arms flail as they argue and wither under her deadly stare.

"I've got her," Frankie insists, crutching to the edge of the embankment to support Alexa.

Jade and Emily crouch in front of me, unlacing my skates.

"It's not that bad," I mumble, though I can't bite back a soft yelp when Mac presses the top of my wrist. *"Shit."*

"Yeah, sorry. We're going to get you all checked out."

"No," I snap through clenched teeth. "No hospital."

"Charlie Porter." The firmness in Alexa's tone scarily matches her mother's as she approaches with Frankie at her side. She crosses her arms over her chest and levels me with a look so intense I shrink back on the bench a fraction of an inch as Alexa launches into her "I told you so" lecture.

She's so powerful that Mac cowers, too.

I take it on the chin. There's no point in pleading my case.

Even my stubborn self realizes when I royally screwed up.

Most people are afraid of normal things—snakes, heights, enclosed spaces, the dark.

Me? I'd rather hang out with snakes in an enclosed dark skyscraper than step foot in a hospital.

Logically, I know it makes no sense. Hospitals are safe places where trained professionals fix you and make you feel better.

But the sterile smells turn my stomach and I swear even my hair tenses as we enter. A lady nurse wearing Ninja Turtles scrubs leads me to a curtained-off examination room with Mac as my escort. "Hi, I'm Nurse Tina. Here you are, have a seat. I'm going to get your intake paperwork taken care of with a few questions, all right?"

I nod, ignoring the sporadic buzz of my phone in my pocket, no doubt my friends checking on me or sending me memes to try and cheer me up. They offered to accompany me to the hospital, but I shooed them off. It's Thanksgiving Day and they all have plans with their families—or secondary families, in Jade's case, since her parents are traveling.

Mac drops into the chair while I hop up to sit on the exam table.

"Full name, please?"

Siiiiigh. "Charlotte Victoria Porter."

"That's a pretty name," Nurse Tina says.

My expression puckers. "I feel like my mom named me that in case I ever trip and fall into the British line of succession. I go by Charlie."

Nurse Tina laughs. "Got it. We'll get your vitals in a minute. What's your date of birth, Charlie?"

"July twenty-fourth, 2008."

"Ah, you're a Leo, huh?"

"Apparently, yeah." I swear I hear a combination of Emily launching into an excitable spiel about how I'm a "Cancer-Leo cusp" and Jade groaning from here.

"So what happened today?" She eyes my jersey. "Hockey injury?"

"It's not that bad," I insist, extending my arm slightly. "Some asshole slashed my wrist with his stick."

"That doesn't sound fair," she says. "Are you currently taking any medications for anything?"

I shake my head. "Just vitamins and stuff."

"Are you a smoker?"

"Nah, I'm an athlete."

"Smart. What about drinking?"

"Nope. Not into it."

"Good. Is there any chance you might be pregnant, Charlie?"

Mac snickers at that one.

I pin him with a death glare in return. "No. Zero. Negative zero."

"Understood. Are you allergic to anything? Any medications?"

"Not that I know of."

Nurse Tina finishes typing her notes. "All right, then. Let's get your vitals checked. Then we'll go back and get that wrist x-rayed."

After the whole height-and-weight, blood-pressure-cuff, fingertip-clamp-thingy, temperature-taking ordeal, I follow the nurse back and let the x-ray techs do their thing. I return to the exam area and climb back up onto the table, situating the ice pack they provide over my wrist.

It only takes half an episode of *Chopped* playing on the tiny TV hanging from the ceiling before the ER doctor calls from behind the curtain.

"Knock knock." He steps inside wearing a mask and smiles with his eyes as he lowers himself onto a rolling stool in front of a computer. "Good news, Miss Porter." He clicks his mouse a few times before turning his monitor toward me to display my x-rayed wrist. "No fractures. Just a mild sprain."

Relief floods my system. "Told you," I fire at Mac. "So can I go now?"

The doctor laughs. "Soon. We'll get you fitted for a splint I'd like you to wear for two weeks. No heavy lifting. You can remove it to shower, but otherwise please keep it on. Do either of you have any questions?"

I shake my head.

"Just confirming," Mac says. "Two weeks of no heavy lifting? I need to make sure my sister heard you loud and clear."

My eyes roll hard. "I got it. Thanks."

"Two weeks. Feel free to take over-the-counter pain medication as needed. We'll get your splint fitted as soon as possible so you folks can get on your way and enjoy your holiday." He strides out with a wave.

Two weeks of not practicing lifts and throws? Geri's gonna murder me in cold blood.

But maybe not as fast as—

"Dad?" I glower at Mac as Dad enters the exam room minutes after the doctor leaves. "You said you wouldn't call him!"

Mac winces. "I texted him while you were in for X-rays. You can be mad at me, but I had to. He would've gotten the insurance statement anyway."

Dad's frown deepens. "Of course he told me. Your brother's a responsible guy—at least, I thought he was, before hearing about this pond match. What the hell *happened*?" Dad steps closer, his eyes landing on my ice-pack-covered wrist.

"Doc says it's just a sprain, no big deal."

"No big deal? You went to play a match against a team you know was gunning for you without a ref. That wasn't a smart move, kiddo."

"I wore my pads! That's where I got slashed, on my glove." It's on the tip of my tongue to explain to Dad what I learned in bio the other day—how my brain's frontal lobe isn't fully developed, which is why teenagers make risky decisions. But he won't really accept that as reasoning, so I hang my head instead.

"That doesn't explain the choice," Dad says, eyeing me as he rubs the back of his neck. "You said you were taking this figure skating competition thing seriously."

"I was. I *am*!" I blow out a hard breath, casting a pleading look at Mac. Between the tension building since entering the hospital and the guilt and shame roiling in my gut from deciding to play out of fear of retaliation, frustrated tears prickle in my eyes. I blink hard like the stubborn ass I am, refusing to let them fall. "Those Winthrop hockey guys—they wouldn't let up."

"They wouldn't have laid off her unless she played today," Mac provides.

"Yeah, and I'm sure as shit not gonna let them bully me more than they already do."

The nurse returns to splint my wrist before Dad can reply. He hangs back, talking in low tones with Mac.

Twenty minutes later I'm wearing my fitted splint as Dad offers me a hand off the exam table and leads me back through the hospital.

Mac slings an arm around my shoulders in solidarity.

Though I know I'm in for a parental earful and some consequences, my whole body releases coils of built-up anxiety the instant I step back into the lobby en route to the exit.

Slowing up my walk through the parking lot, I fish my phone from my pocket, opening the text from Alexa first.

Alexa (9:21 a.m.): Hello??? How bad is it??

"Charlie!" Dad waves me along. "Let's go. I need turkey, beer, and football. You're grounded for the rest of the weekend, by the way. I've got a whole damn list of one-handed chores in mind for you already."

"Ugh, yeah. Got it." I buckle in before replying to Alexa.

(9:48 a.m.): not too bad! just a sprain. two weeks with a splint and no lifting.

Alexa (9:50 a.m.): Thank god. I'm still super pissed at you.

(9:51 a.m.): yeah, i get that.

Alexa (9:53 a.m.): My mom's furious too btw. She's reworking the schedule for the next two weeks to accommodate your unnecessary injury.

It's all too easy to picture Geri leaning over her granite countertop in her bathrobe, angrily tapping away at her tablet as she revises the entire two-week training agenda, cursing me all the while.

"Hey. Gimme that phone, too." Driving one-handed, Dad reaches back with his free hand. "You'll get it back after the long weekend."

My jaw falls. "What? Dad, c'mon . . ."

"Nope. No negotiations. Hand it over."

Before placing my phone in Dad's hand, I fire off one more text to Alexa.

(9:56 a.m.): dad's taking my phone. tell her i'm sorry. i'll apologize in person on monday morning

Eighteen

When we get home, I pop ibuprofen for the pain and tread upstairs for a shower. Then I email Em and Jade from my laptop to reassure them I'm okay—even if I'm grounded and can't meet them at the Beanery again on Sunday after missing Bestie Homework Time a couple weeks ago when I went to New York City. Their return emails definitely carry disappointment in their text-based tone.

Like, I get it, universe. I should've stuck to my plan of not playing and dealt with whatever other fallout would've come my way thanks to Stratford—who for some reason blames *me* for his breakup? Make it make sense!

Thanksgiving dinner doesn't taste as good as it usually does because I'm extra mopey. I spend the rest of the weekend tackling Dad's list of punishment chores and jogging with Mac around the neighborhood, and without my phone I actually manage to catch up on a fair amount of sleep.

As expected, Geri verbally cross-checks me into the boards on Monday morning. Instead of lifts and throws, we'll focus on stroking and flightless spins until I'm cleared to train full throttle.

Throughout that week, each practice I'm unable to lift or throw Alexa when I've been making so much progress adds to my own boiling irritation. I've been funneling all I've got into this training, and as often as Geri reminds me how costly my selfish choice to play that hockey match had been, she can't possibly be more annoyed with me than I am with myself.

Even if a tiny part of me doesn't *totally* regret it, since I've been missing the thrill of a full-speed hockey match like a visceral ache.

On Saturday morning, dread pools in the pit of my stomach while driving to the Winthrop Dance Academy. I strongly consider bailing for the McDonald's next door, but Geri would no doubt find out if I pull a no-show.

Wearing a tank top and cozy tapered joggers beneath my coat, I kick a rock through the parking lot as I shuffle inside and approach the counter. "Hey. I'm Charlie Porter. My coach signed me up for . . . I guess a beginner dance class?" My face twists with disgust. I can't help it.

If it offends the receptionist, she doesn't let it show. Instead, she casts me a curious look. "Studio Two."

"Thanks." Hanging up my coat in the lobby, I enter Studio 2 and scoff, muttering to myself. "You gotta be shitting me, Geri. . . ."

The dozen or so ballet students range in age from about five to seven, all standing at least two feet shorter than me, wearing black or pale pink leotards with matching slippers, some with tutus.

I kick off my Converse by the children's shoes and step onto the floor in fox-print socks, swearing under my breath.

"A new student! Welcome!" The dance teacher looks about my age. Actually—I'm pretty sure she's a Winthrop cheerleader. "Choose a spot at the barre. We'll start in a moment."

The boldest little girl places her fists on her hips and sneers up at me. "You're too *big* to be a ballerina."

My arms cross over my chest. "Yeah? Well you're too small to ride the really fun roller coasters."

She sticks her tongue out at me.

I stick mine out right back.

The door swings open once more.

"Miss Alexa!" A chorusing stampede of dancer-child Funko

Pops flocks toward my skating partner, nearly tackling her in a group hug.

Alexa brightens. "Hey, friends! I've missed you." Her eyes find me by the ballet barre as she sings, *"One of these things . . . is not like the others. . . ."*

"You're hilarious. Did your mom send you to spy on me?"

"Nope! I volunteer sometimes. I started taking classes here when I was even younger than these beautiful mini ballerinas." She smooths her hand down one's hair. "Go on, I'm sure Miss Natalie is ready to start."

"Yes, I am. Thanks for helping today, Lex."

"Oh, it's my *pleasure*." Alexa flashes a wolfish look in my direction as she toes off her shoes and slides on her ballet slippers.

Snoozefest elevator music strains through the studio speaker.

Natalie begins the lesson. "First position!"

Scowling, I spot the little girls pressing their heels together so their toes point outward.

"Seriously?" Scrunching my nose, I attempt the same movement. "Okay, this does not feel natural or graceful—"

"Shhh!" The pint-size Queen Bee in Training shushes me.

Alexa paces down the barre, pausing to rest a hand on my arm. "Just try and follow along, Miss Charlie. You'll get the hang of it."

"I *sincerely* doubt it."

"Backs straight, ballerinas!" Alexa calls. "Chins up!"

"You sound like your mother," I mutter before she pinches my elbow and continues on.

The next forty minutes suck. Changing positions, dipping, bending, crouching, breathing, repeat. My bulkier body definitely isn't built for ballet, every move awkward and stiff. During the session, my thoughts drift almost instantly, alternating between a Big Mac and fries from next door and how sweetly and gently Alexa corrects the children's positioning.

As soon as class is dismissed, I shove my feet into my high-tops and stomp back out to the lobby, craving sleep and fast food.

"Not bad for a first-timer," Alexa says as she glides out from the studio a minute later.

Snapping my gaze upward, a bitter laugh croaks free. "If you think *that's* gonna make me graceful . . ."

"Give it time." She removes her parka from the coatrack. "So are you free the rest of the afternoon? I need to run a skating-related errand and Mom says you're welcome to join me instead of going to the gym—if you promise to get your reps in later." Her eyes swirl with mischief.

"Hmm . . . depends. If it's more ballet, I'm out."

"Nope! We're going on a secret spy mission."

"A secret spy mission?" As if on cue, my stomach growls. "I'm down. Can we drive through McD's first?"

Alexa guides me to her white SUV and reminds me to buckle up. Turning on one of her Swiftie-themed playlists, she swings into the drive-through before veering onto the road. Alexa sings off-key as she merges onto the highway while I pound a Big Mac and shovel fries into my face, mindful not to get salt or crumbs in her nice car.

Ten more minutes pass and I cave. "Okay, James Bond. You gonna tell me where we're going?"

"Nope! Don't worry. We'll be there in under an hour." Her hand reaches over the center console and slips into my not-greasy one, squeezing gently considering the splint. "You trust me, right?"

My stomach flips. "Yeah. I trust you for some reason."

She places her hand back on the wheel. "Good."

By noon, we cross the state border into New Hampshire, exit

the highway, and enter a residential neighborhood. A fresh blanket of snow coats the yards, plowed streets sitting quiet and near empty. Clearly a wealthy neighborhood with substantial ground between each property, mini groves of snow-capped trees separate houses instead of fencing.

Alexa shifts into park and cuts the ignition, reaching across my lap to open the glove box—and snags a pair of binoculars.

"Whoa, what the hell?"

"Told you it's a spy mission." She squints through the device toward one house in particular. "Okay, we're good. Let's go." Tucking the binoculars into her coat pocket, she hops out of the car and waves for me to follow. "Stay close."

"Lex, what . . ." I exit the vehicle, snow crunching beneath my rubber-soled high-tops.

She turns and shushes me before scurrying toward the first tree between two properties. Then she dashes from tree to tree like a ginger gazelle, using their thick trunks for cover.

"We're making footprints in the snow, James Bond," I whisper. "Gonna need to cover our tracks if you're planning on actually stealing something. . . ."

It's probably because I know Alexa is one of the most controlling, morally sound people in my life that I'm not nervous. Instead, I can't wipe the fascinated delight from my expression.

"Don't worry, we're good."

Passing through two houses, the expansive backyards come into view—one in particular earning a breathy *holy crap* spilling past my lips.

An ice rink. A whole-ass ice rink with half-wall boards stands in the backyard of the house we've apparently arrived to scope out.

We stop behind a thicker tree and lean out from either side of it.

"Ha! Knew they'd be at it around now."

Two skaters stroke around the ice—a pair of fair-skinned blonds moving in perfect sync. "Oh shit, is that—"

"Mason and Mallory Ingleborg, reigning national champions." Alexa passes me the binoculars. "I wanted to give you a better sense of what we're up against. The videos don't really do them justice—their emotion when they skate, how intense and crisp they are."

"Damn Dingleborgs." I watch for another minute. "Uh . . . they just landed side-by-side triple lutzes like it's no big deal."

"Yep. But we can do that too, Charlie. I know we've only got another month and a half to prepare for sectionals, but we can get there."

I snort. "With more ballet?"

Alexa's stare fixates on me—watching me watching them. Keeping my jaw stiff, I note how effortlessly they skate together. As if one's a perfect shadow of the other.

"Remember, we don't need to beat them to qualify for nationals. We only need to place in the top four."

"Right. This is the gold standard though, huh?"

"Mm-hmm. For now."

We pass the binoculars back and forth for the next twenty minutes or so, my toes tingling with numbness. I ignore it; they'll warm back up in the car. Alexa's right—seeing them skate in person is a hell of a lot more impactful. Intimidating, too. Not that I'm *afraid*. Just, you know—humbled.

After witnessing a run-through of their routine, I lower the binoculars and arch a brow at Alexa as it hits me. "You've done this with Frankie, haven't you? Driven out here with your little binoculars to spy on them."

Alexa's nose shamelessly scrunches. "Mmm . . . not *exactly*."

I blink. "Wait. Not Frankie. You came out here with your mom, didn't you?" I barely muffle my cackle in time. "That's *hilarious*."

Her sheepish smile spreads wider. "It's not uncommon to check in on each other, get a sense of what you're up against in competition."

"That's why she accused me of being a spy that first time?"

"Yes."

Snickering, I shake my head. "Damn. Skaters are way more intense than hockey players. Like—next level." Stepping out to get a better view, a branch snaps beneath my shoe. The sound spooks a nearby family of deer; they bolt into a thicker thicket of trees beside us, the rustling snagging the Ingleborgs' attention.

"Oh crap, hide!" Alexa grabs my arm and pins me up against the back of the tree, pressing her body against mine with her fingers curled around the lapels of my coat, and together we freeze.

A rush of panic floods my insides. "Did they hear—"

"Shhh!" Alexa smothers her hand over my mouth, expression twisting into a grimace.

I swear I hear her heart thumping as hard as mine beneath our winter coats as voices carry toward us.

"What was that?" Mason asks.

"I heard it too," Mallory says. "Should we go check it out?"

Another forever-long pause.

Alexa's hand lowers from my mouth and braces on my shoulder.

My hands find her waist on instinct and we lock gazes.

I stop breathing.

Her eyes match mine, swirling with the same emotions.

Questioning. Hopeful.

Wanting?

My heart beating rapid fire has nothing to do with maybe being caught by the Dingleborgs.

In what feels like slow motion, Alexa licks her lips, then pushes up on tiptoe, leaning in a fraction of an inch, and—

"Forget it, Mase. Probably squirrels chasing each other."

The prissy voice bursts whatever weird, intense bubble we slipped into.

Alexa steps back, her tempered laugh slightly strained as she puffs out a cloud of cold air. "That was close."

I slump forward, blowing hot air into my bare fist. "Yeah. Too close."

"We've seen enough. Let's get out of here."

We remain crouched as we scurry back to the car, ducking into our seats. The doors shut and our relieved laughter fills the space. Our cheeks match—bright red and frozen.

"So not only are you an Olympic-level skater," I muse aloud while Alexa drives off. "You're a volunteer dance teacher and creepy skater spy in your spare time? I'm learning so much about you today."

Alexa whacks my upper arm with the back of her hand. "I'm not *creepy*."

I laugh harder than I have in a long time. "Whatever you say, Miss Bond. Crank the heat, would you?"

"Hmph."

My cheeks ache from grinning, and for the next half hour, I replay that moment.

The maybe, sort of, almost . . . *moment* moment, wondering if maybe I hallucinated the look on her face, or the way her breath caught when my strong hands found her hips in a nonskating situation.

Exiting the highway, Alexa's playlist cuts midsong as a dull ring carries through the car.

Incoming Call—Konor flashes on the dashboard.

Alexa rejects the call, swiping away the notification.

My grip instinctively tightens around my seat belt strap. "You could've taken it," I say. "I would've plugged my ears or whatever."

"No, that's okay. I broke up with him. For good."

"Wait, what?" My gaze snaps to her profile. I hope like hell I heard her correctly while trying to chill the bundle of bats flapping in my gut yet again. "You did?"

"I did. He was already on thin ice—no pun intended—when I asked for a break. Then when he fist-bumped Gavin after he slashed you with his stick like that?" She shakes her head. "I guess I didn't want to see that side of him before, but my mom always says when someone shows you who they are, believe them. I don't want to be associated with someone that cruel."

"Yeah, I wouldn't either. I'm sorry, though. Breakups suck." Not that I know from firsthand experience or anything.

Alexa pins me with a quick, knowing look. "You're not *that* sorry."

Despite being all warmed up thanks to the pumping heat, my face flares once more at the callout. "Fine, yeah. I'm not. Screw that shithead, he never deserved you."

Alexa emits a sad but fond chuckle and once again reaches over to gently slip her hand into mine.

When she lets go, I can't help but wish she didn't.

Nineteen

When my two weeks of doctor-ordered splinting are up, I'm splint free and pain free. I dive back into training harder than before, eager to make up for lost time. As mid-December hits, Geri announces I'm back on track with drilling jumps, lifts, and throws. In my quest to overcome my setback, I manage to complete several sessions of ballet classes and video yoga, which I grudgingly admit improves both my flexibility and the grace with which I skate.

Lightly falling snow heightens the holiday vibe as we herd into school for the last day before winter break. Paper snowflakes dangle from the ceiling in certain hallways, some people wear Christmas sweaters or reindeer headbands, and cheerful holiday music plays over the PA system between classes.

In homeroom, Mr. Healey distributes our first trimester report cards.

The bell beeps just after I receive mine, and I step out into the hallway before opening the envelope.

Biology—C+

World Cultures—B−

Algebra II—D+

English—C+

Health/PE—A

"Shit, okay," I mumble under my breath, a pained expression overtaking my face. These grades won't be good enough for Quigley to readmit me to Cranford in the spring, but they're not too far off.

"That bad, huh?" Frankie approaches from his homeroom across the hall.

"Not the worst, but not good enough?" I slip the report back into its envelope, knowing Dad will log into PowerSchool to review my grades for himself. I need to be proactive. "Hey, do you think Cyn would tutor me?"

"Sure she would! Ask her today before her second-trimester tutoring schedule fills up."

"Dope. Will do." With a plan in place, hopefully Dad won't be too concerned. "See ya later!"

Parting from Frankie, I head toward bio and note Stratford lingering in the hallway with his arm slung around one of the cheerleaders. Amazing. Maybe he'll stop sneering at me every chance he gets.

After successfully avoiding him in class, I'm running the *Wicked* routine elements through my mind while I limp-swagger on achy feet through the halls. Halfway on my trek from bio to algebra, a familiar hand hooks into the crook of my arm and tugs me into an empty classroom.

I stumble but manage to stay upright, laughing at Alexa—who's clearly super pleased with herself for snatching me. "Dude, really? You miss me that much, huh?"

Alexa rolls her eyes and hops up onto an empty lab table. "I got you a little Christmas present and I didn't want to give it to you earlier with my mom around. Not that—I mean, you know how she is. . . ." She shuffles through her bag and extends a neatly wrapped package with a green bow in my direction.

"You got me a present?" I accept the box, shaking my head. "You didn't have to—"

"It's really not a big deal. Just open it." She curls her fingers around the lip of the table and leans into her palms.

"Why do I suddenly feel like I should be afraid?" Unfolding the wrapping paper, my head falls back as I release a throaty cackle. "Seriously? A box of Band-Aids?"

"They're *custom* Band-Aids!" Alexa snags the box from my hands and opens it, pulling out a wad of bandages and spreading them across her palm for inspection. She obviously put a lot of effort into designing and ordering the thoughtful assortment—maroon Band-Aids with hockey sticks printed on top, forest-green Band-Aids with ice skates, and dark blue Band-Aids sporting the Wonder Woman logo.

"Oh my god, you're such a nerd. These are hilarious." My cheeks warm as she slides the Band-Aids back into the box and hands it to me. "Thanks. They're awesome." A pang of guilt hits and I grimace. "Shit. I didn't get you anything."

I don't have much time to feel like an asshole before Alexa's shaking her head. "You don't have to. I don't celebrate Christmas anyway." A beat passes. "Actually, if you really want to give me something . . ."

Beeeeep!

The warning bell jolts us both upright.

Alexa emits a slightly strained laugh. "Listen, my cousin's getting married New Year's weekend in Boston. I know it's last minute, but do you want to come with us? Not, like, as my date or anything—super low-key, as friends! It's just . . . I was thinking we haven't spent a weekend apart in a while with training, right? And I'm worried we'll, you know, backslide if we—"

"Backslide?" Seriously, could her rambling be more adorable? I shrug in what I hope comes across as a super chill manner. "Sure, why not? I usually hang with Em and Jade on New Year's Eve, but

I'm sure they'll be cool about me getting to go to Boston overnight instead. I'll ask my dad." No doubt he'll take pity on me for having to spend Christmas with my mom.

"Really?" Alexa brightens. "Thanks, Porter. I'll text you the details."

"You're late for class, Miss Punctuality."

"Crap!" Alexa startles. "Bad influence . . ." She hops off the table.

"Proud of it." I nod toward the door. "Get to class, know-it-all."

"You too." Alexa slips out first, casting me one last smile that trips my heart annoyingly fast.

I tuck my new Band-Aids into my bag and set off toward algebra, my limp-swagger shifting into feeling like I'm floating on a goddamn cloud.

Once I share with Dad my proactive tutoring plan with Cyn, Dad gives me enough cash to afford a nice wedding outfit and tells me to consider it my Christmas present.

And as soon as I mention the wedding to Jade and Emily, they whisk me out shopping.

"So not only did she invite you as her plus-one to a wedding, you also almost *kissed*."

"Against a snowy tree? That's so romantic!"

"I think so?" I fidget with the cuffs of the Italian wool suit jacket I'm trying on in a department store at the Winthrop Mall.

Jade leans against the fitting-room wall beside the full-length mirror. She folds her arms over her chest. "What do you mean, you *think so*? She leaned in, right? You said you saw her looking at your lips."

My shoulders hitch. "But what if she was looking at, like, food in my teeth? Or, y'know, she's short, so my mouth is technically at her eye level—"

"Charlie." Emily giggles and shakes her head as she steps up in front of me, smoothing her hands across my shoulder pads.

"Jesus, Porter. You're a goddamn disaster at this." Jade tilts her head to the side and drags her index finger up and down midair before me. "Not *this*. Girl, you rock the *hell* out of a suit. How's it feel?"

I preen, popping the lapels of the jacket as I strike a few obnoxious poses in the dressing-room mirror. The suit's made by a designer who cuts jackets and dress pants for women's bodies. The jacket and trousers are magically a perfect fit, so I don't need any alterations. "I do make this shit look pretty damn good, don't I?"

"Super dapper!" Emily presents two options for the final touch. "Skinny necktie or bow tie?"

"Skinny necktie," Jade cuts in before I even open my mouth. "That way, when Alexa decides she can't resist anymore, she can snag Charlie by the tie and yank her in for a hot make-out session."

"Dude." Heat creeps into my ears and cheeks as I snatch the necktie from Emily's hand, tipping my chin upward while busying myself with tying a full Windsor knot. Dad taught me and Mac how to tie neckties and bow ties before one of his side-gig catering jobs when we were twelve and thirteen. "First of all, I still don't know if she's into girls at all. Even if she is, she basically *just* got out of a relationship, so she probably doesn't want to rush into anything. Also, her mom made it clear we can't do anything to screw up our partnership or whatever right now."

Jade snorts. "Oh, please. So you're saying if you get another shot you're not gonna take it? What if she makes the first move? We all know it's been an embarrassingly long time since you've hooked up with anyone."

I groan. "Shut *up*. That's not my fault. You know there are slim pickings of girls who like girls at Cranford. And I sure as hell haven't been looking at Winthrop."

"Becaaaause you've got it bad for Alexa," Emily provides.

"So, so bad . . ."

"Just admit it, c'mon!"

My head tips back farther and I close my eyes, grumbling under my breath while they wait for my response. They're not wrong—both about my feelings and my level of experience. I've only kissed a handful of girls. A small handful. Two, to be exact. First when I was fifteen in a spin-the-bottle situation at Emily's ninth-grade birthday party, then a lacrosse player at a Cranford Athletics Banquet last year. And I didn't have *feelings* for either of them. Well, a little bit for the lacrosse player—but not anywhere close to this.

"Fine." Summoning as much courage as possible, I blurt my confession aloud. "I like her." Breathing the words into existence for the first time triggers a combo of relief and terror swirling through my chest. It's so good to admit it to the people I trust most, and yet those question-mark variables remain the same—if Alexa likes me too, or if she's straight as a hockey stick shaft? If my feelings could potentially screw things up between us?

Jade and Emily don't seem to care about the confliction written all over my face, high-fiving each other and jumping up and down.

"Finally!"

"Ha! We knew it!"

"It's just a ridiculous crush, leave me alone." I'm not sure why I naively thought my friends would ease up on the teasing once I hopped off the Denial Express. Instead, they launch into a debate over when and how I should tell her, sparking a fresh wave of nausea coursing through me.

"Girl, now you definitely need to make you ditching us on New

Year's Eve worth it. We'll be disappointed if you don't make your move."

"*So* disappointed." Emily fires puppy eyes in my direction.

"Can we please change the subject? I really hate you guys," I declare, even though all three of us know it's not even a little bit true.

"Sure, sure. But you love your hot new suit." Em beams at me through the mirror.

"Almost as much as she loves—"

"*Get out!*" I bellow, shoving a cackling Jade and Emily out of the fitting room.

Did I mention I hate them?

Twenty

Winter break is usually pretty chill for me—some hockey practice and epic PlayStation battles with Mac, lounging around Em's house, playing cards with Dad. This year I've got *two* out-of-town commitments, so I'm bracing myself for the least chill break *ever*.

First up? Weekend Number One, aka *Operation: Get through Mom & Rick's Dinner without Punching a Wall.*

Christmas Eve morning, while me and Mac chuck our overnight bags into the back seat of our car, Dad pulls his old Jeep Cherokee into the driveway next to us after another night shift.

I'm layered in a T-shirt and thick Cranford hoodie, wishing I was enduring another brutal predawn Geri training sesh rather than leaving town to spend the night at Mom's house.

Anticipating my extreme grouchiness, Dad ambles over and extends a large fast-food bag my way. "Here you go, kiddo. A few bacon, egg, and cheese biscuits and hash browns for the road. Make sure you share with your brother." He pulls me in for a one-armed hug.

The greasy goodness hits my nostrils and my stomach predictably gurgles. "Thanks." Lifting my head from the hug, I pout not unlike an overtired toddler. "Sure you don't want me to stay home with you? Being all alone on Christmas must suck." It's not fair, but I guess divorce never feels fair.

Dad shakes his head. "And have your mom call and ream me out over the phone? Nah, not worth it. Don't you worry about me. I'll just be watching football all weekend, enjoying some peace and quiet and all the food in the fridge to myself for once."

"She won't be pissed at you if I have an emergency and need to hang back. We can say I caught a bad flu? Got food poisoning from Mac's cooking so it's Puke City nonstop? Lost my arm in a shark attack?"

"A shark attack where, on our frozen pond?" Mac flicks my earlobe protruding beneath my beanie and snags the food bag from my hand, turning to give Dad a hug. "We'll be fine. Back before you know it." He ushers me into the passenger seat and I cast Dad one last wave as he watches us drive off.

Mac's merging onto the highway when he polishes off his second hash brown and nudges me with his elbow. "Thought you'd be okay with going down to spend time with Mom. You've been sending her our hockey schedules for years."

"That's different," I mutter, wiping the flakes of buttery biscuit crumbs clinging to my hoodie onto the floor.

"Why—because now we have to deal with a four-hour drive?"

I shrug. "It's just different. It's weird there." I'm not sure I've got the words or emotional energy to explain why I hate visiting Mom; maybe it's experiencing life with her upgraded husband and upgraded daughter and how happy she seems without us. If she'd visit for a match, at least I could pretend for a few hours that she never left. That she cares enough to put me first for once, before Kylie. That she could see the product of my years of training and dedication, watch me dominate. That she'd tell me she was proud of who I'm growing up to be despite her absence for half my childhood.

"I hear ya. It is kinda weird." Mac takes a few swigs from his water bottle. "You know why she doesn't come back. All her triggers are in Winthrop."

"Yeah, yeah. I know." Alcoholism recovery 101: Stay away from anything that used to drive you to drink, which was the main factor for Mom's decision to leave. On one hand, I totally get it and I'm proud of her—she worked her ass off in rehab and she deserves this second chance to do things right.

On the other hand, I am and will always be one of those triggers for her. A reminder of what went wrong in her life, or at least a tricky Z-shaped piece of her old Tetris game that doesn't fully fit into her newer, perfectly layered base. "If Winthrop's the problem, she could catch one of our away games. I'm just sayin' . . ."

"Maybe next season. Or the one after that, when you score a roster spot for a D-I school and your games are streamed live for everyone to watch."

"Yeah, true." Focusing on my far future proves much more pleasant than my immediate one. "I'm gonna nap. Wake me up when we get there, I guess."

"Maybe I'll let you sleep through dinner." Mac turns on sports talk radio to keep him company while I drift toward unconsciousness. "Too bad there's not an Olympic event in napping. I'd put all my money on you."

"Hell yeah. Sleeping champion, that's me." The visual of me standing on top of a podium with a gold medal around my neck helps me fall asleep quickly.

Mac pokes me hours later. "Wake up, we're a few minutes out. Figured I'd give you some time to wipe the drool crust from your chin."

Mumbling a few incoherent curses, I sit up and stretch my arms over my head before checking my reflection in the visor mirror. No notable drool. Settling back into the seat, I try mentally preparing myself to reunite with Mom and her family.

We pull into a wealthy neighborhood behind a sign for Windermere Estates. Dirty snow leftover from a week-old storm clusters in gray patches on expansive lawns, along with mini mountainous plow-piles capping the corners of each driveway.

I haven't been to Mom's house in four years, but it's as big as I remember. It's a three-story modern home topped by a sleek, flat roof, boxy with all right angles (Cyn would be proud of my noticing) painted black with silver trim. Like it's trying way too hard to be cool, not unlike my stepdad, who makes a shit ton of money as a trial lawyer.

Speaking of Rick, he's the one who answers the door with a goofy grin on his face. "Honey! The kids are here!" Sporting an ugly Christmas sweater I can't tell if he's wearing ironically or not, he pulls us in for hugs, which I grudgingly accept with a pained smile.

"Hey, Rick. Cool sweater."

"Thanks, Charlie!" Yep, unironically. He tries snagging the end of my bag. "Lemme carry this upstairs for ya—"

"I'm good." I hold tight to the opposite end. "I got it. Thanks, though."

"Ah, right. You and your independent streak. I admire that!" No he doesn't. Rick's nothing if not a strict abider of gender roles. He leads us upstairs and into a floral-themed guest room with two twin beds. "Here you are. You're both a little bigger than you were last time you stayed over—hopefully the beds aren't too small."

Mac claps Rick on the shoulder. "This is good for us. Thanks."

"Your mom's hard at work in the kitchen. Kylie's in the basement practicing a dance routine she's been planning on performing for everyone after dinner. Baby girl loves a spotlight."

"Don't we all," Mac adds, nudging me with a grin.

I roll my eyes, toeing off my shoes and heading toward the door. Taking the stairs two at a time, I nearly slide on the freshly waxed hardwood flooring on my way to the kitchen.

I don't recognize Mom right away with her back toward me and her hair dyed blond. She stands on tiptoe in front of a cabinet, reaching for something beyond her fingertips.

Standing in the same room as her, my built-up bitterness melts away. "Damn. Are you shrinking?"

Mom whirls around. "Char Char!" She holds out her arms and hugs me tight when I approach, her laugh bright against my ear. "Good lord, *look* at you! You've grown half a foot since I saw you last."

Last time I saw her we were almost the same height. Now I'm a solid three inches taller. That's three inches worth of my life she only got the abridged Wikipedia version of through emails, texts, and rare phone calls.

Her hands cradle my face, yanking me from those creeping bitter thoughts.

I study hers, too. She looks a little older as evidenced by the subtle lines in her forehead and faint crowing wrinkles from her eyes when she squints, along with other minor details typically magicked away by FaceTime filters. "Blond, huh?" Yet another attempt to erase her Porter past. I inwardly scold myself for thinking it. It's just *hair.*

She steps back and smooths her hand over her goldilocks. "Ricky loves it. I'm on the fence, but it's growing on me."

"Well, if *Ricky* loves it . . . ," I tease, the open cabinet behind her catching my attention again. "Seriously though, did you need something? I can help."

"Oh, yes! Parsley, please. It should be right—*Macky!*"

Mac barrels forward and folds Mom into a hug.

She does the same thing with him—commenting on his height, pulling back to study his face.

Wanting to give them a moment of privacy, I rummage through the spices until I find the parsley and set it onto the countertop.

I'm barely turned around when a tiny body slams into mine.

"*Oof!* Speaking of someone who's taller . . ." Dropping to my knees, I pull Kylie in for a tighter hug, trying hard to suppress my guilt for thinking shitty things about the kid. She didn't ask to be born. "Hey, kiddo." I sound like Dad, I realize after a beat. What-ever, it fits.

Kylie's light brown hair is woven into two French braids the same way Mom used to style mine. She wears her dance team's T-shirt and shorts, pulling back with a giggle. "I'm almost the tallest girl in my class," she says, matter-of-fact.

Mac pulls her in for a hug next. "We heard you were rehearsing a dance show for us later tonight."

Mom laughs. "She's always gearing up to perform something or other."

"This one's my best one yet! Are you gonna post it on Face-book?" Kylie asks Mom, clearly delighted at the prospect.

Mac and I share a private wince. Neither of us have Facebook, but I'd put money on Mom's page having hundreds of videos of Kylie posted over the years.

"Of course, sweetheart! I bet you'll get dozens of likes like you always do."

Kylie squeaks in excitement.

"How can we help?" Mac asks, moving to the sink to wash his hands.

I follow suit. "Yeah, put us to work." Better than lounging around with Rick watching snorefest golf on TV or listening to high-lights from his latest successful case. He'd no doubt post about all his courtroom victories on Facebook if it was legal, too.

Kylie returns to the basement and Mom enlists Mac's help with the stuffing while I follow her handwritten recipe for raspberry chocolate pie. After thirty minutes of mixing ingredients, rolling out crust, pouring filling, and securing the top layer of dough by press-ing fork imprints around the edge, I snap a quick pic of the prebaked pie along with an apron selfie to send to Emily, who's no doubt bak-ing for her own Christmas Eve feast.

We help clean up before Mom shoos us upstairs to wash up for dinner. An hour later I'm showered and beanie-free, clad in my jeans with the fewest number of rips and a checkered navy button-down shirt cuffed at the sleeves. I'm sitting at the dining room table set for ten beside Mac, in his festive red cable-knit sweater, who's jovially chatting with Rick's sister Isabelle across the table.

As is typical for me in a group of mostly strangers, I spend the salad course quiet and observing, trying to remember the names of those I just met.

Isabelle sits between her twin sons, Evan and Ethan, both freshmen at Syracuse. Beside Ethan sits their older sister, Olivia, who's objectively hotter than her boyfriend on her other side, named Grant. Gavin? Something with a G . . .

"It's so nice to *finally* meet your older kids, Eleanor."

Eleanor? Mom's always been Nora to us, but whatever.

Mom rests a hand on my shoulder beside me. "Aren't they *gorgeous*? Macky's a senior heading to Minnesota on a full hockey scholarship next year. Honor roll, Eagle Scout. What doesn't he excel at, really?"

Mac's cheeks redden and he shakes his head. "Thanks, Ma. . . ."

"My Charlie's a hockey player too—and a figure skater now!"

Isabelle blinks. "Wow, you do both?"

"Yep." I shrink back in my chair, willing someone to change the subject.

"She's a pairs skater," Mac chimes in. "Training for a competition in February. She still hasn't let me watch her throwing Alexa in practice. . . ."

I shoot him a look. "Nobody's allowed to watch practice. Coach's orders."

"Alexa?" Olivia pauses, her fork-speared lettuce halfway to her mouth. "You skate with a girl? Is that, like, allowed?"

"Unusual . . . ," Rick mutters, stabbing his cherry tomato with more force than necessary. "Yet that seems to be the new trend in competitive sports these days. My firm took on a case the other day about a boy wanting to compete in girls' swimming. Whole school district up in arms. What a damn mess."

It's on the tip of my tongue to ask if the boy Rick mentioned identifies as a boy or if he's misgendering someone—and I take a swig of water, preparing myself to launch (and win) a debate with a whole-ass lawyer.

Mac, sensing my tension, cuts in before I get a chance. "Our hockey team's coed, and we do just fine. Reigning league champions, actually." He elbows me. "Charlie can outskate both wingers on my line. Our goalie, Nicole—she's the best goalie in the league."

I release the exhale on a strained chuckle. "Yeah. She's the best."

"Well, good for you and her!" Isabelle raises her wineglass. "Always a beautiful thing when a woman bests a man at his own game."

The low chuckle erupting around the table carries half strained, half genuine.

I zone out as Isabelle launches into a speech about her own children's accomplishments, which in turn fuels Mom's boasting about all of Kylie's dance competition wins, her skiing progress, and her martial arts trophy standing six feet tall.

As we progress into the main course, conversation thankfully shifts to more neutral topics—concerts everyone has attended lately, NFL games, and the Caribbean cruise Rick has planned for Mom and Kylie over spring break.

I'm not even a little bit jealous.

Okay, yeah I am. I'm a shitty liar even to myself.

A weight lifts when we're all excused from the table, my belly full of delicious food as the sole perk of dinner. We carry our dessert plates into the living room, where Kylie made a quick change into her sparkly dance leotard and bosses everyone onto the couches.

I'm shoveling forkfuls of the raspberry chocolate pie I baked into my face as Kylie begins her performance. Her flexibility and natural rhythm are pretty damn impressive.

Then I spot Mom perching on the chaise, silently mouthing the eight-counts along with pride all but bursting from every single pore on her face. She records the performance on her phone as her eyes fill with happy tears, smile wider than a goddamn slice of cantaloupe.

It's a look I haven't seen directed my way in forever and it makes my jaw clench, my raging sweet-tooth appetite plummeting.

Again, I get it. It's really shitty of me to be jealous of a second grader—especially my half sister. It's nothing against Kylie, though. It's everything she gets to experience that I missed out on. Mom cheering her on at every step of every endeavor. Chaperoning her elementary school field trips. Offering middle school guidance through a low-key traumatic and awkward-as-hell puberty. Providing hair and makeup support during her teenage years—not that I wear makeup except for extreme circumstances, but the point stands.

After the performance, Kylie whips out the karaoke machine. Ethan and Evan perform a cringeworthy version of some twangy country song, so I don't even need to fake a headache as I head up to the guest room. Making a quick change into pj's, I flop onto the perfectly made twin bed and pull out my phone for some decompression time.

Bestie Group Chat responded to the baking pic I sent earlier.

Emily (6:49 p.m.): Omg I'm so proud!! My flourless chocolate cake wasn't great but it wasn't bad, either. Progress!! How did your rasp choco pie taste??

Jade (7:17 p.m.): Ayyyy that's great! Em rocks an apron better than you do, Porter. 😛

(8:04 p.m.): yo awesome! i'm down to taste your next attempt at flourless chocolate cake. mine was pretty good but i can't take credit, just followed mom's recipe. jade how's it going with dr. ed and hattie? did you tell them yet??

Emily (8:05 p.m.): OH YEAH did you tell them yet??

Jade (8:08 p.m.): I was getting to that . . . So yes I told them about RISD. They were actually really supportive! If I major in art somewhere they want me to double major in art and something "more lucrative" to give me "options down the line" . . . I'll take it for now.

(8:10 p.m.): dude that's huge!! must be such a weight off, telling them. sooo stoked for you!

Emily (8:11 p.m.): I'm SO PROUD OF YOU!! And now you can spend the rest of your break relaxing at home!

Jade (8:13 p.m.): Hell yeah. Thanks guys. How's it going in Mom World, Charlie?

(8:14 p.m.): weird and awkward as predicted. at least the food is good.

Swiping away from Bestie Group Chat, I pull up my text chain with Alexa.

(8:15 p.m.): how's it going nerd?

Alexa (8:18 p.m.): Mom and I are rocking our Jewish Christmas tradition—Chinese food and a movie!

She sends a selfie holding up lo mein noodles twirled around a pair of chopsticks.

Her good mood is infectious and I grin right back into the phone. Ugh, she's so pretty it's criminal.

> (8:20 p.m.): sounds a hell of a lot better than christmas with mom and rick.
>
> **Alexa** (8:22 p.m.): I hope it's not too bad. I miss you! It's weird when we don't see each other for a whole day.
>
> (8:24 p.m.): miss you too weirdo. what are your plans for christmas day? yoga? reading another "tasteful romance" novel? making a new swiftie playlist? wait . . . does tay tay even have a christmas album??
>
> **Alexa** (8:26 p.m.): 😛 You're a jerk. Our movie's starting. I'll bug you tomorrow. Merry Christmas!

When I stir the next morning, the mouthwatering scents of bacon and coffee waft beneath the crack in the door, rousing me further. I don't bother changing out of my flannel pj bottoms and pull a hoodie over my T-shirt, padding barefoot downstairs with Mac behind me.

"Whoa . . ." My eyes pop comically wide at the state of the living room: the massive Christmas tree still lit from the night before, boxes and gift bags and wrapping paper strewn about like a festive cyclone crashed through. Both Mom and Rick hold their phones out, filming or taking pictures of Kylie as she unwraps gift after gift.

It's the type of Christmas I always thought I wanted. Instead, my earliest Christmas morning memories involve my parents fighting or Mom staying in bed in a depressive funk.

Kylie spots us lingering on the steps. "Char Char! Macky! Santa came!"

"I can see that. Wow. Kinda looks like a whole fleet of Santas came. You must've been really good this year or something."

Mac ruffles my hair. "Unlike Charlie. She always got coal as a kid."

I scoff. "Let's be real. Compared to Mr. Perfect Child, everyone's a bad kid."

Mom motions toward the kitchen. "She's almost through her gifts. I made coffee and boiled water for tea—wasn't sure which you preferred."

Mumbling a thanks, we head into the kitchen. Mac fixes his coffee while I snag a tea bag, adding some milk and sugar to my mug. We return to the living room and ease onto the couch. I will myself to not head back upstairs, wishing I could get over myself and be genuinely happy for the kid.

Mac notices me warring with my emotions and elbows me, leaning in. "We'll head out after breakfast, okay?"

Relief and guilt intermingle inside as I nod a bit too enthusiastically.

"Now that you're awake . . ." Mom reaches beneath the tree for a large box. "Santa brought you two a present, too."

"It's kind of a big one, though—weighed down his whole darn sleigh," Rick adds with a wink behind his coffee mug.

Mac and I glance at each other. We rest our mugs atop coffee table coasters and set the gift between us. Together, we unwrap the present.

The newly released PlayStation console with four games.

"Holy shit," I breathe, momentarily forgetting the seven-year-old within earshot as I snap my shocked gaze up at Mom. *"Seriously?"*

"These are on backorder everywhere! They're impossible to get!" Mac pops up first and engulfs Mom into a bear hug.

"We made some calls," Rick says, accepting his hug from Mac in turn.

I push to my feet and hug both of them, holding on to Mom a little longer than I expect to.

"Merry Christmas, baby," she whispers, squeezing tight.

"Merry Christmas," I croak back. I close my eyes, soaking in as much of her hug as I possibly can, even after convincing myself I don't need it anymore. Who knows how long it'll be before I get another one?

Twenty-One

The emotional whiplash of Christmas settles before New Year's weekend, just in time for my trip to Boston with Alexa and Geri.

"You sure this is a good idea, kiddo? Another weekend away so soon?" Dad asks for what must be the hundredth time in three days. "Your report card didn't exactly light the world on fire—you're barely scraping by with your grades, and you remember what Dean Quigley said?" He doesn't forbid me to go, though, knowing how excited I've been about my new suit.

"It's still winter break. I'll kick off the new year stronger with schoolwork, I promise. I've already got a tutor set up, remember?" I pull him in for a big hug.

"Right, right." He shifts back from the embrace to search my face. "And you'll take care of yourself? No sudden hockey matches or fistfights?"

Mac strolls into my room with his coffee. "Oooh, good point, Pops. Charlie hasn't thrown a punch in way too long. She's overdue for sure."

"Dude, really?"

Mac claps a hand on Dad's shoulder. "She's going to a wedding, not hitting the boxing ring. I think it's great you're getting another weekend off. Weddings are fun!"

They clearly don't know Geri well enough if they think I'll have the whole weekend off.

"Enjoy having the PlayStation to yourself while you can. I'll be back on Sunday night to crush all your high scores."

Beep beep!

"That's them." I shoulder my duffel and snag my garment bag from my closet. "I'll be fine. I'll text you when we get there."

"You better send us some pictures of that fancy Boston hotel!"

"You got it." I fondly pinch Mac's elbow. "See ya." Hurrying downstairs, I tuck my coat under my arm and brave the whipping, frigid winds for the short walk from my front door to Geri's black Lexus SUV.

She pops the trunk so I can toss my bags inside and I barely manage to conceal my laughter at the rear window decal.

Live. Laugh. Lutz.

Once I slide inside, Alexa twists in the front seat, her excitement contagious. "I'm so glad your dad's okay with you coming with us for the weekend."

Geri slides her sunglasses down to fire an intentional glance through her rearview mirror. "I promised him I'd keep a close eye on you and report any concerns. Not that you'll give me anything necessary to report." Her eyebrow arches.

I salute her with an innocent grin. "Nope, nothing at all."

"That's what I thought." Geri turns up her soft-rock station and pulls away from the curb.

Though Alexa invited me as her plus-one, I'm under no delusion this is a date—as Geri confirms with her no-nonsense demeanor in the opulent hotel lobby. She extends room keys to both me and Alexa. "Alexa and I are in the room right across from yours," Geri says. "Set your bags down, change into your swimwear, and meet me at the hotel pool in twenty minutes. We're drilling lifts and throws."

Alexa blinks. "You're not coming up with us?"

"I," Geri starts, pushing her designer sunglasses atop her hair, "am heading to the bar for a much-needed cocktail before we get to work. You two can manage carrying up my bag for me, can't you?"

"You got it, Coach." Before Alexa can react, I snag the handle of Geri's Louis Vuitton weekend bag. "See you at the pool."

Alexa and I step into the elevator and I shake my head, smiling with exasperated fondness. "So that's why she told me to bring a swimsuit? I had a feeling we weren't gonna be sunning ourselves."

Alexa offers an apologetic nose scrunch. "Don't worry. We'll have so much fun at the wedding tomorrow night."

"I'm not worried. I don't think my body knows what to do with more than a day off anyway."

The elevator pings and we step onto the twelfth floor, following the signs toward our rooms.

"Are you disappointed you're not here with Stratford before he was a douche or, like . . . a real date?" I want to kick myself as soon as the words fly past my lips, wishing my niggling anxiety would leave me the hell alone for once.

Alexa frowns. "What? No, of course not." A warm grin spreads across her lips. "I'm glad you're here. It was my choice anyway."

More belly bats swoop through my intestines and I inwardly will them to chill out. Then I extend the handle to Geri's bag once we reach our rooms. "Cool. See you in ten or whatever."

Ducking inside my private hotel room, I drop my bags at the foot of the bed and open the curtains. The bustling city of Boston sprawls outside my window, and I quickly spot TD Garden—the stadium where Dad took me and Mac to see a handful of Bruins games over the years. After changing into my black halter bikini top and black surfer-style swim trunks, I fire off a few texts—one to Dad as promised, another to my group chat with Jade and Emily, and a third to Mac and some of my teammates to wish them luck at tonight's match.

A pang of sadness hits like a harsh check to the boards.

Here I am standing in a fancy-ass hotel room in swimwear when I should be suiting up in hockey gear with my Cranford squad.

This was the deal, I remind myself. I'm fully committed to Alexa and Geri and sectionals, and I'll be back at the Blizzard where I should be next fall. In the hockey rink.

A soft knock yanks me from my thoughts.

"Ready when you are!" Alexa calls.

"One sec!" I snag a towel from the bathroom, draping it around my shoulders. With Adidas slides around my feet, I grab my room key and open the door.

Alexa wears an off-the-shoulder sheer cover-up and a pretty powder-blue swimsuit beneath.

Jesus. Come on, brain. Get it together.

Thirty minutes later, after five freestyle warm-up laps and twenty minutes of lifts, I'm standing in the shallow end of the hotel pool supporting a dripping Alexa in full Superman extension over my head.

Geri reclines on a lounge chair with her legs crossed at the ankles, sipping from her martini glass. "Ten more seconds, ladies. Breathe through the burn."

My arms ache and tremble from the prolonged lift as I desperately try ignoring the gasps and movement around me.

"Whoa, look at them!"

"Check it out!"

"That's awesome!"

"Daddy, can you lift me up like that?"

Children swim around us, their parents joining them or hanging out on the sidelines.

"I thought your mom hates an audience," I grunt at Alexa through gritted teeth.

Struggling to keep her balance, Alexa breathes hard through her nose and mouth, core muscles straining above my hands. "She does, but desperate times. As long as they don't—"

"Hey, you! With the scrunchie!" Geri's shrill tone echoes throughout the indoor pool area. "Put that camera down! Nobody gave you permission to film this!"

"Sorry! Sorry, sorry . . ." The lady cowers, lowering her phone.

Geri's coach voice returns. "Good, Charlie. Now release."

My lips twist with mischief before I haphazardly toss Alexa into the deep end.

Alexa shrieks and after a few seconds, surfaces with a sputtering glare. "You *jerk*!" She swims forward and shoves water at me, unable to suppress her scandalized laughter.

I splash back.

"Girls!" Geri sighs, plucking the cherry from her glass and snagging it from the stem with her teeth. "*Focus.* I didn't realize you wanted to practice throws so badly, Charlie. You'll get your wish."

Groaning, I shake my head with a chuckle.

"Thanks, Porter." Alexa playfully shoves my shoulder.

"Oh, please. You know she was gonna move us from lifts to throws soon anyway."

"Take five," Geri says, swinging her legs over the side of the chair before pushing to her heels. "We'll carry on once I get myself another drink."

Once Geri's out of earshot, picture-taking lady approaches. "Are you two professional dancers?"

Alexa flashes a polite grin back at her. "No, we're—"

"Hockey players." I cut her off with a confident nod. "Pool yoga is great for our strength training." Hitching my thumb toward Alexa, I manage to keep a straight face. Well, *straight*. "You don't wanna mess with this one. She looks all sweet and graceful and innocent, but she's our enforcer. Scrappy as hell. We call her the raging shrimp."

"Charlie." Alexa flushes and rolls her eyes, fingers curling

around my bicep and tugging. "Please ignore her. She's taken one too many pucks to the head. C'mon, stretch out your arms before Mom makes you throw me across the pool three dozen times." Huffing as she turns her back on the lady, she shakes her head—trying but failing to bite back her snicker. "You're ridiculous."

"You love it." A new and exciting brand of pride swells in my chest whenever I make her laugh.

Pursing her lips, Alexa shoots me a threatless glare. "Seriously, though? *The raging shrimp*?" She splashes me again.

I cackle and return the favor.

The next morning it's New Year's Eve and we meet up in the hotel gym for cardio, weight training, and cooldown stretching. In the afternoon, Geri and Alexa hit the hotel spa while I spend the time hanging out in my room, ordering room service on Geri's dime and enjoying a legit break. I paint my blunt fingernails their usual dark shade while chatting with Mac; he shares every detail he remembers about Cranford's victory the night before.

I wrestle down my envy and longing and congratulate him on their win, pretending it doesn't sting that the team seems just as good—or better off—without me.

After washing away the selfish blah vibe with a solid nap and a hot shower, I step into my new wool suit—which looks just as good as it did in the fitting room. Breaking up my black on black, I fasten my lilac skinny tie around my neck to complete the formal look. I FaceTime Jade and Emily and style my hair in loose waves, then pin back the top half before carefully applying light makeup with my best friends' guidance. Sliding my argyle-socked feet into a shiny pair of low-heeled loafers, I take one last look at myself in the full-length mirror and shake out my hands.

It's only a wedding. Chill out, Charlie. No need to be all nervous.

Stepping outside my room, I damn near melt into a puddle at the sight of my skating partner.

Alexa wears a beaded plum cocktail dress with matching strappy heels, her signature red locks pinned into a fancy low knot with a few loose curls framing her face.

"Wow. You look, uh . . ." Adjectives fail me. My single functioning brain cell simply allows me to slow blink.

Her smile dazzles back at me. "Thanks. You look 'uh,' too." With a soft wink, she takes my arm.

"Well. You clean up nicely." Geri's black gown sports a fierce cape billowing behind her as she struts beside us.

"Thanks, Coach. Dope dress. You look hot." Oh. *There's* an adjective. Maybe not the one I was going for, though . . . and I frantically backpedal. "For a mom, I mean. Like a hot mom."

Alexa side-eyes me and only half muffles her giggle.

Amusement dances on Geri's expression. "Why, thank you, Charlie."

We ride the elevator back down to the main floor and find our way to the ceremony space.

While Geri chatters with family members, Alexa chooses our seats.

The far wall boasts floor-to-ceiling glass windows overlooking Boston Common and a setting sun. The aisle running up the center of the room leads to a gorgeous, lily-entwined canopy-type thing.

"That's a chuppah," Alexa provides, tugging me down beside her. "It symbolizes the home the married couple will build together. Pretty, huh?"

"Yeah, for sure." A bearded man strolls up the aisle and takes his place beneath the chuppah. A rabbi, I realize a beat later, waiting to officiate the ceremony. "What else is different about a Jewish wedding?"

"Hmm . . ." Alexa crosses her legs, shifting toward me. "A few things, you'll see. At the very end, the groom stomps on a glass wrapped in a cloth napkin. It's supposed to represent a couple things—overcoming hardships together, something about the destruction of a temple in Jerusalem—I'm not actually sure which temple. I'm sort of a post–Bat Mitzvah Hebrew School dropout." She shrugs guiltily. "Then we all shout *Mazel tov!*, which means *congratulations*."

My eyebrows fly toward my hairline. "And we just hope the dude's foot isn't bleeding in his shoe?"

"Don't worry, they make sure that won't happen."

Other guests fill in as the sunset casts warm colors glowing in the backdrop. I soak in as much as I can of this new-to-me tradition—the wedding party, Alexa's cousin Beth and her almost-husband reciting their vows—and once he crunches the glass beneath his shoe, I jump up beside Alexa and shout, "Mazel tov!"

We clap and cheer as the couple shares their first married kiss. Then they head back up the aisle and Alexa leans in. "Are you ready to hora?"

I frown. "What did you just call me?"

Alexa giggles. "It's a customary dance. It's fun, I promise. But first . . . cocktail hour!"

We follow the crowd to the next room and load up small plates with hors d'oeuvres. Puff pastries, veggies and hummus, mini grilled cheese sandwiches with a dipping side of tomato soup. I'm grateful for Alexa sticking by me as I meet a handful of her cousins.

It's all going pretty smoothly until her cousin Jason—who looks a few years older than Mac—eyes us over his champagne glass.

"You must be Alexa's girlfriend. I'm Cousin Jason." He extends a hand.

I damn near choke on my pig in a blanket as my cheeks flare with warmth, an anxious chuckle puffing free as I shake his hand. "Oh, we're not—I'm not—"

"Charlie's my friend and skating partner for sectionals," Alexa smooths over, not letting go of my arm. Her thumb strokes over the fabric in a weirdly calming yet still spiking-my-heartbeat sort of way.

"Cool meeting you, Jason," I manage through coughs while he walks off. Then I nod toward the bar. "I gotta go snag a soda or something. Got some mini-hot-dog pastry lodged in my windpipe. . . ."

After an hour of mingling, we transition into the ballroom, where we find our assigned table and the live band strikes up music for the hora.

As it turns out, the hora really is easy—and kinda fun, too. We hold hands and dance in a circle around the immediate family of the newly wedded couple. Halfway through the song, someone carries two chairs into the middle and a bunch of bigger guys step forward to lift both the bride and groom into the air during the dance. The couple remains connected by holding either end of a white cloth napkin, the upbeat traditional music providing the rhythm of their hoisting as the newlyweds struggle to keep balance, laughing along.

"You could've lifted Cousin Beth without three men helping you," Alexa mutters into my ear as we head off the dance floor.

I shiver, blushing yet again. "I dunno. The chair might've made it awkward. . . ."

Alexa gasps as she spots an old woman wearing a navy dress with stockings, her mostly white hair containing a few reddish wisps elegantly curled for the occasion. "Bubbe Lil!" She tugs me toward the woman at our table and throws her arms around her in a hug.

"Lexa!" Bubbe Lil hugs tight and kisses Alexa's cheek, leaving pinkish red lipstick behind. "My *verkakte* taxi was late but I made it."

"You made it for the fun part, that's what matters. It's never a party unless you're here." Alexa twists to rest her hand on my shoulder. "Bubbe, this is my friend Charlie. She's skating with me until Frankie comes back. Charlie, this is my grandmother, Lillian."

I extend my hand without hesitation. Old people love me. "Hi! It's so awesome meeting you."

Bubbe Lillian shakes my hand, her eyes sparkling in that intensely bright Goldstein kind of way. "It's my pleasure. My daughter told me all you've been doing to support my Lexa." She speaks with an accent, but I'm the worst at geography so I have no idea where it's from.

My attention flickers toward Bubbe Lil's outstretched forearm. A long-faded but still visible tattoo of a word—no, letters and numbers—is starkly apparent against her wrinkled, spotted skin.

My breath catches as I flash back to eighth-grade history where we learned about World War II and the Holocaust.

Whoa.

Alexa squeezes my shoulder, jolting me back to the present.

"Oh, it's—" I cast Alexa a warm grin. "It's been fun. Definitely a challenge, but I love a challenge." Chuckling, I find Geri across the dance floor with another martini in hand, making her rounds to each table.

"You're a brave girl," Bubbe says, sipping from her champagne flute. "Would you like some? I can order you one. I won't tell." A spark of mischief twinkles in her eyes.

My lips curve upward. "Thanks, Bubbe Lil, but I'm good. I promised Coach Geri I'd stay out of trouble."

Bubbe Lil sniffs. "My daughter needs to loosen up a bit, don't you think?"

"For sure. She seems to be having a good time, though."

Servers arrive with first-course salads and the rest of our tablemates gather.

The salad's mostly a fancy-looking, bitter bit of lawn, but I'm more of a carb gal anyway so I enjoy my dinner roll mostly in silence, admiring Alexa as she effortlessly catches up with more out-of-town family members.

When the band strikes up a slow song, Alexa snags my hand. "Dance with me?"

"Ed Sheeran?" I wince. "We're not gonna do a good job of convincing Cousin Jason we're not a thing if we dance to Ed Sheeran. . . ."

Alexa laughs, shaking her head and tugging. "I don't care what Cousin Jason thinks. I like this song."

"You would." Feigning exasperation, I allow Alexa to lead me to the dance floor. My hands find her waist as her arms loop around my neck.

One glance back and I spot Bubbe Lil firing me two enthusiastic thumbs-up.

"Love how your grandmother tried slipping us some booze."

"She's trouble, that one. Kinda like someone else I know."

My eyebrows raise. "No idea what you're talking about. I'm being super well behaved."

"Mmm . . . you are. I'm a little disappointed."

"Yeah, well. You've got a habit of making me break all my own rules." I level a look at her while my ears warm beneath my hair.

Alexa softens. "I do?" She pauses, considering with a soft hum. "I like that."

"So I was thinking . . ." I know the sudden subject change is probably obvious, but I really need to stop staring at her like I'm the goddamn heart-eyes emoji. "Our routine. We don't have any triples in the program."

Head tilting to the side, Alexa nods. "We don't want to overcomplicate it. It's better to execute clean double jumps than imperfect triples."

"But we can't win without a triple jump. The Dingleborgs have several."

"We don't need to win sectionals, remember? We just need to qualify for nationals."

"We should sneak one in anyway. It'd be cool if we pulled it off." There. Troublemaker status reactivated.

"Oooh, there's the Charlie Porter I know." Alexa considers. "Mom would kill us if we deviated from the program."

"Yeah, but she'd kill us less if we landed it clean. I believe in us."

Alexa steps closer, banishing all distance between us as she hooks her chin over my shoulder. "I believe in us too." Her voice, full of conviction, zaps a shiver down my spine.

The rest of the wedding passes in a blur of eating, dancing, more eating, and more dancing. We return to our rooms before midnight, my feet aching in yet another new way, but I've got no regrets.

Changing out of my suit and into a pair of polka-dot sleep boxers and a faded Cranford hockey tee, I wash off my makeup, brush my teeth, and flop backward onto my hotel bed.

It's 11:57. Jade and Emily are still awake waiting on midnight, asking for pics and details via text.

I'm midresponse when a soft knock raps on the door.

Eyebrows drawing tighter, I set my phone aside and shuffle barefoot to open the door and find Alexa—also washed up for bed—on the other side. "What's up?" Gaze sweeping downward, I note her tank top and drawstring cloud-print pj pants along with those adorkable purple narwhal slippers adorning her feet. Snickering, I hold the door open. "Cute slippers, nerd. Not surprised you brought—"

Alexa stands on tiptoe, hooks her soft hand around the back of my neck, and presses her lips to mine in the most tender way.

My brain shuts down as I slam my eyelids shut, soaking in this very moment before I can fully register it happening.

This can't be real.

Alexa Goldstein is kissing me.

Alexa Goldstein is *kissing* me.

Alexa Goldstein is kissing *me*.

I release the door in favor of wrapping an arm around her middle, and we take two steps into the room so the door closes behind us with a soft click. It takes a few more seconds for my sluggish, shocked mind to catch up. When it does, I respond with enthusiasm and hoist her into the air on instinct—just as I have several hundred times on the ice, in the gym, and in the pool yesterday.

When the kiss comes to its natural end, I carefully guide Alexa back to the ground. Leaving our foreheads pressed together, my eyes crack open half-mast.

"Happy New Year," Alexa rasps as she stares at me beneath heavy lids, her dazed grin stretching wide. Her free hand cradles my cheek and when she speaks, her voice carries with soft huskiness that ignites a fire in the pit of my stomach. "Is this okay?" She licks her lips. "I feel like I've wanted to do that forever."

Swallowing the massive lump in my throat, I puff out a few notes of a shocked, decompressing chuckle. "Course it's okay." A fresh colony of bats launches in my stomach, my heart thumping so hard I'm pretty sure it's actively beating out of my chest. "Happy New Year to you, too. Um. Your mom. Is she—"

"She's asleep. I was kinda hoping I could . . . hang out in here for a little?"

"Hang out?" I smirk, nuzzling our noses together. "Is that what we're calling this?"

"Mm-hmm." Alexa tugs me back toward my bed as she presses another soft kiss to the corner of my mouth.

An impish smile stretches across my face. "Are you gonna keep the narwhals on while we . . . hang out?"

Alexa tips her head back and laughs. "Shut up, Charlie."

"Make me." My challenge carries hoarse and an octave deeper than intended. My lower lip snags between my teeth as my gaze drinks her in fully, wondering when I'll wake up from this perfect dream.

"Oh, I fully intend to," Alexa murmurs after a heartbeat, hopping onto my bed and urging me along.

Crawling over her, my body naturally settles atop hers, kissing her more thoroughly this time. Mid-lip-lock, I lace our fingers before pinning her hand against the pillow above our heads.

The purple narwhals hit the floor soon after.

Twenty-Two

After falling asleep curled around Alexa, I wake up big-spooning a hotel pillow instead.

I'm sure it was all a perfect dream until I check my phone—and my heart trips all over again.

> **Alexa** (7:35 a.m.): Sorry I snuck out, I didn't want Mom realizing I spent the night. Meet us downstairs for breakfast at 8:30? 😉

A wink face.

Score.

I flop onto my back and cast an arm over my eyes, replaying as much as I can remember from the night before, desperate to sear the fresh memories into my mind for eternity.

Dressing in my typical plaid shirt, jeans, and Converse, I check myself in the mirror once more and wrestle my hair into a messy bun.

A darker patch of skin stands out over my neck's pulse point and a stunned snicker croaks free as I recall just how it got there. Hurriedly yanking my hair tie back out, I brush my hair over my shoulder in an effort to cover it up, then head toward the elevators.

The hotel's breakfast buffet isn't super crowded yet.

My favorite shade of red pulls my attention almost instantly and I snag a ceramic plate as I approach.

Her eyes lift while she hits up the cereal bar, pouring Honey Nut

Cheerios into a bowl. "Good morning," she says casually.

Almost casually. A timid smile plays on her lips and I can't help but mirror it.

"Great morning," I reply, following her to the hot-foods station. I'm piling a mountain of scrambled eggs and bacon atop my plate when I feel her eyes on me. "You can take a picture if you want. Hang it up in your locker . . ."

Her cheeks heat. "Charlie . . ." Faux admonishment tinging her sigh, she serves herself a normal serving of eggs. "I've never done that, you know. With a girl."

The change of tone eases the teasing from my expression. "Oh yeah?" Not a big surprise considering her history of keeping away from girls as a general principle. "So should I apologize now or later for ruining guys for you?"

Alexa groans. "You're the worst."

She's still smiling though.

"Really, though." I survey her profile while spooning mixed fruit into a bowl. "You okay? You don't, like . . . regret it or anything?"

"More than okay," she says. "No regrets here."

Relief sags my shoulders. "Dope."

"So dope," she mocks.

It's my turn for my cheeks to warm. "Where's your mom? Is she . . . um, will she be cool if she finds out . . ." *About us?* Wait. Maybe better not to assume things, Charlie. It was one night. Maybe there's not an "us" yet. ". . . you might be into girls, too?"

"She's checking out at the front desk; she'll be here shortly." It's Alexa's turn to pin me with a mischief-tinged grin. "And my mom's bisexual, Charlie, so I don't think my little revelation will bother her."

I damn near drop the fruit spoon. "Wait—*Seriously?* Dude, double score for my team!"

"*Our* team, apparently," Alexa corrects. "Let's go find her. She's been dying to tell us about our free skate routine."

We find Geri cradling a venti Starbucks drink in the dining area. Despite my mental pep talk to play it cool, I struggle keeping my puppy eyes at bay over breakfast.

So does Alexa.

We take turns stealing looks at each other across the table while Alexa daintily chews her smoked-salmon-and-cream-cheese-topped bagel and I shovel heaps of eggs and bacon into my mouth.

Her shoe playfully taps mine and I return the favor.

Geri sips her coffee, tapping her tablet as she carries on with business as usual. "I finished mapping out your free skate. You two will skate to a ballad from the musical *Finding Neverland*. Compared to our *Wicked* piece, it's a perfect complement. The music's softer but more moving. It's based on a true story about the writer of *Peter Pan* and his dying girlfriend. They create Neverland as a place where they can always—" Geri cuts herself off and frowns, lowering her oversize sunglasses down the bridge of her nose. "Are you two even listening to me?"

I snap my attention to Geri, warmth coloring my cheeks. "Sorry, Coach. Yep. I'm with you."

"Of course," Alexa says, unable to tame the giveaway grin behind her teacup.

Geri glances between us, eyes narrowed. "Oh, for the love of . . . thank god you're not poker players or you'd both be broke."

I jam another forkful of scrambled eggs into my mouth to avoid talking.

"Mom, don't worry. We know what's at stake."

"You better not forget," Geri says. "I had a feeling it was only a matter of time before you two figured out—whatever you needed to figure out." Her gaze lands on me once more. "If I didn't think it would help your on-ice chemistry I wouldn't be as quick to give my blessing here."

Blessing? I inhale sharply and choke on some eggs, erupting in a coughing fit while reaching for my glass of water.

Alexa casts me a concerned look before my coughing subsides.

Wait. Geri's cool with . . . whatever line Alexa and I crossed last night? *Holy crap.* My undercaffeinated brain spirals in a thousand different directions.

I insert a strip of bacon into my mouth.

Geri arches a semithreatening eyebrow at me. "I trust you'll keep your priorities in order."

My chin jerks upward and bobs in a near frantic nod.

Alexa laughs.

"Very well then." Geri flips her tablet around. "Listen up while I run through your free skate elements."

We turn to face Geri more fully as we continue eating our breakfasts.

I'm mostly paying attention, stealing another quick glance across the table.

My breath catches as I spot a faint yet definitely noticeable red mark standing out against the pale patch of skin beneath Alexa's ear.

I muffle my pleased grin with another heaping bite of breakfast potatoes.

Now I'm definitely convinced I'm not still dreaming.

I get home too late for me to catch Jade and Em at the Beanery, but I text them a pic of my favorite bruise of all time as evidence of my excellent weekend.

Emily (3:21 p.m.): AAAAAHHHH YESSSSS OMGGGG

Jade (3:22 p.m.): GIRL. IT WAS THE SUIT, WASN'T IT? SHE COULDN'T RESIST THE SUIT.

(3:23 p.m.): it was definitely the suit.

Emily (3:25 p.m.): So happy for you!!! Do we get any details??

(3:26 p.m.): sorry, babes. i don't kiss and tell.

Jade (3:26 p.m.): But you'll snap pics of your hickey??

Emily (3:27 p.m.): We'll expect a full report next Beanery Sunday!

January kicks off with a more rigorous training schedule. Geri choreographs more of our free skate and we practice both *Wicked* and *Neverland* before and after school both on mats and on the ice. I find myself tapping out the rhythm of the routine elements on the edge of my textbooks during class and against the side of my hot chocolate mug after dinner, and running through each step in the shower while humming the songs under my breath.

In figure skating, preparation is just as much mental as physical— like hockey.

And while my physical state grows stronger than it's ever been, my mental state . . .

Well, I'm taking it day by day.

It's just—the stress is kind of a lot now, with the competition a month away.

A week into winter trimester, I'm striding through the library with my stomach growling for lunch when I pull up short in the office doorway.

Instead of sitting across from each other as they usually do, Frankie and Cyn sit on the same side of the table.

My head tilts to the side as I drop into a chair across from them. "What's going on?"

"What's going on?" Cyn asks, scoffing. "What's going *on*?" She turns to Frankie. "Can you believe this bitch has the audacity to ask what's going on?"

Frankie groans. "Girl, *you and Alexa*! How dare you casually dine with us here all week and not mention—"

"Drake, c'mon!" My face reddens and I laugh, shaking my head. "That wasn't only my secret to tell, okay?" Telling Jade and Emily was different—they were my friends first and for way longer. My stomach flips in a jazzy somersault as I casually retrieve the turkey and cheese sandwich and chips from my lunch bag. "So she told you?"

Frankie's lopsided smile remains plastered to his face. "Only after I needled it out of her after practice this morning. There's definitely been a change in how you two are skating together. It's way more intense—like, chemistry off the charts. I've never seen Lex skate with so much emotion." He clutches his chest in a dramatic fashion. "I'll try not to take it personally."

Cyn snickers and elbows him. "*You* don't make her feel all hot and bothered on and off the ice. . . ."

My eyes roll. "I'm glad she told you. I'm really bad at lying."

Cyn opens her bag of Cheez-Its and considers. "So what now? Are we inviting her to our secret lunch hideout now that you're dating?"

"Um—I don't think we're dating?"

Frankie blinks. "Why not?"

"I don't know! We haven't talked about it yet. We've been busy as hell and focused on competition, if you haven't noticed. . . ." I bite into my sandwich, tucking a wad of masticated turkey and cheese into my cheek as I continue. "Besides, she's been hanging out with the nerds in her physics class ever since she ditched Stratford. It's been good for her!" It's almost like I maybe helped her reprioritize friendships in her life. I'm equal parts proud of her for making efforts to kindle relationships with new friends and pleased with myself for being a positive influence.

Cyn chucks a square cracker at me. "Okay. Obviously you should still ask her on a *date*, doofus!"

Frankie nods. "Insider intel . . . Alexa may or may not have mentioned to me she was wondering if you'd ask her or if she'd have to make the first move again. . . ."

The cackle Cyn releases echoes in the library office.

My jaw drops, a deeper shade of red painting my cheeks. "Oh my *god*, fine! Jeez, I'll ask her right now." Pulling my phone from my back pocket, I swipe away a text from Mac and another text from Emily sending a screenshot of her Cranford basketball team schedule, making a mental note to respond to both later. Then I tap Alexa's most recent text.

(11:06 a.m.): hey. you free tomorrow night?

It's after I hit Send that panic strikes, my gaze snapping up to Cyn and Frankie looking very much like approving older siblings. "Shit. I've never planned a date!"

"Don't worry, girl." Cyn glances at Frankie before leaning forward. "I'm an award-winning fanfic writer. Romance happens to be my specialty."

"Romance *and* math? Damn, what a combo. You're so powerful."

While we wait for Alexa's response, Cyn and I compare our schedules and choose a time for our first tutoring session this Sunday afternoon—literally the only regular open block of time I have where I'll have any functional brainpower. I'll need to cut Beanery dates with Jade and Emily a little shorter than usual, but they'll understand. They want me back at Cranford too—and I need to get my grades up in order to make that happen.

My phone buzzes.

> **Alexa** (11:08 a.m.): I might be. Depends what you have in mind. Another jumping practice? Yoga session? Dance class?
> (11:09 a.m.): a date. you and me.
> **Alexa** (11:10 a.m.): Finally. Thought you'd never ask. 😊
> (11:11 a.m.): you know me. i've got a cool reputation to maintain. can't be planning things too far in advance.
> **Alexa** (11:12 a.m.): Mm-hmm. Tell Frankie I said thanks for the assist.

I tell Alexa I'll pick her up at seven. Then I set my phone face down and grin across the table. "I've got a date tomorrow night." A flash of mischief crosses my expression. "And I actually have an idea she might really like."

Frankie leans forward, bracing his chin in his palm. "It better not involve hockey pucks. Let's hear it. . . ."

"So are you gonna tell me where we're going?" Alexa eyes my profile from the passenger seat. She looks gorgeous, but that's nothing new, wearing a gray merino sweater with black jeans and her hair styled down in loose curls.

"Oooh, a dose of your own medicine. How does it taste?" I push up the sleeves of my mulberry Henley and toss her a quick grin. "Don't worry, we're not going too far."

Outside of athletics, preparation has never been a priority for me. Yet I want tonight to go well so badly I spent every free second between practices and workout sessions and dance class and eating meals last night and today making sure I sweep Alexa off her skates.

Before picking her up, I headed over to Hopkins Pond and dusted the freshly fallen snow from the picnic table to set the scene for our date. As we pull back into the parking lot, I'm relieved my setup remains untouched by children or raccoons or any other nosy creature.

"You can't stay away from the ice, can you?" Alexa mocks as a callback to my own ribbing of that same flavor back in Rockefeller Center.

I shrug. We step out of the car, boots crunching on snow.

She pulls up short when she spots the picnic table covered with a black cloth weighted down by two twinkling Yankee candles I pilfered from our home coffee table. Melting with sappiness, she takes my hand. "Damn, someone went all out on the romance aesthetic," she notes, standing on tiptoe and pressing a kiss to my cheek before tugging me toward the table.

"I had fierce competition with all your romance novel characters."

She laughs.

"Wasn't sure what you'd be in the mood for, so you choose first. . . ." I motion to the three thermoses standing between the candles, which I've labeled "Chicken noodle," "Creamy tomato," and "Lobster bisque."

"Oooh. *Souper.*" She drops onto the bench and urges me down beside her.

I groan at the pun. Reaching into the basket I carried from the car, I pull out a Tupperware container of cheddar biscuits. "Baked these earlier today with Emily's help. We had to physically fight Mac from taking more than one." I pause for a fond eye roll, leaning back into the bag. "And for later, dessert . . ." I produce a larger thermos. "Hot chocolate."

"Yum! This is perfect and adorable. Perfectly adorable. Thank you." Alexa reaches for the creamy tomato soup. "Us reds need to stick together," she says, uncapping the top and pouring a serving into the lid.

It's near freezing but we're both basically immune to Vermont cold. The pond sits blissfully empty and the sky hangs extra black overhead, the stars dazzling even harder. I pour myself a cup of lobster bisque and snag a biscuit to dunk into my soup.

"So," Alexa starts, angling her body toward me while taking a biscuit for herself. "Not where you pictured yourself four months ago, hm?"

My bright chuckle puffs as visible chilled air. "Nowhere close. Can't complain though. Sure, it's been tough . . ." Understatement of the century. "But the pros for sure outweigh the cons."

"You might even miss Winthrop a little bit when you go back to Cranford next trimester, hm?" A flicker of sadness glints in her brown eyes.

"*Hell* no. I'll never be a Snow Leopard." I soften in the next beat as I process the look on her face. "I'll miss you, though. And Frankie and Cyn." I pause. "Even Mrs. Milford . . ."

Alexa laughs and knocks my boot with hers. Mission to lift her slightly dimmed spirits accomplished. "If you miss Mom's schedule so bad you can come cheer on me and Frankie at five a.m."

A dash of anxiety hits. "*If* we place high enough at sectionals so you guys can compete at nationals, you mean."

"We will," Alexa says, curling her free hand around my wrist. "I bet we'll even place higher than fourth. We've really got something special going together, Charlie."

The determination in her eyes when she talks about skating

flashes fierce as ever. It's one of the things I admire most about Alexa—her passion for her sport, her unrelenting drive to improve. To not only win but dominate. It mirrors my own, and that's why we make such a great team.

"Then you'll need to get used to skating with Frankie again. . . ." The thought settles uneasily in my chest. I try hiding my weird mix of emotions with a sip of soup. I shouldn't be sad about stepping back after sectionals. That's been the plan all along, after all.

"Don't you worry about that. We'll be okay." She thoughtfully chews a bite of biscuit, washing it down with some soup before breaking the beat of comfortable silence. "I never thanked you for doing this. I know you're getting a college scout hookup in the deal, but it still means so much to me. And I was horrible to you at first; I never really apologized for that."

I shake my head, effectively cutting her off. "Hey, no. You don't have to apologize. I was a dick right back. We worked through it though, yeah?"

"Considering we're on a date right now? I'd say so," Alexa says.

"Considering *this bitch* started landing triples? Wobbly, but still landing! Putting up with your evil twin was worth it. How many people can say they've landed a triple lutz? That's a brag badge I can carry for life, dude!"

"Damn right! And you'll only improve from here."

"Yep. Like our date," I say, a flash of mischief painting my face. Reaching beneath the table, I pull a small duffel bag onto the bench beside me, unzipping it to produce two pairs of figure skates with a familiar logo emblazoned on the side.

"Charlie Porter, did you *steal* from the Blizzard?"

"*Borrowed*," I amend. "I'm totally gonna give 'em back on Monday. Nobody will even notice they were gone. If I told you to bring skates it would've ruined the surprise."

"Surprise, hm?" Eyeing me, she finishes off her cup of soup and shifts on the bench to swap her heeled boots for the rental figure skates capped with the blade guards I'd affixed before packing them.

I do the same, hastily tying the laces before standing and extending my hand, which she takes without hesitation.

We amble toward the edge of the empty pond, the glowing moonlight overhead setting off cool colors reflecting in the ice. Hazy blues and greens and purples.

"The only rule for tonight," I say as I remove my blade guards and lead her onto the glassy surface after she does the same. "No choreography." I haven't forgotten how blissfully happy Alexa was, skating without Geri watching. Without a goal or agenda. "No rules."

Her face lights up when she realizes she gets another opportunity to do that—this time with me right beside her.

"Well, in that case . . ." Her grin twists with that same intensity I've grown to appreciate. "Race you to the other side!" She pushes off and darts away from me at full speed.

"What—cheater!" I cry into the icy night air, my skates powering behind her as I work hard to catch up.

She beats me to the other side, cackling in victory until I tackle her to the soft snowbank, powdered flakes kicking up and swirling around us. "I WIN!"

"No way! You're *a hundred percent* disqualified!"

Alexa's prodding my side, waxing on about her victory over the speedster hockey star. "You're the one who said no rules! You can't disqualify me for that!"

Too determined to engage the next part of my plan to rise to the fresh-banter bait, I fish into my pockets and pop one of my freshly cleaned earbuds into her ear, hooking the other into my own. Then I pull my phone from my opposite pocket and press play on the Taylor Swift playlist I arranged for a moment just like this—tracks curated so it's only the mushy, happy Taylor songs, not the ones about dudes and breakups.

Alexa's giggles subside when her favorite singer's vocals croon through the earbud, her expression shifting from self-satisfied to emotionally touched. The gesture steals her breath in a gasp and she leans up to capture my lips with her own, pouring her affectionate appreciation into the kiss.

With a serenade of Swiftie songs providing a steady, heartfelt undercurrent throughout the rest of our date, we do everything we're not allowed to do during practice. We race a few more times, we free skate without worrying about form and technique, we dance together both fast and slow, and we kiss until we're warmed from the inside out.

Hell of a first date, if I do say so myself.

Twenty-Three

We start holding hands off-ice after that. I encourage Alexa to stick with her new physics friends for lunch, but I rework my routes between classes to escort her from one to the next when I can.

Frankie and Cyn verbally dunk on me, but they're also thrilled and supportive, so I don't mind. Cyn's trying to get her long-distance girlfriend to visit and quickly mentions a double date whenever that happens. Frankie's weirdly tight-lipped about his love life, no matter how much we plead and prod.

After those five long days of training and classes and more training, Alexa waits for me outside the locker room after our second practice the following Friday. "Sure you're up for this?"

We linger in the empty ice rink as the cheers and jeers from the jam-packed hockey rink echo from the other side of the Blizzard.

"I'm sure." I can't miss the chance to support my team—especially my brother—as they take on Winthrop for their first regular-season matchup. It's not as crucial as the Winthrop Cup or any sort of playoff game, but our epic rivalry always draws a full crowd of rowdy spectators. "Sure you wanna go with me?"

"Of course!" Alexa grins and links our fingers. "This totally counts as another date, by the way."

"Sweet. Popcorn's on me."

Armed with a bucket of fresh-popped, lightly buttered popcorn, we cross the complex to the other rink and find seats halfway up the bleachers eight minutes into the first period. No score yet.

Forcing out a hard breath, I will away the tension suddenly

gripping my shoulders as my chest pangs. Despite everything—my own choice to pursue figure skating, the support of my friends and family, my new girlfriend—yearning churns in my gut.

A sophomore takes my spot on the second-line shift—the line I'm supposed to lead this year.

My mouth tugs into a scowl when I spot Gavin Davis gunning for Mac even harder than he usually goes after anyone.

"Hey." Alexa nudges me gently with her elbow. "I'm sorry you're missing another chance to score on Konor. I know how much you wish you were out there right now."

Swallowing hard, I cast Alexa a sad smile. "Doesn't matter. I'll be out there again soon enough. Besides, I got the girl."

"You definitely got the girl," Alexa says, tossing up a kernel of popcorn and catching it in her mouth.

"Any room for me?"

Our gazes snap upward and find my dad hovering over us, wearing a Cranford hoodie, amusement dancing in his eyes.

"Of course! Hi, Mr. Porter!" Scooting down the bleacher row, Alexa pats the now empty end spot beside her.

"Thanks, Alexa. Mitch is good," Dad says. Preferring being addressed by his first name is something he has in common with Geri, but he won't want to hear that. He checks the scoreboard and when the whistle blows, he pulls a bag of my favorite sour gummies from his pocket. "Here, kiddo." Reaching over Alexa, he hands me the treat, then casts an apologetic look to my date. "Didn't know you were coming or I would've—" He hitches his thumb over his shoulder. "Want me to grab you something from the snack bar? What kind of candy are you into?"

Alexa gently settles a hand atop his forearm and softens. "Oh, thank you, Mitch—but I'm good! Charlie got us popcorn already and maybe she'll even share some of her sour gummies. . . ."

"*Psh.* Never." Except I tear open the package and offer her first choice anyway because I guess I'm a sucker or something. Biting the head off my sour worm, I quirk a brow her way. "For future reference, what kind of candy *do* you like best?"

"All kinds! Anything chocolate. Starbursts, Jolly Ranchers, Skittles . . ."

"Skittles, huh?" A devilish flicker twists up my lips as I lean over, lowering my voice so Dad can't hear. "So you're telling me you're kinda digging your taste of the rainbow so far. . . ."

Alexa blushes nearly as red as her hair and she fires a half-hearted glare my way before leaning closer. "*Behave,*" she whispers back, taking my hand in hers and resting both on my knee.

I assume Dad's solely focused on the hockey game, but after a minute or so, he pointedly catches my gaze. His eyes flicker down to our joined hands and he looks back to me with an unspoken question written on his face.

For a suspended moment, I hold my breath. I never outright came out to my dad, but, like . . . I didn't think I ever had to? I never thought I'd be dating anyone anytime soon, for one. And two—well, he's always been a pretty open-minded kind of guy.

I offer a sheepish shrug in return, unable to keep my lips from twitching into a grin.

Dad simply offers a quick thumbs-up.

Exhaling with a depressurizing chuckle, my focus returns to tracking the puck.

"What's so funny?" Alexa asks, clearly having missed the non-verbal exchange on either side of her.

"Hm? Oh . . . I was just thinking I wish I made a sign that says 'SUCK IT, STRATFORD.'"

Alexa leans into my side. "No need to rub it in his face."

"You're no fun."

The game carries on.

Winthrop scores two goals in the second period, my lips twisting into a pucker as I grumble a few swears under my breath.

It's a tight game as per usual. Mac scores an impressive backhanded goal to close the gap, but Cranford loses by one. My mood sours along with that of all the other Cranford supporters.

"Tough beat. They needed you out there," Dad says as we slowly make our way back down the bleachers toward the lobby.

I know he means well, but my stomach plummets. "Wish I could've played."

"You'll get 'em back next season," Alexa insists, with Dad nodding in support.

"You need a ride home?" Dad asks Alexa before his eyes drift to me. "You gonna wait for your brother?"

Alexa shakes her head. "No thank you—I've got my car. I can actually drive Charlie home a little later, if that's all right?"

"Fine by me. I'll see ya later, kiddo. Sorry for crashing your party here. . . ." He motions with his index finger between us before heading out of the complex.

"Bye, Mitch!" Alexa slips her arm through mine. "Do you wanna grab some hot chocolate or something? Maybe take some space from all this?" She nods back toward the still emptying hockey rink. "Or . . ." A somewhat devious look glazes over Alexa's expression as she once again leans in and lowers her tone in both volume and pitch. "Maybe we could go . . . check out the pro shop?"

My brow knits. "The pro shop's closed, Lex."

Alexa rolls her lips inward, a fresh flush streaking her cheeks. "Yes, it is. And you still remember the code to get in, don't you?"

It takes far longer than it should for my single brain cell to unpack the heart of Alexa's suggestion. My eyes tear from the hockey rink and I blink at her. The way she's looking at me jolts a welcome tingle down my spine and my lips quirk in an impish smile. "Alexa Michelle, are you suggesting what I think you're suggesting?"

She offers a cool shrug in return, her thumb skimming over my knuckles. "We haven't been alone since Saturday. . . ."

Opportunities haven't really made themselves known since Geri's kept us so damn busy. But now?

"Troublemaker," I fire back with a soft laugh.

We're back in spy mode as we weave through the gathered post-game crowd of parents and friends waiting for players in the lobby. Then we sneak up the stairs to the empty, dark Blizzard pro shop, crouching as I input the code to open the locked door and lead her inside.

Alexa tugs me toward the fitting room before her lips seal over mine and, magically, I no longer give a single shit about another brutal loss to Winthrop's hockey team.

Another Saturday hits and my schedule's more crammed than ever thanks to the mandatory costume fitting slotted in between dance class and weight lifting with Mac. It takes two whole hours for Geri's hired stylist to take our measurements while discussing—or more like debating—colors, fabrics, and appropriate hair accessories and makeup for both our *Wicked* short program and our *Neverland* free skate.

At least I'm able to culminate the busy day with another date night. This one's less creative—dinner and a movie—but I never really care what we do, as long as we do it together. After dropping Alexa off before her curfew expires, we continue texting well into the night, and I'm unwilling to give up the floaty feeling of whatever happiness hormones work through my system in exchange for sleep.

It's worth it, even if I'm more tired than usual on my rest day.

Whatever, it's fine. I'll go to bed earlier tonight after catching Em's season opener basketball game.

In the morning, I ride my bike to the Beanery, exhausted but happier than I've been in a really long time. Pushing inside with my bag hitched over my shoulder, I deeply inhale the pleasing aroma of espresso beans and head toward our normal round booth. Jade and Em are already hard at work, my regular hot chocolate waiting for me to drink.

Arriving, I drop with a serene groan. "You guys are the best," I declare, picking up the teaspoon to swipe some whipped cream into my mouth.

Then I realize something's off.

Jade barely glances up from her sketchbook.

Emily's near-constant light of positivity isn't half as bright as it usually is. She looks up at me with sad eyes. "You missed my opener last night. I scored fourteen points."

"What?" I frown. "Your game's tonight. I have it in my calendar—"

"You must've put it in wrong," Jade says. "Not surprising, considering how distracted you've been lately."

"Shit." I deflate, raking a hand through my hair. "Em, I'm so sorry. I really thought it was tonight."

Emily sighs. "We reminded you last week. I guess you forgot."

My throat tightens. "I did, yeah. My fault for not checking the calendar, too. I've had so much going on, extra training and everything since the competition's in a month. It'll be back to normal soon."

Jade pins me with an unimpressed look. "Extra training? How often are you with your girl when you used to spend weekends with us? You see her every morning and during and after school every damn day, and now she gets your Saturdays and some Sundays, too." Jade takes a breath. She softens a beat later when she notes the rush of anxiety gripping my entire being. "Look, the three of us keep it real, right? We don't do the talking-behind-each-other's-back thing. So I'm telling you we understand you're busy as shit with figure skating and practicing hockey with Mac and trying to get your grades up and learning how to balance a new relationship on top of it all—but we miss you."

My teeth bite into my lower lip, my shoulders sag, and my grip tightens on the crossbody bag strap still slung across my chest. I glance to Emily, who nods in agreement with Jade, and a wave of guilt-tinged nausea rises in my stomach. "Yeah, I hear you. Shit. I'm really sorry, guys. I'm glad you said something. I'll try to balance everything out a little better, okay?"

"Cool, that's all we're asking," Jade replies. "And for the record, we're happy for you and Alexa. Genuinely."

"*So* happy for you. For both of you!" Emily says, her rare sad eyes tweaking my heart. "I get it—it's not easy balancing a boyfriend or girlfriend with friendships. It helps me to make sure I spend one weekend night with Brian and one with you guys as much as I can." She pauses, shifting into a more encouraging expression. "You can even invite her to hang with us sometimes, if you want? We really like Alexa."

"Yeah? She'd like that." I consider. "Not all the time, though. It's still gotta be the three of us. Especially when—like you said—I get to see her at school and practice and stuff, too." Soon it'll be switched if I get back into Cranford for spring trimester. But I'll worry about the readjustment there when the time comes. Em's right—no matter where I'm going to school, balance is key.

"Your hot chocolate's gonna get cold," Jade points out as she settles back into her sketching.

"Oh, right." With a calming breath, I allow myself to enjoy my drink now that Jade's and Emily's moods have notably improved. "Friday night, right? Cranford hoops game two?"

Emily nods. "Friday night. Yep."

"I'm there no matter what," I promise. "Then diner food on me after the game. Milkshakes included."

Jade grins. "We'll hold you to that, Porter."

Twenty-Four

For the next several weeks, I do a much better job balancing my best-friends relationships with my girlfriend relationship on weekends, while dedicating as much of myself as possible to skating *Wicked* and *Neverland* to the best of my ability. I also manage to bring my grades up thanks to Cyn's tutoring help, my average hovering around a B in most subjects. Even math!

On sectionals competition day I'm so anxious it's a miracle I don't puke in Geri's Lexus. With Frankie chattering beside me, my knee bounces uncontrollably for most of the drive to upstate New York, and I'm wishing I could channel my fearless pre-hockey-match confidence into my pre-figure-skating-debut energy.

"Hey . . ." Alexa turns from the front seat as we approach the Polar Vortex Ice Center in Schenectady. "You've been quiet this whole ride. You okay?"

Before I can answer, Geri's eyes dart to the rearview mirror. "She's focused. Running the routines over and over in her head. Right?"

"Yep." I pop the *p* for extra oomph.

I shoulder my bags and we enter the complex, then stand off to the side while Geri waits in line for registration. My attention flits to the double doors leading to the parking lot, knowing Dad and Mac are en route behind us with Emily and Jade in the car.

"We can do this," Alexa assures me with a grin, taking my hand. "Fourth place. I bet we can place third or even second today."

A few knots of tension loosen in my tight shoulders, which I credit to whatever girlfriend magic Alexa wordlessly performs when she takes my hand. "Yeah? That'd be pretty cool."

"Why not first? Anything can happen," Frankie adds.

"Heeeey, Goldstein! Drake!"

Speaking of first place, we whirl around to find the top-spot favorites—two matching faces with turned-up noses, both puckered around the mouth.

Frankie heaves an overdramatic sigh, summoning a snippiness not quite hitting its mark. "Ingleborgs, twelve o'clock."

Alexa squeezes my hand. "Mallory, Mason. It's nice to see you both again." As if we hadn't gone on a road trip to specifically spy on them a couple months back. As if Mallory hadn't psyched out Alexa at one of their junior competitions years ago, leaving an indelible mark on her heart.

"Nice to see you, too." Mallory's grin carries a bloodthirsty edge—I recognize it from our most intense hockey matches. This bitch thinks she won already. She's nearly drooling with hunger as she shifts her focus to me; I can almost see the cartoonish thought bubble forming over her head. *Fresh meat.* "And *you* must be her new partner. Is it true you never figure skated before this season?"

"Yeah, that's me. I'm Charlie." I don't bother extending a hand; instead, my chin jerks upward in greeting.

"The hockey player," Mason says.

Clearly they've done their research.

"Hockey player *and* pairs skater," Frankie corrects. "Charlie does both. She's versatile like that."

Mason's attention drops to Frankie's walking boot. "We heard there's a chance you might be back for nationals. If you two qualify, of course."

"We will," Alexa says as though it's a done deal. "Frankie's physical therapy is progressing ahead of schedule."

Mason brightens.

Mallory elbows him.

"What?" Mason shrugs. "When we repeat our gold, we want to make sure we're going up against the best of the best."

"Mmm . . . I suppose so. Still, we're all very eager to see you skate, Charlie." She casts me a wolfish smile before her attention snaps back to Alexa. "We heard your mom single-handedly took on the National Figure Skating Association's board and got the rule book changed so a 'pair' is no longer defined as one male and one female skater."

I blink. "Wait, really?"

Alexa's grin stretches wider, pride glittering her eyes. "Yep! She had the backing of the ACLU and everything."

"Wow." Mason eyes me up and down. "I hope all that was worth it."

"Alexa. Charlie. Franklin." Geri waves us over.

Mallory cracks her gum. "Good luck today, ladies."

"You too," Alexa says, tugging me away before I can glare at them.

"Your mom really did that? She got the rules changed so we could skate together?"

"She did."

Frankie laughs. "Damn right she did! Geri's a badass boss lady."

Geri casts a grin over her shoulder. "Astute assessment, Franklin."

As we follow our coach, my heart once again tweaks as if preparing me for the loss of stepping aside for Frankie's on-ice return. Obviously Frankie should come back for nationals—not only is he officially Alexa's partner, he's ridiculously talented and he's my friend, too. I only care about Alexa scoring a medal and earning more points toward her eventual Olympic run. This is still her sport and not mine, hard as I've been working to jam my hockey-shaped puzzle piece into a space that doesn't totally fit.

When we reach the Skaters Only entrance, Frankie hugs each of us before promising me he'll find Dad, Mac, Emily, and Jade and then exiting to save seats in the stands.

Geri leads us into our assigned locker room, each area sectioned off to give skaters a modicum of privacy. I slip behind the black curtain to change on one side while Alexa changes on the other. As I wrestle on my black high-waisted trousers and loose-fitting black peasant-type top, leaving the crisscrossing tie at the collar undone, my hands shake.

"You getting all Elphie'd up over there?" Alexa calls from the other side. "Remember, the short program doesn't count as much as the free skate. If we mess up in the short, we can make up ground with *Neverland*."

"Got it," I reply. "Okay, I'm dressed when you are."

She opens the curtain and we sit side by side in front of our designated vanity, Geri dumping various hair and makeup products before us.

Staring at myself in the mirror wearing my *Wicked* routine getup somehow makes this more real. My pulse thumps harder and I fiddle with the hair tie on my wrist, snapping it a few times in an attempt to quell the storm of nerves simmering inside.

"Charlie, French braid," Geri commands while she situates eye shadow palettes, face paint, and lipsticks before her.

"I've got her." Alexa steps behind me, finger-combing my hair as she begins to weave a French braid as directed by her mother. "Hey. Keep breathing. You're so prepared for this. We've been working our butts off."

Geri fusses with bobby pins. "As long as you skate a clean program, that's what matters. You've done it on our home ice—you can sure as hell do it here, too."

A closed-circuit TV behind me displays the current skaters performing their short program, officially kicking off the competition.

I watch in the mirror as a male skater confidently and effortlessly tosses his partner into the air, catching her one-armed.

"Don't watch that," Geri snaps. "Keep your attention right here on us. If you watch them and they fall, you'll get overconfident. If they do well, it'll stir the nerves. That reminds me—phones off, ladies. No distractions. A single text or social media post can mess with your whole mindset. We're in the distraction-free bubble now until the end of both programs."

Once again, I nod—even though I'm not sure my nerves could stir any harder. I'm a goddamn blender stuck on high speed right now.

Alexa finishes my hair, then Geri maneuvers my chair to the side to face her directly, paint palette in hand. She dips the tip of her makeup sponge in Wicked Witch Green and carefully paints my whole face, witchifying me. "I've seen you lift cleaner than him. Don't think about your competitors. What we lack in routine difficulty you'll make up for with routine sharpness, cleanliness, and emotion. You'll skate your programs to the best of your ability—we can't ask for more than that."

Alexa squeezes my shoulder before turning to apply her own makeup—much simpler than mine with pink lipstick and sparkly eye shadow. "And if we fall, then we get up and keep on going. No matter what, we finish."

Thirty minutes later, we stand together rinkside in full makeup.

The pair before us—Mason and Mallory Ingleborg—perch on the judging bench to receive their scores.

"That's called the Kiss and Cry," Alexa explains. "It's the area where you sit and wait to receive your official scores. Each second feels like an hour and you're plastered on the jumbotron in high-def so everyone can see the panic in your face. It's absolute torture." She scrunches her nose. "Don't worry—we'll get ourselves through it when it's our turn."

"Oh, awesome. For the record—I don't kiss *or* cry in public, so. I'll be the rock here."

The crowd erupts as Mason and Mallory are declared the new leaders.

Shocker.

Glancing up at the crowd, I spot Dad and Mac along with my best friends across the ice and suck in a sharp inhale through my nostrils. Shit's getting real. They've never seen me skate before. Not like this, anyway. This is my first chance to prove it's all been worth it.

"It's only the short," Alexa mutters, tugging at the hem of her sheer beaded sleeve. Her Glinda the Good pink-and-white costume boasts a heart-shaped bustline and ribbon crisscrossed down her back like a corset, its flowy skirt hitting midthigh. Her hand braces against my shoulder to pull my focus again. "Charlie, stay with me. It's you and me at the Blizzard. The audience, the judges—pretend they're not here. It's only us." Her assurance effectively melts a chunk of the tension lodging beneath my shoulder blades.

I force another deep breath. "Yeah, it's only us. We've rehearsed this a million times. We got this."

The announcer's voice booms over the rink speakers. *"Our next pair for this afternoon's short program . . . Alexa Goldstein and Charlie Porter from the Blizzard Skating Club of Winthrop, Vermont."*

We remove our blade guards and Geri accepts them; her lips press into a thin line as she delivers a steady, firm nod.

Alexa pins me with a wink before skating out to center ice, then holding her position.

The crowd cheers.

A few seconds later, I skate out and stop behind her, taking her waist.

"Don't forget to breathe," she whispers before the soft strains of "Defying Gravity" stream through the rink's speakers and we begin our routine.

Holy shit. Without my hockey pads, I might as well be naked out here.

Summoning every ounce of courage in my body, I push off my toe pick and will everything besides Alexa and our music to fade away. Reminding myself I'm doing this for *her*, my body moves far more gracefully than I've ever imagined it could as we skate through our opening choreography sequence, my limbs loosening as we stroke side by side and lead into our first jump.

The announcer's voice sounds a light-year away, carrying in a calm, quiet manner over the hushed crowd.

"Here's their first jump, a double axel—"

Blowing out a hard exhale, my arms draped in front of and behind me, I crouch and hit my toe pick hard, landing with a steady crunch beside Alexa at the same exact time.

"—beautifully executed by both skaters!"

Relief and excitement surge at once. I shift to skating backward as Alexa approaches, her expression fierce yet soft at the same time—and I take her waist for our next element, raising her above my head as she twists into position.

"A twisting lift . . . gorgeous. The steady height, her effortless hold after the twist—and the transition into a spiral sequence . . . in perfect sync. Well done!"

The track intensifies midsong, which amps up the speed and power in the second half of our program.

"Double salchow, double toe loop . . . strong execution once again from both skaters!"

We link hands for another choreography sequence, our natural chemistry guiding my hands down the side of her body while she grips my forearms, foreheads pressed together for a brief, steadying moment.

"Wow, you can really feel their bond out there—impressive for a pair who've only skated together for half a season."

She smiles.

I smirk back.

Shirking the rest of my nerves, we stroke our way to another series.

Double lutz, single toe loop.

Death spiral.

One-handed lift.

All clean minus a slight over-rotation on my lutz, but I catch myself before I fall.

After our closing choreography sequence—Alexa and I cup the backs of each other's necks with opposing arms and our legs extend horizontally, spinning steady as helicopter blades until we strike our final pose—the crowd rockets to their feet as a *wall* of sound hits us from every direction.

Raucous applause.

"We've all just witnessed history here, folks! The first same-sex pairing to perform a routine at a sanctioned National Figure Skating Association competition. And they nailed it!"

My arms—now trembling with adrenaline—wrap around Alexa as I curl into her, panting a disbelieving chuckle against her ear.

I swear I feel her impish grin spread wide against my temple. "Those ballet lessons really paid off, huh?" She pulls back, taking my hand and lifting it between us while waving to the spectators with her other hand.

I follow suit, spotting Dad, Mac, Jade, and Em on their feet, yelling through cupped hands and fist-pumping wildly.

We bow and then skate in perfect sync off the ice.

Geri bursts with pride as she hands each of us our blade guards, which we affix to our skates and follow her to the judging bench.

We sit together in the Kiss and Cry area, my face flushed and breathing labored as our eyes lock up on the scoreboard, Alexa damn near breaking my fingers.

She's right. Each second feels like a whole goddamn hour.

Then, the scores—

GOLDSTEIN/PORTER
PAIRS SHORT PROGRAM
TECHNICAL SCORE: 38.66
PROGRAM COMPONENTS SCORE: 40.82
SHORT PROGRAM TOTAL: 79.48 (SECOND PLACE)

The crowd erupts again.

My free hand claps over my mouth.

Geri clutches both of our shoulders from behind. "Second place," she croaks, releasing the breath she's been holding. "Second place going into the free skate."

"We did it!" Alexa squeals, smiling brighter than the goddamn sun.

"Holy shit." Dazed, I once again find Dad and Mac waving and clapping across the ice.

I wave back.

"Charlie?" Alexa's voice carries softer now, concern etched between her eyebrows. "You're bleeding."

Licking my lip on instinct, the sharp, metallic taste of blood coats my tongue. "Dammit . . ."

"Here." Geri plucks a tissue from her pocket and clamps it over my nose. "Follow me. We need to change and do fresh makeup for *Neverland*."

I take over pinching my nose. "I'm fine," I mumble behind the tissue. "We crushed that shit. That's what matters."

Geri guides us back toward the locker room. "You did well, but it's only the short. The free skate is much weightier toward your final score. I have notes for you on some corrections—"

"Mom, can we stop Charlie's nosebleed before we start harping on her?"

"Oh. Yes. Of course." Geri gathers my garment bag for the next routine and extends it toward me with a bottle of face wash. "Go scrub your face, get all that green makeup off, and change into your next costume."

Nodding, I remove my skates and step into my Adidas slides, shuffling toward the bathroom down the hall. I always thought a hockey victory was sweet—but the thrill of a hockey win hardly compares to the plane of bliss I'm flying on after crushing that performance.

Hanging the garment bag on a stall door, I bow my head over the sink and remove my *Wicked* makeup. Patting my face dry, I note my nosebleed mercifully decided to stop as an unmistakable "*Shhh!*" carries from the larger accessible stall.

I freeze for a beat before whirling around . . . spotting two pairs of shoes beneath one door.

Correction—one pair of shoes, one shoe and one walking boot.

"Uh—Frankie?"

The door opens with a cartoonish creak and Frankie clears his throat, his cheeks blazing. "Charlie! Hey! You guys really slam-dunked it out there!"

My brows knit as his stall mate peers around him.

Mason Ingleborg, sporting equally reddened cheeks. "Hi, Charlie!

Wow, impressive performance, rookie!" He exhales with a strained sort of laugh. "I should get back to my sister. Nice, er—catching up with you, Frankie." With that, Mason ducks his head and rushes out of the bathroom.

My arms fold over my chest, eyebrow arched in a near-Geri-type question mark. "Seriously? You're hooking up with the enemy?"

"I know it looks bad . . . ," Frankie says, rubbing at the back of his neck as he ambles out of the stall. "I promise—we don't let our relationship mess with each other's skating. We've been, uh . . . kind of long-distance dating for a while now? Alexa knows. She knows I'd never do anything to sabotage us, and I'm really hoping you know I'd never—"

"I know," I say, my shoulders loosening after hearing Alexa's cool with it. Still, I can't help but tease, shooting him a playful glare. "Really, though? Between programs?"

Frankie chuckles. "In my defense, we don't get a lot of time to see each other."

"Did you even wait to watch us skate before sneaking off?"

"Of course I did!" Frankie launches himself forward and braces his hands on my shoulders. "You were fantastic, girl! I'm so proud of you. Felt pretty amazing, huh?"

A disbelieving puff of laughter escapes. "Yeah. Wild. But it's only the short."

"Go on," Frankie says, nodding toward my garment bag. "Get changed, then we'll mentally prep for the free skate."

Frankie leaves and I duck into the larger stall to change into my *Finding Neverland* costume. It's a new pair of high-waisted trousers—brown this time, with a few patchwork fabric scraps on the knees—with a gray Henley shirt and a pair of suspenders. I'm really trying to sell that early-1900s impoverished-writer aesthetic.

Considering we're once again slotted to skate middle of the pack and we need to wait for four pairs to skate their short programs and another four to perform their free skate routines before us, the mental preparation between programs proves pretty challenging.

Geri tosses a zip-up jacket over the closed-circuit TV in the locker room so we can't watch the other performances.

Cozily ensconced in our protective bubble, Alexa and I play a few card games to keep our minds sharp and focused. When the Ingleborgs are called out to the ice, Geri summons Lex and me to walk through our routine one more time in our small space. We finish our skateless rehearsal when a sharp rap carries from the open doorway.

"Charlie!"

Our gazes snap toward the voice, Geri and Alexa's expressions contorting with confusion.

The color drains from my face as I stare at the uninvited guest. It takes more work than it should to summon my chill along with my voice in the next beat. "Mom?"

Twenty-Five

"Hi, hon!" Without invitation, my mother rushes inside and throws her arms around me.

A full two seconds pass before my arms raise and awkwardly return the favor.

It takes a hell of a lot to shock Geri—particularly when she's locked into coach mode—but even she stands unmoving. She no doubt would've immediately yelled at literally anyone else in the world to banish them from our midperformance bubble, but instead she blinks at me in bewilderment.

Pulling back, a stunned quiver carries in my voice, which I hate very much. "Mom, this is Alexa, my skating partner. And that's her mom and our coach, Geri."

"It's nice to meet you," Alexa says, stepping closer to Geri, who nods once.

It's only been a month and a half since Christmas, when I didn't expect to see her again for many months or even years, considering her history of making and breaking plans—particularly when the invitation involves her watching one of my competitions.

Hockey competitions. She wasn't invited to *this*.

With introductions out of the way, I take Mom's elbow and lead her out through the doorway for a modicum of privacy. "What are you doing here?"

"Surprising you, of course!" As if she'd ever showed up unannounced before. Mom beams, her eyes taking a tour of my body. "God, *look* at you. It was one thing seeing you over Christmas, but all done up and ready to compete? You're so tall and strong and *beautiful*." She reaches out to hold the tail end of my braid, skimming her thumb over its gathered ends.

"Thanks . . ." My voice cracks on the single syllable. I've never been so torn. I want her to be here and watch me kick ass—but I also don't want her anywhere near here. It doesn't make *sense*.

"I was talking with Macky and he told me about your big competition today. Kylie wants to be a figure skater, have I told you that? She decided after you left on Christmas Day. We started her with lessons right after the new year. She looks *so* cute in her little figure skates and she loves it, so I figured it would be *so* great if I could take her to watch her big sister perform!"

"Wow, that's—that's great," I stammer, a few notes of a shocked, uncomfortable laugh squeezing free. Part of me wants to murder Mac with his own hockey stick for telling Mom about the skating thing. And yet deep down, I'm beyond thrilled she *finally* showed up. It's not a hockey match, but it's still an opportunity to prove to her I turned out okay not because of her, but in spite of her. I'll show her I'm a badass competitor and make her realize what she's been missing out on. What she all but gave up on.

"I'm sorry we missed the beginning, Char." Again with the *Charlotte* Char, not the *Charlie* Char. "Traffic was absolutely horrendous. But I found Macky in the stands and dropped Kylie off with him and your father and they're saving me a seat so I can watch your free skate. Maybe we can all grab dinner—you know, after you win your gold medal today." She winks.

"Oh, um . . . sure? Yeah, we can do that, I guess. But nobody wins medals today. It's only a qualifier for the big national championships, which I won't even be skating in because—"

"Charlie." Probably overhearing my conversation and noting the discomfort in my tone—something my own mother seems oblivious to—Geri stands at the doorway with her arms crossed. "I'm sorry to interrupt, but I need to prepare my skaters for their next routine."

Mom at least has the wherewithal to look appropriately chastised. "Oh, that's right! I'm sorry, hon—didn't mean to mess with any preperformance mojo up in here. Good luck out there, both of you!" She pulls me in for one last hug and smacks a kiss to my cheek, leaving lipstick behind as she bustles out of the athletes-only space.

Slow blinking, I turn back to Geri and Alexa. "Sorry. I had no idea—"

"Of course you had no idea." Geri grabs a tissue and wipes the lipstick off my cheek.

Alexa takes my hand and squeezes. "Are you okay? What do you need?" I can tell by the look on her face she's more concerned about me at this moment than our upcoming performance.

"I'm good," I say, easing into a more natural smile—which is never difficult with Alexa. "Really. No idea how she snuck back here, but I'm okay." I shift my gaze to Geri, whose expression reads as unconvinced. "I'm serious, Coach. I'm ready to go out and crush this thing."

"Good," Geri says. "Because we're up next."

Moments later, the coordinator peers around the doorframe and glances at her clipboard. "Goldstein and Porter?"

Rinkside, Geri collects our blade guards, kisses Alexa's forehead, and squeezes my shoulder before retreating to her seat.

My jaw clenches as I track Mason and Mallory Ingleborg landing one of their signature triple-doubles to end their routine, the cheering crowd leaping to their feet.

"Hey . . ." Alexa takes my hand. "Don't think about them. It doesn't matter what score they get, okay?"

"Okay." I will myself to relax. Spotting Mom and Kylie now sitting with Dad and Mac, I brace myself for the preperformance nerves to bodycheck me into the metaphorical boards like last time. Only . . . they don't hit. Instead, there's only confidence.

Well-earned confidence stemming from months of intense hard work and dedication.

Lingering confidence from nailing our short program and earning a standing ovation from this crowd.

Surging confidence to take full advantage of showing off my skills to my mom, who finally showed up this time. Maybe for her one and only time.

"Lex." I catch her elbow before she steps onto the ice, my free hand bracing her cheek. "This is gonna be our last chance to do this together. Why don't we have a little extra fun with it? Give 'em something special to remember us by. Say . . . I'll toss you higher for a triple on our last throw instead of a double?"

Alexa shoots me an admonishing faux glare. "Troublemaker. I don't think that's a good idea."

"C'mon. We can do it! You said we could at your cousin's wedding, remember? We've done it in practice!"

"Not always *cleanly* . . ." Alexa counters, confliction crossing her expression. She steals a quick glance to her mother.

I cut another look to my mom in the stands before sliding my hand down to Alexa's shoulder for another solid squeeze. "Lex, think about it. Think how cool it'll be! Think about how a sick triple throw would wipe that smug-as-hell look from Mallory Ingleborg's face. It'll give you a chance to really screw with her head leading up to nationals. *Payback* for her messing with your head years ago."

Alexa peers over at Mallory Ingleborg, who's sitting at the Kiss and Cry striking obnoxious poses and blowing kisses to the camera in her face. Alexa takes a deep, steadying breath before glancing back at me. "You make me break all my own rules too, you know. Okay, yes. Mom won't be happy, but she'll be less mad if we land it, and I've got a good feeling about this. About us. Let's do it."

The announcer's voice booms over the rink speakers. *"Ladies and gentlemen, once again from the Blizzard Skating Club of Winthrop, Vermont . . . entering the free skate in second place . . . Alexa Goldstein and Charlie Porter!"*

We skate together hand in hand toward center ice and settle into our positions.

The soft, enrapturing flute solo leads into our free skate routine: *Neverland.*

"A beautiful opening sequence with palpable emotions bolstering each skater's movements . . ."

The entire crowd—my mother included—melts into the background when Alexa strikes me with one of those heartfelt smiles reserved only for me. We stroke toward the perimeter of the ice, preparing for our first jump sequence.

". . . leading into their first side-by-side jump, a double salchow, double toe loop combo—"

Exhaling sharply, I crouch on count, strike my toe pick, and launch into the air beside Alexa; we land with a satisfying crunch on a single beat.

"—flawlessly performed by both skaters!"

A second-place finish flashes before my eyes as we shift into our first lift with impressive, near-perfect form.

"They transition into a serpentine lift . . . stunning."

The middle of our routine carries on with only minor missteps on my part—nothing worthy of significant point deductions from our score.

"Side-by-side double flip, double loop . . . and a strong execution once again from both skaters!"

Alexa's smile shines so bright it's nearly blinding and impossible to not mirror in this moment. We stroke through another few sequences, our deep bond and palpable care for each other helping one move flow seamlessly into the next.

"And their final component—a double salchow throw . . ."

Our last big move. As we glide with linked hands, I cast Alexa one questioning glance she reads for what it is: *Are you sure about this?*

Alexa responds with a single, firm nod.

Grounded in pure trust and a desire to leave one lasting impact on the judges and spectators—well, now one spectator in particular in my case—I take Alexa's waist. We count back in our heads and I launch her into the air with what I believe is enough force and height for Alexa to complete three full rotations in the air—

Only it's not. I catch a flash of Alexa's panicked wince as she spins out of timing and under-rotates her landing, crashing onto her back.

Thwack!

Her skull bounces off the ice.

A sympathetic symphony of groans accompanies the fall in sur-round sound, sinking into the marrow of my bones.

Alexa's eyes remain closed and her body lies scarily still.

My heart stops cold. *"Lex!"* Terror powers my skates as I reach her side first, dropping to my knees and reaching out to her shoul-ders.

Geri's booming voice freezes my hands before I make contact. *"Stop, Charlie!"* She runs hard toward us on her flat boots. "If she has a neck injury, you can't move her head." She kneels at Alexa's other side, casting me a withering glare. "What the *hell* were you thinking?"

"I—" My explanation lodges in a golf-ball-size lump in my throat, tears stinging my eyes. "We—I thought—"

"You thought you were superwoman out here, didn't you? You

care more about overperforming than Alexa's safety."

"No! No, I—" I choke, my hand settling over my thundering heart as I glance back down at Alexa. Her chest rises and falls—thank god, she's breathing—but the acknowledgment does little to settle the agonizing guilt crashing through me. "I'm sorry," I croak, shaking my head. "I'm sorry, Lex. Geri—" I look up at her. "I'm sorry. I thought we could—I shouldn't have—I messed up and I'm sorry."

The paramedics dash onto the ice with a stretcher.

"Oh, you're sorry? She could have brain damage! She could be paralyzed! But that's all fine because you're *sorry*." Geri snarls. "Back away from my daughter."

I wipe my nose on the back of my hand and push onto my skates, allowing the paramedics to approach her directly.

Adrenaline, terror, and sorrow war for dominance in my trembling body. I hug myself in a weak attempt to self-soothe as paramedics secure a brace around Alexa's neck and shift her carefully onto a stretcher.

Geri remains by her side as she's carried away.

Left alone on the ice, I bow my head and spot the blood smear where Alexa's head made contact.

Dropping back to my knees, I bury my face in my hands and break one of my Kiss and Cry rules, openly sobbing in front of several thousand horrified spectators.

Twenty-Six

I'm frozen near center ice, crouched beneath the shame-powered microscope of thousands of judgmental eyeballs until a warm, comforting hand presses down on my shoulder.

"C'mon, Charmander." Frankie reaches for my hand and tugs me back to my skates, urging me away from the spotlight.

A low yet steady pity clap trails behind me and I wonder why they're not booing instead. Throwing shit at me from the stands. Disqualifying me instantly. I wish they would.

"Your dad and brother and friends are waiting for us in the parking lot. We'll meet Geri at the hospital."

"She won't want me there," I mumble, leaning into Frankie. "Not after what I did."

"Who, Geri?"

"Yeah." I pause, considering. "Both of 'em."

"That's not true. Go on and change real quick, I'll wait right out here."

Mom and Kylie leave while I'm changing, not bothering to stick around to say goodbye or check in about that dinner she offered. In any other circumstance I'd probably deflate, but right now I'm relieved.

I barely speak on the ride from the ice rink to the hospital, even as Dad, Mac, Jade, and Em praise my skating and try cheering me up.

Wow, kiddo, you did great out there! I'm sure Alexa's gonna be just fine.

Holy crap, you're actually good at figure skating!

Don't be too hard on yourself!

Accidents happen!

Why don't they get it? It wasn't an accident, not really. It was me once again back in cocky hockey mode, trying to show off for one big selfish moment of glory while putting the important things—first my hockey team, now my skating partner—in jeopardy.

It's the Winthrop Cup blown shot all over again.

Only this time, I may have permanently injured my girlfriend.

The entire car ride I stare unfocused out the window, reflecting on all the progress I've made, and I'm not even talking about skating. I've grown from throwing punches to squirting water guns to doing my best to ignore those d-bags in the hallways. I've been better at managing my recklessness, my impulsiveness. I learned how to put others before myself and support someone else's ambitions—not only Alexa's but Frankie's, too. Then at the first major opportunity to show off for someone who doesn't even really deserve to see me at my best, I throw all those personal-growth wins directly in the garbage.

Progress, my ass.

We arrive at Schenectady's nearest emergency room not long after the ambulance, the same spike of anxiety lancing through my body upon registering the sharp antiseptic scents particular to a hospital. I curl up on one of the waiting room chairs, hugging my knees to my chest with my earbuds blaring music, trying to drown out not only the hospital itself but my own punishing thoughts.

Dad pours himself a Styrofoam cup of coffee and sits beside me, his quiet, steady presence offering at least a little comfort while my mind replays my botched throw over and over again. The look of fear twisting up Alexa's face once she realized I messed up. The sound of her skull smacking the ice, leaving a smear of blood behind. Geri's venomous snipe.

Back away from my daughter.

Over the next hour, Jade and Em take turns sitting on my other side, trying to comfort me with words of reassurance or distract me with memes.

Mac hits up the vending machines and offers me a bag of sour gummies.

I shake my head, instead accepting the cup of water offered by Frankie.

Another episode and a half of an HGTV show airs on the mounted screen before Geri steps into the waiting room, all of us snapping to attention and straining to face her. I yank my earbuds out and shove them into my pocket.

"Alexa's awake. We're incredibly lucky—the scans show no bleeding on the brain or evidence of significant traumatic brain injury. She has a concussion, which is the best-case scenario considering the force of the impact." Her eyes dart to me, her jaw setting. "She's asking to see you."

I damn near fall out of my chair as I unpretzel my limbs, wincing at the stiffness that set in over however long it's been.

Geri leads me back through the ER hallways, keeping two steps in front of me and not bothering to look back.

My hands burrow into my hoodie's pouch and my shoulders tense toward my ears. I can't resist stealing curious, nosy peeks into the half-curtained or fully opened triage spaces, wondering what's wrong with the patients in each one. Almost all of them are old people, reminding me how Alexa shouldn't be here at all.

Finally, Geri whirls around and stops before one of the closed curtains, leveling another look at me. "Don't take too much time. She needs her rest."

"Right," I croak, squaring my shoulders and forcing a deep, shaky breath as Geri pulls back the curtain enough for me to slip inside.

"Hi." Half reclined on a small bed wearing a hospital gown and an easy, stoned sort of smile, Alexa reaches for me. "C'mere."

The sight of her here, looking frail and dazed with glassy eyes and the natural rosy color drained from her cheeks, triggers another brutal pang of guilt and regret constricting around my heart. "Hi." It's almost impossible to ignore the wires and monitors poking out from her hospital gown connected to the machines beside her, each beep setting my teeth on edge as I shuffle slowly to her bedside. "Did they at least give you the good drugs?"

"Oh yeah, for sure. Headache's all gone for now." She curls her fingers over my forearm. "I'm sorry, Charlie."

I blink. "*You're* sorry? No, I'm the one—"

"We made that decision together, remember? I'm sorry I scared you."

My lower lip quibbles and I catch it between my teeth, willing my quick-thumping pulse to settle with little success. "I'm still sorry. You have no idea how sorry I am. I should've been more careful. We didn't need to do that big move."

"But we still qualified for nationals, thanks to you." Alexa takes my hand and squeezes. "Mom checked the standings. Fourth place. We did it." Her hazy happiness kicks up a notch.

Meeting our goal should make me feel better, but I can't even summon an ounce of give-a-shit. My gaze drops to her slight fingers on my arm—the IV taped to the back of her hand—and my eyes burn with stinging tears I refuse to let fall. "Why are you being so nice to me? I almost *killed* you. *Paralyzed* you! I thought your skull cracked, there was blood on the ice and—"

"Charlie." Alexa squeezes my arm, shaking her head with a slight wince. "Stop thinking that way. Those things didn't happen."

"But they *could have*!" I reach up with my free hand and rub my eyes, willing the emotion back down. "I'll never forgive myself for this."

"You need to. Because I forgive you, Charlie. Injuries happen in sports, remember? We've landed the triple throw a dozen times in practice."

Her instant forgiveness somehow only makes me feel shittier. "I'm glad you have Frankie back now." Before the competition I'd been jealous of him, not looking forward to stepping back even when the plan never called for me to continue on. But at least he won't do anything rebellious or dangerous. He's not like me.

Alexa nods. "We're both so grateful for all your help. I'll need a few weeks off to fully recover, then Frankie and I will get started training and rehearsing for nationals. And now . . ." She heaves a wistful sigh. "You won't need to skate with me anymore, and I know you're going back to Cranford soon, but we can still . . . keep going. Off the ice."

My brow knits. I can't wipe Geri's terrified face, the murderous look she pinned me with, out of my head. The woman who'd somehow filled in as the only stable mother figure I've had lately. And now she's pushed me away, too. "Lex . . . I can't."

"You can't what? Just because we won't be competing together . . . we can still skate together on the pond, right?" Hope shines in her glassy eyes.

I grimace, my own eyes also glassy—though not from a concussion. "I can't *do* this. Don't you get it? I'm a goddamn liability. I'm no good for you. I don't deserve . . . this. Us. Not anymore."

"What?" Alexa slips her hand down to take mine, lacing our fingers. "No. Charlie, look at me."

I've never felt more like a coward, but I summon what little courage I've got left to meet her gaze.

"You and me . . . we're two halves of a whole. I know you know it. We're great together, both on and off the ice."

"I know," I say with a sniffle. "But I still . . . I'm in over my head. I'm so damn selfish. You should be with someone who's gonna keep you safe, not put you in the hospital." Blowing out a hard exhale, I release her hand. "You heal up quick, okay? You and Frankie are gonna crush it at nationals."

A deep frown curls at the corners of Alexa's mouth, tears welling hard and fast in her bright brown eyes. "Charlie, please. Wait—"

"I can't," I rasp, shaking my head. "I'm sorry. I'm so glad you're gonna be okay, but I've gotta—I'm gonna go home."

Her lips purse, jaw setting in that adorably bossy kind of way. "Don't you dare walk away from me, Charlie Porter!"

"Rest up, Lex."

Stepping back around the curtain, Geri stands with her arms crossed and offers a quick nod of what feels like appreciation. Gratitude for stepping away from her daughter.

My heart—already aching like hell—splinters into pieces. But I'm doing the right thing. I'm sure of it. Nodding back at Geri, I wipe my tearstained cheeks with the cuffs of my hoodie on my slow shuffle to the waiting room.

"She's okay," I confirm to everyone else. I'm talking physically. She's not okay emotionally.

And now I'm just . . . numb. Numb and exhausted.

Dad pushes up from the chair and pulls me into a hug, dropping a kiss to the crown of my head. "Let's get out of here, huh? Let's go home."

Frankie catches a ride home with us since Alexa will need to stay in the hospital overnight for observation.

All of us remain quiet on the car ride back to Vermont, the

steady chatter of sports talk radio filling our silence. We make it home around nine.

I drag myself upstairs without dinner and turn on the shower as hot as I can stand it, my skin raw and pink after I've finished attempting to scrub off every cell from the new worst day of my life.

The next morning, I wake in a cold sweat. A wicked case of panic thumps through my veins and I shakily climb out of bed, desperate to rid myself of the buzzing, uneasy energy holding my body captive.

After a record-speed morning washup, I pull on a sports bra with a T-shirt and my Cranford hoodie on top, a pair of tapered sweatpants, and thick socks. On my way out, I mutter a "be back soon" at Dad, who's sitting at the kitchen table with coffee and a morning paper. Then I stomp my feet into snow boots and grab the car keys, ducking out of the house.

I drive on autopilot and find myself approaching Hopkins Pond.

I can't explain how desperately I need to skate. It's the only thing that really clears my head and I crave the steadying rush now more than ever, hoping it might quiet the monster clawing through my chest.

Opening my trunk, I spot my three pairs of skates with their laces all tangled up with each other.

My hockey skates—collecting dust from months of neglect. My figure skates. My old hockey skates turned pond skates. I reach for those before freezing midgrab, snagging my figure skates instead.

Who gives a shit if I wreck the blades? Not like I need them anymore.

Shuffling to the same bench where I sat with a sprained wrist a couple months back, I choke out a sob as I swap my footwear for the same skates I wore when I almost seriously injured Alexa. Lacing them up, I trudge a few feet on snow-caked grass toward the empty pond and remove my blade guards.

The instant my blades touch ice, my body returns to a state of equilibrium I only ever feel while skating. I solo-stroke a few warm-up laps, the morning sun reflecting off the ice from above and making me wish I snagged my sunglasses. Pushing my sleeves up, I grit my teeth and put my toe pick to work.

Maybe it's an act of self-punishment, but my nerve-riddled brain decides I can't leave until I land ten clean triple jumps.

And suddenly Geri's stuck in my head, berating me for my mistakes.

Stroke, stroke, stroke, reverse, crouch, hit the toe pick, launch, three spins—

Crash!

I hit the ice hard, skinning a few layers of skin from my left elbow, blood beading at the site.

The sting barely registers. Try again.

Stroke, stroke, stroke, reverse, crouch, hit the toe pick, launch, three spins—

Crash!

This time I almost break my ass. My tailbone's gonna be sore as hell for a week, but whatever. I've had worse hockey injuries.

Minutes creep toward an hour and my muscles scream for rest, limbs trembling from overexertion.

Landed triples: six.

Wipeouts: thirty-one . . . ish? I lost count.

Grinding my molars through the pain, I wipe my sweat-soaked forehead with the back of my hand and push toward the end of the pond, preparing for another jump with both elbows and knees bleeding, my ass cheeks numb from impact while no doubt already blossoming with bruises.

After another hour, I drop back onto the bench and pull my boots back on. Standing, I take one more moment to appreciate the orangey morning sun rising over the pond. My heart wrenches yet again upon noting how the sun's fiery reflection around its edges matches Alexa's hair color. I flashback to our on-ice slow dance during our first official date, the way her eyes stared through mine and into my soul.

Shoving that thought into my brain's recycle bin, I force my focus on the positive. On my friends, on returning to Cranford. To life *almost finally* going back to normal. I register my body's return toward equilibrium, and a surge of appreciation for the people in my life significantly lowers my anxiety.

I toss my busted figure skates into the trunk and drive away from Hopkins Pond without looking back.

Twenty-Seven

Mercifully, after Dean Quigley signs my official readmission letter for the following Monday and start of the third trimester, Dad signs me out of Winthrop High School a week early.

"This is probably the coolest thing you've ever done," I say as I descend the Winthrop High stairs for the final time. Part of me wanted to see Frankie and Cyn during our brief trip to the main office to take care of my student withdrawal paperwork, but I'm mostly relieved I didn't see anyone else. I'll text them later.

Dad's eyes narrow. "Cooler than my tattoos? Or that time I let you and Mac talk me into dressing up as Luigi for Halloween a few years back?" Mac dressed as Mario. I was Bowser, because of course I was.

"Hmm . . ." I steal one last look at the snow leopard statue by the flagpole, relief cascading through my body as I climb into the passenger seat of Dad's Jeep. "Okay, it's tied with those things." I cast him a grateful look. "Really. Thanks."

"Don't thank me. I know you need the break. You scared me pretty good for a little while there." He twists the key to fire up the ignition and rolls out of the parking lot. "So my conditions for your week off: First, you need to get some real, solid sleep every night. I'll be taking your phone by nine thirty to make sure you do."

My gut instinctively wants to argue, but then I realize I'm no longer texting a girlfriend well into the night, so it doesn't really matter. "Okay, yeah. Sleep sounds excellent. I feel like I can sleep the whole week."

"Yeah, I know. A solid nine to ten hours per night should do the trick with getting you good and refreshed for Cranford. I also made you some appointments you're overdue for. Regular pediatrician checkup. Dentist. Dermatologist."

"Therapist?" I ask, my ears warming beneath my hair. "I know you probably didn't think to set that one up, but it's probably good for me to start up again, right? Especially with—"

"Your mom showing up like that, unannounced, then bailing when the going got rough? Yeah." He cuts me a warm, supportive look. "Good thinkin', kiddo. Lord knows Nora put my ass in therapy for years after she cut out. I'm surprised you didn't want back in sooner."

We laugh. Every family needs a little trauma bonding, right? As a treat.

Dad turns the radio down a notch. "I'm proud of you, y'know. I know I don't say it. . . ." He keeps his eyes on the road, but that's intentional. We Porters don't really do heartfelt conversations, especially not face to face. "The way you threw yourself into a new sport like you did, gave it all you had from the start, how fast you were able to compete at that level? Gotta be some sort of record somewhere."

A rush of intense emotion lodges in my throat. I blink back a sudden prickle of tears. "I do know you're proud," I say, reaching across the center console to give his forearm a pat. "You never needed to say it because I always knew. You always show up for me."

"Damn right I do," he says. "Now, the third term of our agreement? I took tomorrow off. You and me are gonna spend the morning skatin' and shootin' around the pond before it starts to thaw."

My eyebrows fly northbound. "Oh yeah? It's been a minute since you laced up. You still got game, old man?"

He gives me a playful shoulder shove. "I got plenty of game. You'll see."

I smirk. "Looking forward to it."

Alexa (8:16 a.m.): Hi. I wanted to wish you luck on your first day back at Cranford.

Alexa (8:28 a.m.): Frankie's full weight bearing on his skates! Thought you'd want to know.

Alexa (9:09 a.m.): I get that you're avoiding me, but do you think maybe we can talk soon? I know you don't want us to be together but it feels so weird not talking after spending so much time with you.

Alexa (9:22 a.m.): I miss you.

Alexa (6:26 p.m.): Fine, Charlie. I get it. Have a nice life.

I lean against my new Cranford locker and open our text chain for what feels like the hundredth time this week, my thumbs hovering over the keyboard and hesitating. It's been four days since I've started school refreshed and rejuvenated thanks to Dad's self-care camp, and I *want* to reply. I want to talk with her. I miss her, too. Like hell.

But then the moment of her skull whacking the ice flashes behind my closed eyelids and another swell of panic surges in my chest, reminding me I should leave her alone. She's better off if I leave her alone.

"No phones are permitted to be out of pockets or lockers during the school day, Charlotte."

My gaze snaps from my phone to the headmistress as a weak, sheepish grin tugs at the corners of my mouth. "Sorry, Dean Quigley. Bad habit I picked up from those Winthrop delinquents."

"Mmm . . . yes, well. You'll find your Cranford stride again in no time." She reaches out and adjusts the collar of my maroon polo shirt.

A teasing glint sparkles in my eye. "I bet it's been pretty boring around here without me making your days interesting, huh?"

Dean Quigley sniffs and lifts her pointy chin. "I'm extremely content with having minimal *disruptive behaviors* to address, but I do appreciate your concern." She raises a slender hand, pointing her index finger at me. "One toe out of line . . ."

"I know." My nose scrunches. "Seriously. You don't have to worry about me."

"Good." The Quigs relaxes into a tight-lipped grin. "It's good to have you back, Miss Porter."

It's pretty damn jarring swapping schools two-thirds of the way through the school year, but I'm not complaining. Continuing at Winthrop would've been even more difficult; my spy skills have never been good enough to evade Alexa all day every day. Better to cut and run.

Shaking thoughts of Winthrop High, I head to study hall in the library, making my way to the back corner table where Emily and Jade sit amid stacks of textbooks, their Cranford-issued laptops open in front of them.

"Finally," Jade says as I drop into my seat beside Emily. She pops to her feet, happiness radiating from her entire form. "I have an exciting announcement."

Em and I glance at each other.

"Oh my god, did you get in?" Emily asks.

Jade doesn't answer, but instead lifts a tube from the side of her book bag. She unscrews the lid and pulls out a rolled-up piece of canvas. Unfurling it, she uses her impressive wingspan to hold her creation out so the both of us can see it. Experience it. The master-piece before us.

My mouth falls open. "Holy shit . . ."

"That's *incredible*!" Emily bursts, staring at the gorgeous oil painting with the title "Duality of Woman" inked in the lower right-hand corner.

Jade painted a triple portrait of all three of us. She situated herself front and center with her eyes closed, her form split down the middle with one half of her silhouette tattooed in primary-colored science equipment—flasks and Bunsen burners, chemical equations, genetic Punnett squares. She painted her other half tattooed in secondary colors—pencils and brushes, painting palettes, spattered paint, sculpted clay.

Her detailed, tattooed rendition of Emily stands to her left on the page, in the same style with Emily split in two—celestial bodies symbolizing her love for astrology on one side, with baking imagery on the other.

I'm on the right. Jade portrayed my two halves so perfectly—hockey on one side, figure skating on the other. Reds, blues, and yellows for hockey, greens, oranges, and purples for figure skating.

"I'm representing Heart and Mind," Jade explains, shifting her gaze to Em. "Emily's Body and Spirit." Then she nods to me. "And I painted you as Grit and Grace."

I don't realize I'm experiencing too many feelings until a tear slips down my cheek. Seriously, what is it lately with me no longer having a death-grip control over my emotions? I quickly flick the pesky tear away and glance toward Emily, who's full-on crying.

"So did you get in?" Em croaks, sniffling. "You better get in with that masterpiece. I'll beat the crap out of whoever rejected you if you didn't—"

"I got in," Jade says. "No need to threaten anyone on my behalf. RISD summer program, here I come."

All three of us squeal, ignoring the shushes from our classmates and the librarian as we rush around the table and tackle Jade in a proud hug.

"One more thing," she says, disengaging from the embrace to pull a stack of flyers from her bag, extending one to each of us. "A few of my pieces are gonna be featured in the Winthrop Art Center Student Art Show in early April. They're giving me my own corner in the exhibit, which is so cool. . . ."

Em and I beam at Jade.

"This is the coolest!" Em exclaims.

"I wouldn't miss it for anything," I assure her. "I'll even triple-check I put the right date in my phone this time." I haven't missed one of Em's basketball games since I screwed up with the first one. I sure as hell won't forget Jade's art show.

A few weeks later I'm settled into academic and social life back at Cranford. It's mid-March and I'm sitting next to Dad as our Caribou hockey team sweeps down the ice led by Captain Mac. It's the first playoff match against Greenfield High, and despite my readmission, I'm not allowed to play because I wasn't on the roster all season. Which—valid, I guess, and yet my insides twist and ache with envy and longing.

We're up by two in the third period when my phone buzzes in my pocket. I open my lock screen assuming it's a text from Jade or Em since we have plans tonight to grab burgers after Emily's game. But instead of a text, it's an email.

To: cvporter4@cranfordprep.org
From: jpnicoletti03@pennstate.uni
Subj: Invitation

Greetings, Ms. Porter,

I recently received a call from Coach Goldstein, who spoke very highly of your athletic ability, your dedication and superb work ethic, and the passion you exude for not only hockey but all of your pursuits. My staff would like to extend to you an invitation to our weeklong Summer Skills Clinic for rising high school seniors at our Pegula Ice Arena near our main campus from July 12 to 16. You will find travel, food, and lodging details, along with a more specific daily schedule, attached to this email. This opportunity will be offered at no cost to you.

We hope you'll join us and we look forward to getting to know you both as a person and as a player. Please respond with your intent to attend no later than April 30.

Regards,
Jaime P. Nicoletti
Head Coach
Nittany Lions D-I Women's Ice Hockey
The Pennsylvania State University

"Oh my god." My free hand flies to cover my mouth, eyes widening as I read the email again. Then a third time.

"You good, kiddo?" Dad's attention pulls from the match to me beside him.

Puffing out a disbelieving snort, I show him my phone. "Geri, she—she held up her end of the bargain. I got invited to the Summer Skills Clinic at Penn State. I'll have all week to show my stuff and . . . damn, this could lead to an offer—or at least the scouts swinging back through in the fall to catch me in action!"

Dad wraps his arm around my shoulders and squeezes tight. "That's my girl. Check you out with your own personal email invitation."

My head's spinning throughout the rest of the game, spirit

soaring as I cheer for Mac and the team without the brick of bitterness sinking my stomach. They win the game and suddenly, for the first time all damn year, I finally feel like a winner too.

We exit the hockey rink and Dad heads to the bathroom.

I know I shouldn't, but I can't ignore the pull to drift across the main lobby. Through the doors to the figure skating rink, Alexa and Frankie skate at full strength. I instantly recognize our *Wicked* short program routine—a few of the elements upped in difficulty with Frankie back in his rightful spot. Geri nods her approval throughout.

When Alexa and Frankie finish their routine and strike their final pose with heaving chests gulping for air, Alexa's gaze flits toward the doors first.

She spots me and her expression instantly shifts, her dazzling grin falling into a stony frown. She wrenches her attention away and storms off-ice.

Geri strides after her.

Frankie casts me an awkward wave, holding up one finger.

Against my better judgment, I wait for him. He exits the rink a minute later on his blade guards. "Hey, stranger."

"Hey. You guys rocked that routine in there. Really made me look like amateur hour. Nationals won't know what hit 'em."

He chuckles. "Thanks, Charizard. And thanks . . . for all of it. I don't think I ever properly thanked you for stepping in for me, for pulling out a qualifier placement so we could even have this shot at the national championships."

I shrug. "No sweat. And by that I mean *so much* sweat, but it was worth it. Some parts were even pretty fun, in a torturous kinda way." My focus wanders over Frankie's shoulder into the figure skating rink once again.

"You miss it, huh?"

My spine snaps straighter. "What, pairs skating? Crashing all the time, cuts and bruises everywhere on my body, those horrifically tight pants? *Psh.* Nah . . . it's your sport, Drake. Not mine."

"No, Charlie. It's yours, too. If you want it to be." I've never been a good liar and Frankie knows me well enough to recognize when I'm not telling the whole truth. His voice carries gentler. "You don't have to choose between figure skating and hockey, y'know. You can have both."

"I can't. Not after I made that selfish call and really hurt her. Besides, this is your spot anyway."

Frankie shakes his head. "Hey, stop beating yourself up about that. Mistakes happen. And don't you worry about me. There's a lot up in the air for next season. You and Lex . . . there's something really magical there. It's obvious how much more she skates with her heart when she skates with you. Even Geri believes it, whether she'll admit it or not."

My eyebrows knit. "What's up in the air?"

"I can't really say yet," he says. "Will you come with us to Ann Arbor next month? Second weekend in April. Be with us for the competition?"

I wince. "Like hell Geri wants me anywhere near there. And Alexa too, for that matter." My phone buzzes in my pocket, reminding me about my recent email invitation, and excitement once again surges. "Oh hey, could you do me a favor and tell Geri I said thanks? She'll know what it's for."

"Maybe you should tell her yourself. Geri's calmed down a lot now that Alexa's back on track. And Lex . . . I know she misses you."

Reaching up, I squeeze the back of my neck. "Yeah, well. I screwed that one up." Shaking my head, I refocus and nod back toward the hockey rink. "We've got our championship game scheduled for that same weekend and we're definitely gonna get there. I can't bail on my team, even if I can't play, so I can't go anyway. But thanks for offering." I hesitate only for a beat before stepping forward and pulling him in for a tight hug. "Thanks for—all of it. Not only the skating support but the lunches, having my back at Winthrop. Those six months would've been a lot worse without you."

He hugs back hard. "Hey, no problem. What are friends for? And tell your brother I said to go kick some hockey-championship butt."

"Break a leg at nationals," I say, instantly recoiling with a head shake. "Not literally this time."

Frankie's laugh choruses with mine. "Yeah, no. I'm over that broken-bone life for real. Thanks, Charlie."

With one last quick hug, I rush out of the Blizzard—keeping my head down so I don't accidentally make eye contact with Geri or Alexa.

Twenty-Eight

As predicted, Caribou Hockey wins the following three play-off matchups. All of Winthrop buzzes with anticipation as we're set to rematch against the shithead Snow Leopards in the league championship next Sunday afternoon.

I'm jazzed about Jade's big art show tonight because I'm beyond stoked for her. It's a bonus perk that I get to dress up in my suit again, the invitation including a "formal attire recommended" note at the bottom.

Emily comes over to help with hair and makeup. She lets out a low whistle as she reenters my room after applying her makeup in the bathroom. "Damn, Charlie. I almost wish you were my date tonight."

I gasp. "Flyin' Brian's gonna be *devastated*. It'll be a hard enough blow to his ego once he realizes I wear a suit better than he does."

Em giggles. "Let me see. Strike a few poses for me." She holds up her phone and prepares to take some pics.

With a light laugh, I strut around my bedroom, pinning her with a few obnoxious, smoldering stares.

"Work it, Porter! *Wooo!*"

My hand slides into my pocket, which I assumed was empty, and my eyebrows knit as I pull out the rectangular piece of plastic.

It's the room key from the hotel we stayed in for Alexa's cousin's wedding. My face falls, heart plummeting as I recall just how damn *happy* I was that night. The start of me and Lex skating over that line from newfound friendship to so much more.

Emily's voice tugs me from my reverie and she peers at the key card, with its hotel logo. Then she rests a hand on my upper arm. "Hey. You wanna talk about it?"

She and Jade have been really great treading gently around the Alexa topic over the past couple months. They know I miss her. They occasionally urge me to text her back or swing by the Blizzard after one of her training sessions for a quick conversation, simply to give me some better closure. And while I agree with them on that point, I remind them I'm too damn cowardly to text her back, let alone show up for a face-to-face convo.

"I'm good," I assure Emily as I toss the key on my bedside table. "We should get going soon, right? Set up your treats display?"

"Def! Let's head down. The guys are probably ready to go." Emily's springy floral dress flows around her as she leads the way down the stairs, where Mac and Brian wait wearing unwrinkled dress shirts, pressed slacks, and ties.

Brian's eyes sparkle upon seeing Emily all dressed up. Then he looks at me and frowns, mumbling to Mac. "Should we be wearing jackets, bro?"

Mac shakes his head with a chuckle. "Nah. Charlie's extra when it comes to formal wear."

I strike a pose, tugging the lapels of my suit jacket. "Damn right I am. C'mon, let's go."

Mac drives, Brian navigates, and in the back seat Emily and I protect the four large Tupperware containers between us full of cup-cakes, cookies, and brownies. For the past few months Emily has been nailing her grain-free baking attempts—so much so that last week Emily asked Jade if she could provide baked goods for Jade's exhibit visitors, and Jade was all too grateful to accept.

The Winthrop Art Center is a hip gallery in the heart of town a few blocks away from the Beanery. We arrive twenty minutes before tonight's event officially opens, rushing to find Jade hanging her favorite oil-painting pieces around her designated display space.

One look at her and Em and I openly gape.

"Seriously, Jade? What the hell?" I cry with faux frustration.

Jade juts her hip to the side and tosses her hair twists back over her shoulder. "You're not the only girl who can rock a hot suit, Porter."

"*Daaaamn.* Okay, fair enough." After a quick tripod selfie in support of Jade's big night, we get to work.

Emily assigns Brian and Mac the task of unloading her sweet treats onto the refreshment table nearest to Jade's station. While they handle that, she and I stroll around the space and admire Jade's work—not sketches hastily doodled in notebooks (which are impressive in their own right), but medium-to-full-size paintings framed or on bare canvas hanging on a white wall for maximum impact. Jade's RISD portfolio centerpiece is mounted most prominently and we silently admire it under the warm lighting, appreciating every detail.

My loud mouth breaks the silence. "This makes me want tattoos even more," I declare.

Jade hums. "You know what? Me too."

Emily grins. "Oooh, we should get bestie tats when we graduate next year. Jade can design 'em."

"First RISD over Haverford Science Camp, now *tattoos*? I'm not sure how many of these life-altering decisions a mother can take." Hattie Douglas stands beside Dr. Ed. They're both wearing seriously expensive-looking formal wear and matching wide grins.

Edward holds out his arms first. "Hi, baby."

Jade all but leaps into her parents' arms, sunshine radiating from all three of them. "I'm so happy you guys could make it."

"We wouldn't miss it."

Emily sniffles beside me, dabbing the corners of her eyes with a tissue.

I nudge her with my elbow, amusement curling on my lips. "Dude, *keep it together*."

Once the Douglases disentangle their arms, Hattie and Dr. Ed move toward us next. "Get in here, girls! We've missed you, too!"

"Back at you!" I hug both of Jade's parents alongside Emily, then I nod behind me toward the walls featuring Jade's work. "Check out your girl's latest. She's pretty freakin' amazing."

Their gazes follow my head nod.

Dr. Edward's eyes fill with tears while Hattie audibly gasps. They step forward to take a closer look, Jade launching into her spiel about her inspiration, materials used, and hours dedicated, along with her plans for every piece after the exhibit closes.

Em and I step back to give Jade some family time while more attendees fill the gallery.

Soothing jazz music streams throughout the space, and while Emily turns to restock some of her baked goods, I pluck two champagne flutes from a pyramid-shaped drink display, handing one off to Em. "Sparkling grape juice."

"Ahhh, right." Emily accepts her glass. "Student event, so no booze. I was wondering why it wasn't guarded by someone checking IDs. Cheers, though!" She clinks her glass against mine. Then she takes a sip and glances toward the door, doing a double take. "Um . . . Charlie?" She clears her throat.

I whirl around and damn near drop my drink.

Alexa meanders through the exhibit nearest to the door. She's more goddess-like than I remember in her beaded green formal jumpsuit and heels; the strikingness of her whole look honestly feels like a personal attack.

Emily's lips roll inward. "Do you want me to run interference or something?"

Before I can answer, Alexa shifts and spots me. She hesitates before casting a soft wave.

"No, it's okay. I should probably—what you guys said about closure? I'm gonna—yeah." Steeling my nerves, I shove my free hand into my pocket. My shiny loafers suddenly seem to weigh twenty pounds each as I make my way toward her.

Alexa, noting my approach, meets me halfway. "Hi," she croaks. She's not yelling. That feels like a win off the bat.

"Hey. Didn't know you had a thing for art. . . ."

"Jade invited me," she blurts, a faint flush pinking her cheeks. "Oh, I don't think I was supposed to tell you that, but I didn't want you to think I stalked you here or anything."

"She did? I wouldn't think that anyway." I glance back over my shoulder in time to spy Jade looking on, shooting me a hard look. Her voice floats through my head without her mouth moving.

Grow a pair, Porter.

I should probably be furious with her for inviting Alexa behind my back, but I'm not. Not now that Alexa's here, calm and curious.

Turning back toward her, a few notes of a decompressing chuckle puff free to break the awkward silence. "So, how are you?"

Alexa folds her arms over her chest in a self-soothing type of way. "I'm all right, I guess. As well as I can be a week out from nationals. Mom almost didn't let me leave the house tonight, but I promised I'd only stay for a little. I just . . ." She blows out a hard breath. "I needed to see you. Are you okay?"

"Me?" I blink. "I'm fine. You're the one who had to heal from a concussion and immediately throw yourself into even more intense training."

"Yes, you. You didn't answer my texts. You didn't come back

to school when you should have. I've been worried." Despite everything, her eyes swirl with concern. "I've also been confused and heartbroken and furious, for the record."

My eyes drop to my carbonated juice. "Yeah, I get it. You have every right to be. That was shitty of me for making you feel those things. I'm sorry. Truly."

"Feeling sorry doesn't *solve* anything." An impatient huff emits through her rouge-painted lips. "I don't need you to be sorry. Charlie, look at me." She reaches out and curls her fingers beneath my chin, urging my head upward until my eyes lock back on hers.

The depth of emotion I find in her steady, intense gaze steals my breath.

Her words, shaky yet certain, release in a lower tone meant only for me. "I need you to understand that I'm *hurt*. You hurt me, but not the way you think. I'm not mad about the crash and my injury. I'm hurt because you walked away from me. You walked away while I was too weak to fight for you to stay, and that wasn't fair. I deserved that chance. We'd been through too much together for you to just— abandon me like that, Charlie. You *abandoned* me."

Her words strike my chest and ripple through me harder than a collective unobstructed check into the boards from an entire pro team.

You abandoned me.

Those three words echo in my ears and play on repeat, shooting a haunting chill down my spine. How long have I agonized over my mom leaving me? Not being there when I needed her most? And now here I am—doing the same thing to someone I care a hell of a lot more for than I'm brave enough to admit to myself.

There are so many things I want to say. I want to apologize a billion times over. I want to own up to my shitty decision to walk, explain why I did that, or at least attempt to explain. I want to tell her

I'm working with a therapist to try and get better. I'm *trying*.

Though with Alexa standing here before me looking as strong and beautiful as ever, even in the midst of such an emotionally charged conversation—it's suddenly clear as Zamboni-fresh ice.

I'm not trying *enough*.

I'm hiding from her. From my intense, overwhelming feelings. I'm keeping everything buried and tucked away to deal with later—because I haven't been brave enough to face my real issue.

The truth is, I walked away so she couldn't walk away first.

I abandoned her the instant something felt insurmountable, before *she* had a chance to abandon *me*.

Before I formulate any words that come close to articulating any of those things, she's releasing my chin and taking a step back, smoothing down the bodice of her beaded jumpsuit in an attempt to regain some composure.

"There. I've said what I've been wanting to say." She takes a deep breath, swallowing against the lump of emotion coating her tone. "I hate how things ended between us, but I'll forever be grateful for your help and I truly want what's best for you."

What's best for me? *You're what's best for me.* It's right there, on the tip of my tongue—but the moment my lips part, a wave of bottled-up feelings all but strangle me, and I'm forced to close them again before some sort of broken, pathetic sob escapes instead.

Clearly sensing my internal struggle, Alexa summons her best smile. It's the saddest damn smile I've ever seen, which only serves to shatter what's left of my heart into dust. "One more thing. We'll be live on ESPN next Saturday. Promise me you'll tune in? If not for me, then watch for Frankie."

The mention of Frankie and ESPN somehow dislodges whatever thorn was trapped in my windpipe. My grin twitches with a mirroring pained sadness. "You think I'd be able to skip you finally getting your revenge over the Ingleborgs and putting the *gold* in Goldstein? I won't miss it."

A brief sparkle returns to Alexa's eyes, but it's gone in a blink. "Thanks, Charlie. Take care of yourself, okay?"

I nod, my shoes rooting to the spot while Alexa walks past me to, no doubt, greet Jade and appreciate her artwork. After a minute or so, I duck through an archway into an adjacent exhibit. I face someone else's portrait of an old dude on the rear wall, hoping anyone passing by will mistake the tears streaming down my cheeks for me being intensely moved by the artwork.

I manage to keep my shit together throughout the next hour, not selfish enough to make a scene in a space dedicated to celebrating other people's accomplishments.

After the event, Jade's parents take her, me, and Emily out to a nice Italian restaurant. I know Jade and Em sense my heartache— it's a rare meal when I'm not fighting them for an extra breadstick or polishing off my entire bowl of spaghetti and meatballs. Instead, I remain polite, albeit quiet, knowing what a special treat it is for Jade to have her parents in town for a visit. Graciously thanking both of them after we finish, I take my leftovers box and hop into Emily's car since the three of us plan to sleep over at her place.

I wait until we're washed up with pj's on before curling up on Emily's queen-size bed, finally letting everything spill. I share the way I pressured Alexa into that triple throw, ultimately ending in her concussion and the all-consuming guilt racking my body ever since. How I left her there at the hospital when she begged me to stay, unable to face not only what I'd done but the deep-rooted fear she'd leave me for it. My gold-medal-caliber ghosting. Then I tell them about the harsh but true words she struck me with at the gallery tonight. The feelings she stirred calling back to my issues with my mother.

The deep, terrifying realization that I might be just like her.

While I ramble on in semicoherent sentences, my best friends listen. Emily strokes my hair while Jade offers tissues, both of them not daring to cut me off as they absorb every detail.

When I finally crest for air, I sit up and blow my nose. They take a pause to process, and it's Emily who speaks up first.

"I don't want to diminish your feelings, Charlie. They're all totally valid. I think Jade and I are well aware you've been doing a not-so-hot job getting over Alexa—"

"Hence the invitation tonight," Jade cuts in. "Which I'm not sorry about, by the way. Something had to give."

"I know, I get it. I'm not mad." I sniffle. "And it's also why I don't feel guilty being the center of attention right now on your big night, since you triggered this conversation."

Jade waves me off. "Please. My big night's over and it was *amazing*. This is important, and it's been a long time coming."

Em nods. "It's pretty clear to both of us you're miserable without her. I think we're all in agreement when I say she brings out the best in you, and from what you've told us, I'm pretty sure you bring out the best in her, too. So if you still want to be with her, you simply need to . . . unabandon her."

"Simply?" I frown. "It's not that easy."

Jade offers me a fresh tissue. "No, it won't be easy. But if she's what you want, then it'll be worth it."

Gentle teasing carries in Emily's voice. "Also, please. Since when do you shy away from hard work? I get that you were training a thousand hours per week learning all those fancy figure skating moves, but really, Char. If *you* can curate a romantic Taylor Swift playlist, you can do anything you set your mind to."

My hoarse laugh bounces off Emily's bedroom walls, Em and Jade laughing along with me.

My ribs hurt from crying, and laughing doesn't help the ache, yet cuddling with my best friends soothes my soul in a way nothing else can.

They're right. I'm the only one standing in my way here. If I want to fix this, I need to prove to Alexa I'm not an abandoner. I need to show up for her in a *big* way. I'm not sure how yet, but I'm desperate to figure it out somehow.

Porters never back down from a challenge, after all.

Twenty-Nine

I spend the week trying to plan my grand romantic gesture to win back Alexa, but nothing big enough comes to mind. Saturday morning, Jade and Emily come over bright and early and the three of us whip up a big breakfast. Mac joins us as we all pile eggs, bacon, and pancakes onto our plates, settling in around the living room couch and coffee table. Bracing myself to experience more Alexa-related emotions, I turn on the TV and flip to ESPN airing the Pairs Skating National Championships live.

"Turn it up, Char!" Emily squints at the list of skating pairs displayed on the screen. "Ooooh, they're skating first!"

I turn up the volume, wondering how Geri and Alexa might feel about that random draw.

"—and welcome to this year's National Junior Pairs Figure Skating Championships. We're broadcasting live from the Onyx Ice Arena in Ann Arbor, Michigan. Sixteen pairs have qualified for today's competition and only three will stand atop the podium at the end of the day. Last year's gold medalists, Mason and Mallory Ingleborg, of Deerfield, New Hampshire, are currently favored to repeat—"

I grumble. "Of course they are."

"—with two other pairs coming in as favorites with a chance to win the title? Richard Hastings and Amanda Royal, of Rochester, New York, and Frankie Drake and Alexa Goldstein, of Winthrop, Vermont. Though it should be noted Frankie Drake limped off the ice *after warm-ups, and it's unclear how healthy he'll be as he skates through today's programs. . . ."*

My face falls. "Wait, what? *Shit*."

"Frankie reinjured his ankle?" Jade snags her phone to, no doubt, jump on social media in search of more details.

"Maybe he's just sore. . . ." Wishful thinking, I know, but I can barely eat I'm so damn anxious for this to go well for them. My eyeballs glue to the TV as Alexa and Frankie skate onto the ice, their matching grins flashing in HD on our large screen as they ready themselves to kick off the competition.

My heart tweaks and soars in the same moment as the familiar *Wicked* track—with Frankie pulling off that green face paint far better than I ever could—fills our living room through surround-sound speakers. They look amazing. The camera pans close before they begin, showing their expressions focused and ready. And though I'm not the one skating, I hold my breath on every jump combination, every throw and lift, unblinking throughout the entire routine.

On the final jump sequence, Frankie over-rotates and uses his newly healed ankle to plant harder and stop himself from falling. Ever professional, his wince near instantly morphs into a genuine smile—so quickly I wonder if I'm the only one who catches it.

Then Alexa physically supports his balance with her arm around his middle as he skates one-legged off-ice.

"Oh no, is Frankie hurt? They looked so great during their performance!" Emily shifts on the couch.

Jade emits a low whistle. "Doesn't look good to me. What do you think?"

During the tense Kiss and Cry, a grimacing Frankie unlaces his skates as they're announced to have earned a respectable score despite having no other pairs to compare to just yet.

Scrambling for my laptop, I frantically google the National Pairs Figure Skating Rule Book. My finger tracks the text on my screen as I read aloud. *"In the event a pairs skater is injured between programs during competition, an alternate skater from the same club may be named replacement in his or her stead."*

Jade leans forward. "Charlie, does this mean—"

"I'm going to Michigan." The words burst free before I take any time to think them through, but I need to do this for Frankie. For Geri. For Alexa most of all.

This is it. My chance to show up for Alexa when she might need me most.

Jade holds up her phone. "They're scheduled to skate last for the free skate. You can fly out soon, make it there in time."

Emily's posture snaps straighter. "Oh my god, seriously? You're gonna skate with Alexa?"

When Em asks directly, I hesitate. Making snap decisions hasn't served me well in the past, so I take a moment to think through this. Is the idea of skating in front of an even more massive crowd this time high-key terrifying? Absolutely. Does the Neverland routine spark extreme anxiety after my botched throw injured Alexa last time? Of course.

And yet I can't abandon her again. Not when she might need me more than ever. "Yes. If she'll let me. No doubt Frankie will consider pushing it on his bad ankle, but he sure as hell shouldn't—he couldn't even put any weight on it when Lex helped him off-ice. He's a competitor through and through, but I don't want him hurting himself permanently, and neither do Geri and Alexa."

Dad had been cleaning up in the kitchen, listening in. He steps into the garage before shuffling into the living room. "You're gonna need these." He drops a pair of skates beside me.

My figure skates. Cleaned and buffed, their blades extra shiny. I gasp, reaching out to accept them with shock and awe written all over my face. "But I wrecked these on the pond. How did you know—"

"I found them in the trunk," Mac says with a cool shrug. "Saw them busted up, figured you didn't have the heart to put them in an actual garbage can. I got the blades replaced. The boots are professionally cleaned, too."

My eyes snap to Mac, breath catching. "You did that for me?"

He smiles through a mouthful of eggs. "I know you've been missing skating. Figured it was only a matter of time before you decided to get back on that horse. Porters aren't quitters."

"Damn right we're not." Dad claps Mac on the back.

A stunned chuckle escapes and I nod. "Wow. Okay. So I'm really gonna do this. I'm going to Michigan?"

"*We're* going to Michigan." Jade's phone chirps. "Just booked us a twelve o'clock flight with my emergencies-only credit card. Hattie will understand."

"Oh my god." I scramble to my feet. "I gotta pack my stuff!"

"You'll be back for the match tomorrow, right?" Mac scans the three of us. "You've got return flights, too?"

"Don't worry, Cap." I ruffle Mac's hair on my way to the stairs. "I won't miss our shot at redemption."

Triple redemption, if I've got any say in it.

Mac against Winthrop High hockey.

Frankie, Alexa, and me against the Ingleborgs.

Me against myself.

This time, I've gotta be different. Unselfish. No matter what happens, I'm going to stay.

And there's nothing I want more than to help Alexa earn her gold medal—whether it involves me stepping back and cheering her on if Frankie's okay to skate, or taking over and skating the shit out of that routine. The right way this time.

Ninety minutes later, the three of us race through the Burlington Airport, completely winded as we barely make it to the gate right before they seal the door. Then we board our flight from Vermont to Michigan. I sit between Emily and Jade. During the two-hour flight, I fasten my earbuds in and alternate between mentally reviewing our free skate—just in case—and listening to my chill-out playlist, my knee bouncing all throughout takeoff and a while after.

I may have pure intentions, but the reality is that I haven't worn figure skates in two months. Do I remember the *Neverland* routine? Every beat of it, without question. We drilled that shit so hard I couldn't forget it if I tried. Am I still in shape? Hell yeah. I've been working out off-ice consistently. Still, the cold fact remains— I haven't practiced *figure skating*.

Ugh, I *really* hope Frankie feels fine. He trained his whole life for this—surely he's generally more prepared to skate for a national title even when he's not feeling 100 percent. Best-case scenario? I'll sit in the crowd with Em and Jade, cheering Alexa and Frankie on to victory.

I'm bracing myself for the alternative. That's why I'm making this trip, after all—to be a safety net for Alexa, as I've trained to be since September.

As soon as the plane touches down, Jade taps her phone off airplane mode and loads the ESPN app. "Okay. The free skates are halfway through."

I peek at her screen. "They're still slated to skate last, that's good." *Knee Bouncing: The Sequel* strikes as the plane taxis to the gate. "Are we gonna make it?"

"Maybe." Emily scrolls frantically through the competition social feeds. "Someone posted that Frankie and Alexa announced they'll make a game-time decision whether or not they'll skate."

"Good. That gives us more time." I consider texting Alexa, but there's no point. She, Frankie, and Geri are safely ensconced in their midprogram distraction-free bubble, purposely shutting out the world so they don't psych themselves out while no doubt agonizing over whether or not to push Frankie to skate on an injured ankle.

"Okay, the tenth pair's starting now." Jade pops up before the plane connects to the tunnel thingy, pitching her voice louder. "Make way, passengers! Future national pairs figure skating champion coming through!"

"Jesus, Jade . . ." Laughing, my stomach flips as I sling my backpack over my shoulder.

Emily snags my bag carrying my skates from the overhead compartment and we rush up the aisle first, apologizing to the pissed-off flight attendants and pilots.

We book it through the Detroit airport, Jade hailing a Lyft, which waits for us when we reach the exit.

I dive into the back seat, frantically undressing.

"Eyes on the road, my guy." Jade casts a hard glare at the driver from the front passenger seat. "You gotta get us to the Onyx Ice Arena as fast as possible."

"I'll do my best, ladies. Buckle up."

While I twist to pull on my brown patchwork costume pants and socks for the *Finding Neverland* routine, Emily tracks the live stream. "The Ingleborgs are up now."

"Don't tell me if they crush their long." No doubt they will. I peel off my hoodie and swap it for my gray Henley shirt, tucking it into my pants while I fish into my bag for my suspenders.

"They did really great, Char. Solidly in first place."

"Figures." I roll my eyes. "No pun intended."

Emily raises her phone to show me the ESPN app. "Oh, look!"

The announcers flash to Alexa and Frankie off-ice.

"After devastating falls from Amanda Royal and Richard Hastings, all eyes will no doubt be on Alexa Goldstein and Frankie Drake. If they can pull off a solid free skate, they stand the best chance at knocking the reigning champions off the top of the medal podium. They'll need to go all out as the Ingleborgs nailed their routine—possibly because Mallory Ingleborg recently announced a retirement from competitive figure skating after this season to pursue a more traditional collegiate career."

I watch Emily's phone while tugging on my skating socks. In the performers' tunnel, Alexa paces back and forth in her light blue beaded costume as Frankie sits on the bench, a pained look fixed on his face while he massages his ankle. Geri looks on with concern, shaking her head—clearly visibly torn as to whether or not to encourage Frankie to skate.

"We gotta *get there*." Goddamn traffic jam.

"Fourteenth pair's skating now," Emily says.

I pull my hair back into a low messy bun and slide my feet back into my boots.

Bouncing on the seat, I quietly perform my calming breathing exercises and stretch my arms and legs as best as possible within the limited space.

Jade monitors her traffic app, commanding the driver through an alternate route.

"The fifteenth pair just stepped onto the ice. Alexa and Frankie are up next, Charlie."

The driver zooms to the entrance and pulls to a sharp stop, brakes screeching.

I bolt from the car with my bags in hand, Emily and Jade following close behind.

Right before entering the rink from the lobby, I yank off my

Converse and jam my feet into my figure skates, hands shaking with an injection of preperformance nerves as I lace them up.

Jade talks rapid fire to the security guard at the door, explaining the situation while motioning to me and my skates.

Security lets us through.

We pass through the double doors, the judges' voices boom through the (holy shit, *pro-hockey-size*) arena, scoring the second-to-last skaters.

Emily takes my shoes. "Hurry, Charlie!"

Jade scans the ice with her analytical eye and points to the table where four judges sit with bulky headphones secured over their ears and microphones propped before them. "I'll go let the announcers know there might be a change of plans so it's official. Go on and crush it out there, would you?" Jade winks and rushes into the rink. "If Frankie skates, we'll save you a seat."

"Thanks, guys. I owe you big-time."

My skates are laced, and Emily offers a reassuring squeeze on my arm. "Go kick some butt, Porter!"

"You got it, Em."

Geri stands beside the rink wall door, anxiety tightening every muscle in her face.

I rush closer as Alexa steps onto the ice first to a cheering crowd.

Frankie takes one step onto the ice and I snatch his suspenders from behind, tugging him back.

Geri gasps.

"What the—" Frankie whirls around, his jaw falling comically slack. *"Charlie?"*

"Hey, are you good to skate this?" I ask, my gaze flickering down to his right foot and back to his eyes.

"What—" He swallows hard, glances at Geri, and freezes.

I shake his shoulder to pull his attention back on me. "Dude, the ankle. Are you at eighty percent or twenty percent? Because I sure as hell can't beat your eighty percent, but I might do better than your twenty." Holy shit—look at me doing *math*! "Unless Geri wants me to bounce out of here, which I totally get."

Geri considers us both as we stand before her in matching routine outfits. "It's your decision."

She must know we both have Alexa's best interest at heart.

Frankie shakes his head, exhaling with relief as he steps back. "It hurts like a bitch and a half. It's all yours to skate."

I wince. "You're sure?"

"*A hundred* percent. This is your routine, Charlie. Yours and hers." He urges me ahead in his place. "Get out there."

Alexa turns around at center ice, confusion and concern etching in her brow as her partner doesn't immediately follow.

Skating toward her with a bashful sort of smile flickering, I roll up my sleeves and glide to a stop in front of her.

Her eyes pop wide, color draining from her face.

"You look like you just saw a ghost," I say, stopping a foot away from her. "Which, that's fair, since I've been basically ghosting you. Like a dick."

"Charlie—"

"I'm so sorry," I burst, my arms falling to my sides, palms open. Guard down, anxiety up.

Tens of thousands of people mutter confusion all around us.

I push on, my focus solely on Alexa. "Lex, I was selfish and a coward and I shouldn't have walked away like I did. My reaction and the ghosting all stemmed from my issues with my mom that I should've dealt with way sooner—but I'm working on it now and I'd do anything to go back to that moment in the hospital and do things differently. Literally anything. You deserve someone who's gonna show up for you no matter what, and I still want to be that person for you. *Please* give me another chance. I miss you every day. Like hell."

I may or may not have blacked out during that epic ramble. Didn't exactly stick the landing there. But as with skating, I'm hoping what I lack in technique I make up for with enthusiasm and heart.

Alexa exhales in a barking, stunned chuckle. "You wanna make it up to me?"

I glance down to my skates, then back up to her. "I mean, yeah. I'm here, aren't I?" If this doesn't prove I'm all in, what will?

"Triples," she says, planting her hands on her hips with a challenging sparkle in her eye.

It's my turn to pale. "*What?* I can't! I can only land them, like, one out of every five attempts. I won't hurt you again—"

"Stop. Listen. We took a risk together, Charlie, and it didn't work out. Reaching higher than you should doesn't mean you're a bad person. Sometimes the risk is worth it." She points up to the leaderboard. "We're behind and we need two flawless triple-double combos instead of the double-singles we've practiced to have a shot at first place. This isn't a qualifier. This is for a medal, and I want to put the *gold* in Goldstein, dammit!" Her eyes alight with that fierceness I've grown to associate with the thrill of a big victory on the line. "If I didn't think you could, I wouldn't ask you to, but this is how you'll make it up to me. Two triple-doubles. One in the opening sequence, the other in the final sequence. Plus the triple throw."

The announcer taps his mic. *"In a last-minute injury substitution— Alexa Goldstein will be performing her free skate with partner Charlie Porter, also from the Blizzard Skating Club of Winthrop, Vermont."*

"Okay," I croak. "Triple-doubles. If you think I can."

"I know you can." Her perfectly shaped eyebrows arch as she tilts her chin upward. "I'm the know-it-all, remember?"

I snort. "Guess you got me there." Blowing out a hard, calming breath, I extend my hand for our opening pose.

She takes it, her eyes flickering toward our point of contact. As she spots one of my Band-Aids—the green one with the figure skates—curled around my pinkie finger, her smile softens. She winks.

The flute solo from our free skate track fades in and we share one intense, steadying look before gliding forward together for our first intricate choreography sequence. Immediately, we skate more in sync than the last time we attempted this routine, whisked away in our own little bubble in Neverland.

Our second chance. The one neither of us thought we'd ever get.

Maybe it's the magic of the moment for me—not only a hockey player but also a *figure skater* returning home after months away. And despite my lack of practice or warm-up, I slip right back into place without missing a beat. My worries fade away and there's nowhere else in the world I'd rather be right now than skating here with her under the brightest spotlight there is.

"And here's their first jump combination—double lutz, single loop . . ." The announcer whispers into his microphone as we turn backward and count off, crouch, and hit our toe-picks to launch into the air side by side in perfect sync, landing together with a satisfying, singular crunch. *"It's a triple-double! Alexa Goldstein and Charlie Porter upped their technical difficulty with a triple lutz, double loop, and a clean landing for both skaters. Wow!"*

We transition into a bold lift. I hoist Alexa into the air, skating down ice while twisting her over my head helicopter style. The crowd applauds as she gracefully slinks back down my body and I hold her around the middle, dipping both of us into a tight spiral, our joined hands extending upward.

Our next choreography sequence carries on without error. The lyrics backing us keep me away from the intimidating Onyx Ice

Arena, my mind safely tucked in the clouds with Alexa as we skate in perfect tandem, stroking back up ice to pick up speed.

"—another jump combination—and another surprise triple-double! Triple salchow, double toe loop. Beautiful execution!"

Resisting the urge to pump my fist in an unchoreographed reaction, we twirl side by side at center ice, shadowing each other in our sit spins.

"—if they keep this up, they could possibly earn enough points to overtake Mason and Mallory Ingleborg—"

This isn't about a medal for me. It never has been.

This is about proving I can be more than a practice partner.

It's about proving I care about more than myself—in a partnership, on a whole team.

That I've got what it takes to compete in this super-intense sport I've fallen in love with.

That I can both show up for and keep up with the super-intense *girl* I've fallen in love with.

Keeping Alexa as my sole focus, it's easy to shut out the thousands of spectators as we skate through the rest of our program, the music winding down to our big finale.

Controlling and channeling the energy in my body, I breathe hard as Alexa skates up to me at full speed. Taking her by the waist, I twist her in my arms. We lock eyes, count back from three together, and I launch her into the air with perfect force and height this time.

Alexa twists not two but three times midair, landing with a steady swoosh on one foot, her back leg kicking out and arms extending to the side.

The crowd *roars*, bursting through our faraway Neverland bubble.

My smile splits wide and I take her hand, skating back toward center ice as we gracefully finish our final sequence.

Squinting in the spotlight, I find my best friends in the stands yelling and jumping in place with everyone packed in around them.

I finally notice the bulky TV cameras with their ESPN logos emblazoned beneath the lenses.

Alexa curls into me.

I duck my face into the crook of her neck, full-body trembling with a massive dose of postperformance adrenaline pumping through my veins.

We cling to each other at center ice as the cheering continues— far louder than it had for the pair before.

Flowers and stuffed animals flood the rink all around us.

Eventually, Alexa pulls back and beams at me, tears streaming down her cheeks.

I grin, reaching up to brush them away with the pads of my thumbs while barely managing to blink mine back.

Skating off-ice, Alexa rushes into Geri's waiting arms.

I accept the water bottle and a tight hug from Frankie, nerves once again spiking as I stand before Geri . . . after risking Alexa's neck again. But we landed it this time. With that fact in my back pocket, I summon all the chill I can muster and cast her a dorky salute. "Not bad, huh, Coach?"

She steps forward and wraps her arms around me for a hug so tight a soft *oof* escapes. "Thank you, Charlie." Her eyes swim with watery pride when she pulls back. "You were incredible."

Relief floods my system, dizzying in the best way.

After fastening our blade guards, Alexa laces our fingers and tugs me toward the judging bench for the Kiss and Cry, Geri standing behind us as we huddle together and collectively hold our breaths.

The scores flash on the jumbotron above.

The crowd erupts.

Geri *screams*.

Alexa once again throws her arms around my neck.

I quit breathing altogether.

GOLDSTEIN/PORTER
PAIRS FREE SKATE
TECHNICAL SCORE: 64.68
PROGRAM COMPONENTS SCORE: 80.82
FREE SKATE TOTAL: 145.50 (FIRST PLACE)

"They've done it! Combined with the short program score, Alexa Goldstein and Charlie Porter edge out the Ingleborgs to win gold! Wow, what a comeback performance—a crowd favorite featuring a cold-skater fill-in and nailing their routine? The first same-sex team not only skating in a Pairs Skating National Championships event— but earning gold? History made in more ways than one! Or should I say herstory! *Either way, surely the performance everyone here will remember for quite some time."*

On shaky legs, we keep our hands linked as we walk on blade guards up a narrow red carpet to the three-tiered podium now affixed at center ice. Stepping up to the middle, tallest platform, we bow our heads and accept our gold medals from the president of the National Figure Skating Association.

I admire its weight and shininess for a moment before hopping off the platform, approaching Frankie. Then I remove the gold medal from my neck and hang it around his.

Tears slide down Frankie's cheeks as he tugs me in for another fierce hug. "She's all yours now," he mutters into my ear. Pulling back, he sniffles.

My head cocks to the side. "What's that supposed to mean?"

He laughs. "Don't worry, it's all good. I'll explain later. Get back up there with your girl."

I nod and clap his arm before returning to the podium.

Alexa looks on with an achingly fond expression. "You earned that gold medal just as much as Frankie. We can get a third made—you both deserve one."

Shrugging, I slide my arms around her middle. "Nah, we'll just have to win another one next year instead. Maybe of the Olympic variety?" My eyebrows wag. "Besides, I don't need a medal when I've got the biggest prize right here."

Alexa rolls her eyes, looping her arms around my neck. "You're such a cheeseball. . . ."

"You love it. C'mere." I dip down and kiss her, ignoring the popping flashbulbs, cheers, and wolf whistles all around us—Geri, Frankie, Emily, and Jade the loudest among them, while I'm sure Dad and Mac are celebrating just as loud from home.

Lex and I remain lip-locked as I lift her into the air.

Which is kind of our thing, you know?

Six Months Later

A week into senior year, I finish my classes for the day and the good brand of anxiety swoops in. I'm standing in the bathroom with Jade and Emily on either side of me as the dull chatter of a gathering crowd filters inside.

Jade brushes out my hair, pinning a few strands out of my face.

"C'mon, guys. I can't be late. You know I'm gonna put a hat on in a few minutes, right?"

"You're not late—you're the lady of the hour! The party can't start without you," Emily declares, straightening the knot of my tie and plucking a piece of lint from my Cranford-issued sweater vest.

I chuckle, fidgeting before taking a deep, calming breath. Then I peek out from the bathroom and baby bats take off in my stomach.

School dismissed for the day thirty minutes ago, and since then the hallowed lobby of Cranford Prep transformed for a ceremony. *My* ceremony. Specifically—my official letter of intent signing. The Cranford Prep official backdrop stands facing the main doors, and several rows of chairs line up in front of it. Before the backdrop, a table dressed with a thick black cloth displays three hats turned out toward the gathering crowd. Behind each hat, the letter of intent for each university.

All three of my full-scholarship commitment offers waiting for my decision.

"All right, let's do this." With a steadying nod, I stride out from the bathroom and wave, surprised by so many butts in the seats. My classmates, several teachers and coaches I've given gray hairs to over the years. Flyin' Brian, Matty, Nicole, and the rest of my teammates clustered together. Dad and Mac sit in the front row on one side and Jade and Emily scurry over to join them. On the other side of the aisle, Alexa sits between Frankie and Geri. Cyn sits on Frankie's other side.

My mom's a no-show yet again, but that's no surprise. Lately I've been better at focusing on who shows up for me when I need them rather than who doesn't. The people in the first two rows are my family, blood or not.

A gentle hand settles over my shoulder.

Dean Quigley grins with pride and pulls me in for a hug before motioning for me to sit behind the table. Then she clears her throat. "Ladies and gentlemen, esteemed colleagues and guests, members of the media. Welcome to Cranford Preparatory School. It's always a special occasion when we get to celebrate the wonderful accomplishments of our students—whether they be academic, athletic, artistic, or philanthropic in nature." She cuts me another glance. "This one's a particularly proud moment for me. Miss Charlotte Porter has been a pain in my rear end since a decade ago when she pranked her first-grade substitute into quitting."

The gathered guests laugh.

I offer a sheepish shrug, sharing a grin with our headmaster.

"But I'm delighted to report she's grown into a responsible, dedicated young woman with a bright future ahead of her. Particularly today, with quite an important decision to make. So without further ado, allow me to officially introduce our letter-of-intent honoree this afternoon. Charlie Porter."

Casting Quigley a salute, I clear my throat and lean into the skinny microphone propped in front of me. "Wow, that's the first time you've called me Charlie. Thanks, Quigs."

"Don't push it, dear." Dean Quigley stands off to the side.

Staring out at the people who came to support me, I take a moment to take in the moment. "So. Hey. Thanks for coming, everyone. It's been a hell of a year," I start, puffing out a stunned laugh. I cut a glance toward the Cranford trophy case—the Winthrop Cup back in its rightful home as of this past weekend, the silver tiered trophy standing proudly beside the league championship trophy Mac held over his head after he led the team to victory last spring. "I still can't believe I've got not only one hockey scholarship offer but three. All three of these programs are incredible, and I'm so humbled and honored they want me to play for them."

The three hats and intent letters laid out before me belong to D-I women's hockey teams: Penn State, Northeastern, and Wisconsin, all top-tier universities with deep and rich sports legacies, state-of-the-art facilities, and coaches who will train me up to the next level.

"Before I share my decision, I need to thank a bunch of people. First—Dean Quigley, you kicking me out of school for almost my entire junior year turned out to be the best thing that ever happened to me." The small crowd chuckles and Alexa tosses me a wink. "Thanks for never giving up on me for real. For welcoming me back and giving me another chance."

"My family. My dad; my big brother, Mac; and my two sisters, Jade and Emily." I focus among them and swallow the sudden lump in my throat. "Thanks for being the best. For supporting me in every possible way. Not sure how I scored the best family around, but I'm so damn lucky and I appreciate all of you so much."

"To my coaches. Coach Doug, who's gambling on giving me an assistant captain's patch this season. I won't let you down. And

Coach Geri . . ." My gaze finds hers across the aisle. "Thanks for taking a chance on me. For developing me not only as a skater but as a responsible human, and for pushing me to achieve more than I ever thought possible. For seeing a good person in me when I couldn't see it for myself. Thank you."

Geri daintily dabs her eyes at the corners and nods, working hard to compose herself as Alexa's head rests against her shoulder.

"Frankie, my dude. I would've had the worst time at Winthrop without you and Cyn. You've stuck by me through thick and thin this past year and I'm so grateful to have you in my corner." My eyes flicker to Mason Ingleborg—Frankie's new competition partner for this upcoming season—sitting behind him. "But you better watch your step, 'cause Lex and I are coming for you guys at regionals tomorrow."

Frankie and Mason shout a teasing boo, which lacks all heat and carries only happiness and respect, while the rest of the attendees cheer and jeer for a few lighthearted seconds.

"And last but certainly not least . . ." My focus finally wholly lands on Alexa—who's full-on crying, her smile rivaling the sun. "*Seriously?* You can't be a mess before I even start talking about you. What the hell. . . ." Fond laughter bubbles up from everyone else and I fish into my pocket for a tissue, rubbing my eyes. "All right, Alexa Michelle. What can I say? For some inexplicable reason, you trust me time and time again to launch you up into the air with nothing but solid ice below. Even when we fall—even when we screw up—we stick together and we run it again. You make me a better person in every way and I've never experienced this kind of support outside my family, and I promise—no matter where this college thing takes me—I'll always be here to catch you. No matter what."

Alexa wipes her cheeks and mouths those three most special

words, which never fail to strike me square in my chest and erupt like confetti.

After a moment of silence passes, Dean Quigley motions to the table before me. "I believe it's time to make your decision known, Miss Porter."

My posture straightens and I lean forward into the mic again. "Right. But before I sign one of these and put a dope new hat on, I'm excited to announce that all three of these universities have accepted my gap year deferral for one year after graduation—so I can make an official Olympic run with my girl."

The crowd gasps and bursts into applause. Geri and Alexa, along with my family—who already know about this slight detour—clap along.

"Speaking of," Geri cuts in. "I don't mean to rush your big moment, Charlie. But you're due for practice in twenty minutes."

Another round of laughter fills the Cranford lobby.

"Right, yeah. Got it, Coach." Picking up Dean Quigley's fancy fountain pen before me, I glance down at all three offer letters through blurry, tear-filled eyes.

I'm still super shitty at math, but with one last glance up at my people in the front row—all of them radiating with pride as I scrawl my signature on a paper and reach for a hat—I realize however I slice this equation, whichever path I sign onto for my future, the outcome's the same.

I can't lose.

Acknowledgments

What an immense privilege it is to be able to contribute an original story to the ever-growing body of YA literature centering queer love with a happy ending. This whole process has been a dream come true and earning this opportunity has been the greatest honor of my life. I could not have accomplished this without the support and encouragement of so many incredible people.

To my all-star literary agent, Claire Friedman of InkWell Management: I'm forever grateful for your belief in me and this book, your wizard-level communication skills, your sharp instinct for helping me mold story ideas, and your genuine, encouraging spirit. I wouldn't want anyone else in my corner to help me navigate every step of this publishing journey. Thank you for gifting me the opportunity to do what I love.

To my brilliant editor, Sarah Homer of Harper: You're amazing and it's been an absolute pleasure working with you to bring Charlie and Alexa to readers. Thank you for loving my girls as much as I do, and for your thoughtful vision and patient guidance to help me make their love story shine as bright as possible on the page. Thank you for being gentle and understanding with a rookie author and supporting me every step of the way.

Thank you to the editorial, design, marketing, and publicity teams at HarperCollins who helped give *Love/Skate* its extra pop and sparkle: Erika West, Mary Magrisso, Megan Gendell, Susan Bishansky, Nicole Goux, Julia Feingold, Alison Donalty, Audrey

Diestelkamp, Abby Dommert, and the sales team.

To Elayne Becker, whose invaluable feedback not only set Charlie and Alexa's story on the right path but also made me a stronger writer: Thank you for touching an underdeveloped version of this story with your talented brain and nurturing heart.

To Aimée Carter, my dear friend, publishing industry Obi-Wan, and the Roy Kent to my Ted Lasso: I wouldn't have had the courage to pursue book writing without your initial nudge and supportive guidance. Thank you for showing me I had the tools to make this dream a reality and lending your genius plot mind, writing advice, and cheerleading along the way.

To Kat Jenkinson, my #1 Scrabble sister: I treasure our friendship even more than I treasure our docs. (You know the ones ☺) Thank you for always reminding me to be kind to myself and also for being the best curator of funny internet content when I need it most.

To Leeanna Chetsko, speed-reader extraordinaire: Thank you for being the best beta reader a "binch" could ask for. I appreciate your eyes on my words every time. Thanks for always being willing to listen to my book brainstorm rambles.

To Bethany Zaiatz, Charlie and Alexa's #1 proud auntie: Thank you for creating absolute banger character playlists, being my go-to character fashion consultant, and always hyping me up when the doubt gremlins creep into my brain.

To my agent siblings, Maggie Horne, Jenni Howell, Jo Schulte, Rachel Moore, Dinesh Thiru, Skyla Arndt, Maggie North, Robin Lefler, Amy Goldsmith, Courtney Gould, Mary E. Roach, Jenna Voris, Marlee Bush, C. G. Drews, Allison Saft, Olivia Worley, Alli Hoff Kosik, and every other member of Claire's Hype House: Thank you for being so instantly welcoming to a newbie and keeping our group chat a safe, uplifting space.

To my wildly talented writer friends, whom I've been the luckiest to collaborate with over the years, Randa Tolbert, Karel Le Berre, Elissa Hillier, Roxy Irizarry, Clare Richardson, Shawn Mostafa Nadolny, and Megan Rufenach: Whether we wrote together days, months, or several years ago, you made me better simply by sharing your words with me. Thank you for providing a mutually trusting creative space to help me grow as a writer.

To my favorite librarians in the whole world, Deirdre McKeon, Sherry Hazlewood, and Randi Gordon: I've lost count of the number of times you've helped me during emotional moments along this roller-coaster publishing journey. Your unwavering belief in me and my writing deserving a spot on library shelves helped keep me going through the really tough or heartbreaking days. Thank you for being wonderful friends.

Thank you to my amazing friends who provided support and encouragement by reading my writing, listening to me stress about the publishing process, checking on my well-being, or celebrating my small wins along the way: Shana Album, K. G. Bautista, Nancy Bianchini, Margie Britton, Isadora Cabral, Andrea Clipsham, Teresa Costanzo, Tara Cutler, Holly Delauder, Dana Diamondstein, Claire Evans, Rachel Flood, Kari Hansen, Kaylee Hillier, Karolina Kayko, Sarah Kindler, Kristina Koppeser, Katia Kordek, Anna Krammes, Miranda Leiggi, Dottie Mazullo, Anastasia Mela, Shannon Menickella, Jillian Oliver, Jazmin Postell, Dawn Rice, Steve Shank, Rachael Slutsky, Liia Smith, Jackie Templin, Tom Thomas, Dana Wynne, Maureen Zdanis, and Michelle Zimmer. I'm so fortunate to have you in my life.

I'm so grateful to have experienced my formative childhood years receiving unwavering love from my family, who not only accept but celebrate who I am. Thank you to the best aunts and uncles: Elisa Corson, Darren Corson, Sheri Melcher, Michael

Melcher, Lori Herrmann, and Fred Segal. Thank you to my awesome "little" cousins, whom I had the privilege of witnessing grow from adorable babies all the way to kindhearted adults: Jill Gorham-Segal, Marisa Corson, Lexi Segal, Dylan Corson, Kayla Melcher, and Sam Melcher. I love and appreciate all of you beyond words.

To Grandmom Marlene, Pop-Pop Herby, Grandmom Sandy, and Pop-Pop Harvey: I realize how fortunate I am to have had all four of you for so long—and yet never long enough. Though you're no longer here with me, you've left indelible thumbprints on my heart. You're on every page. "Love you thiiiiiiiiiis much and back again!"

To my brother, Matt: It took me writing a few stories in various genres to realize "supportive brother figure" is a character type I instinctively include, and though it wasn't intentional, it absolutely stems from our relationship. From our competitive childhood antics like taking turns practicing WWE moves (you) and karate moves (me) on each other, to intense sleeping bag races down the staircase, to beating each other up at the bus stop over a lawn soccer game (sorry, Mom), we've always had each other's backs when it mattered most. I'm so proud of the dude, the teacher, and the father you've become. The smartest decision you ever made was adding the world's best sister-in-law, Christa, to our crew. Love you both to the moon and back.

To my nephew and godson, Brayden: You're only three right now, so you have no idea how much joy you bring to my life, but you will. I promise.

To Mom and Dad: I'm not sure what I did to deserve hitting the parental jackpot, but I'm grateful for you both every single day. Thank you not only for wholeheartedly supporting my education and writing endeavors, but also for dedicating so many childhood weeknights and weekends to my karate/soccer/softball practices/games/tournaments, for never discouraging me from lacing up my

Rollerblades to play street hockey with the neighborhood boys, and for always encouraging me to pursue my passions in life—especially when they led me down an unexpected Rainbow Road. You're the best.

And finally, to my steadfast wife, Veronica: Thank you for reminding me to stretch, take brain breaks, eat, and drink, and for nourishing me when I forget to do so myself during my marathon drafting/editing days. Thank you for your patience when my mind drifts to plot knots and character arcs in the middle of "us" time, for helping me talk through new book ideas, for understanding my writing- and nonwriting-related needs, and for supporting me relentlessly, without hesitation. Thank you for opening my eyes to the importance of LGBTQ+ representation in every form of media and inspiring me to contribute to it. Thank you for teaching me how to love with my whole heart, and for loving me with yours, unconditionally and forever. This book is both for you and because of you. This is our resistance.